Harlem After

MIDNIGHT

TITLES BY LOUISE HARE

THE CANARY CLUB MYSTERIES

Miss Aldridge Regrets
Harlem After Midnight

Harlem After
MIDNIGHT

A Canary Club Mystery

Louise Hare

BERKLEY
New York

BERKLEY
An imprint of Penguin Random House LLC
penguinrandomhouse.com

Copyright © 2023 by Louise Hare

Library of Congress Cataloging-in-Publication Data

Names: Hare, Louise, author.
Title: Harlem after midnight / Louise Hare.
Description: New York : Berkley, [2023] | Series: A Canary Club Mystery
Identifiers: LCCN 2022052038 (print) | LCCN 2022052039 (ebook) |
ISBN 9780593439289 (hardcover) | ISBN 9780593439296 (ebook)
Classification: LCC PR6108.A7335 T54 2023 (print) |
LCC PR6108.A7335 (ebook) | DDC 823/.92--dc23
LC record available at https://lccn.loc.gov/2022052038
LC ebook record available at https://lccn.loc.gov/2022052039

Printed in the United States of America
1st Printing

In memory of Karen Clarke

Harlem After Midnight

Thursday, 17 September 1936, 1 a.m.

SHE LET OUT a sigh as she fell, an exhalation so sweet and soft that not a soul heard it, not even the cop who'd passed by the building not two seconds before; it was the smashing of china and the subsequent thud of her body landing hard against the stone steps three stories down that made him turn and look.

Patrolman James Freeman was only a few months into his new career. If you can't beat 'em, join 'em. Forget that his brother hadn't spoken a word to him since. The paycheck sure made up for it. Or it had done up until this very moment.

He noticed her arm first, thrown above her head but in an elegant manner, her fingers beautifully positioned like a dancer's. His eyes traced along to her face. So beautiful and still, her cheek resting against the cold step, her hair curling down toward the sidewalk. Her eyes were closed, her face serene, as if she had just fallen asleep, though the rest of her body was in chaos, sprawled upside down with legs twisted and one foot almost kicking the front door of the building.

A broken angel. He was as frozen as she was, staring down at her like a fool. But then she opened her eyes.

A cough. Blood leaking a thin trail from her mouth. A groan that changed its timbre from pitiful to panicked as she tried to move but couldn't. Freeman ran forward, the spell broken, and dropped to a crouch beside her head.

"Ma'am? You all right, ma'am?" He cursed himself. How in the hell could she be? He tried to remember his training, but his mind had gone blank. "Don't move. I'll get help."

Her eyes rolled shut and he looked around. The street wasn't quite empty, but the closest people were way down on the other side of the road. He could shout but he didn't want to draw a crowd. He looked up. She'd fallen from this building. He could see the open window, a curtain fluttering out from the dark, no light visible from the room, but he could hear music playing. A party? Freeman jumped up and rang the bell, pressing his finger hard against the button until he heard the thud of footsteps from within, a man calling out to hang on, can't you have a little damned patience, don't you know what time it is?

"Sir," he said, as soon as the door swung open, "there's been an accident. You got a telephone in there? You gotta call for an ambulance. And the police."

"Ain't you the police?" The man looked him up and down suspiciously. He was in late middle age and had clearly been in bed when Freeman had rung the bell. A dressing gown hung loose over his pajamas, and he didn't look very happy to see a cop on his doorstep.

Freeman didn't know how to explain, so he just stepped aside, letting the man see past him to the woman behind. "Sir, you gotta ring 'em now. Before it's too late. Please."

The man flinched as he saw the woman, but he stepped forward. "My God."

"Sir, please, I just need you to let me know if you can make the call." Freeman felt the situation slipping from his grasp. It wasn't supposed to be this hard. A face like his was supposed to make it easier for Harlem residents to trust the police, only too often it felt like they trusted him less. "You got a telephone, or no?"

He heard footsteps from inside, heels tapping against floorboards, and then a younger woman appeared from behind the man. "Bill, what's going on?" Her eyes widened as she took in the scene before them. "Jesus help us!"

"Lynette, go into my apartment and call the police," the man told her, tying the belt of his dressing gown around him before stepping outside. Lynette did as she was told, vanishing back inside the building. "Son, I'm a doctor. Forgive the shock; I just wasn't expecting . . ." He knelt and checked the woman's pulse. "Weak, but she's still with us. For now."

Freeman glanced back up at the window. No sign of anyone else up there. "You know who she is?" There was a dark halo around her head now, a pool of blood that was spreading quickly.

"I've seen her around. Visiting the couple on the top floor. There was a gathering of some sort. A celebration." He shook his head as he followed Freeman's upward glance. "She fell, then?"

"Looks like." Freeman spotted something in the woman's hand. Her arm was twisted underneath her, so that he had missed it at first. A small book. "What is that?"

The doctor pulled it out gently, with the woman moaning softly as he disturbed her. He handed it up to Freeman. A passport. Not American, but British, according to the embossed letters. Freeman squinted in the poor light to make out the name, handwritten in black ink, that peeked out through the cut-out oval in the front cover.

Miss E. Aldridge

AUTUMN IN NEW YORK

1

Tuesday, 8 September 1936

I'D BEEN IN the apartment for only fifteen minutes but already it felt like home. The bedroom that would be mine for the next fortnight was perfect; I might never want to leave. The bed was immaculately made with blue cotton sheets and a pristine white comforter tucked into the foot, the floor made of the same sturdy varnished wood that ran through the entirety of Claudette and Louis Linfield's home. Clean towels had been folded and placed on a cozy navy blue velvet armchair that sat in the ideal position, in a corner close to the window, where I could sit and catch the last rays of sunshine at the end of the day. Claud had even laid out a selection of her favorite books on the bedside table to ensure I had something to read before going to sleep. She was a librarian by trade, so I supposed the habit ran deep.

"You about settled in?"

Claud Linfield had a constant easy smile. Even though she and her husband had been complete strangers only a couple of hours earlier, I already felt that there was no place safer in the whole of New York than in this cozy apartment.

"Yes. Thank you." I moved to let her join me at the window, looking down into the street that was so different from the narrow London streets that I was used to. Wider, the buildings far taller, everything just that little bit bigger and brighter than back at home. "It's so kind of you to let me stay. I know that I could have stayed on at the hotel, but—"

"Hotels are for those without their own people," she told me. "Far as I'm concerned, you're with Will and that makes you family. He's as good as a brother to me and Louis."

Will Goodman. The reason I was in Harlem and no longer a resident of the luxurious but impersonal Sherry-Netherland hotel. We'd met on the voyage over from England. A cliché of a story: I had been a passenger; he was the bandleader, playing to the rich and famous every night in the Starlight Lounge on the HMS *Queen Mary*. It had been quite the voyage, and the addition of a whirlwind romance had left my head spinning. Perhaps it was foolish to throw my lot in with a man I'd only just met, but I trusted Will. There were so many others whom I couldn't, so when he'd offered to arrange for me to stay with friends of his, I'd agreed without a second thought.

"You all grew up around here, you and Louis and Will?" I could see a group of young boys playing down in the road, shrieking and laughing loudly, until a woman stuck her head out of a window across the street and called out a warning for them to keep it down. Some things weren't so different from home.

Claud nodded. "Went to the same school, and Will and Louis went to college together."

"Really? I didn't know that." Louis was a pediatrician at the local hospital. Had Will studied medicine as well? Doctor to musician was an odd career change.

"Come through, Lena. I know you English love your tea, but I hope coffee will do." Claud left the room before I could quiz her about Will.

Will and Louis were already in the lounge, and they had both chosen to drink beer. The Linfield lounge induced further envy. High ceilings and tall windows, the sashes lifted to let in a breeze and offset the warmth of the early September evening, the fading light bathing the room in a natural glow. An unlit fireplace sat center stage with a sofa and two armchairs arranged around it.

We were three stories up, at the top of what had once been home to a single family. Now the Linfields lived above two other couples. An older doctor friend of Louis's, a mentor from his medical school days, owned the building and occupied the ground floor as well as running a private practice from the basement. Above him lived his son, a dentist who shared the basement business with his father, and his wife, along with their small son. I was yet to meet them, but it struck me that yet again I was among people whose lives were very different from my own. I had left school with the bare minimum of qualifications; in my world they had never seemed that important. I was never going to be a doctor or a dentist or a teacher. Those occupations just weren't for people like me. Or so I had thought.

Claud and I took the sofa, with the men already settled in the armchairs. They might have been brothers, Louis and Will. They sat in the same way, one leg straight out, the other bent with their beer bottle resting on the thigh. On the ship, Will had always been dressed in a formal suit, his bandleader persona permanently on display. Now he had dressed down in looser, wide-legged trousers, his shirtsleeves rolled up and no tie in sight. He looked right at home, and I felt my breath catch in my throat as he looked up at me and smiled.

"So, you two met at sea, huh?" Louis was speaking to me but grinning at Will. I could guess what he was thinking. I'd been worried about what they'd think of me, a woman of loose virtue, but it seemed as though Claud and Louis weren't the sanctimonious type.

Will took a swig of his beer. "I already told you, didn't I? Lena and I got to talking since she's a singer. Same line of work. Just a shame the job she had lined up fell through."

"All this way for nothing?" Louis shook his head. "A real shame. At least now you get to have a vacation. Do the tourist thing and see the sights."

"That's true." I took the cup of steaming coffee that Claud handed me and I wondered when it would be acceptable, if ever, to ask for a beer like the men. "I managed to get a ticket back to England in a fortnight, but until then this city is my oyster. Thank you again for putting me up. It's really very nice of you."

"I, for one, am just thrilled to meet a friend of Will's," Claud told me. "We hardly see him these days, and when he does show up, it's just a flying visit, no news to report." She aimed this dig directly at Will, who shuffled uncomfortably in his chair.

"Will doesn't bring many friends home, then?" I avoided his gaze as it shifted to me. Of course I wanted to know. If he made a habit of bringing women back to Harlem, better I found out now.

"Lord no! You're the first in the whole time he's been working on the ships. How long is it now—five years? Six?"

"Too long." Will's tone made it clear he wasn't in the mood for Claud's teasing.

"Too long," Claud agreed. "It really is nice to know that he's not been as lonely away at sea as I've been imagining."

Louis's laugh was wheezing. "Oh, come on, now!" he said as Will began to protest. "We're only teasing. It's what friends do, isn't it? No need to take it so serious."

Will looked almost shy as he glanced at me. "I don't want Lena to get the wrong impression, is all."

"That you're a man who doesn't share his affections with every girl who crosses his path? I'd think that'd be a good impression to make." Claud eased the barely-sipped-from coffee cup from my hand. "You want something a bit stronger than that, don't you,

Lena? I can tell." She got up to go to the kitchen, barely more than an alcove that had been sectioned off from the lounge.

I looked guilty enough to cheer Will up. "Lena, Claudette Linfield is my best friend, as good as a sister and a mother too, plus a mind reader to boot. You're in safe hands with her."

"But you do have a sister as well?" I was trying to remember what he'd told me in a rush as we'd temporarily parted at the port the day before. A reminder that I really didn't know very much about him, nor he me.

What I did know was that Will usually stayed with the Linfields when the ship was docked in Manhattan. However, on this occasion, in order to preserve my reputation (though it was far too late for that) he would stay with his sister overnight before returning to the port in time to sail the next day. Stepsister, I reminded myself—he'd been very clear on that for some reason. As much as it was disappointing that our last night together would be spent sleeping in separate beds, I knew how lucky I was to have these last few hours with him. My love affairs tended to end with a lot less civility than this one would.

"You know, I've been telling Will to come home and settle down instead of wasting the best years of his life away at sea," Claud told me, returning with a glass full of beer, ignoring the fact that the man himself was sitting right there.

"Life doesn't seem *so* bad on the ship," I told her, trying to stick up for him. "You don't have to worry about rent, for one thing, or how to afford food. Things run like clockwork, and the people are nice."

"But isn't it dull? Living the same day, over and over again. Same people. Same sights. Anyone of interest only hanging around long enough to get from A to B." She gave me a sharp look, and I knew that I was the "anyone of interest," but I had to disagree on one point. At least on the *Queen Mary*'s last crossing, life had been far from dull. I only wished it hadn't been.

We'd decided, Will and I—had agreed between us—that the

events of the previous few days were best left alone. I had brought up the subject tentatively and been glad when Will agreed readily. When I told him that I wanted to put it all behind me, he had thought he understood. There was no easy way to explain to new acquaintances that I'd been at the center of a murder investigation. That three people had boarded the ship in Southampton alive and been carried off from the New York docks in a coroner's van. It felt like a dream—a nightmare—now that I was sitting with these very normal people. How could they understand?

Besides, as far as almost everyone was concerned, the culprit had been found out and appropriate action taken. Apart from me, only the murderer knew the truth, and no one would believe me if I told them what had really happened. Even Will was more in the dark than he knew. Still, I knew that it was in his best interest to be ignorant. When I'd felt scared and lost on the ship, he had been the one person I trusted, the only person I could find shelter with. It was another reason I'd decided to risk following him to Harlem rather than staying in my fancy hotel. Some of my fellow passengers knew where I was booked to stay. I didn't think they would come looking for me, but sometimes it was better to be safe than sorry.

"You'd be surprised at what goes on at sea" was all I said to Claud.

"Well, I just think you're so incredibly brave to have traveled all that way alone, Lena." Claud pressed her lips together and shook her head. "See, that's why I'm glad I've got Louis. I'm far too chicken to do things like that. I'm not intrepid in the least."

"You never know—you could surprise yourself one day." I managed to smile, a lump forming in my throat as I tried to push down the memories of what had actually happened. I took a sip of my beer and struggled to swallow it down. What I wouldn't give for a martini, or anything stronger. Something to take the edge off . . .

"But do you have to go back to England right away?" Claud pressed, and for the first time I began to feel uncomfortable. So many questions. "What if you were able to find another job in New York?"

"I suppose—well, I haven't given it much thought." I didn't even know if I was allowed to stay much longer. I'd never traveled before. My passport was brand-new, and I'd literally never left England before, so I didn't know how things worked in America. I had no ties to New York, no bank account or home address, none of the usual mundane things that made life tick along easily. Yes, both my parents had been American, but how to prove that when one was dead and the other would likely rather die than confess to being my parent?

"Well, I think—"

"Claud?" Louis interrupted his wife. "Didn't you say you needed a hand in the kitchen? To carve the meat?"

She stared at him blankly, blinking as she realized she was being told to shut up and leave me and Will alone. "Oh, yes. Come on, then. Dinner won't serve itself."

Will came and took her place beside me on the sofa as she and Louis disappeared into the tiny kitchen. I'd never seen him look nervous before. Usually, it had been me standing before him and trying not to make a fool of myself.

"Is everything all right?"

"All right?" He paused. "Why wouldn't it be?"

"You don't seem yourself." He seemed tense, but I couldn't understand why when he was the one on familiar territory.

"Oh." He looked down at his hands. "I guess . . . There's something I wanted to tell you."

I groaned. "Oh God! How bad is it?"

"Huh?"

"Are you going to tell me that you're married? Or that you have a secret child stashed away somewhere?" I gave him a gentle nudge with my elbow. "Come on, then, out with it."

Will grinned as he realized I was teasing, though he looked a little too relieved. Not a wife or a child, then. "No. This is . . . It's a good thing. I hope." He looked worried. "I just don't want you to think that—"

"Oh please, just spit it out." The suspense was doing nothing for my nerves.

"It's just that I got someone to take my place on the ship for this next trip coming up. I'm not leaving tomorrow. I'm staying in New York and then I'll travel with you when you sail back to England. If that's all right. With you."

"You'll stay here? And sail back with me?" I could hardly believe it.

"Sure. An old friend owed me a favor. He helped out once before, so he knows how it goes, and it's only one return crossing. The band will hardly have time to miss me."

I grinned through my disappointment. For a brief moment I'd thought he meant that he was going to come back with me, to live in England. But that was daft. We barely knew each other. Who would move to another continent for someone they'd only just met? That sort of romance belonged in novels and in movies. But Will was staying in New York. For me. "It's a good thing," I confirmed.

He leaned forward and kissed me lightly on the lips. "Gives us a little time to get to know one another."

"You think I'm worth getting to know, then?" I was fishing and he knew it.

"I've decided it's worth finding out if you're worth getting to know." He laughed and dodged the teasing swipe I aimed in his direction. "I mean, c'mon, Lena. We're both full-grown. We know this ain't some fairy tale or romantic movie. Likelihood is, you'll go back to London and I'll go back to leading the band and sailing back and forth until they get sick of hearing my kind of music. But it'll be nice to live like a regular person for a couple of weeks. And if I was a regular person, I reckon I'd be wanting to spend my time with you."

"I suppose that's romantic." I knew it was too much to expect the man to uproot his entire life on a whim. Besides, maybe after a fortnight with Will I'd decide he wasn't the one for me anyway. "Have you told your sister you'll be staying?"

"Bel'll be fine with it," he assured me. "I guess you'll get to meet her sooner or later. And Joey—you'll love Joey. She's my niece. Ten years old and smarter than anyone I ever met. Her daddy died when she was just a baby, so I try to be there for her, you know? 'Specially since my mama's gone too."

"A father figure." I understood. My own father, Alfie, had been everything to me. Will knew that. It was one of the few things that he did know about me.

"I'm not around much, obviously, but I do what I can. And Bel . . . well, she's just Bel."

"You don't get on?"

"It's complicated." He said the words with heavy sentiment. "But hey, while you're here we can do whatever you want to do. Go dancing. Walk through Central Park. And Claud mentioned you'd spoken to her about going with her to the library tomorrow?"

"Yes," I said, "I want to have a look through the old newspapers and the like. Alfie did used to live here, after all. I can't help wondering if there's any record of him."

Or of any family he'd left behind. It was something I'd had in mind since leaving London, but now, with so much free time on my hands, it felt like kismet. There was so much that Alfie hadn't told me about his past. Maybe there were no more skeletons to find, and God knows I'd be grateful for that, but I couldn't help wondering. I hadn't really been sure where or how to start, but when Claud suggested the library archives, they seemed like as good a place as any. Since Alfie had died, I'd felt untethered. Rootless and drifting. Even if I found nothing, I hoped the search might give me purpose.

All these years, I'd thought I knew my father better than anyone else in my life. Now I was afraid that wasn't true. He'd kept a whole host of secrets, hoping to protect me, but things hadn't worked out that way. I hoped that someone who had known him as a young man would be able to shed some light on the man he had been before I'd been born. I wanted confirmation that the man I'd placed on a pedestal my whole life deserved his place there.

"Family is complicated," I said aloud, echoing Will's earlier words. We had talked frankly about friendship and how our friends had become as good as family to us.

"Sure. But as long as you got friends, things ain't so bad." He smiled as he pulled me in for a longer kiss, and I let myself relax.

Will was right. Friendship was worth a lot, and so far he had proved himself a true friend.

2

Tuesday, 8 September 1936

"DINNER IS SERVED!" Claud carried a platter of chicken to the
dining table, which sat by the window at the back of the living
room. Louis followed with the vegetables and Will was on drinks
duty. A fancy dinner for a Tuesday night, but then, I was guest of
honor. My usual diet consisted of whatever I could afford: bread and
soup and sandwiches that I could devour on the hop. On the ship the
food had been exquisite, but meals had been tension filled, to say the
least, so the simple act of sitting at a table with people I liked was a
novelty.

The meal was a lighthearted affair and if Claud and Louis were
anything to go by, Will was every bit the man I had thought him to
be. Principled, kind, talented. Though I had to keep reminding myself: There was no future for us beyond the next few weeks. Post-
poning his return to the ship was not a permanent commitment. I
couldn't let myself get carried away by the small gesture of his sticking around awhile longer. It was hard, though. It was a glimmer of

hope after so many bitter disappointments, and it had shone a light on that part of my brain that invited optimism and craved romance. That part that remembered the kisses we'd shared on deck after everyone else had gone to bed, and still felt the rasp of Will's unshaven chin against my thighs after I'd decided that since there was a good chance I was going to die, I'd have one last moment of pleasure. My face flushed hot at the memory, and when I looked up, Will was staring at me. Had he read my mind? Or maybe he was plotting a way for us to reenact that scene. The only downside to my sleeping under the Linfields' roof was that Will, for the sake of propriety, would not be.

"Walk with me to work tomorrow morning," Claud invited me. "I'll show you where the records are kept. Was your father from New York originally or did he come from someplace else?"

It was a shock to realize that I had no idea. "He definitely lived here for a few years before he went to England. He left here in 1908, I think, or 1909. He didn't like talking about the past, so I don't know much at all. Only that he was a musician and that was why he traveled to Europe, to get work. He played piano, just like Will."

"Only better, or so I've been told," Will joked. I had said that, but more to annoy Will at the time than because it was true. "We should ask around the clubs as well. Some of the old-timers might remember him."

"I see how your mind works," Claud accused. "You just want an excuse to take Lena out dancing."

"I don't need to come up with excuses. I'm more than happy to ask her outright." Will rested his hand on mine and I felt my whole body light up. "You won't be coming along, then, Claud?"

"I never said that. Of course, not during the week, but Louis and I don't mind a night out at the weekend, do we?"

Her husband nodded. "And don't forget, this Saturday is a special occasion."

"It is?" Will looked puzzled. "Is something happening?" He

burst out laughing as Claud's eyes shot daggers at him. "As if I'd forget your birthday, Claudette. As if I'd dare!"

"I feel honored that you'll be home for once. I can't remember the last time I got to celebrate my birthday with you." Claud looked moved. Whether the decision to stay had been about me or a combination of things, I was glad he was getting to spend more time with the Linfields.

"We're having a quiet family dinner here first, but then there's a rent party happening a couple blocks over," Louis told me. "The perfect opportunity to meet everyone Will's ever known. Best way to find out what you're getting into."

"Hey, hey, hey!" Will held his hands aloft. "Don't encourage her. A man needs to keep some secrets to himself. 'Sides, Lena's not interested in what we got up to in high school."

"You mean the time you and Louis got caught trying to brew up moonshine, or the time you disappeared on the trip to the natural history museum, and it turned out you'd snuck into a jazz club by posing as the musicians?" Claud asked.

"I doubt you've done anything worse than I have. I know you don't have some deep dark secret to hide." I was teasing, but then I saw Claud and Louis exchange a look.

Will hesitated a fraction too long. "Exactly."

"I mean, unless you count the time we accidentally set fire to one of Will's mama's wigs." Louis started to tell me the story, which involved some cheap hooch, a box of matches, and a costume that apparently made sense to Will and the Linfields but left me mystified, and by the end we were all in stitches.

We'd all done things we weren't proud of, me most of all. I'd certainly never set fire to a wig and then thrown it out into the street for chaos to commence, but I had a list of wrongdoings as long as my arm, even if none of them had been committed with malice. If Will did have a secret, then he was in good company, and if the Linfields could forgive it, then it wasn't worth worrying about.

I STILL FELT all at sea. I'd adjusted so quickly to the motion of the ship that I'd barely noticed it after a day or two, but adapting back to dry land seemed more difficult for some reason. When I lay down, I could feel the gentle motion of the ship, not a violent movement but enough to make me feel disoriented.

"I hope you're not missing your fancy hotel." Will was lying on the bed beside me, both of us fully clothed and the bedroom door wide open. Our shoulders touched, but that was as far as I dared to go with Claud's and Louis's voices audible from the small kitchen, our pleas to take over the washing up ignored.

"I'd rather be here." I laced our fingers together, my right hand and his left. "Claud and Louis are good people. It's good of them to let me stay. It's good of *you* to let me stay."

This bedroom, after all, was usually Will's when he was back in New York. He didn't usually live with his sister, and as he'd told me earlier, they didn't have the easiest relationship.

"You're worth a few nights' sleeping on Bel's old couch," he assured me. "I'd rather sleep on Claud's, but I know she'd be suspicious. She'd think I'd be creeping in here all hours, having my wicked way with you."

"And wouldn't you?"

He kissed the back of my hand. "Of course. Which is why it's safer for everyone that I stay with Bel."

"I'm looking forward to meeting her and Joey."

"Sure, baby, you'll meet 'em soon enough. Though you should know we're nothing alike."

"You love Joey, though." I'd noticed how his tone softened whenever he spoke his niece's name.

"She's a good kid. I know what it's like to miss out on having a father around. I can't be here as much as I'd like to be, but . . ." He sighed. "Bel did just what my mama did. Fell for the wrong fella and now she has to deal with the consequences. At least she's not made the mistake of marrying the first man to show an interest. Mama did that; it's how Bel and I are related. My mama, her papa, and suddenly we were expected to be a happy family."

"Bel's father was no good?"

"A gambler. Ma met him when he was on a lucky streak. He showed her a good time and she thought he could provide for us, so she married him. He moved in, went through her savings like water, and she ended up having to work two jobs to keep the roof over our heads. He disappeared when I was twelve and Bel was ten. Owed money to the wrong people. To this day I'm not sure if he ran himself or if he was made to disappear. Either way, he left us worse off than when it was just Ma and me."

"And Bel's husband was like that? A gambler?"

"He used his fists." Will's tone was hard now, and I think we were both wishing we'd never embarked on the conversation. "But he's gone now, for good. Got run over by a garbage truck of all things."

I winced. Perhaps divine retribution was real. Still, I'd come to the Linfields' in the hope of a quiet fortnight, away from thoughts of death and murder. "Let's talk about something happier. What about the party on Saturday?"

We chatted for a while but were both painfully aware that our hosts were waiting for Will to leave before turning in to bed. It wasn't late by our standards, only nine o'clock, but the Linfields were normal people with normal jobs—larks, not night owls. It seemed disrespectful for Will to outstay his welcome, so we kissed good-bye at the front door and I went to the window to wave him off. Bel lived only a couple of blocks away, he'd said. I was curious to meet her. Whatever Will thought about her life choices, I knew that I was in no position to judge. People always looked down on women living unconventional lives, and I had never been one to follow the rules.

IT HAD BEEN a long time since I'd heard the sounds of a household waking: the whispered conversation of a couple trying not to wake their guest, the creak of pipes as the water is turned on, the diminishing whistle of a kettle being whipped from a stove top. I turned onto my back and stared up at the high ceiling. A home, but not my home. Where was my home now? Not the rented room in Soho that I'd been kicked out of and certainly wouldn't miss. The only vague plan I had was to go and stay with my best friend, Maggie, who had only her beloved dog, Cecil, to keep her company now that her husband was dead and gone, but that could only be temporary. As much as I loved her, things had altered between us. We'd left a lot unsaid on our last meeting, and the thought of confronting everything that had happened left me nauseated. Even worse was the prospect of not talking about it, of tiptoeing around each other like strangers when before we had been closer than sisters.

I checked my wristwatch: a quarter to eight. Claud had said that we'd leave at half past to go to the library. I sat up in a mild panic. What should I wear? I'd packed for this trip under the strangest of circumstances, and I'd left my trunk full of evening gowns in storage at the Sherry-Netherland hotel. Bad memories had soaked into their silk like cigarette smoke, and I hadn't wanted to bring them into the Linfields' house. In my trusty carpetbag were stuffed a couple of day dresses, toiletries, clean underwear, and a wad of banknotes—half in British pounds, the rest dollar bills, as many as I'd risked changing in one go without arousing suspicion. Enough to go shopping with, for everyday clothes. That had been the idea, anyway.

There was a knock on the bedroom door. "Lena? You awake?" It was Claud and she came bearing a very welcome gift: a steaming cup of coffee, strong on the cream and sugar.

"You're a godsend," I told her.

She was already dressed in a sensible brown skirt and cream cotton blouse. She sat at the foot of the bed. "I can't start the day without a cup. Louis'll tell you what a nightmare I am without it."

"I'm exactly the same." I took a sip and wondered how long it would take her to get around to telling me what was on her mind.

"Bel Bennett's invited us over for lunch," she said. "Will's sister." I wondered if Will knew. "I speak to Bel often," she continued. "She's had her troubles, but she cares about Will a great deal, whether he knows it or not."

"Family can be tricky" was all I could think to say. A gross understatement. I was intrigued at the prospect of meeting Will's stepsister, though. I hoped that Will wouldn't mind, but then, he had said himself that I'd meet her sooner or later. Besides, how bad could she be?

"Well, I'll let you get dressed. Louis is just out of the bathroom, so it's all yours, and you can help yourself to the oatmeal in the pan in the kitchen. There's bread and butter too if you prefer." She got up and left me to it.

I lay back and drank my coffee. What was Will doing right at that very moment? Was he just waking up like me, or was he already up and about, facing the day? He hadn't told me what else he'd be doing while he was back in Harlem. We had arranged that he would come over for dinner again at the Linfields' that night, but before then I had no idea. He must have business to take care of. But then, he usually didn't stick around this long. He should have been going back downtown today, off to the port to board the *Queen Mary*, back to that mean little cabin that was his home at sea. Perhaps he just wanted to spend some time alone for once, to stretch his legs and stroll around these streets that were so familiar to him, to recapture old memories. I realized that I was going to be late if I didn't get a shift on, and leaped out of bed, determined not to make Claud late for work.

Claud's library was on 135th Street, an impressive three-story building that suited her down to the ground, as if they'd been made for each other. She knew everyone we passed, introducing me to her fellow library workers without breaking stride.

"I'm just an assistant, but I've been here long enough I can pretty much do as I like," she told me with a wink. It was a whistle-stop tour of the building. "You won't be interested in the children's books. I guess you want to check out old newspapers?"

"I suppose so." I had no idea where to start, but it felt important to make some effort to discover who my father had been before I'd known him. The life-changing revelation of meeting my mother on the ship had disturbed me. It wasn't that Alfie had lied to me so much as he'd withheld information. It made me wonder what else he might have kept from me. Nothing, I hoped, but I'd be lying if I said I wasn't a little apprehensive. I loved my father. He was the best man I'd ever known, and I understood why he'd not told me the truth, but I wished to God he had. A little warning would have saved me an awful lot of trouble.

"Births," Claud advised as we landed at the archives. "Start out there, the year he was born, and work your way forward. The *New York Times*, but we've also got copies of the *Christian Recorder*, which is a Black newspaper. And if nothing turns up, then I know a couple of the church ladies who've been around forever. They know everyone in Harlem, it seems like, so we can interrogate them on Sunday."

She left me with a smile and an intimidating pile of yellowing old newspapers. Alfie had been born in August 1889, but all I had to show for a couple of hours' work was ink-stained fingertips. I wasn't even sure what I was hoping to find, or perhaps not to find. No more surprises.

It had been a shock to discover my long-estranged mother on the *Queen Mary*, and to then have to watch as members of her family—I would never think of them as my own—were picked off by a murderer who was either deranged or devious, depending on your point of view. Eliza had promised me money, compensation for almost three decades of neglect, but it felt like a payoff. A crafty maneuver to ensure that I didn't tell her legitimate children who I really was. If Alfie had any living relatives here in New York, might they be more welcoming? More like real family? But Alfie had come from nothing. People with no money hardly ever ended up in the papers. Births, deaths, marriages. Perhaps a tragedy befallen or a crime committed could earn you the right. No news was good news.

It was still too early for lunch, so I decided to look up Francis Parker. Rich folk were a different matter. It was no surprise that my maternal grandfather featured fairly frequently. I had met him only briefly, this divisive figure, a man heading toward the end of a life even before the cyanide had choked it from him, but on these aged pages he was a man in his prime. Making enemies and money with dizzying rapidity as his firm, Parker Godwin, raised itself from fledgling company to behemoth predator, swallowing up all before it.

My mother's birth was listed in the *New York Times*. The daughter of Francis and Eleanor, born into a cage of immense privilege, which Alfie had failed to free her from. Down the rabbit hole I fell, reading every article I could find on the Parkers, then the Abernathys: my mother's society wedding, then the births of first Frankie and then Carrie.

I'd come to find Alfie, I reminded myself, but it seemed futile. He'd been a penniless musician his whole life. His story had always been that he'd struggled to make a living in New York and had traveled to England because he'd heard there were opportunities for Black musicians there. If only he hadn't been stuck with a baby daughter when he was barely an adult himself, perhaps he would have made a go of things. Whenever I'd asked about my grandparents, he'd only told me that they'd died before he left America. There'd been no mention of siblings, and as I was an only child myself, it had never struck me as unusual. Alfie, though, it had turned out, was the king of omission. There were things he'd kept from me: my mother and her wealthy family, why she'd really walked out on us. If he'd still been alive, I could have demanded the truth, but Alfie had died thinking that his secrets would go to his grave with him. Perhaps some of them had. Without even a birth notice to go off, how was I supposed to find out anything about the father who had meant so much to me and yet had kept his past hidden? It seemed an impossible task.

Alfie

IT WAS ROUTINE by now, a bad habit that he hadn't worked out how to shake. Waking up just as the sun had passed its peak and decent people were thinking about the end of the working day, about what to cobble together for dinner and how much they were looking forward to putting their feet up. The relative quiet of the lodging house was beginning to be disturbed as those with regular jobs began to arrive home, eager to change their clothes and eat before turning in. Out on the street, two stories below, he could hear familiar voices greeting one another over the sounds of horses' hooves from a cart or wagon, too slow and steady for a carriage.

Alfie stared up at the stained ceiling, the cracks that were now so familiar to him. He could hear the scuttle of some beast beneath his bed. A cockroach if he was lucky. He'd have to get up soon. His bed wasn't even his own; he shared its broken-down springs with a long-shoreman who worked early shifts, living an opposite life to Alfie's. Time was, he'd considered himself a cut above. Not for him, working the menial jobs that the average Negro was forced to take. No waiting tables, no factory work for low pay or breaking his back down at the port, no *Yes, sir. No, sir.* It had all seemed incredibly straightforward at the start of it; he still couldn't quite see where it had gone wrong.

"Where to this evening, my good sir?" Smiles burst in through the door, slinging his bag onto his cot before landing his behind on it so hard that Alfie worried that one of these days he'd fall straight through to the floor.

"What time is it?" Alfie struggled up to sitting, his throat as dry as wood shavings.

"Just after four." Smiles wrestled with the laces on his shiny black boots. "Jimmy got a big tip today. Wants to throw it away at the craps table. You in? Think lady luck's still on your side?"

What had happened the night before? There had been gin, lots of it, he could tell from that sour taste at the back of his throat, from the thick coating on his tongue. He tried to swallow but his mouth was too dry, and he felt his stomach twitch. It had been a while since he'd eaten a proper meal, but at least he hadn't been sick.

Thank goodness his mother couldn't see what had become of her son, though he knew she must be worried. He'd been forced to leave home in such a rush, there'd barely been time for good-bye. He'd sent a note as soon as he'd reached New York but he'd been too scared to include an address. He'd promised to write, to send money home, but with funds hardly flowing in his direction, he'd been too ashamed to send a thin envelope, lies scribbled across a sheet of paper because he couldn't bear his family's knowing the truth.

But wait—a memory returned from the night before. A couple of hands at the poker table, but that wasn't his game, and he hadn't wagered a lot. Leaning over the side of the cot, he saw his trousers lying in a crumpled heap on the floor and grabbed them up. One empty pocket but in the other a couple of folded bills. Twenties. His winnings?

"You know they gonna want some of that back," Smiles told

him, his permanent white-toothed grin on show. "Come on, see if I can catch some of that luck off of ya."

"Maybe."

He shook his head, trying to clear it. The night was a series of images in his head, a zoetrope of a life clinging on to the rungs of the ladder, some of the pictures clear, others blurring into obscurity. After the poker there had been more drinks. They'd gone to a place just off Sixth Avenue, a popular club well-known among local sportspeople. Someone had won big on the horses and showed off his magnanimity with champagne all around. Alfie remembered lifting a glass to the fella.

"Who was that white fella you was with last night anyway?"

White fella? The next image clicked into place. More champagne, and then he'd seen that there was no piano player on in the back room, so he'd taken himself back there and sat himself down. This was why he'd moved to New York, after all, though he hadn't really tried to make a living out of music. Not yet. He'd thought that talent enough would get him by, but it turned out that you also had to know the right people.

The only luck he'd had so far in New York was with a woman, Victoria. She'd come in with friends the first time, rich white folk slumming it. She'd been back a couple of times since with a male acquaintance who Alfie knew was inclined toward young men rather than women. Alfie had seen her eyes on him, had been trying to act aloof around her, but on her last visit she'd thrust her hand down the front of his trousers in the alleyway round the corner and showed him what he could expect more of if he wanted it. He didn't trust women like her. Why act like a whore when you didn't need to? He was the son of a dressmaker. He knew that even the clothes that she wore to the Tenderloin were worth more than he'd earn that month. She was just playing a game, but he wasn't completely averse to participating on his own terms.

But Victoria hadn't been at the saloon the night before. He'd played a couple of ragtime pieces that he'd heard elsewhere. Reading music wasn't his forte but he had a perfect ear for a tune. He only had to hear the music once and he could re-create it, not identically but close enough, often adding improvements, in his own humble opinion. A change in the rhythm, a slight key change, or sometimes a complete moving of the notes from major to minor or vice versa. It was what he was known for back home, and it was only his own fault that in the Tenderloin he was better known for losing his dollars at the craps table than for his musical abilities. At least, he had been.

The next sequence of events clicked back into his memory.

"He offered me a job."

"Finally!" Smiles grinned. He'd never understood Alfie. Had always thought that he was a useless dreamer. A fool who'd end up on the street before doing the right thing and getting a regular job with regular pay, same as everyone else. Smiles played horn himself, but he didn't trust it to pay his way. "A job doin' what?"

"Playing piano." Alfie felt as confused as Smiles looked. It might have been his dream, but it turned out that he'd never quite believed it would come true. "He wants to hire me to play piano."

Someone had called out to play "Go Down Moses." He'd remembered how his father used to sing it, had surprised himself as his liquor-reddened eyes welled up at the memory. The room had fallen still as Alfie sang, his fingers nimble despite the gin and the champagne, his voice not his own but that of Alfred Aldridge Senior. When he'd finished the song, there had been silence. The same expectant quiet that Alfie knew from theaters when the gaslights turned down and the curtain lifted. And then the requests had come in thick and fast and he'd somehow, miraculously, kept up. Barely a gap between songs, his glass kept full of champagne, the tips dropping into his pocket, and he'd been carried away by the music, taking a break only when his bladder demanded. The man had approached him then, as Alfie weaved his way along the alley outside to find a safe spot to urinate, his fists clenching as he sensed danger.

"I just came to say that I thought you played well," the man said, either not noticing Alfie's defensive stance or ignoring it. "Do you play professionally?"

Even in his half-drunken state, Alfie could see that this wasn't the typical sort of fella who came to the bar. Plenty of white people came along, but they were usually just day-trippers like Victoria, the Tenderloin their zoo, a sideshow. They'd come in for one drink, their eyes wide as they took in the sights and sounds. The girls would giggle if a Black man dared to flirt with them; the men would make jokes or try to make conversation, showing how they understood the struggle of the Black man. *Slavery was a truly terrible thing, but we got rid of it.* Which is what it all came down to in the end. *We saved you. Be damned grateful.*

But this man was different. For one, he'd come to the bar alone. And this man was rich, not so young, probably the same age that Alfie's father had been when he died a few years before. He was dressed smart, like a lot of the fellas at the club, but this man had a gold watch that looked like it weighed him down. There was a weariness about him generally, a slowness to his gait and to his speech. Though Alfie came to realize that the man spoke in a leisurely way because he could. Where Alfie had learned to talk fast, to get his words out before Jessie could interrupt or his mother told him to be quiet, this man was used to people stopping to listen to whatever it was he had to say. People trusted his opinion, and this man thought that Alfie could play professionally.

"I reckon I'm better than most who do." It was no time to be bashful.

"I'd agree with that." The man pulled out two cigars from his inner jacket pocket, offering one to Alfie. "You never wanted to make a career of it?"

Alfie took the cigar. "I do. I just haven't had time yet. I just arrived in town."

It was sort of a lie, depending on how you looked at time and its passing. It had been just shy of nine months, and the great expectations he had arrived with had so far been forgotten along with his intentions to follow his mother's instructions and stay on the right path.

Cigars lit, Alfie followed the man through to the main room at the front of the saloon, where they took seats out of the way.

"Forgive me." The man stuck out his hand for Alfie to shake. "They call me Tar."

"Alfred. Alfred Aldridge."

"Good to meet you, Alfred. Well, let me get right to it. I need a boy like you to come along and play a private concert."

"A private concert?" Alfie's eyes narrowed. He'd heard of all sorts of odd shenanigans going on uptown.

"My wife's birthday," Tar clarified. "Nothing out of the ordinary, but she's been a little unwell, you see. She heard some of that ragtime music being played—one of our daughter's friends learned to play a tune on the piano, but he's not a patch on you. Now, usually I'd take her out to the theater to see a real show, but she's too ill right now so I thought I'd bring the music to her."

"Oh." Alfie couldn't see a catch in this. A sick woman wouldn't be any bother at all. Easy work. "Thank you, Mr. Tar. That's kind of you. I can do that."

"Excellent. Though it's just Tar, not Mr. Tar. A nickname, you see. Works kind of nicely round these parts."

Alfie supposed the man didn't want people to know who he really was. It should have alarmed him, but Tar had just slipped him two crisp twenty-dollar bills, so he was ready to overlook his misgivings.

Now, the next day, with Smiles staring at him, waiting for an answer, he pulled out the card the man had given him. He was to go along to the address at three o'clock sharp on Saturday afternoon. Tar would have a suit for him to borrow and a grand piano waiting for him.

"He's my new boss."

He'd give the craps a miss tonight, head over to the club early, and see if he could practice some of his best tunes. For the first time in nine months, Alfie smelled opportunity. Maybe he'd even be able to finally send some money home and make his mother proud.

3

Wednesday, 9 September 1936

"YOU 'BOUT READY?" Claud popped her head around the door. "Bel's place is just a five-minute walk."

"Let me just wash this ink off my hands." I got up gratefully, astonished at how quickly the time had passed. I felt nervous all of a sudden. What if Bel didn't like me? I was messing around with her stepbrother, after all. Might she be protective of him? Whether she and Will got along or not, she was family. Her opinion would count for something.

Claud loved to chat. I'd learned that already, but it was a soothing trait rather than annoying. She told me about a poetry reading at the library the following evening; about the woman she'd just been dealing with who'd expected Claud to know exactly the book she meant, just from the description of there being a dog in it; about the fact that Will paid for Bel's apartment, each subject gliding so smoothly from her tongue that I almost missed this last, most interesting fact. I shot her a glance, but her face looked entirely innocent. Had she meant for me to infer something from this knowledge?

Bel Bennett's apartment was up two flights of dark, narrow stairs, this building not half as nice as the Linfields'. I spotted mold on the walls higher up, the smell of damp almost muscular as it shoved its way into my nostrils.

"Damned supe won't do a thing about it." Claud waved a hand at the black patterned spots on the wall. "I swear Joey's lungs are so bad in the winter because of it."

If I was honest, it reminded me of my old address in London. The uncared-for look of the place, drab and dour, people living under its roof out of necessity rather than because they had some great desire to make a home there.

Claud knocked at the door of apartment 3b.

"Just a minute!" I heard a muffled curse before the chain slid back and the lock clicked, and then I tried to rearrange my face to hide my shock as I saw Will's stepsister for the first time. The woman who threw open the door to the apartment was my age. Dark blond hair, hazel eyes, and a face made up like a movie star's. If you didn't know any better, you'd never think that Mabel Bennett wasn't white.

"I'M NOT SURE what I expected," Bel said. "It's been a long while since Will brought a young lady home to meet his family."

I just smiled. I supposed it was reassuring that I wasn't just another name on a long list of women whom Will had seduced, but there was something in her tone that made me take note. Or perhaps it was the look that she and Claud exchanged, as if they both knew something I didn't. Bel did seem nice, though, funny and clever. She'd served up ham and potato salad for lunch and had quizzed me about my life in London. I'd stuck to safe topics, slightly overplaying my theater experience and making the Canary Club, my previous place of employment, sound less grimy and sleazy than it was in real life.

"I got ice cream for dessert, ladies." Bel reached across from the small table we were crowded around, grabbing the carton from the windowsill behind her. "Vanilla. I know summer's sort of over, but it's a special occasion, after all."

Claud groaned and checked her watch. "I wish I could, but I need to get back to the library. No rest for the wicked, but, Lena, you stay. Unless you wanted to go back to your newspapers?"

"No," I said quickly. It had been an interesting morning, but I didn't think there was much more to be gained from being cooped up in the library. Besides, perhaps with Claud gone Bel would open up. I was curious as to why Will's mood was so tepid when he talked about her. "I can stay for some ice cream if that's all right, Bel? And I'll come and find you at the library afterward."

Claud got up to leave and Bel pointed me in the direction of a low, ancient-looking sofa on the other side of the small living room. Compared to the Linfields' apartment, Bel's was closer to my usual standard of living. The living room was cramped, with hardly any spare space once you took into account the sofa, the round table with its chairs that barely fit around it, a coffee table with a selection of fashion magazines that must have been Bel's, and a stack of classic novels—Hardy, Dickens, and Brontë—that I assumed belonged to the studious Joey.

Beside the sofa was a Victrola perched on a stool. "You must know Billie Holiday," she told me. "I heard her sing over at the Apollo last year. I'd kill to have a voice that sounded like hers."

"It's unique," I agreed. "Do you sing?"

She shrugged. "Not really. I can hold a tune but I'm not like Will. Now, that man, whatever else you might think of him, he can sing." Another hint that their relationship was tricky. "Mostly I pour drinks in a bar over on One Hundred Thirty-Third. It's nothin' special but it keeps food on the table and some nights the tips are good. I thought about trying out as a dancer years back—I even got an audition at the Cotton Club when it was still up here in Harlem— but sometimes it's better to be less noticeable, you know?"

Bel didn't strike me as a wallflower. If anything, she reminded me very much of the various women I knew in London. She reminded me a little of myself, if I'm honest. Her hair professionally waved, makeup applied, her eyebrows plucked high so that she reminded me a little of Myrna Loy. And her clothes . . . If Claud dressed like you'd expect for a librarian, then Bel certainly didn't. Neither, though, did she wear the clothes of a woman who worked in a bar. She wore an emerald green dress that reached just past knee length, long in the sleeve. She looked like a rich housewife, not a woman who surely had to fight to make each cent last.

"It must be hard," I said, "doing all this on your own."

"It's . . ." She looked away, her lips pressing together, as if there was a lot she wanted to say but nothing she felt she could. "We make do, you know? Will helps. He don't need to but he does and I'm grateful for that. And I'm here when Joey wakes up and I don't have to leave for work until she's fed and just got her homework to do before bed. This is a safe building. I'm not a bad mother."

Her tone was a little defensive and yet I didn't think I was the reason. I couldn't imagine how it must be. My own life was chaotic at best, but at least I had only myself to worry about. When I made mistakes, they were mine and I was the only one who suffered. The idea of having another person, someone to be responsible for, made me shudder. Bel was a heroine as far as I was concerned.

"You fancy a beer?" Bel got up before I could answer, and she came back with two full mugs. "Cheers!"

We clinked mugs. I'd never been a big beer drinker, but after a week of gin hangovers it was a nice change. I offered Bel a cigarette and we lit up, leaning back against the couch like we were old friends. I wondered what Will would say. Did he even know I was here? There was nothing of him that I could see in the apartment.

"Will sleeps here on the couch," Bel told me, seeing me look around. "He's a light traveler, if you haven't realized that already. His real belongings, the few things he cares about, he keeps at Claud and Louis's."

"You and Will." I thought for a moment of how to phrase the question and then just threw the words out there. "I get the impression that you may have had a falling-out at one time or another."

"You could say that." Bel's laugh was dry. "It's complicated. We were really close once. When we were kids. My old man, he wasn't the best father. Marrying Tish Goodman was the best thing he ever did for me, though it wasn't so great for her. He could be violent when things weren't going his way. And he spent every penny we had. Will stood up for me and Tish when he could, and when Pa left it was a relief. Tish's wages could go on the things we needed, and not into the pockets of other lowlifes. Life was good, for a while. And then I met my husband and, well, I think Will was disappointed in me. Still is, though he'll never say as much."

"Your husband wasn't the best?" I didn't want her to know Will and I had been talking about her behind her back.

"I wouldn't give up Joey for anything, but sometimes—well, don't we all wonder what our lives would be if we'd just changed one decision?"

I couldn't disagree. I found myself warming more and more to Bel. How could I not? We had a certain amount in common. I knew how one decision could change a life.

I let Bel change the subject to something lighter: fashion. When I mentioned that I needed to buy some new clothes, Bel's face lit up.

"Well, we must go shopping," she said. "Come on, Lena. I can show you where to find the best bargains. Or we can pretend that we have money and go to Fifth Avenue. B. Altman and Saks. It's not often I can afford to buy more than a little makeup in those fancy stores, but I love to try on the clothes. Pretend just for a moment that I'm a movie star. Not that you ever actually see a movie star in those stores. Usually, the places are full of old crones. As if they can do any justice to those beautiful clothes!"

Bel Bennett really was a girl after my own heart. We shared another bottle of beer and made plans for Friday. I could get a new dress for the Saturday-night party. There'd be dancing, after all, and other women.

"You need a dress that'll blow Will's socks off," Bel said with a wink.

I felt my cheeks redden as she read my mind. It felt awkward, though, talking about her brother that way. Stepbrother, I reminded myself, but still. There was so much I didn't know about either of them, and the obvious tension in their relationship would have had my thoughts running wild if I hadn't put them on a tight leash.

When we'd been stuck at sea, with a murderer in our midst, Will had come to represent sanctuary. It had felt as though he was the only person I could trust. But then, how could I possibly know everything about a man I'd only just met? Events happening around us had helped us to forge a bond that was perhaps stronger than it deserved to be.

The sound of a key in the door was a happy distraction from these less cheerful thoughts.

"Joey, honey, come and meet Lena. Uncle Will's friend." Bel welcomed in her daughter.

Claud had called Joey adorable, and she wasn't wrong. Smartly dressed in a pale blue dress, her white socks pristine and her hair pressed into two neat braids. Her skin was a few shades darker than her mother's, but she had the same wide eyes. She carried her books under her arm, and dropped them onto the table by the door as her face lit up with excitement.

"Pleased to meet you, ma'am." She actually dipped into a little curtsy as she smiled shyly at me.

"Oh! Well, I'm very pleased to meet you too, Joey." I was charmed beyond belief.

"Ain't she a doll?" Bel looked proud. "And smart too. Top of her class in English and math, her teacher tells me."

"Very good." I wished I were better at talking to children.

"You're from England?" Joey asked. "Have you ever met the king?"

I burst out laughing. "Oh no! I mean, yes, I'm from England, but I'm not anyone important. The king doesn't have the faintest idea who I am."

She muttered the word "important" under her breath, copying my intonation, so different from how Americans pronounced it. "You should write to him. I wrote to the president once."

"She likes to hear Roosevelt when he speaks on the radio," Bel told me. "So I said she should write and tell him what she thought. Honestly, this girl! She makes me feel as dumb as a box of logs."

I wanted to ask if the president had replied, but Joey looked so proud that I didn't, in case he hadn't. She deserved to look proud. I'd never have thought to write to anyone in power, as a child or otherwise; by adulthood I'd learned to be cynical. Even when I'd been in close contact with a member of Parliament, it had never crossed my mind to discuss policy with him. We had been in the middle of a torrid love affair, the illicit excitement driving our relationship rather than anything we actually had in common. We didn't talk about anything of national importance. It had only been a few weeks since I'd last seen him, but I felt ashamed now when I thought of James Harrington. I'd left an old version of myself behind in London, I hoped. The new Lena wasn't interested in wasting her time with married men. I hadn't quite decided what it was that she did, but I had made a start and that counted for something.

Bel and I shared another bottle of beer while Joey sat at the table eating up the leftovers from our lunch. When she was done, the little girl washed up her plate without being told, before pulling her schoolbooks from her bag. I'd never seen a child so keen to learn. Bel and I were discussing the relative merits of Clark Gable and Cary Grant when a second key rattled the lock.

"Hey!" Will looked out of place, too big for the cramped room.

"You two look like you're gettin' along." He didn't look altogether happy about it.

"Thick as thieves!" Bel giggled and lifted her half-full mug in salutation. "I love her! Well done, Big Brother. Could it be that Will Goodman is finally moving on with his life?"

"There's nothing to move on from," he said shortly. "C'mon, Lena. I told Claud I'd come get you in time for dinner."

"Is that the time?" Bel looked at the clock on the wall and cursed mildly. "Damn it, I was trying to be good and get you back nice and early."

"Are we going to be late?" What time did normal people eat dinner anyway? It was barely past four o'clock, but I hated to think of Claud going to all that trouble to provide a meal, only for me to turn up late.

"It's fine," Will assured me. "I just know what Bel is like. She'd keep you here all night if I let her."

"I wouldn't actually. I have work to think of." Bel took my mug and hers to the kitchen. "We manage pretty well, you know, when you're not here . . ."

Will's eyes were glued to the floor, as though the curling corner of the old rug were a great puzzle to him. "Let's go, Lena. Bel, I'll see you later. And you better be asleep when I get back, kid." He gave Joey a quick hug and opened the front door, ready to leave.

"Bye, Uncle Will. Bye, Aunt Lena!"

"Good-bye, Joey."

I felt my mouth curl up in a wide smile. *Aunt Lena.* It sounded nice. As an only child I had never imagined having nieces or nephews of my own. Maybe if Maggie's wish had come true, I'd have been godmother to her babies. But that hadn't worked out. There was so much to tell her when I got back to London. So much that I didn't know where I'd begin.

DON'T
BLAME ME

4

Wednesday, 9 September 1936

"YOU FIND OUT anything interesting at the library?" Will broke his silence as we stepped out onto the street. I could almost see the tension flood from his body as we left the building.

"Not really," I said. "I don't want to give up, but it seems like a hopeless task." The library had always felt like a dubious place to start, but in lieu of any other information I had at least tried something.

"I was thinking." Will stopped to light two cigarettes, passing one to me. "Alfie was a musician, so how 'bout I take you out tonight, after dinner? Chances are that Alfie played some of the clubs round here. Might be that some of the old fellas remember him."

"What a brilliant idea!" More than the slight chance of finding some old-timer who had known my father thirty years ago, the idea of a night out with Will excited me. Claud and Louis were wonderful people, but their presence in the apartment rather stifled opportunities for romance. We were short on time, but it was too soon to give up on the electric attraction I knew we'd both felt at sea. Surely, he wanted the same, for us to be together for as long as possible. Why else would he have arranged to spend all this time with me? I let the back of my hand brush against Will's and felt triumph when he took hold of it.

Claud served up meat loaf with greens and, to my relief, made excuses for herself and Louis when Will suggested they come out with us. "I'll give you a key, Lena. I'm afraid us old married folk need our sleep. We got work in the morning."

"Where you headed to?" Louis looked less happy about staying in than his wife did. "Pod's?"

Will shook his head. "I thought we'd try somewhere low-key for this evening. We need to find the old fellas, not the young bucks. Might help to start off somewhere I can be heard over the music."

"Not just about the dancin', then." Louis winked at me. "You know Bel is working at Leon's club? That might be a good place to start."

"Leon's? Nah, I know the fellas who go there. I'd be surprised if they can remember what happened to 'em last week, let alone thirty years ago." Will shoveled meat into his mouth, his expression closed.

What was it with Will and Bel? I thought back to conversations we'd had on board the ship. Our first meeting had gone so badly, Will seeing immediately that I was, well, just like Bel. A Black woman who looked white. Was that why he'd been so standoffish at first? Had I reminded him of his stepsister and his uneasy relationship with her?

I glanced at Claud, who was listening intently to Louis's account of his day at the hospital. He was on the front line of life and death, saving lives or at least helping people through ill health and injury, calming their fears and being their rock. He had a solid career, a job that would always be needed. I wondered again how Will had ended up leading such a different life. Claud would know, but whether she'd tell me or not . . . No, best to get it from the horse's mouth, so to speak. Will and I would go out and have a few drinks, loosen up, and I could gently interrogate him. A few innocuous questions to test the waters. If I was going to live in Will's world for the next few days, then I wanted to get to know him.

THE BAR WILL took me to first was down a flight of steps not far from Claud's library on 135th Street. It was a small place, hardly even a bar at all, more like someone's living room. A trio of old-timers sat at the bar. It was nothing fancy, but since I had the same dress on that I'd been wearing all day, I was grateful. There were a couple of sticky-looking tables opposite the bar and Will escorted me to one.

"Sit down. I'll get you a drink."

"But don't we need to speak to people?" I asked, looking at the men, who were looking at me as if they were travelers stranded in the desert and I were an oasis.

"Reckon it's safer if I go, don't you?" Will was barely concealing a smirk. "What do you want to drink?"

"Surprise me," I said, hoping it wouldn't be more beer but not knowing what else might be safe to drink.

I lit a cigarette and watched Will at work. I'd never have felt comfortable in a place like this without him. Annoying but true. He was tall and looked like a man whom other men didn't mess with. Someone who could handle himself in a fight if he had to, but his nature was that he'd never be the one who started it. The three men at the bar gave him their full attention, regretfully turning away from me.

A gramophone on the bar played a record that kept jumping; the music was too loud for me to be able to eavesdrop on the conversation. This had been a speakeasy, I realized. Outlasting Prohibition but only just, from the looks of things. The wallpaper was peeling from the walls and the ceiling was bubbled from years of condensation.

Shoved against the back wall was a piano from another century, a handsome-looking instrument that had been hard done by to be left in such a dilapidated setting. Through a doorway behind the bar was a set of stairs leading upward, and I saw a woman in a dressing gown shuffle past, calling out something unintelligible to the man behind the bar, who replied with a shrug and a grunt.

"Any luck?" I took the glass that Will offered on his return and sniffed it. "Whiskey and ginger?"

Will grinned as he sat down. "We're not on the *Queen Mary* anymore. No martinis or champagne." He had the same, plus a bottle of beer on the side.

"I know. I'm not complaining." I took a sip. I wasn't a huge whiskey drinker, but I didn't mind it. And it was a change from beer.

Will took a swig from the bottle. "None of them recognized Alfie's name, but they mentioned a fella I know, Leon Jones. He used to work downtown back then, but now he runs his own club not far from here."

"Downtown?" My knowledge of New York geography was limited to the three locations I had visited so far: the Sherry-Netherland hotel, an apartment on the Upper West Side, and our immediate vicinity in Harlem.

"It's back down toward where the ship came in. Used to be that whole area was where the Black folk lived, before Harlem became the place to be. It makes sense that Alfie lived there rather than here now that I think about it. Used to be that the theaters and the clubs round the Tenderloin and Tin Pan Alley were the place to be."

"So chances are, Alfie played there!" It was barely a crumb of information, but it was something. I felt a bubble of excitement swell in my stomach. I'd tried to tell myself that this was just a casual search. That if I didn't find anything, it wouldn't matter. Had I been lying to myself? "We should go to Leon's club after we finish our drinks." Will didn't answer. "What's the matter?" I suddenly remembered the conversation over dinner. Leon's club, Louis had said.

"That's where Bel works?" Will nodded and I reached out and took hold of his hand. "Is it so very bad if we go for a quick drink there? We don't have to stop for long. This Leon chap might not even be there tonight." I tried not to sound as though I were talking to a child, but I could see in his frown that I'd not succeeded.

"You think I'm being an idiot." His hand slipped away from mine as he leaned back in his chair, his gaze fixed on the wall behind me.

"I'm confused," I clarified. "Maybe you are being an idiot, but how the hell am I supposed to know?"

"What does that mean?" His tone hardened.

"It means that I thought this—by which I mean, whatever it is that's gone on between you and Bel—was none of my business. We've only just met. I know it's not my place to stick my nose into your past." And God knows, I knew what real family secrets were. "But this is affecting me now. I'm happy to go to Leon's place alone if you point me in the right direction, but I don't understand how you can be so reluctant to even go to Bel's place of work. I mean, Claud told me that you pay her rent. You're staying at her apartment, so it's not like you won't be seeing her anytime soon."

"I pay Joey's rent," Will corrected me. "And I'm only staying there because you're sleeping in the bed that's usually mine."

"This is my fault?" I tried to stop myself, but I was damned if he was going to pin the blame on me. He'd invited me, after all; it wasn't as though I'd begged for a place to stay. I drained my drink. "I thought we were going to have a nice night out, the two of us, but it seems as though that's not going to be possible."

Will caught hold of my arm as I got up to go. "Wait! Don't go."

I looked down at him. "Give me a good reason why not."

"Because I am an idiot. You're right." He spoke quickly. "Because I don't want to ruin whatever this is. Please. I can explain and hopefully you'll understand." His hand slid down my arm until our palms met. "It's pretty common knowledge around here anyway. It's a long story but I'll give you the short version."

I took a gamble and sat back down, still holding Will's hand. With his free hand he slid his whiskey across the table to me.

"I told you that Bel's daddy married my mom." He fiddled with his beer bottle. "We were all in elementary school at the time, me, Louis and Claud, Bel a couple grades below. Claud . . . Well, you know Claud. She took Bel under her wing and let her play out on the street with us. Bel's pa was violent. A poor excuse for a man, Claud's mother used to call him."

"You were all very close," I noted.

"We used to look out for one another. It's how we were raised and that never changed, not until Bel took up with this fella Henry Bennett. Smart kid—he was in my class at NYU." I'd been wondering about that since Claud had mentioned about Will and Louis being students together. It must have shown on my face. "Hey, I wasn't always a penniless musician! Once upon a time I thought I might make something of myself." He forced his mouth to turn up into a smile but he was not an actor; his honesty was what had drawn me to him. "Henry was a charmer. Most of the kids in our class were white, you understand. Someone burned a cross on campus that year, some KKK shit, so we stuck together, me and Henry. We sat together in class, studied in the library afterward. He made me read *The Crisis* and go to NAACP meetings. We planned to go to law school after, learn how to stand up against injustice. We wanted to make people listen to us. He was smarter than Louis, who was always the smartest fella I knew growing up. I trusted him. That summer Claud wanted to go on a picnic in Central Park. Really, she wanted to go to the zoo, but she didn't want to admit it 'cause the zoo is for kids." He looked down at his hands. "There was no reason for Bel not to come. Like I told you before, Claud was like a big sister to her."

"That's where she met Henry." It made sense. But the Henry I was picturing now was far from the useless layabout I'd pictured when Will had called him a piece of work the day before. I'd imagined a heavy drinker, a gambler, a sharp-suited scoundrel. Now he emerged as a quieter man. Intelligent, charming, dangerous in a way you didn't see coming.

"Nothing happened that day. Just a little friendly conversation between the two of them. Henry was always a flirt, so I kept an eye on Bel, but it seemed innocent enough. It was a month or so later. I'd been studying down at the library one Saturday, trying to get ahead for the next semester, and I got home just in time to catch him at it. Ma was out at work and Bel had thought I'd be catching up with Louis after I finished with my books. To be honest, I would've been except that he was having tea with Claud's parents. Putting in the work, as they say, ready to propose the following year. He's always been a plan-ahead type of fella."

"I'll say." I lit another cigarette. "So, Henry and Bel—were they . . ."

"They were just talking, but . . . she was only seventeen! We were twenty, we were older, and we—well, we were men. It's different. He acted like the gentleman, but I just didn't like it. The way he'd snuck around, giving me excuses for why he couldn't come to the library." Will shook his head. "He lied to my face."

I could understand why he'd been angry, but I could also see it from Bel's point of view. What young woman wouldn't be swayed by the attentions of a dazzling future lawyer? "He knew what he was doing," I murmured.

"It's not just that he lied to me. He was a ladies' man. Bel wasn't the only girl he'd fooled around with that summer. He even tried to sweet-talk Claud one time, though she soon set him straight, and it was as well that Louis never found out." He shook his head as I smiled at the thought of it, the straitlaced young librarian ticking off the opportunistic rascal. "I told Bel what he was like, but she didn't listen. She didn't want to know that he was cheating on her, even though everyone saw him with a different girl on his arm each week.

I tried to show her once. Dumb of me, I know, but I thought that she might believe it if she saw it with her own eyes. Instead, she stopped speaking to me."

I could understand Will's reasoning, but getting involved with other people's affairs was a destructive business, no matter how good the intentions. I couldn't blame *all* my recent troubles on her, but if my own best friend, Maggie, had ditched her own useless, cheating husband earlier, then at least one life would have been saved. Maggie, like Bel, had walked down the aisle knowing in her head, if not her heart, that Tommy would never be faithful. Now he was dead. Which brought me back to Henry Bennett.

"You said Henry died in an accident, didn't you?" I asked, wary. I knew how easy it was to get away with murder if you knew the right people. Or if you *were* the right people.

"An accident? Yes! That was nothing to do with me." Will held his hands up in protest, joking because he didn't realize that I wasn't. "No, it was some sort of divine retribution, I swear. Joey had just been born, and, well, the one good thing about Henry was that he did provide. He studied by day and worked every evening to make ends meet. He looked smart in his suit, so they put him on the door at the Cotton Club. Just Black enough to add a little authenticity without scaring away the tourists, you know? Of course, he was surrounded by women every night and he couldn't keep his hands off the showgirls. Even the white girls and even the married ones. A husband came home from work early and caught him at it one afternoon. Chased him out into the street, where he got mowed down by a garbage truck. Tragic." Will drained his bottle. "I do mean that, by the way. I never wanted him dead. I just wished that Bel hadn't fallen for him." For a moment his gaze softened, as if he was remembering the Henry Bennett he'd first known. There was regret there, I thought, perhaps over the loss of an old friend, even though the friendship had died long before the man himself.

I knew what it was like to find out that a friend was not the person you thought they were. Wasn't that why I was putting off contacting Maggie? Because as close as we'd been for most of our lives, I wasn't sure she was the person I'd thought she was.

"You can't think about what might have been," I said, instructing myself as well as Will. "Bel made her own choices. She might have been young, but so was Henry, in the grand scheme of things. So were you. And it's all in the past, after all. You can lose years thinking about old mistakes, and that's no good for anyone." Alfie had certainly believed so. He'd left New York behind and never thought about the city again.

He shook himself back to the present time. "Come on, then, let's get this over with. Let's go find Leon."

As we emerged from the bar, I hesitated in the stairwell, where no one could see us, pulling Will close for a kiss. Family was complicated and I felt honored that Will had trusted me enough to confide in me, even as I was rather certain there was still more to his story.

5

Wednesday, 9 September 1936

LEON'S WAS A different world from the bar we'd come from. The pavement outside was thronged with people, a queue having formed, punters eager to gain entrance. I could hear the music, that joyous abandon of a band trusted to entertain the crowd in whatever manner they saw fit and understood why. I was torn, eager to go in but feeling underdressed and awkward. This was a proper club, a place for serious revelry, and people had dressed accordingly.

Will saw my hesitation. "We can always come back tomorrow night."

"You don't get away with it that easily," I told him, pulling him to the end of the line. "We don't have to stay all night. Just long enough to find out if this Leon character is around, and if he knows Alfie."

"It's gonna be loud in there," he said. "If we came tomorrow, early on . . ."

"Stop it." I raised myself onto tiptoes and kissed him to soften the blow. "We're here now. Bel's not going to bite. I know it's annoying, but it won't kill you to spend five minutes in her company now."

"It's not the company that annoys me. It's the asking for a favor," he muttered.

"So let me ask," I told him. "It's my father we're trying to find. My father, my favor. It makes sense that I'm the one to owe her."

"I s'pose." He sounded unsure, but his demeanor brightened.

The queue moved quickly, but I was disappointed to find that the band was just taking a break as we made it inside and the tables were filling up with hot-and-bothered couples taking the opportunity to put their feet up for fifteen minutes.

"You wanna sit?" Will asked.

"I'll come to the bar with you," I said. There was something in those little round tables that reminded me of my old London haunt, the Canary Club, and I didn't want to be alone with those memories. "Let's talk to Bel together."

We pushed our way past people until I spotted Bel, leaning over the bar as she poured whiskey for a man whose eyes were firmly fixed below her chin. Her blouse was low-cut; she probably made a fortune in tips. I saw Will clock the gent's gaze and sighed to myself. Her clothing wasn't the reason why Will got so frustrated with her, but it wasn't helping. Should I say something to her about it? No, I decided. If someone told me that I should wear something more conservative I'd tell them to stick it. And I'd never liked feeling like the pot telling the kettle what to do.

Will lifted his hand in greeting and Bel made her way along to us. "Didn't expect to see the pair of you in here tonight." She was looking at Will with a raised eyebrow as she said this, leaning over the bar toward him as she stared him in the eye.

"This ain't a social call," he said, brusque, not breaking gaze.

"You won't be needin' a drink on the house, then?"

I put a hand on her arm, ending the ridiculous standoff. "That's very generous of you, Bel. Yes please. But the main reason we're here is to talk to Leon if he's in. Turns out that he might have known my father all those years ago."

Her face softened. I'd told her all about Alfie that afternoon. I'd thought she'd seemed sympathetic to my loss; it was time to find out if that sympathy was genuine.

"You're in luck. He's in tonight. I can get one of the boys to go fetch him from upstairs." She glanced back at Will. "Did you want a drink, then, or not?"

We did, and Bel turned away to make them. "Could you do me a favor?" I asked Will. "Can you let me talk to Leon alone?"

"Alone?" His brow furrowed. "I don't think that's a good idea."

"I'm not going to go anywhere with him," I said. "I'll be right here, only I'm thinking that maybe he'll talk more if it's just me. Feminine charm and all that." I wasn't doing a very good job of convincing him. "Go and talk to Bel or something. You don't even need to take your eyes off me. Just move a few feet away."

He agreed reluctantly, but his dark mood had descended once more, and it was too loud to bother asking him why while we were in the club. Raised voices weren't exactly conducive to heartfelt conversations. We fell silent as we waited for our drinks and, in the mirror behind the bar, I saw a woman staring at the back of my head, her eyes narrowed. Slowly, trying not to make it seem obvious, I turned toward Will so that I could just spy her out of the corner of my eye. I was being a fool; she was talking to the friend she was with. I was getting paranoid. Probably she hadn't even known I was there.

Two more whiskey and gingers, and then another pair before Bel's boss showed his face. Still, we hadn't paid for them, so it seemed churlish to complain about how long he had made us wait. Assuming that he knew that we hadn't paid.

Leon Jones was an unremarkable-looking man. In his midfifties, a little overweight but not enough to entirely spoil the hang of his tailored gray suit. His hair was shaved close to his scalp to minimize the effect of his growing bald patch, and his mustache was well tended. People moved out of his way as he walked, like a prophet parting waves, and I felt my mouth go dry. I'd been expecting a Tommy Scarsdale character, a greasy aspiring businessman who was out of his depth, but Jones was a man who commanded respect. He greeted his customers as he passed, a man of the people, and they were eager to respond.

"I heard you wanted to talk. Been a while." He stared at Will as he spoke. "You back in town?"

"Just temporarily. And it's not me who wants to talk," Will said. He glanced down at me, and I gave him a small nod. "If you'll excuse me, I just need to pay the bathroom a visit."

"Sure." Jones nodded, then turned to me, picking up my hand and lifting it to his lips like some old-fashioned gent while his eyes tracked the rest of my body. "I see why Goodman's sticking around awhile. Haven't set eyes on that cat in years." He smiled at me, showing a gold tooth. "What might your name be, sugar?"

"Lena." My voice cracked on the second syllable, and I cleared my throat as quietly as I could manage. "Lena Aldridge. Pleased to meet you, Mr. Jones."

He nodded and let go of my hand. "Leon, please. So, what can I do for the two of you?"

"Sorry, sir—Leon." He watched me with a bemused grin on his face. "My father's name was Alfie. Someone mentioned that you worked in the clubs downtown—this would be around thirty years ago—and that you might remember him. They said that if anyone did it would be you." I hoped my attempt at flattery wasn't too blatant.

"You English?" He nodded when I confirmed as much. "I can tell, you know. I been to London a few times myself back when I was a younger man." He took a minute or so to light a cigar, carefully snipping the end, then caressing the exposed tobacco with the flame so that it lit evenly. His lighter looked gold. Expensively engraved. "Arthur, you said?"

"Alfie," I corrected him. "Alfie Aldridge. He was in London by 1909, but before that I—we—think that he played piano downtown."

"Alfie Aldridge." Jones looked as though he was searching through his memory. Bel slid a tall glass of Coca-Cola to him while he waited for inspiration. "Piano player from the Tenderloin days. That's where it all went on back then, before there was such a thing as jazz, when it was all about ragtime." He puffed on his cigar. "Light-skinned fella?" I nodded and tried not to look too excited as he took a sip of his sugary drink. "I might know who you mean. Quiet sort of cat. The ladies couldn't take their eyes off him. They loved themselves a bit of café au lait in them days. Still do, if we bein' honest. I figured he'd either moved up in the world or else he realized there was more money to be made on a lady's arm. Lucrative business in them days, acting the gigolo. Everyone loves a pretty young man. Or woman." His grin was a leer in my direction, and I was glad Will wasn't there to witness it.

"Do you know if he had any family?" I asked, ignoring Jones's insinuations.

He shrugged. "Everyone minded their own business in them days. Folks was coming in every day from elsewhere, 'specially from down south. We was living on top of one another down there. All sorts went on. Nothing like this place." He threw out an arm to indicate his own fine establishment. "No, ma'am, the clubs and saloons down there, things was casual. All the booze was under the table 'cause no one was licensed to sell it. This is before the nonsense of Prohibition, of course, which was another fine time to be in the know. Downstairs there'd be music and dancing; upstairs you could lose the shirt off your back at the craps table. There'd be girls on every street corner, willing to help a man sleep a little lighter if his pockets was too heavy when he walked out."

I didn't have time for Jones's romanticizing. It didn't sound that different from Soho, if I was honest: people doing what they had to in order to get by. "So you don't remember anything else about this man?" Maybe it was just as well. Did I want to find out that Alfie had made a living as a gigolo in his youth? Shame was an awfully good reason for not wanting to talk about the past.

"Faces came and went. I only remember that fella 'cause of the ruckus he caused one night. Couple of us had just opened up a club off Sixth, my first business, if you like. One of my business partners had sorted the entertainment and the fella I'm thinking of, he used to come in and play the piano occasionally in the evenings. We never hired him, not officially, but he could play any tune you asked him to. Like a human player piano. 'Maple Leaf Rag,' though. That was his signature. Played it every night, sometimes two or three times if he got asked to."

My heart thudded as he spoke. It *was* Alfie, then. If you'd asked me to name one tune that I remembered him for, it was that one. I'd asked him once why he played it so often and he'd said it was for the memories. To remind him why he'd come to London in the first place.

"Some rich white fella. Used to be a regular in that place. Tar, they called him. I remember, 'cause he was about as white as they come!" Jones laughed at his own weak joke. "Two of 'em was friends up until something happened. Kid came in one night and started playin', just like always, but soon as Tar walked in, he stopped and got up. Next thing I know, punches are bein' thrown, the table's been flipped. Kid was screamin' somethin' 'bout his sister."

"His sister?" I took a step back. Alfie had sometimes talked about his mother—I knew she'd died before he left America—but never anyone else. Certainly never a sister.

"I think." Jones's brow furrowed as he tried to put himself back in that bar almost thirty years earlier. "Yeah, I'm sure. 'Cause all he kept screaming was *she trusted you*. And I remember the fella just laughed and said that if their mother had brought them up right, the

57

girl would have known better. Something like that. Struck me as pretty sick, if I'm honest, though I wasn't surprised. Rich white folk like that, they throw money around and expect to get away with anything and everything."

I nodded, feeling a little sick. "What happened after that?"

"The boy ran out—crying, mind you, by the time they was through. Tar paid up for the damage. Wad of notes in his wallet like he owned a bank. Never saw either of 'em again after that night." He finished his drink in one gluttonous gulp and checked his watch. "That's all I know, so if you'll excuse me, I got a business to run and a band who should've been onstage five minutes ago."

He left me feeling paralyzed. Leon had given me more questions to ask and not many answers. Could Alfie really have had a sister? Did I really have an aunt I'd never heard of before, let alone met? I wanted to believe that Leon was thinking of some other young man, who just happened to look like my father and play piano like Alfie had, even down to the tune he always played. I could imagine the "Maple Leaf Rag" was in many a piano player's repertoire back in the early 1900s. It was possible. I lit a cigarette and finished my drink. I had just a name: Tar. The nickname of a rich white man. Not much to go off. But what if I really did have an aunt out there? Wasn't it worth trying to find out more?

"Let's get out of here." Will appeared out of nowhere, steering me into my coat and out the door before I could say anything about it.

"Wait a moment!" I dug my heels in, literally, once we were outside, and turned away from the queue of patient people still eager to dance on a weeknight. "For pity's sake, Will, what's wrong with you?"

"It's late, is all," he said, not meeting my eye. "Claud will worry that something's happened to you."

"No, she won't. She knows I'm with you." I riffled in my hand-bag for my cigarette case, giving up when Will handed me a cigarette, already lit. I inhaled deeply as we started to walk. "What's going on? Why are you being so . . ." I stopped there, biting off the harsh words that threatened to pour out. I was on edge, I knew. Partly thanks to Leon but more due to Will and his decidedly off manner.

We walked on for a minute or so in silence before Will sighed heavily, pulling me to stop beside him. "Baby, I'm sorry. I know I'm acting strange; it's just that I'm not used to being off the ship for so long. I guess I got itchy feet or something." He smiled sheepishly and bent to kiss me. "I'll be better. Promise."

There was a strange distance between us that hadn't existed when we were at sea. As if the reality of my entering his world, trespassing even though I had been invited, had washed away the comfort we had found in each other. Will was keeping something from me. I knew it for certain; it was why we'd left in such a rush. Something had happened in that small window of time between his leaving me with Leon Jones and his return. Nothing to do with Bel, for she had been behind the bar, never out of my eyeshot. Someone else had rattled Will. He dressed it up as if he was concerned for me, but was it more concern on his own behalf? What wasn't he telling me?

There was history all around me here, and none of it good. Alfie and Will. They weren't so different, after all, but they weren't alike in a good way. Not in the way that I'd hoped. Two good men, but their secrets were beginning to feel overwhelming. I'd carry on my search for Alfie and this long-lost sister. Harder to deal with was Will. He walked right beside me, but I didn't know how to ask him the questions I wanted answers to. What price was I willing to pay for that knowledge? I might very well find out the truth, but if it ended our friendship, our romance, whatever you could call it, would it be worth it?

Harlem After Midnight

Thursday, 17 September 1936, 2 a.m.

THE WOMAN WAS clinging to life as they loaded her into the ambulance, but Garson knew better than to count on ever getting from the horse's mouth the truth of what had happened. Even if she survived, she'd been banged up pretty good. Would she remember what happened? Fifty-fifty. He looked up at the window she'd fallen from. If it weren't for the vicious stone steps beneath, he'd have given her better odds. As it was, it was a miracle she'd made it this far.

"We know whose apartment that is?" he asked the young patrolman, pointing up to the window. Freeman looked pale and he kept his eyes averted from the pool of blood that had been left behind.

Freeman glanced down at his notebook. "Linfield. They're a married couple. There was a gathering there tonight. Several people were in the apartment, but they all claim not to have seen what happened. It's a bedroom window. The party was mostly happening in the living room, and they'd all been drinking."

"You questioned them?" Garson's eyebrow raised. Damned rookie taking matters into his own hands and messing up the system.

"No, sir." Freeman swallowed hard. "No, I only went up there to secure . . . to make sure that everyone stayed put. Till you fellas got here. They was quick to speak up, though, sir. I just thought it best to listen. In case anyone said something useful."

"Hmm." Garson reached into his jacket pocket for his cigarettes.

The boy had the right idea, he had to admit. When liquor was involved, people let things slip. Give them time, though, and they'd start to sober up. He wondered what state the revelers would be in when he got up to see them. A woman falls from a window, from a room away from the party itself. Even banged up from the impact, she was a good-looking woman. It would be one of the men, probably. Or a jealous rival. There would be a story there. He just had to figure out who was willing to tell it.

"She was holding on to this." Freeman passed him the woman's passport. "It's British."

"Shit." God knew this was the last thing he needed. Dealing with international bureaucracy would probably be a nightmare, not that he had any experience in it. Maybe his boss wouldn't mind dealing with the Brits. McLennan liked to think he was a cut above even though he was just another Irish cop. Garson pocketed the passport. "She was visiting the Linfields?"

"Yep. They seem like decent folk. He's a doctor; she's a librarian."

"And they were having a party? On a Wednesday night?"

"They'd all been over to the Apollo," Freeman explained. "Amateur Night. It was a bit of a celebration, if you get my drift. A couple of the guests had been performing."

"Including her?" Garson stared after the ambulance as it pulled away.

Freeman shrugged, embarrassed. "Sorry, sir. Like I said, I wanted to wait for you. Didn't want to step on no toes, you know? This is just what I picked up while I was getting them all to wait in the one place."

"Okay." Garson lit a cigarette. "Take me up. Let's find out what really happened here."

Alfie

June 1908

THERE WAS RICH and then there was wealthy, though Alfie had never realized this difference until he was shown into the drawing room of Tar's house. The fact that the man owned an entire house should have been a giveaway. Alfie hadn't asked for enough money. Ten dollars for the afternoon was what they'd agreed, on top of the money that Tar had already paid him, double what Smiles and the other fellas back at the boardinghouse earned in a week working in construction. Alfie ran a finger along the frame of an oil painting and wondered what Tar had paid for it. A staggering amount, he was willing to bet.

The room was grand. High ceilings, polished wood floor, not a speck of dust in sight. There was one long sofa, piled up with cushions, and several uncomfortable chairs dotted around the room. A fire blazed away even though it was June; the curtains were drawn, but electric lights blazed the room into a strange and eerie light. It was a sunny day out and Alfie wondered why they didn't pull open the drapes and save their money. He wondered if his Victoria lived in a house like this. She'd vanished from his landscape, not seen in the Tenderloin for over a week now. Returned to the less grubby life she belonged to, he supposed. He couldn't blame her. This house, this life, was safe. Comfortable.

In the corner sat the grand piano. Ebony wood, the lid propped open so that the internal workings of the instrument were on show. The piano gleamed and the keys were pristine. Did anyone ever play it? Alfie looked around. The maid who'd begrudgingly led him to the room had disappeared as though she was ashamed to be in his vicinity. She'd dared to look down her nose at him even though all she did was sweep hearths and wash windows all day. He was a musician. A man of talent. A man getting paid a considerable amount more than her for a lot less work.

A modest win at craps the night before had given him enough money to invest in new clothes for the occasion. A shirt that was actually white, and trousers that weren't darned to within an inch of their life. It was an investment rather than an expense. If he looked the part, played the part, then surely Tar would keep him on. No one got tired of listening to music, and Alfie was great at keeping up with the latest songs straight out of Tin Pan Alley.

Where was Tar? Alfie hadn't expected an effusive greeting, but he had thought that Tar would meet him. Tell him what he wanted him to play. The house was silent. Should he just begin? Was that his job, to break this terrible peace that made the house feel more like a museum than like a home?

Alfie lifted the stool lid. No sheet music. He lowered the lid and sat down. It was a Saturday afternoon. Too early for the sort of ragtime tunes he whipped out in the Tenderloin? It didn't feel quite the right setting, even though ragtime was what he'd been playing when Tar had approached him. What about something more classical? Or had Tar chosen him for his race? Some white fellas, they loved a Negro spiritual but were too ashamed to admit it to their own kind.

Alfie had shied away from these; he wanted to play more modern music, show that the Negro had more than one string to his bow, but he could play "Deep River" if that's what was required. He closed his eyes and smoothed the tips of his fingers along the keyboard. Yes, he could play whatever it was that Tar wanted, just as soon as Tar told him what that actually was.

"My goodness, Sallie!" A girl stomped into the room, startling Alfie. "Will you look at the time? Did I not ask you to come get me as soon as Mama's luncheon had been served? I'm going to be late."

Alfie's first instinct had been to duck down and, once he'd done that, he couldn't exactly sit back up. His natural common sense told him that this girl wasn't expecting to see him sitting at the piano. Would she scream if she saw him now? Think that he had been lurking there, just waiting for her? It was too late now. If she'd walked in earlier, when he was standing by the piano, running his clean palm over the high gloss of the wood, that wouldn't have been so bad. He could have explained his presence quite easily, he thought; what sort of criminal waited around in the drawing room where any member of the family could walk in and see him? But now that he'd sat down, the bulk of the pianoforte shielding him from sight, he looked suspicious. Like he was hiding.

The girl was around his age, nineteen or so. A Gibson Girl. Well-fed, straight-backed, and tall, though he thought the height of her golden hair, in the pompadour style that was all the rage, gave her an extra couple of inches. She stood before the mirror above the fireplace, turning this way and that to make sure that not a strand was out of place. Her dress looked similar to one that his sister, Jessie, had made back in Jacksonville for rich folks. Gallons of pink muslin and lace that draped her from neck to ankle, her waist tugged in tightly. He wasn't sure it suited the girl; Jessie could have made a better job of it, made sure that the dress didn't swamp the neck of its wearer as this one did.

The Jacksonville dress had been sold to a rich widow who wanted to wear it to her daughter's wedding. Jessie had bent over her work, hour after hour, until her head ached so badly she'd had to stop. The money had been worth the sacrifice, though the woman hadn't been grateful. Would it kill these people to show a little gratitude? Alfie could tell this girl was of the same stock. Entitled and arrogant. He slouched down farther, more convinced that he couldn't let her see him.

"Sallie!" The girl bellowed and Alfie heard hurrying footsteps along the corridor. "For the love of God," she muttered under her breath.

"Miss?" It was the maid who had shown Alfie in, less snooty now and very much more out of breath. If he stood up now, would she vouch for him? Too risky.

"Didn't you hear me?" The girl turned on her heel. "I told you to come get me when it was time to leave."

"I'm so sorry, miss, only your father wanted me to let in the—" The maid's eyes were flitting around the room, and Alfie realized she was looking for him. He was the reason she'd been distracted. He kept his head down and hoped for the best.

"Where is he?"

"Miss? You mean the—"

"My father, you foolish girl." Tar's daughter took one last glance in the mirror. "Tell him I've gone out with Gertrude Young. I shan't be back for dinner; I'll dine with the Youngs."

"Yes, miss." Sallie gave up explaining, though she did give the room one last look over before being shooed out ahead of her mistress.

Alfie sat up once the coast was clear, the front door of the house slamming closed as the young mistress left. He dared to dart across to the window and peer around the curtain to catch a better view of her as she climbed into a gleaming gray-and-gold automobile. Tar's daughter might have said that she was going out with Gertrude Young, but the person waiting in the Model K roadster was most certainly not female. Black hair slicked back with brilliantine so that it shone as brightly as his autocar, a waxed mustache, and at least five years on his young companion. Tar surely didn't know what his daughter was getting up to. Alfie knew what a girl from his part of town would be called for doing similar, but he hadn't known that so many rich girls were prone to the same predilections. Weren't they too busy calling upon one another and sifting through prospective husbands? He'd thought Victoria to be extraordinary, not of her type, but perhaps she was just following a traditional rite of passage. Her own minor rebellion before settling back into the life set out for her.

"Ah, there you are."

Alfie jumped as Tar entered the room, jacketless, his shirt collar unbuttoned. A casual look, but then he was at home. "Sir."

"Quite a different view than you're used to, I'm guessing?" Tar came and joined Alfie, just seconds after his daughter and her clandestine beau drove out of sight.

The quiet, tree-lined street was indeed very different from life down in the Tenderloin. Not a single Black person in sight, though Alfie was sure that behind closed doors there were plenty of them, hard at work as cooks and maids and manservants.

"It's a nice street," Alfie said eventually.

"The neighbors think I'm vulgar. New money. Like it's a crime to do an honest day's work. My wife chose this house." Tar leaned around Alfie, replacing the drapes and closing out the street.

"You don't like the house?" Alfie looked up in surprise. Wasn't Tar living the American dream? A mansion in a fancy part of town. Actual real-life chandeliers hanging from the ceilings and a fleet of staff to take care of the menial tasks.

Tar shrugged. "The house is fine. It's like any other. Eleanor likes being close to her friends; it's them I can't stand. Round here every morning, drinking a gallon of tea and pretending that they don't look down their noses at me. Most summers we leave this cesspit and sail to Europe."

"All that way?"

"Son, one day maybe you'll get to travel. Do it soon, before you get saddled with a wife and children." Tar clapped Alfie's back and steered him toward the piano. "I'd do anything for my wife. And she loves music, which is why you're here."

"You want me to play for your wife?" Alfie was confused.

"That's what I said, isn't it?" Tar showed a hint of the lack of patience Alfie had seen in the daughter. "My Eleanor, she's sick. Has been for some time. Most days she can get herself dressed, spend a couple hours in here with her friends. Then she's in bed for the rest of the day. She can't go out and hear music at the theater like we used to, so I thought, why not bring the music to her?"

If Alfie thought it a bit odd, he knew better than to say so. "Sir, I can play just about any song. Some classical too, if your wife prefers. I learned Brahms and Beethoven from my teacher back in Jacksonville."

"No, no." Tar gestured for Alfie to sit at the keyboard. "Play her what you were playing the other night. She wants to hear the new music. The stuff she's missing out on." He smiled suddenly and Alfie wasn't sure it suited him. "I'll just go get her."

Alone again, Alfie fought the urge to run. He couldn't put his finger on it, but today, when Alfie was stone-cold sober, there was something unnerving about Tar. Who was he? His accent didn't fit his grand house, though he was trying hard to smooth it out and slow down his speech. Today Tar spoke like a man who worked hard for a living, who got paid only for the work done and so spat his words out because they didn't earn him a dime. He was a man who hadn't grown up with money, or not this volume of wealth at least. He showed off his riches through his walls, cluttered with oil paintings, through his spoiled daughter's expensive clothing and jewelry, by paying Alfie to come and perform a private concert for his ailing wife. And Alfie didn't even know Tar's real name.

"Here we go, darling." Tar returned with a middle-aged woman, pushing her unwieldy chair on wheels before him. "Young Alfred will play whatever you like. Your very own Carnegie Hall!"

Alfie got up and gave a small bow, as if he were indeed about to take the stage at a world-renowned concert hall. The woman smiled and nodded gracefully. Her movements were slight, as if they pained her. Her fingers were bony and he could see that she had no strength, her left hand weighed down by hefty rings. She looked as though a breeze could scatter her into a cloud of ash.

"I hope my husband is paying you a decent sum?"

"Yes, ma'am. I'm very grateful for the opportunity." He hated that he sounded so subservient, but it was such an odd situation. He'd been expecting a party of people. Men of influence who might be able to give him a leg up in the world of music. This was just . . . odd. "Would you like me to play anything in particular to begin with?"

"Whatever you please," she said as Tar settled her before the fire, tucking a blanket around her legs.

In looks, she was an aged version of her daughter, though her countenance was far preferable. Her accent was refined, unlike her husband's. Perhaps the money was hers, Alfie pondered as he retook his seat. And what was wrong with her? He dared a glance up as Tar sat down heavily on the sofa behind his wife. She smiled and gave him another nod of encouragement.

All right, then. He'd start off with his signature and go from there. "Maple Leaf Rag." If she didn't love that, then he was in trouble.

6

Thursday, 10 September 1936

"GOOD NIGHT?" CLAUD asked, leaning out of the small kitchen into the living room as I shuffled in, yawning and half-asleep still. "Coffee?"

"Please." I was grateful she'd asked. I hadn't had a clue how to use the strange coffeepot in the kitchen. I'd already discovered that tea wasn't an option unless I wanted to go out and buy my own, along with the teapot and the other bits and bobs necessary. Like much else in America that I'd seen so far, everything in Claud's kitchen was recognizable but just that little bit different from what we had at home.

"Did you find anything out?"

"Yes. Maybe. An aunt, perhaps." As soon as that word—"aunt"—passed my lips, I felt a little sick. Could Alfie really have turned his back on a sister, so that he would never mention her name again? No matter what she'd done, I couldn't imagine my father being that coldhearted. Then I remembered Eliza. He'd never spoken her name aloud either. I knew why he'd exorcised Eliza from our lives; she'd deserted us and left us penniless while she returned to her family's wealth. Had this sister done something equally callous?

"Goodness, an aunt? And you never knew?" She leaned against the doorpost. "You get a name for her?"

"No. It was that Leon chap who told us, but he wasn't sure. He used to know a man who might have been my father, and that man had a sister." I bit my lip. "It might be nothing. He didn't know her name. Just a strange nickname for a man who the chap—maybe Alfie—had an argument with. A rich white man who went by the name Tar. That was all he could tell me."

"Doesn't ring a bell." Claud's disappointment quickly switched to amusement. "But you went to Leon's after all? And Bel was there?"

"We ended up getting pointed in that direction." I decided to push my luck. "Will told me what happened with Henry Bennett, though I still don't understand why Will's so odd around Bel."

"He told you? That's good. That's good." She smiled as she repeated herself. "I told him you'd understand."

"Of course," I said. "Who wouldn't understand an older brother being protective of his sister? And that Bennett chap sounds like he had it coming to him." Not to make light of a man getting run over in the street, but it had been only his own fault.

"I got a lot of time for Bel," Claud told me. "She's fun to be around. But she's made more than her fair share of mistakes, and I think Will's just had enough of cleaning up after her. He pays the rent for Joey's sake, not hers."

"He said as much."

I'd told Will everything that Leon had told me, but we hadn't talked much after he'd walked me home. He'd kissed me at the door and promised to do better. We'd go sightseeing the next day and start over. I'd held him close and agreed. It would be daft to fall out over something that didn't really affect me. Although, just as Will had helped me out on the *Queen Mary*, perhaps there was a way of me repaying the favor. I was an outsider with no ulterior motive. If I could help Will and Bel to understand each other a little better, wouldn't that be a good thing? Meddling in other people's business had gotten me in trouble in the past, but I couldn't see how the situation with Will and Bel was similar in any way.

"Will's taking me to the Empire State Building," I told Claud as she handed me a steaming cup of coffee and sat down opposite.

"Wowee," she breathed. "You mind telling Louis 'bout that? 'Cause I've been on at him to take me since it opened. They say you can see five different states from up there if you peek through one of their telescopes."

"That seems . . . amazing."

"Doesn't it? That's why I want to get up there and see for myself!" Claud laughed. "Louis's scared of heights, but don't tell him I said so. If he has to go any higher than the fourth floor, he gets dizzy. At the hospital the nurses draw the curtains across the windows so that he can't see out."

I couldn't imagine the solid, no-nonsense Louis being scared of anything. "I would never have guessed," I said.

"No." Claud fired up a cigarette and refilled our coffee cups. "It can take years to get to know a person. Who they are, what they're capable of." She smiled and added sugar to her cup. "I'm glad that Will confided in you. Secrets like that, they just aren't worth keeping. And—don't take this the wrong way, but I can tell that you're not a girl who's led a sheltered life. You know that good people are capable of bad things. Heat of the moment and all that."

Heat of the moment? Was she talking about the incident Will had told me about, when he'd walked in on Henry with Bel? Come to think of it, he'd never actually said what happened after that. Had he just dragged Henry out by his collar? Or had things taken a more violent turn and ended in a fistfight? Either way, Claud made a good point about me understanding that human nature wasn't just black-and-white.

"My best friend's husband died before I left London," I told her. "It's awful, but when I realized that he was—gone . . . I was glad. Which is a terrible thing, really, but he treated her so badly." I took a sip of coffee and tried not to let the worry line in my brow show.

"You feel guilt, though. About being glad he's gone."

"I do," I admitted. "You shouldn't speak ill of the dead, they say, but why? Tommy wasn't a good man. He'll be in hell right now; I'll tell you that much. And maybe he's there with Henry Bennett."

"Henry." Claud shook her head. "Such a charming man. Clever and handsome. I completely understand how Bel fell for him. Lord knows, if I hadn't been loyal to Louis already, maybe I'd have fallen for his sweet words. Silver-tongued, isn't that what they call it? If the man could just have kept his pants buttoned up a little more often, he and Bel would have been living the high life. That's what makes it saddest of all. He had talent. He'd just graduated from law school when it happened. He and Bel were married. They had Joey . . . It was a tragedy, really."

"Will talks about him like he was the devil incarnate," I said, confused. "But you don't think he was that bad?"

"He was a flawed man," she corrected. "It's a sin, lust, of course, isn't it? But with Henry it wasn't as straightforward as Will likes to make out. Henry only ever loved Bel, and I think they had an understanding of sorts. She married him, after all, and she knew what he was like. That's what Will can't forgive. That after everything that happened, she still went ahead with the wedding."

After everything that happened. This was the vital piece of information that Will hadn't shared. The way Claud had phrased it—*she still went ahead.* Something else had happened between Will and Henry. After he'd walked in on them that time, much later, when there was already a wedding being planned. "Did Bel know how Will felt? About the wedding, I mean, not generally."

Claud raised an eyebrow. "Well, Henry didn't exactly go to Will asking for permission. How could he?"

We both jumped as we heard a key in the front door, the belated knock on the wood as Will let himself in. I knew that I was nervous about Will overhearing me question his best friend, but why was she so nervy, hardly able to look at me as she called out a greeting to him?

"Morning!" he called back.

Claud smiled and squeezed my arm as she began to clear away the coffeepot. "You two have a nice day. And look! Blue sky. You're going to get quite a view."

I nodded and managed a smile as Will walked over, his face beaming, and leaned down to kiss my cheek. I almost pulled away but caught myself in time. It was evident now that Will had only told me a sanitized half of the story. On the one hand, I could understand why. This was a temporary romance. All the omens foretold that once I reached Southampton in a couple of weeks' time, that would be the end of us. Was it even fair of me to demand answers when there were so many secrets that I was keeping to myself?

THE WEATHER WAS glorious, the sun bringing a glow to the brownstone buildings, glinting off the cars as they passed us on the street. It wasn't as warm as it looked, though, and I was glad to have brought a jacket out with me.

"We'll take the el," Will told me. "It'll take us straight down to Thirty-Fourth Street, plus you'll get a good look at the city."

We climbed up the steps at the station and were just in time to catch the next train headed south. I wasn't like Louis, scared of heights, but for some reason the journey was disorienting. I was used to buses and to the tube. Shooting through the tunnels in the dark felt safe. What you don't know about can't hurt you. Up here, the train made a rattling sound, rocking its way along the tracks above the street with nothing to catch us if the driver missed a turn. "Precarious" isn't a strong enough word to describe it.

"We'd just land down there, on those poor people," I said, thinking aloud.

"It's safe," Will assured me, taking hold of my hand in reassurance. "Think how many trains they drive along here every day, no problem."

"Would Louis get on one of these?" I asked. I had no previously known fear of heights but this felt very real. A fear of falling was very rational, a very different proposition from the abstract idea of it.

"No," he admitted. "But Louis can barely survive in that third-floor apartment. Claud had to promise him that they'd move somewhere on a lower floor when they were able, but now she's got the place looking so nice he can't bring himself to suggest it."

"And I bet Claud knew that when she promised him."

"Undoubtedly." He grinned. "I love that you're getting along with them."

"I can see why you're so close to them." Was this the right time to bring up Henry Bennett? Probably not. "Claud cares about you a lot."

"Yes."

He fell silent for a moment, then leaned across to point out where we were in relation to Claud and Louis's apartment; to Morningside Park, hidden for the most part behind the buildings, a snatch of greenery catching the corner of my eye if I concentrated my gaze on the cross streets; to the neighborhoods that we passed through on our way south. Every so often we pulled into a station and let New Yorkers on and off the train, their attitudes reminding me of my own beloved Londoners. The men in suits flicking open their newspapers, eager to make sure that everyone could see how industrious they were, reading the financial pages before they had even arrived at their work desk. Workingwomen in smart dresses looked destined for the secretarial desk; those in full makeup were shop workers. Maggie and I had always played a game on the tube to pass the time. We'd pick a passenger and give them a name. A job. A husband, wife, lover, or not. What their life was like, where they lived, whether they were happy or sad. We took clues from their attire, their hand- bag, their hairstyle, the station they'd boarded at.

"Watch out—this is Suicide Curve up ahead."

Will chuckled at the look on my face as I shivered at the idea of it. How anyone could bear to walk along those tracks, at that height, just to throw themselves off, was beyond me. I'd die of fear before I got that far, but plenty managed it, Will assured me, so many that apparently a significant number of passengers walked down to the next station to avoid seeing it happen.

The train hurtled down Ninth Avenue, and then it was the vast Central Park I was trying to spy across the carriage. Hell's Kitchen looked disappointingly ordinary, not a place I was keen to explore, and then Will was pulling me to my feet and we were disembarking. I can't lie; I was immensely relieved to have my feet flat on the ground, the buildings towering above me, as felt correct.

I don't know what I expected. Some sort of fanfare, a marching band, a huge banner proclaiming that the ordinary revolving door we passed through led into the tallest building in the world. Instead, the Empire State Building looked quite like any other building.

"Most of it's just offices," Will told me when I remarked as much. "It really is just like any other building, apart from the observation deck. And the fact that when you get up there, you'll feel like you're on top of the world."

There was no way on earth that Claud would get Louis up to the top, I decided, my entire body feeling like jelly as we stepped into the lift—elevator—and the operator announced our next stop as the 86th floor. It was such an odd feeling, the swift propulsion upward, unnatural. My ears protested and Will winced as my fingernails bit into his hand.

"Almost there," he told me, pulling me close.

Thank goodness. The operator opened the doors, and I took a few wobbly steps forward, trying not to feel sick, my hearing muted as my ears seemed full of bubbles, the sounds popping in and out as I tried to get to grips with my surroundings.

"You gonna be okay?" Will looked half-concerned, half-amused.

"I'll be fine," I assured him. "Let's go and see what all the fuss is about." We might as well make the ordeal worth it.

Outside on the deck the wind was blowing gaily, reminding me of our time at sea. Down on the ground the day had felt still and warm enough for a light jacket. At more than eighty stories high, the breeze was far more noticeable, enough to make me shiver.

"Want to take a look?" Will bounded over to one of the telescopes positioned at intervals along the deck. We'd arrived early enough that the deck was half-empty and it was no difficulty to secure a position along the fence, my eyes desperate to glance down and see just how high up we really were. "Don't look down! Or just look down a little. That's the Chrysler Building right there. And then behind, you got Central Park."

My nausea passed and my ears finally popped, and I enjoyed letting Will show me the sights of his city. For the first time since we'd arrived in New York I was with the Will I'd met on the ship. A confident man who had been at home in his surroundings. Odd that the only time he wasn't himself was when he was actually at home. I let him lead me on a lap around the building and steeled myself for the inevitable.

"Seen enough yet?" he asked, joking.

"Can we sit down for a moment?" I asked. "There's something I want to ask you."

7

Thursday, 10 September 1936

"I NEED YOU to tell me everything," I told him once we were sitting down. "The whole truth about what happened with you and Henry."

"What d'you mean?" He tried to laugh it off, but he couldn't look me in the eye. "Did Claud say something?"

"Enough to let me know that you only told me half of the story." I put a hand on his knee. "I don't care what it is that you're holding back. Truly, I don't." I hoped that when he did finally tell me that this proved to be true. "What I care about is that something's coming between us."

"There ain't nothing going on," he told me. "It's just family history. In the past. Nothing for you to worry about."

"I'm not perfect, Will. You know that." I pushed away the knowledge that he didn't know the half of it. "But it's not history. It's not in the past if it's still affecting you."

"Fine." He changed his posture so that he faced straight ahead.

Away from me. He took off his hat, straightened his tie. "There's no easy way to say it, I guess. That's why I've tried to avoid it, knowing that you'd think different of me."

"You don't know that."

"Yeah, I do." He began to fiddle with the band of his hat, smoothing the felt with his thumbs.

"Will, just tell me." I thought about touching his shoulder, laying a hand as comfort, but didn't think I could bear it if he shrugged me off. "Whatever it is, I've heard worse, believe me."

He didn't say anything for a long moment, time enough for my imagination to run wild. What was the worst that he could reveal? That he'd killed a man? Well, he could join the list of people I was on first-name terms with who could say the same. Then I thought about Bel. She was a good-looking woman and only a stepsister, not a blood relative. I'd heard of stranger things than two people, thrown together in the same household, falling in love. Was that it? Will had been in love with Bel all these years and that was why he'd been so furious about her marriage to Henry, a man who wasn't good enough? It would explain why he'd been so standoffish with me when we'd first met. Did I remind him of her? My heart sank. Had I just been a second-rate replacement?

"I was in prison," he said. His head hung down in shame as I felt relief rise in my chest. "For assaulting Henry Bennett."

"That's it?" I asked, wanting to be sure. "That's what you were scared to tell me about?"

"*That's it?*" He looked at me in disbelief. "That's a pretty big deal, don't you think? Most people would say so. I got a criminal record, Lena. Why d'you think I spend my life at sea? I got sick of people staring at me when I played clubs here, talking about me, or not letting me play in the first place. I got violent tendencies, they say." He shook his head.

I had to smile. "No, you don't. I know you don't. There's not a chance in hell that Claud wouldn't have warned me if you did, and she's known you almost your whole life. She might be loyal to you, but she's a good person above all else."

"She is that," he agreed.

"So, what happened?" I could guess, the pieces finally beginning to slot together. "You caught Henry with a woman who wasn't Bel and lost your temper?"

"He was just such a bastard about it." Will's tone had lightened considerably, his body relaxing slowly as I watched him cast his mind back, his head shaking as he remembered his former friend's betrayal. "We were out dancing, me and a girl I'd been seeing, Claud and Louis, Henry. Bel should've been there, but she was sick, so she said. I hadn't seen her in a good couple days. She was locked away in her bedroom, calling through the door to say that she looked terrible and she wouldn't show her face until she was better." He shrugged. "I was so busy back then. Studying, plus I had a job packing groceries to try and make ends meet. Ma was still alive. I think she knew what was going on, but she'd told Bel not to tell me."

"Henry had hit her?"

"Yup. I found out by accident. He was out on the dance floor, flirting with the girl I was with, and I was already close to seeing red. I left because I was worried I was going to lose it. Only when I got home, Bel was in the kitchen. She'd thought I'd be out all night, which, to be fair, I usually was."

I tried not to wonder about the girl Will had been with, whose night had been cut short. Who was she? Claud would know. I didn't want to interrupt Will's flow of conversation.

"She had a black eye—well, it was fading because she'd been hiding it from me for a couple days. I made her sit down and tell me what had happened. Which is that she had got upset with Henry over his philandering. He'd gone to storm off and when she'd grabbed his arm to pull him back, he'd shaken her off and then . . . I guess he punched her. She had a huge bruise on her ribs too, when she lifted up her sweater, and that was when I lost reason. I didn't stick around to ask any questions, just went straight back out to find him. I caught him coming out of the club with some other girl he'd picked up." He paused to look at me, scrutinizing my face for any sign of condemnation. "I beat him down. I couldn't have stopped myself if I'd tried."

"For good reason," I told him. "You did it for Bel."

"That's no excuse." He grew serious. "Afterward I could barely remember doing it. That floozy he was with, she sat up in the witness box and told the court that I had looked like a crazy person. Like a monster. Just hitting him, over and over again, even when he was down on the ground." He looked me in the eye. "I could've killed him, Lena, honestly. I think I could've. He ended up in the hospital and I ended up in jail. Bel married him anyway, so what was the point? It's not like he changed his ways."

There it was. The click of a puzzle piece slotting into place. This was what Claud had meant: *after everything that had happened.* Bel had known full well that Will had tried to protect her, and she'd turned her back on him and married the man who'd beaten her, who presumably carried on beating her long after the wedding cake had gone stale. Why? There was one good reason I could think of, and I wondered how long it was afterward that Joey had been born.

"Maybe she didn't have a choice," I suggested, and he grunted an acknowledgment. "These situations . . . I remember being a young girl like Bel was then. It's not like being a man. We have other things to consider."

I'd always been lucky, never fallen pregnant, though I'd taken the odd stupid risk over the years. In fact, only the year before, I'd suffered through a terrible few days thinking that I might be pregnant. Had even rehearsed how to break the news to my married lover, now former. Given a real choice I wouldn't even have told him, but I knew he knew people—doctors who could carry out a safe abortion without alerting the authorities—and had the money to pay for discretion. I couldn't imagine that a girl of seventeen would have the money for that. Bel would have been facing a back-street quack with no guarantee that she'd be safe. That or worse, living with the shame of an illegitimate child. Henry Bennett might be dead, but at least she and Joey had his name. There was no shadow cast upon a widow and her child. That garbage truck knocking Henry Bennett from this life and into the next might have saved Bel from a fate far worse.

The silence stretched out between us and I was worrying that I'd spoken out of turn when suddenly he sat up. "You're right. I know you are. Claud's said the same to me a hundred times."

"Us being right doesn't make you feel better, though."

"Nope." He took hold of my hand and kissed the back of it. "But sometimes it helps to hear the truth. Me and Bel have had other arguments over the years. It ain't just about what happened with Henry, but that's where it started."

"I'm glad you told me." It was a relief, if anything. "I understand why you didn't want to tell me. It can't have been easy, rebuilding your life after what happened."

"Is that what I did?" He smiled wryly. "People might say that I've been avoiding doing just that. Sailing back and forth across the Atlantic with strangers. Hoping no one finds out what I did."

"Your band aren't strangers. They're friends. And they know, don't they?" It was a wild guess, but he nodded. He wasn't a secretive person, not usually. "So, then. Just because you grabbed hold of an opportunity, it doesn't mean you've been hiding away. You've been doing what it takes to provide for your family."

"I guess so."

I remembered suddenly about my plans for the following day. "Talking of your family, you don't mind that I'm going shopping with Bel tomorrow?"

"No. I'm glad you two get along. And I'm sure buying a few new dresses will put the smile back on your face."

"What do you mean?"

I tried to look affronted, but he had a point. I'd been out of sorts since we'd left the ship. After what had happened, how could I not be? But I had fled to Harlem—to Will—because he made me feel safe. I could be myself around him. My recent past was a patchwork of other people's mistakes, nothing to do with me; at least that was what I wanted to believe. Why shouldn't I be allowed to fall in love? Even if it was to be short-lived.

"What time do Claud and Louis get home usually?" I asked. "They keep to a regular schedule, I suppose?"

Will shrugged. "Sure. Around five, I guess. Why?" His expression changed as he understood what I meant. "Claud'll kill me! I promised her there'd be no raunchy stuff—her words, not mine—under her roof."

I checked my watch. Not even noon, and I'd seen Claud making sandwiches for herself and Louis that morning. Not planning on popping home for lunch. "What's the worst that can happen? I can afford a hotel if Claud kicks me out."

"I'm not worried about you. Think what she'll do to me!" But the fear wasn't great enough to stop him from getting to his feet.

I barely noticed the elevator journey back down to terra firma, or the rickety journey back north on the el. I don't think we spoke much; we didn't need to. It had been a long time since I'd felt that addictive rush: lust, anticipation, the excitement of discovering someone new. It wasn't going to be our first time sleeping together, but it was the first time that it would be something real. At sea, on the ship, there had been so much else going on. I'd been barely surviving, not sleeping, and Will had been a sanctuary. What had happened between us there had felt temporary, with the translucent fragility of a fever dream. When I had left Will's narrow bunk on the *Queen Mary*, I had half expected never to see him again, to discover later that he was a figment of my imagination that appeared only when I was most in need. Here, in New York, we were real. Solid and made of flesh.

As expected, the Linfields' apartment was empty when we got back. There was something decadently louche about making love in the middle of the day, the curtains not pulled, the afternoon sunshine glowing against every inch of our bodies. When Will decided we should perhaps eat something, to keep our strength up, he walked to the kitchen without a stitch on and I thought I had never seen anything so magnificent. We ate rolls with thickly spread butter and slabs of cheese, careful not to drop crumbs in the bedclothes, before turning our attention back to each other. It was as though when I heard Will's confession the barriers between us had been demolished. We might both be troubled souls but there was a kinship in that, so strong that I had to push away the knowledge that in less than a fortnight I would be sailing back to England. Though, did I really have to? Will kissed a line from my forehead to my navel, and the last thought I had before he moved lower was, *What if I stayed?*

8

Thursday, 10 September 1936

"SO, HOW WAS it?" The first words out of Claud's mouth when she got in from work.

"What? What was . . . Oh!" I stammered so badly that I might as well have just owned up immediately. I saw Claud's eyes narrow and she shot Will a look that could have withered a rose in full bloom. "We had a lovely day," I said quickly, as if firing the words at her at pace would make her more willing to believe them. "You really should go up there—up the Empire State Building, I mean. Maybe with a friend? I can tell you right now that Louis would hate it!"

"The sky was incredibly clear. We could see the whole city." Will met Claud's accusatory glare and didn't blink once.

"Hmm. Well, I got hamburgers for dinner. Lena, if you feel up to peeling a few potatoes, that'd be much appreciated. And we're out of beer." Claud disappeared into the kitchen to drop her shopping bags.

"I'll run out and get some. You need anything else?" Will got up, a smirk on his face from having gotten away with it.

"I got everything I need." She reappeared in the doorway, hands on hips. "How 'bout you?"

Will shrugged. "Can't complain."

"You had a nice day out, then? What else did you do?"

Will was ready for her. "We walked around, talked. You know how it is. The weather was glorious."

"And that ain't always a guarantee this time of year. God blessed you with the sunshine."

"He truly did."

It was like watching a Wimbledon final, two people at the top of their game, neither one willing to give an inch. I was just thankful that neither of them seemed to require me to get involved. Claud gave up and stalked off to her bedroom to get changed out of her work clothes, but I saw her glance through my open bedroom door and was very glad that I'd made the bed once we'd vacated it. With the curtains blowing gently in the breeze from the open window it would look the very picture of wholesome innocence. I hoped.

"I'll be back in ten." Will bent to kiss me. "And don't let her bully you!" He pushed his lips together and mimed the action of a turning key. "She'll try and trick you while I'm gone, but don't you let her."

"But she knows," I hissed.

"So what? Long as you don't confess, she can't do anything." His face broke out into a huge grin. "She wouldn't do anything about it anyway, but she'd never let you forget it. It ain't worth the aggravation, trust me."

I went into the kitchen and made myself useful, unpacking the shopping, putting away anything that wasn't needed for the dinner that Claud was planning to make. I'd made a start on peeling the potatoes by the time she joined me, tying a pinny around the waist of her housedress.

"I'm not a judgmental woman," she said, "but I need to make a point to Will. You understand?"

I almost fell for it, so gently did she speak, but caught myself just in time. "We had a nice day." I kept my tone light, not lying as much as avoiding the topic. "It was good to talk properly. About what happened to Will, you know? With Bel."

"Ah yes. I wondered if I'd said too much this morning, but I guess he really did tell you everything?"

"I understand it now, why he's so angry with Bel. Not angry," I corrected. "I suppose it's a mixture of things that he feels. Disappointment. Guilt. All those things that make us feel bad about ourselves." Claud was an easy person to talk with; it was still taking all my wits to stop myself from blurting out how Will and I had really spent the afternoon.

Claud leaned against the sink and watched me thoughtfully. "You know, I wasn't sure when Will asked me if you could stay here. Nothing personal, of course—I hadn't even met you then—but I was surprised. So surprised that I guess that's why I said yes. Will hadn't brought a girl here before. Not ever. He's almost back to the Will I grew up with, but I don't think he'll ever quite be the man he was."

"Prison took something from him?"

"Sure. I mean, how could it not? He'd worked so hard at college, expected to get into a good law school, and it ended up all being for nothing." Her gaze misted over and I knew she was remembering the boy, the young man who had almost killed Henry Bennett and had as good as killed himself at the same time. "We were all shocked when it happened. Louis and me, we were there that night, in the club. I didn't see much, but Louis ended up taking care of Henry while the cops came and took Will away. Just a horrible situation. We were all friends, you see, and we . . . well, we didn't know what Henry had done. Not for a long time after. We couldn't talk to Will and of course Henry was full of shit, tellin' anyone who'd listen that Will had lost it, that he was crazy, that he was in love with his own sister and that was why he'd gone mad. Jealousy, that's what Henry told anyone who'd listen."

I felt that sickly twinge of shame, knowing that the same thought had crossed my mind, briefly or not. "And I suppose Bel didn't put anyone straight."

"Not then." Claud shook her head in disbelief. "She told me on her wedding day, would you believe? Will had been found guilty by then, Henry making quite the stir in the courtroom, so Louis told me. Bel wanted out of Will's mother's house since she was hardly welcome any longer. Tish had guessed the truth of it, since she knew what Henry had done to Bel, but without Bel herself coming forward . . . And it seemed pretty likely that Will would be found guilty whatever Bel said. You can't beat a fella unconscious no matter how much of a bastard he is."

"No," I agreed. "But why tell you on her wedding day? Like a confession?"

"She was drunk." Claud's tone made it clear what she thought of that. "Silly little girl, I think she knew it was the wrong decision. If Will's mother hadn't made it clear that she wasn't welcome in her home any longer, she might have had the courage to walk away. But after all that trouble, and what with Will rotting in jail, I guess she didn't dare."

"Before she told you, did you really all think that what Henry said was true? That Will was in love with Bel?" I tried to imagine what that must have felt like, to know that it wasn't just random strangers who believed a lie, but his closest friends. Claud and Louis.

She sighed. "I didn't know what to believe. I'd never known Will to lose his temper like that. Henry was . . . well, he made it sound like the truth. If he'd lived much longer, he'd have been an incredible lawyer. Bel would've had the house she dreamed of, even if she had to put up with his nonsense."

"His *nonsense* left her relying on Will for charity and Joey without a father." What a weasel of a man. If he'd still been alive, I would have felt violent toward him myself. I hadn't even met the man, but he brought back bad memories. All the times I'd seen Maggie's husband flirting, or worse, with some young girl he'd promised the world to. Tommy Scarsdale was now dead, but I wouldn't grieve for him. His funeral had taken place while I was halfway across the Atlantic, and although I felt a slight twinge of regret at not being by Maggie's side that day, I knew that she too was glad to be rid of him. "What a mess," I said, meaning a lot more than just the shadow of Bel's adulterer husband.

"It is that," Claud agreed, "but this is all history now, Lena. It was awful, all of it, but Will was only in jail for just over a year in the end. Henry was gone by then and Joey had just been born. Bel's been trying to make things up all this time. Don't hold it against her; she was just a kid herself when this all happened."

I was slightly regretting the decision to spend the next day shopping with Bel. I knew it wasn't fair to judge her for something that had happened a decade ago, but it was difficult not to let Will's revelation affect my feelings toward her. But I'd gotten along with her like a house on fire the day before. And maybe she could help me out. Leon had given me one clue to follow up on when it came to my father, but it wasn't enough. Bel was the only other person I knew who mixed in those circles, who knew the older fellas who might have once come across Alfie. Bartenders were the priests of the nightclubs. If ever I'd needed to know anything about anyone back in London, I'd gone to Vic, the German bartender at the Canary Club. He had the ear of everyone, from the boss to the muscle on the door, from the regulars who leaned against the bar to the young waitresses who loved to gossip as they waited with their trays. If Bel and I became friends, she surely wouldn't mind asking a few questions from behind the bar at Leon's.

The front door slammed shut and I heard male laughter, Will returning from the shop, Louis from the hospital.

"Not a word," Claud warned. "Let's have a nice dinner, just the four of us, and we can plan what to have for my birthday dinner."

I nodded, having completely forgotten about Claud's birthday. Bel could help me pick out a present the next day. Something extra special, partly to make up for having flouted her rules, mostly because she had been such a welcoming hostess. And I needed something new to wear. I did some quick sums in my head, working out how much money was left hidden away in my old carpetbag. I had meant to save some for when I got back to London, but would it hurt to spend a little more now? I'd get Bel to show me where I could send a telegram to London, let Maggie know which ship I was taking and that I'd be arriving home sooner than planned. A lot sooner. Just as I'd always been a shoulder to cry on for her, her big empty house in Hampstead had been a place I could stay whenever I had the need. If I arrived back with just a couple of pounds to my name, it was still more than I'd had a few weeks ago.

When we sat down to eat, Will was full of good humor, he and Louis trying to guess who might be in attendance at the party. Will seemed to know an awful lot of people, and I wondered again why he hadn't tried to make a new start in New York. People had long memories, but it seemed like he still had friends in Harlem, and not just the Linfields. Harlem's loss had been my gain, I reasoned, but it seemed such a terrible shame. Had it really been impossible for him to return to college, to finish the education that he'd worked so hard to gain?

"Bel asked if she could bring Joey for dinner. She can't go to the party, of course, but I suggested she sleep here until we get home," Claud said, and Will nodded.

"It's a special occasion, after all. And last time I went to a Harlem rent party it was dawn before we left." He shoveled mashed potato into his mouth. "You don't mind a late night, do you, Lena?"

"Not at all," I replied. Late nights had been my stock-in-trade ever since I'd gotten my first singing gig at the age of fifteen.

Claud looked pleasantly surprised, as if she'd expected there to be a minor argument about it at the very least. I saw her and Louis exchange glances before her husband brought the subject on to how much booze we should take, and where they could get their hands on a keg of beer.

I couldn't remember the last time I'd been invited to a party. A drawback of working every evening bar the Lord's day; I could never be counted on to make it. Alfie and I had celebrated birthdays with nice dinners or small cakes, whatever we could afford at the time. When we were younger, Maggie and I would go out dancing after my last set had finished, dashing into bottle parties before the doors were locked and pressing up against unsuitable men. Even after she'd married, we'd carried on, knowing that Tommy would likely be out just as late, making his own fun with a girl who wasn't his wife. It hadn't been until Maggie had lost her first baby that she'd slowed down. Stayed in and stopped staying out late.

Looking at Will, then, the easy smile back on his face after a couple of days' absence, I let myself relax. There'd be plenty of time to worry about Maggie when I got back to London. In the meantime, Will was right in front of me, and good men don't grow on trees.

9

Friday, 11 September 1936

WE STARTED THE day nice and late. What with Bel's occupation
keeping her out late, it was eleven o'clock before she called round at
Claud's, where I had filled the morning by trying on each of my
clean dresses, pairing them with various accessories until I was satisfied that I could bear to show my face in the sort of fancy department
stores that Bel had threatened to take me to. Quite some feat too
when you keep in mind that I had only two clean frocks left. Laundry was a task I hadn't yet undertaken in New York. Hopefully after
our shopping trip I could put it off for another few days.

"I thought we could start off with Bloomingdale's and then head
down from there," Bel said as we walked toward the elevated. I was
beginning to feel like an old hand at this, my nickel in my fist, looking like a real New Yorker. "And then whatever else happens, we have
to finish with a late lunch. In fact, I've already got the perfect place
in mind, somewhere that Will won't take you to."

"I'm sure he would." I followed her onto the train, determined that I wouldn't let Bel put Will down. I hoped we'd have a nice day together, but my loyalty rested firmly with him.

"Oh." Bel looked at me awkwardly as we sat down. "I didn't mean it like that. I should have said 'can't,' not 'won't.'"

It took me a moment before the penny dropped. Bel and I could go to a fancy restaurant because we looked enough like the other patrons. White. Will might be able to get a job at one of those places, but he'd never be allowed in as a paying customer.

"Do you go to those sorts of places often?" I asked, curious. In London, my passing was less of an issue. There was no official color bar, though I'd heard enough stories to know that it did exist unofficialy. Will had told me in no uncertain terms that things were different here. There'd be no lowered tones and embarrassed looks. Just a stern word and the expectation of obedience.

Bel shrugged. "Can't afford it too often, or find a man who wants to take me." She laughed but it was a brittle sound, as fragile as the dead leaves that were starting to be seen on the sidewalk below us as we rattled past Morningside Park.

"Well, if I'll do, then I'd be glad to take you." I squeezed her arm. It couldn't have been easy for her, bringing up Joey alone on just her one wage. And as much help as Will gave her, it couldn't have felt good to be so reliant on him to pay the rent. Not after what had happened.

"I think you'll find, Lena, that *I* am taking *you*. This is my city, after all. Just 'cause I'm a little down on my luck doesn't mean I don't still know where's good to go. Far as anyone else is concerned, today we are two ladies without a care in the world. And why should we care, seein' as how our good husbands are out working hard to keep us in heels and silk stockings? That's our story, and you're an actress, after all." Her smile was genuine this time and I felt the thrill of her words.

Maggie and I used to do the same thing. Putting on our nicest dresses, spending hours on our hair, before waltzing past the doormen at Harrods as though we could afford to buy the entire shop. When Maggie got married and could actually afford to buy clothes from Harrods and Selfridges, the excitement vanished. There was a great pleasure to be had in trying on a ball gown that cost a year's rent money, in imagining myself the sort of woman who could afford such a luxury. Who was she? Where was she from? Which man would she kiss under the clock at midnight?

"What's your plan?" Bel asked as we cut across Central Park. We were surrounded by trees and other greenery, but above us towered those incredible buildings. From this perspective, I could appreciate just why they were called skyscrapers. "Is this practical shopping or fantasy shopping?"

"I suppose a bit of both. I need something to wear to Claud's birthday tomorrow, but I like the idea of trying on some ridiculously priced ball gown."

"I have a penchant for fur coats," Bel confessed. "My husband always said he'd buy me one once his law practice got up and running, but . . . you know what happened next."

"I'm so sorry," I said.

She waved away my pity. "Oh, he was a womanizing bastard and he got what he deserved. The only shame of it is that I'd like Joey to have more. She's the one who got let down. I knew what I was marrying."

"If you don't mind me asking," I said carefully, "why did you marry him if you knew what he was like?"

For a moment I thought she wasn't going to answer, that I'd ruined the day before it had even gotten started. "Because I thought I could change him. That after what had happened with Will—he did tell you?" She stared at me, wide-eyed, worried that she'd given away his secret, until I nodded, and she looked relieved. "After all that trouble, Henry had to be worth it, right? Otherwise, I'd just wrecked Will's life for nothing. And I knew everyone blamed me for what happened."

It made an odd sort of logic. I was hardly immune from making my own mistakes, after all. I could understand how Bel might have felt that Henry was her only ally. Claud had said that Bel had been as good as thrown out, Will's mother unable to even look at her after her son had been convicted. Easier to walk down the aisle and think of a new life, one that came with the promise of security and a fur coat. Even Henry Bennett himself couldn't have predicted what would happen.

"There does come a point when you have to leave things in the past," I told her, sounding wiser than I had any right to. "How can you plan for the future if you cling on to that one night? I don't blame you. Will's doing the same, but if you moved on maybe he could too."

"You think?" She looked hopeful.

"It's worth a shot, isn't it?" I linked arms with her. "But for now, I say, let's ignore the past. Let's try on some fur coats and some expensive frocks and act like we can afford them, but they're just not quite what we're looking for. We can pretend to be rich ladies who don't need to work for a living."

"We can be sisters," Bel said, putting on a remarkably passable English accent. "Two sisters from London whose father is here on business and has left us to our own devices for the day."

"And Daddy has the money, so we can't possibly pay for anything," I added.

It was the most fun I'd ever had acting. Bel and I rampaged through ladies' wear in Bloomingdale's and Bergdorf Goodman. I hadn't found anything I wanted to buy, but Bel had been bold enough to ask the keen assistant at Bergdorf's to put a hold on the most ridiculous mink coat, floor-length with fur so thick that Bel's slim figure disappeared within it, leaving her with just a head popping out the top, like some overpriced version of the Cheshire cat. Shop assistants tripped up in their eagerness to help these two wealthy young women. The accent seemed to be the key and I was having so much fun that I'd forgotten that there were actually people in New York who knew me, and knew that I was just Lena Aldridge, daughter of a deceased music hall piano player who hadn't a penny to her name other than the wad of warm dollar bills that had been come by through chance.

We'd decided to go down to Macy's and do some serious shopping for Claud's birthday, when my luck ran out. Bel was about to flag a taxi when I recognized that I knew the area. The Sherry-Netherland hotel was just across the street, more or less, and I'd meant to call the front desk and check if anyone had left a message for me. Perhaps Maggie, and even if not, I should really send a telegram to London. If she'd read the papers maybe she'd already heard what had happened on the *Queen Mary*. She'd be worried.

"Go and check," Bel said. "We can get the doorman to hail a cab for us when you're done."

The lobby was hectic, and Bel ran off to use the bathroom while I waited in a queue to speak to a receptionist. My feet were aching; we'd done a lot more walking than I'd realized. I took off one shoe and sighed as I rested it against the cool marble floor, closing my eyes in relief.

"Lena?"

My eyes sprang open on Eliza Abernathy, one of the few people I knew in New York and one of the last I had hoped to see. Every time I saw her it took me a moment to remember that she was actually my mother. It was thanks to her that I'd been duped into accepting the free ticket to come to America, not that she knew it. The last time I'd seen her she'd been walking off the *Queen Mary*, a broken woman escorted by her rather more legitimate son and daughter. It wasn't that we'd left things on bad terms, more that I'd had the distinct idea that I didn't really matter to her any longer. And why should I when she had a father and a husband to bury? It was a biological fact that I was her daughter, nothing more.

"Lena, thank goodness! I thought you'd run back to England

without saying good-bye." She stood there, looking immaculate in her expensive black silk dress, her makeup perfect as always and her blond curls salon fresh. The society wife still. "I was going to leave you a message, but they told me you'd checked out after only one night."

"I'm booked to go back to London in a week or so." I remembered my manners. "How have you been? And the children?"

"Oh, you know." She looked a little embarrassed, glancing around her. "I was just passing, and I remembered that you were staying here. I came out for some fresh air more than anything. There's so much to take care of. The funerals and . . ." She bit her bottom lip. "This isn't the place for a reunion, Lena, I realize that, but can we talk? Come to the house. It'll just be the two of us." She glanced around her once more, and I realized she wasn't alone. She riffled through her handbag and pulled out what can only be described as a calling card, a small rectangle embossed with her name and address in gold lettering, and handed it to me. "Come for lunch Tuesday. One o'clock. My telephone number is there if you need it."

And then she was gone, not even waiting for me to agree or say anything at all. Not that I felt able. The last thing I wanted was to go to lunch with Eliza Abernathy. I had gone to Harlem precisely to avoid the Abernathy family and the memories of what had happened to us on the ship. But I would go. I already knew as much. Eliza was an unpulled thread, and she was one of the few people who might be able to answer questions about Alfie. She hadn't known him when he lived in New York—they had met in London—but they must have talked. How could they not, knowing that they both hailed from the same city all the way across the ocean?

"Who was that?" Bel knocked me back into reality as she returned, her makeup refreshed.

My mind raced. I was caught out. "Just a fellow passenger from the ship. She wanted to say hello." I could feel my face turn red.

"I'm going to sit down. My feet are killing me." Bel disappeared, leaving me still in the queue. At least she hadn't noticed my lie.

Finally, the man at the front accepted that since he was not a guest at the hotel, they could not accept or take messages for him, and we all shuffled forward. Eventually it was my turn, and after all that, no messages. A relief that there was nothing from the police back in London. Disappointing that no one had cared to find out if I'd made it to New York safely.

I was all alone. No father; a best friend who maybe wasn't any longer. I looked down at the calling card still clutched in my hand. Eliza hadn't asked where I was staying. It wasn't as if she could find me if I didn't show up, but didn't it make sense to go? It could be that she'd known Alfie's sister. She owed me some answers. Anything she could remember from her brief affair with Alfie could be vital. I wanted to see how she lived, and I wanted to know if her offer of financial support was still available. At least I could have some security from my usual money worries. My thumb traced the raised letters of Eliza's address. She'd said it would be just the two of us. I had to trust her on that.

10

Friday, 11 September 1936

IF I WAS preoccupied as we continued our shopping mission, then Bel didn't seem to notice. She filled the quiet with commentary on everything, from the best place to grab a bargain or a dress that had been copied from a movie star's photograph, to sharing snippets of tourist information. I smiled and muttered the odd rote phrase to make sure she knew I was listening, but there was a buzz inside my head, growing gradually louder, and I could feel my armpits begin to grow damp. I'd not felt this since leaving the ship. The disturbing sensation that something was happening outside of my control. Was it just from seeing Eliza? I wasn't sure, but I didn't like it one bit.

We struck gold at Macy's, Bel sticking to the green that suited her with a bias-cut crepe number that looked dressy without being too ostentatious. I found a discounted silk knee-length dress in a shade that the store assistant called ultramarine, plus a couple of practical knitted skirts and blouses for day wear.

"And now I'm really starving. Let's eat." Bel led the way out, throwing her arm up to stop a passing cab. "With a bit of luck we'll have missed the lunchtime rush."

We bundled into the back of the taxi and Bel gave the driver instructions. It seemed like she was in charge, so I didn't pay much attention, just gazed out the window as we drove, heading back along the way we had previously walked, turning up Fifth Avenue.

"I hope you like oysters," she said. "You're in for a treat if you do, though they do have other options. Last year I was seeing this guy for a while. He used to take me to this oyster bar. They make a stew that's so good that even though he bored me half to death I kept seeing him just for an excuse to go and eat there."

I couldn't judge her motives; I'd done worse than spend an evening making small talk with a dullard just to get a free dinner.

We pulled up outside a train station—Grand Central, Bel told me as she whisked me inside. Midafternoon, the concourse was busy but not too crowded as I followed her, clutching my shopping bags in both hands. The concourse was ridiculous: vast even compared to the great stations of London, the ceiling so far above our heads that it may as well have been the sky. We headed down a ramp and eventually arrived at our destination.

"Oh, I hope you like it." Bel was nervous, less sure of her recommendation now that we were actually here.

"It looks wonderful," I assured her.

If I had expected a cramped space beneath a busy train station, then I had been wildly wrong. This was a huge restaurant by English, if not by New York, standards. White-clothed tables were set out under tiled arches, the room only half-full of dining guests, but Bel took me to the counter instead.

"This is where you get the real experience," she said as we hopped up onto stools, our shopping bags at our feet. "You could go anywhere and sit at a table."

The menu was extensive, and I felt as though I were on the ship again, the choices overwhelming. I glanced at Bel, who was busy catching the eye of the bartender. He winked as if he recognized her and I wondered just how often she came here, and with whom.

"Two beers, please, Jake," she ordered, pulling out her cigarettes. "My friend here came all the way from London, England, and I told her this is the place to come."

"All this way, huh." Jake smiled at me as he reached up for glasses, and I found myself returning the favor. He was very easy on the eye. I wondered if it was just the oysters that kept Bel loyal to the place. "You staying long?"

"Not as long as I hoped," I admitted. "Only another week or so."

"Lena's a singer. She came here for a job, but it fell through." She leaned her cigarette forward into the flame that Jake offered.

"Tough luck." Jake commiserated, moving his lighter toward my own cigarette.

"I'm trying to convince her to stay. There must be a heap of places looking for a singer. I mean, why waste the trip just to turn around and go home?" Bel was full of surprises.

"Sure would be a shame." Jake blessed us with a white-toothed grin as he placed our drinks before us. "Enjoy, ladies, and give me a wave when you need me."

Bel sighed as he moved on to a couple of gents down the bar. "All right, so maybe it's not just the oysters that make this place a favorite."

"You haven't . . ." I paused, not knowing how to phrase the question politely.

"God no!" Bel looked appalled, then laughed. "I mean, I wish. But a young, good-looking fella like him—he wouldn't want to get stuck with someone like me."

"Why not? He's not that much younger than you."

"It's not my age." She spat out the words and I knew I'd said the wrong thing. "I'm only twenty-eight! And everyone says I look younger."

"You do. Definitely," I murmured.

"It's Joey. No one wants to get saddled with a kid, not even a brilliant kid like her." She took an angry drag from her cigarette. "Even my boring Wall Street guy ditched me once he realized I wasn't just going to open my legs and be grateful for a few free dinners. He said he didn't want to be paying to bring up another man's child." She took a large slurp of her beer. "Not even thirty years old and already on the scrap heap."

On the face of it our lives were very different. My father had never remarried, and I had fallen for more than a handful of the wrong men but never got hitched or ended up widowed with a young child, but there was something in her resignation that I recognized. Before a stranger had shown up at my Soho lodgings and offered me the opportunity of a lifetime, I had been feeling much the same way as Bel. Done and dusted at twenty-six, nothing going the way I had hoped, dumped by my married lover and struggling to make ends meet. We weren't that dissimilar, then, after all.

I took a more measured sip of my own drink. "You know, life has a way of surprising you. It might seem as though you're on the scrap heap, but things can change. Look at me, for instance. If you'd told me three weeks ago that I'd be sitting here, in a restaurant in New York, drinking beer and eating oysters with a new friend, I'd have laughed and thought you were mad."

"It really happened that fast?" she asked, a note of hope creeping in.

"Really," I confirmed. "I mean, look, things haven't quite worked out the way I wanted, but still, it's been quite an experience." That was putting things mildly. "I'd never left England before, never been to sea before. I might not be going onstage on Broadway, but I feel different now. Like I could do anything. Go back to London and show up at auditions that I was too scared to try for before."

"You're a new person." She clinked her glass against mine. "Cheers to you, then, Lena. I'd kill to have a second shot. But you're sure that

London is the right place for you now? It seems easy now that you're so far away, but wouldn't it be easier to start again in New York?" She smiled, teasing. "I reckon that Will would stay if you were going to be here. He's never been serious about a girl, not since, well . . ." Her mouth twisted in regret. "I'd like to see my brother happy."

It was the second path, the one I'd been trying not to think about. The short-lived romance that I'd hoped would jolt me out of dwelling on recent events now felt like something more. But Will worked on an ocean liner, and I had nothing tying me to New York but him. No job. No friends, except Claud and Louis and Bel, who were only borrowed from Will. Added to which, being so close to Eliza and the Abernathys had already proved to be dangerous. If I could bump into Eliza by accident so easily, how long would it be before others worked out where I was?

Home was London, I reminded myself. Home was Maggie, who might need my help. And I had so much to tell her. Things that I couldn't possibly write down in a letter. I had been disappointed not to hear from her, but what was I expecting? Her life had gone on in London. A funeral. A whole mess to sort out: Tommy's estate, the Canary Club and its dubious accounts, a host of shady characters who had conspired to get rid of her feckless husband. As loyal as I already felt to Will, Maggie had to be more important. Our years of friendship were worth more than a short romantic dalliance.

"I very much care for Will," I told Bel carefully, "but it's too early to tell if it's serious."

"You're not in love with him, then?" She raised an eyebrow. "You've gone all red, Lena."

"It's just the alcohol," I snapped, then felt like a real heel. "Bel, I know you want the best for Will. I do too. I'm just not sure that I'm it. You barely know me, after all. Will barely knows me." I couldn't bear to imagine what Will would say if he ever found out the whole story of what had happened on the *Queen Mary*. None of it was my fault, exactly, but I had kept the truth from him nevertheless. Now that he'd told me his own terrible secret, mine weighed a little heavier on my soul.

"I don't need to know you inside out," Bel went on, and I felt my body relax. "I see how my brother is after knowing you only a few days. He's a new person. And you just told me that so are you. So maybe you don't know yourself as well as you thought."

I felt her words ignite a small spark of hope deep inside me. They had a decidedly complicated relationship, but Bel knew Will. She'd lived under the same roof as him for years, on and off. There was nothing in it for her to push us together, other than to secure Will's happiness.

Jake returned to take our orders and I followed Bel's lead, taking a chance on the oyster stew. I could see the chef making the stew fresh behind the counter. No cook myself, I found it fascinating how swift he was, throwing ingredients into his pot, his lips singing lyrics to a song that I couldn't quite hear. It was as good as any performance onstage.

Bel wasn't as fascinated as I was, and we settled into talking about less fraught issues: who the guests at Saturday's party would be, where I could get my hair done for the aforementioned event, then on to Joey's recent school report on the NAACP, which had resulted in a letter home warning Bel that her daughter seemed to have access to upsetting materials.

"Like what?" I asked, and lit a fresh cigarette.

"Lynchings." Bel looked irritated. "As if that sort of thing happens here! It's not something that Joey should be worried about. But she will read the newspapers. And Claud lets her take whatever books she likes from the library. I've told Claud to show her the children's books. Look at pictures or what have you, but no. My damned daughter takes after her father. The one good thing about Henry was that he believed in justice for everyone. I guess in this case the apple hasn't fallen far from the tree."

In my naïveté I asked, "What's so bad about that?"

Bel blew smoke out of her nostrils. "On the face of it, nothing. But when my ten-year-old girl is standing up before a class of kids and reading aloud about the violence that gets done down south, well, no wonder the teacher thinks I'm filling her head with these horrors."

"I understand why you might not want her to be exposed to violence," I said, "but you must be proud. That she doesn't sit there and accept that bad things happen."

"I'm always proud of her." Bel seemed needled. "But there's a time and a place for talking about these things, and a kid living in New York City doesn't need to be worrying about what happens to Negroes down south."

Our food arrived and I concentrated on the oyster stew, which was surprisingly good. The perfect meal for a day that, while not quite cold, had given up the promise of autumn. The warm creaminess of it felt like luxury, the culinary version of the fur coat that Bel had tried on earlier. Jake brought us two more beers to wash it down with, and I added the stew to my list of things I would miss about New York.

The problem with New York, I admitted to myself, wasn't that I couldn't live here. It was that living here with Will would be complicated. Bel and I had spent a marvelous day together, looking around, walking the streets, joking with shop assistants. All that was possible because of how Bel and I looked. People saw us and thought we fit in. We had everyone fooled, but if I had been with Will all day, I knew, I wouldn't be half as content as I was sitting at that counter, my belly full and my shopping bags safe beneath my feet. No matter what Bel said, I wasn't sure I was ready to enter the world that Joey wanted to right.

IT AIN'T NECESSARILY SO

11

Friday, 11 September 1936

IT WAS OVER our second round of beers that Bel came up with the plan. She'd asked me how my investigation into Alfie was going, and after a moment's hesitation I told her what Leon had told me.

"A mysterious aunt?" Her eyes lit up. "Well, we have to find her!"

"How? I don't know her name. Or if the man Leon knew was even my father."

"Hmm." She stared off into the distance, thinking. "Now, there is one fella I know who was around then. Plays trumpet down at the Ubangi and has done since it was Connie's. By which I mean he's an old-timer. I know he and Leon go back a real long way. If Leon knew your father, there's a good chance this fella did too."

"All right." It was worth a shot. "I don't think Will had any plans for this evening, so I suppose he won't mind if I suggest this."

Bel pulled a face. "Oh, Will won't come. He hates that place."

"Really? Why?"

"Full. Of. Tourists." She laughed. "Connie's was whites only. So was the Cotton Club when it was open. They all used to come up to Harlem to have a good look around. Like a trip to the zoo. The riots last year spooked them all off. That's why the clubs that were too good for colored folk have all died off. The Ubangi opened up and they ain't as fussy, but you'll still see more Negroes working there than drinking there." She drained her glass. "Come on, let's get the bill. I got the night off and I'm in the mood for a little music this evening."

I wasn't surprised that Will wouldn't be keen to go somewhere like the Ubangi. Alfie had left New York almost thirty years earlier and yet it seemed like not much had changed, if anything had. I just hoped Will wouldn't mind my going, and with Bel.

"The Ubangi?" Will pulled a face.

"Bel thinks there's someone there who might have known my father," I told him quickly. "We won't stay for long."

"There's the card game over at Rufus's," Louis reminded him. "It'd be good for you to catch up with the fellas. They always ask after you."

I stifled a yawn. The early-afternoon beers had made me sleepy and even a cup of strong coffee when I'd gotten back to the Linfields' hadn't helped. Claud had brought home pork ribs, macaroni cheese, and corn bread from a local restaurant. I wasn't that hungry after the oyster stew, but I dug in quickly, seeing that Louis and Will would demolish anything that wasn't snatched up in time.

"Haven't seen Rufus in years," Will said around a mouthful of food.

"That's what I'm talking 'bout," Louis pointed out. "Come on, man. You don't need to worry about the money. Small stakes. Half the fellas can't afford much more than a few dollars here and there."

"It's not the money I'm thinking of. I can't just desert Lena. She's my guest."

"You're hardly deserting me." I laughed. "If anything, it's the other way around."

"The show don't start until after midnight at the Ubangi," Will said, but I could hear his tone soften.

I put my hand on his. "Why don't you go and enjoy yourself? You don't have to worry about me. I have my mission, after all. I have to at least check if this chap did know Alfie or not."

"Fine. I guess I can trust Bel to look after you." Will turned his attention back to Louis. "Besides, if I remember rightly, last time we played cards you ended up owing me forty bucks. That'd go a ways toward some good liquor for the party tomorrow."

"Don't you dare," Claud told her husband, and I saw him and Will exchange a grin as soon as her back was turned.

BEL CAME OVER and we got ready in my room, doing our makeup side by side like old friends. The clock struck ten and Bel poured out the gin. Claud had retired to bed early and Louis and Will had headed out to their card game. "We'll leave here at eleven. The Ubangi gets going late, but we want to catch Smiles before he gets caught up."

I nodded; it made sense, but the gin was turning my stomach a little and I was suddenly exhausted. I was thinking about making coffee when Bel suddenly jumped up.

"Time to go!" She gathered her jacket and purse.

I followed her outside and along the street, my prayers answered when the Ubangi turned out to be only a ten-minute walk away.

"It's an odd crowd," Bel said to me under her breath as we arrived, "and an odd old show too." The doorman nodded as he caught sight of her and we skipped straight past the queue, paying our cover charge to emerge into the packed club. To my surprise, almost all the revelers were white, dressed to the nines and sitting around tables facing an empty stage. "Tourists," Bel said, giggling, and I knew then why Will didn't like the place. "Plus, this place caters for a bit of everything, if you know what I mean."

I didn't, but I had more pressing concerns on my mind. "Where do we find Smiles?"

"You don't want a drink first?"

I shook my head. "Let's get business out of the way first." I could already feel the gin thudding a tame beat at the back of my head. If I drank much more, a seedy hangover the next day would be a certainty.

I followed Bel, the two of us weaving our way between the tables, avoiding the singing waiters who were serenading a couple seated to one side of the room. I'd assumed we were headed backstage, but instead we stopped at a table in a corner. A large Black man sat there, smoking a cigar and drinking Coca-Cola. When he saw Bel he grinned widely, his whole face lighting up in a way so contagious that I couldn't help but return the smile, and I saw how the man had gotten his nickname.

"Been a while, darlin'," he said.

"Too long, Smiles," Bel agreed, sitting down and gesturing for me to do the same. "This is Lena. Lena, this is Smiles."

"Pleased to meet you." He stuck out a hand, warm and calloused. "What can I do for you two lovely ladies? And make it quick—I'm onstage in ten."

"You've been on the scene for a while," Bel started, and he began to laugh.

"Just call me old and have done." He stubbed out his cigar and took a sip of his drink.

I decided to get right to the point. "My father used to play piano downtown. I'm trying to find people who knew him."

"You English?"

I nodded. "But he wasn't. He would have been young when you knew him, not even twenty years old. I just . . . I found out recently that he had a sister. It's really her I'm trying to find out about. His name was Alfie. Alfie Aldridge."

His eyes hooked onto mine as soon as he heard the name. "Yeah, I knew Alfie."

I felt a sudden breathlessness. "Really?"

"Sure. We lived in the same boardinghouse for a while. Must be twenty-five, thirty years ago." His gaze softened as he traveled back in time. "Is he— The way you talk, like he's in the past . . ."

"He died last year," I confirmed. "Tuberculosis."

"Damn." He shook his head. "Not a good way to go out. My condolences."

"Thank you. I suppose you got to know Alfie quite well? And his sister?" You surely couldn't live in the same house as someone and not know they had a sister in the same city.

"Jessie?" He took the bait. "I only met her the once. Quiet thing. He'd left her behind in Florida, only she came up after him. He acted like he was angry with her over it, but I knew he was glad to see her."

"Florida?" Alfie had never mentioned anywhere in America other than New York.

"Back then folk was arriving every day from down south. I got the impression that something had made him leave, but he never would talk about it. Restless. That was what he was. Never got himself a regular job until some white fella offered him a heap of notes to play private concerts for him." Smiles lit another cigar, taking his time as I bided mine. "He moved out of the boardinghouse when Jessie came; that's why I only met her that one time. They found rooms to rent with a friend of hers. Can't remember the friend's name, but I do remember that she looked like trouble. A dancer, and back then dancers didn't just make their money up onstage, you know what I mean?"

I did. "I don't suppose there's anything else you can tell me about Jessie?"

He shrugged but had the decency to look regretful. "Sorry. Never set eyes on her again." He glanced at his watch. "Ladies, I'll

have to love you and leave you. Feel free to keep the table, though."
Reaching beneath his chair, he retrieved a black instrument case and
then he was gone.

"Well, at least you have a name now," Bel said.

"Jessie." It wasn't much, but it was something. She was real. Jessie Aldridge, my aunt.

Bel waved in the direction of one of the waiters. "Come on, let's
get a drink and watch the show. The night is still young."

I was exhausted, and it was after midnight, but I felt that I owed
her to stay for at least a little while. She'd led me to Smiles and kept
quiet while I'd spoken to him. The lights went down and came back
up in the middle of the club, where the show was to take place. First
out were the dancers, but the next act explained why Bel had called
it an odd old show.

"Gladys Bentley," she told me as the entertainer strode out in her
smart tailcoat, hair slicked down, followed by a troupe of immaculately dressed young men. "She's the reason everyone comes here."

Within minutes I understood why. Her voice was powerful, and
she commanded her stage like it was her God-given right, but it was
what she sang that had the audience blushing and laughing in equal
measure. When we'd arrived, I'd been so intent on finding information that I'd not noticed much of the clientele. As Gladys sang to two
men close to the stage, teasing them with her risqué lyrics, I watched
them turn to each other and kiss.

"You're not shocked, are you, Lena?" Bel grinned at me.

"Nothing I haven't seen before." Which was true. I'd sung at the
Shim Sham back in London several times and had to dive out during
a police raid that they claimed was over the lack of a liquor license,
but which I suspected was more to do with the action on the dance
floor.

"Have you ever kissed a woman?" she asked me, and in the darkness I could sense her eyes, keen for any flinch I made.

I took my time answering. There was something off about her

manner. She wasn't flirting, and I'd never had any inkling that she was interested in me in any way other than as a friend since I was Will's lover, but there was something so intense about her. "Actually I haven't," I said eventually, which wasn't quite true, but was all she was getting.

She fell silent, disappointed by my casual answer and my refusal to ask her the same question. We drank another cocktail, and then, as the house lights came back up, I got up to leave.

"But there's more!" she protested.

"I'm sorry. I'm too tired, and it's Claud's birthday tomorrow, after all. Today," I corrected, and silently groaned at the lack of sleep I was going to get. "Stay if you like."

"No." She grumbled as we made our way out and all along the street, telling me about the performers we'd missed and how she never got to have fun nights out. She was drunk, I realized. We separated at the corner and I felt relief walking away from her. I'd enjoyed the time we'd spent together up until that night. What had changed? I couldn't put my finger on it. Or maybe I was just being daft. I'd drunk a lot myself. It had been a long day and she'd done me a huge favor in taking me to talk to Smiles. Bel was fine and the next day everything would be back to normal.

Except that, of course, it wasn't.

Harlem After Midnight

Thursday, 17 September 1936, 3 a.m.

NAMES HAD BEEN taken down, people sent on their way home. There'd be some mighty sore heads the next morning, but none worse than that of the woman who must now have arrived at Harlem Hospital. The only people who remained were those closest to the victim; they were seated somberly on the sofa in the apartment's living room. Garson lit a cigarette and watched them. He didn't know them exactly.

He'd realized too late that he knew one of the party attendees, though only by reputation. Will Goodman. He'd heard the whispers, must have been a decade or so ago. A man driven to violence through love, or lust. Goodman had gone to the hospital in the ambulance, and Garson hadn't been quick enough to put two and two together, but he'd sent Freeman on over to keep an eye on him.

The scene of the crime, for that's what he had decided it was, was now quiet. Evidence had been taken, fingerprints extracted from the apartment's occupants for elimination purposes, although Garson knew there was little point. This woman had been hurt by someone she knew. It was that sort of crime. Passion, love, hatred. He leaned against the doorframe and surveyed the bedroom. The sash window was still raised, the curtain waving like a proud flag in the breeze. Walking over, he found the sill to be low, hitting below waist height on him. The woman would be shorter, though. Not an accident. Not suicide: In his experience, people didn't tend to attempt to kill themselves at parties, especially not in someone else's home. Too messy. Too complicated.

He leaned out, looking down at the steps below, ash falling from the tip of his cigarette. The woman's fingernails had been torn. She'd fought back against her attacker. He—and it must be a he, to throw a full-grown woman out of this window—had meant for her to die. Whether it was spur-of-the-moment or not, it would be murder if she died. Garson hoped she didn't; his life would be that much easier if the woman woke up and told him exactly what had happened. Hell of a lot more straightforward than piecing together evidence and constructing a motive from pure conjecture.

12

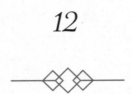

Saturday, 12 September 1936

IT WAS WILL'S turn to wake me with a cup of coffee bright and early. Though the gesture was lovely, I wished I'd had a little warning. It was the first time he'd seen me without a scrap of makeup, and I quickly yanked the net from my hair, hoping the curls it had been guarding were safe. My mouth was dry from the cocktails at the Ubangi, and the threat of a headache hung over me like a dark cloud on a sunny day.

"Does Claud know you're here?" I asked. The last thing I wanted was for her to suspect that Will had sneaked back into the apartment in the dead of night, even though I wouldn't have kicked him out if he had.

"She does," he confirmed. "I brought breakfast for you all. Bacon and eggs, some fresh bread. Louis's no doubt frying it all to a crisp as we speak."

"The birthday girl gets the morning off." I took a sip of the coffee and tried not to wince. Goodness, it was strong! At least it would wake me up. "Is Bel here?"

"Nah." Will lay down beside me on top of the bedspread, his socked feet nudging mine, which were cozy beneath the covers. "You two had quite the night, by all accounts. She's still sleeping it off. How are you feeling? Did you find anything out?"

I filled him in on what Smiles had told me, that the existence of my aunt had been confirmed but that I had nothing much else to go on. "Gosh, I'm exhausted." I yawned. "Forget the late night—we walked miles yesterday on our shopping trip."

"You get something for Claud?"

A daft question. "Of course!" I passed him my coffee cup to hold and leaned over, reaching beneath the bed. "I hope she'll like it."

I'd spotted the necklace as Bel tried on rings at the jewelry counter in Saks. Perhaps it wasn't Claud's usual thing, as she only wore a plain black watch and a wedding band. But she'd been admiring the silver chain that Bel wore around her own neck the other day and wishing she had something similar to show off on her birthday. The chrome-and-crystal necklace I'd bought wasn't ostentatious, and I thought it would look nice with the navy dress Claud had showed me she was going to wear.

"She'll love it." Will kissed me. "Thank you for getting her something so thoughtful."

"Why wouldn't I? She's been a wonderful hostess. I was only worried that Louis might be planning on buying her jewelry."

Will snorted. "Lou don't believe in jewelry. He believes in bank accounts and investments for the future. He'll treat Claud like a queen all day, but he'll have bought her something practical. Something for the kitchen or a new pair of work shoes. That's what he always does."

"And what did you get her?" I had to hope Claud had a few nice gifts. Sensible shoes or a new pan were hardly a girl's dream gift.

Will showed me a square, neatly wrapped present. "A record?" I guessed.

"Friend of mine works over at the Apollo. This is actually one of Claud's own records; I just borrowed it so that he could get Billie Holiday to sign it for her. Maybe it ain't much, but I think she'll like it."

"She'll love it." I twisted awkwardly, trying not to spill hot coffee as I kissed him. "You know, if you fancy getting me an early birthday present, I'd take the same."

He chuckled. "I don't actually know when your birthday even is."

"March," I told him. "Maybe an early Christmas present would make more sense."

We sat in silence for a moment, and I wondered if Will was thinking the same thing as me. That it might be nice to spend Christmas with a loved one.

I would happily wait until March for a signed Billie Holiday record if it meant I could receive it from him. Bel had made a good point the day before. Would it be so terrible to try to stay in New York?

I was too old to get a job as a chorus girl—even if a venue would accept me, there was no chance in hell I was going to spend my evenings dolled up and shaking my behind along with a bunch of sixteen-year-olds. "Undignified" wasn't the word. But I could sing. It was what I had clung to these last few years. And I wasn't the worst actress out there. The setup couldn't be so very different here than in London. There'd be auditions during the day, and, if need be, Bel knew people. There might be a job going at Leon's or somewhere like it. And Will would be passing through every fortnight.

"Actually, Teddy Hughes—he's my friend at the Apollo; I met up with him last night—he's coming to the party tonight. I thought I might speak with him about work." I felt him shift his weight, trying to get comfortable without jolting me and my cup of coffee.

"You're thinking of becoming a landlubber?" I tried to make light of his words, even as they were an effective bombshell, scattering all my future plans to the four winds.

"I guess." He was staring up at the ceiling when I dared to glance across at him. "It's just an idea. He might say no."

"Why? You're an amazing musician. You were playing for Cole Porter on the ship, for goodness' sake! And you said he's a friend. Why wouldn't he put in a good word for you?"

He turned to face me. "You know why. People round here, they know what I did. A lot of 'em believed what Henry said about me. His being dead don't change that. If anything, it's worse for me that he isn't around to help clear my name. The respectable establishments, they don't want trouble."

"But it's been years," I reminded him. "People have short memories, and they grow old enough to have done some pretty daft things themselves. Speak to Teddy. Didn't someone mention the other day about them having an amateurs' night?"

He bristled. "I'm hardly an amateur."

"You know that isn't how it works." I put my cup down on the bedside table and rolled toward him. "I mean, it's a foot in the door, isn't it? You're brilliant, but when was the last time anyone in New York heard you play?"

"It's been a while," he admitted. "You get a few nos from the places you want to play at, it seems a harder fall when you get a yes from a place you wouldn't choose to drink in."

"So, then. This could be the opportunity you've been waiting for," I said, leaning in to kiss him. "I wouldn't tell you to do it if I didn't know that you'll wow them."

I understood his reluctance. It was hard, once you'd become comfortable in one place—for him, the easy rolling day-to-day of the ship musician; for me, the lack of challenge that a guaranteed spot at the Canary Club had offered, allowing me to pour all my energies into my father's ill health and medical requirements. It was hard to pull away from the familiar and take a risk. To take a chance when you weren't sure if you'd lost that spark. That je ne sais quoi that had given you a foot in the door, only for you to loiter for too long at the back of the room rather than marching straight up to that spotlit stage.

Will kissed me back at first, then pulled away. "What about you?"

"What about me?"

"Amateur night. I'm in if you're in."

"I'm not the person we're talking about," I reminded him.

"No, but you don't exactly have a job right now."

"I've got a berth booked on a ship bound for England in a week and a half."

"So you've got nothing to lose." He cupped my chin and moved back so that he could look me in the eye. "Wouldn't it be so much easier to walk into an audition in London and say you played a theater in New York? Impressive, even?"

He had me there. I'd taken it as a joke when Bel had first mentioned it, but it had been a long time since I'd sung in front of a theater audience. The Canary Club had been my life for too long and, though it didn't have the worst crowd in Soho, there were nights in that basement when I'd found myself singing at a wall of chatter and drunken laughter. It would be something else to get up on a real stage, sing to people who had come there to listen, to discover new music and new artistes. Unless, of course, they didn't want me. But maybe it'd be worth the risk. God, I missed it, even that postage-stamp-sized stage at the Canary. Wasn't that why I'd fallen for the ruse that had brought me to New York? The opportunity to do something real, to play a role of substance, had been too tempting to turn down. But then, on the other side of the coin . . .

Rejection. The greatest fear. It wasn't rational. I knew I was a good singer. I had the reviews (well, a couple of yellowing notices from the *Evening Standard*) and once upon a time I had harbored great ambition. The odd bit part had come my way, and I enjoyed the fact that although Tommy and I had always had a relationship based on absolute detestation of each other, he had kept me on at the Canary because he knew my talent brought in the punters. But over the years, that safety net had eroded my confidence. Because if I had a guaranteed job, why put myself through the agony of auditions where half the girls were blond and pretty, usually younger than me these days—the epitome of what middle-aged men wanted to see on their stage? It was different for Will. Men didn't need to look good in a dress or walk that tightrope that a woman did, of looking pure and untouched, but also as if she could show a man a good time.

"I'll tell Teddy we come as a package deal," Will said softly, as if he could read my mind.

"I don't need favors!" My words came out harsher than I'd intended, and I softened my tone. "I just don't want some stranger feeling sorry for me. If he asks me to sing—and I haven't decided if I want to yet—then he'll be asking because he thinks I'm good."

"I know that." He wasn't ruffled by my outburst. "I just thought it'd be kinda nice. Like when we teamed up on the ship."

That had been a good day, I remembered. I'd been just a member of the audience when Will had invited me up onstage to join him. Those unexpected moments were always the ones that stuck with you, when there was no pressure to make a mark, just an unbridled joy at performing.

"I forgive you," I said, smiling at the way his eyebrows shot up. Clearly, he hadn't been apologizing but he had the good sense to stay quiet. "Is Claud up and about, do you know?"

"Lou was taking her breakfast in bed. If he hasn't burned it beyond recognition." His face told me that Louis was not as skilled in the kitchen as he was at his workplace. "I told him we'd just grab some rolls and not to bother cooking for us."

"We probably have a little time before they notice that we're still in bed." I fiddled with the top button of his shirt, making my intentions clear.

"Oh, I'd say we have a whole heap of time." He cottoned on quickly.

There were worse ways to start the day, I have to say.

"BUT IS THERE enough food?" Claud was fretting, pacing a straight line between the kitchen and the center of the living room, which we were setting up for the party.

"There's enough here to feed an army," I assured her. "There are only six of us!"

We'd spent the afternoon cooking. Well, Claud had. I'd been her eager assistant, though, dredging chicken thighs in bowls of flour to be fried, mixing up corn-bread batter, and whisking egg whites in a bowl until my arm ached and the whites were ready to be piled on top of a lemon meringue pie. There was food everywhere, in various states of preparation. Claud had made a feast, the pièce de résistance being a five-tiered caramel cake, which Louis placed at center stage on the dining table.

In the living room Will was tinkering on the piano, Louis telling him what was getting the Harlem folk on the dance floor these days. I was glad to see Will taking the idea of Amateur Night seriously. It would do him good, whatever happened.

"Should be plenty good music," Will said. "Teddy's bringing his horn, and I'd be surprised if Earl didn't show up."

"True, true." Louis straightened up with a groan, leaning his back into an arch. "Oh Lord, I'm gettin' old." He stretched his arms overhead. "You think we got enough beer to take over to the party?"

"Yes." Claud interrupted before Will could suggest otherwise. "We got beer enough to drown ten men. There's half a bottle of whiskey left over from Christmas, for when you fellas get melancholy later. I even got some gin for our English rose here." She winked at me. "And vermouth 'cause I want Lena to teach me how to make a martini."

"Coo-ee!" There was a knock on the door: Bel.

"You're late," Will said, letting her and Joey in. "I thought you said you'd come over at four."

I noticed Claud roll her eyes in Louis's direction, her husband nodding in agreement, and glanced at the clock. Five thirty. We'd just finished all the food preparation. Perfect timing as far as Bel was concerned. I got the distinct impression this wasn't the first time.

"Happy birthday, Aunt Claudette," Joey said, handing over a present.

"I hope you like it," Bel said. "It's from both of us."

"I'm sure I'll love it." Claud sat down on the sofa, patting the seat beside her for Joey to sit. She ripped off the paper. "Oh."

"What is it, honey?" Louis came to take a closer look, then backed off with more speed, shooting a desperate glance in Will's direction.

Something was wrong, but it wasn't until I inched a little closer myself that I realized what Bel had done. It was a pair of photographs in a beautiful walnut frame. On one side, Bel's wedding. The bride stood proudly beside her husband, my first look at Henry Bennett. He didn't look anything like I'd expected. Just an ordinary man, not that good-looking and not much taller than Bel. You'd walk past him on the street without a second look, and yet he'd managed to cause enough trouble to outlive him by a decade and counting.

On the other side of the frame was what I guessed was a christening. The godparents, Claud and Louis, with baby Josephine in Bel's arms. All the important people in Joey's life save one: Will. It didn't need to mean anything, and yet I could tell that it meant everything.

"Shall I put it on the mantelpiece for you?" Bel asked. "Pride of place, I hope?"

"Sure. Yes." Claud was staring at Will, who hadn't moved, though he'd surely seen it. She cleared her throat. "Thank you. Thank you, Joey. What a lovely idea."

"Mama showed me the photographs just the other day and I thought it'd be nice if you had them. Since Mama's always said that we'd be lost without you and Uncle Louis." Joey smiled, her face troubled. Poor little mite. She could see that something was wrong but she didn't know what.

"Such lovely photographs, Joey," I said, trying to sound breezy. "Now, I really must get ready before the other guests arrive! Will, you were going to help me with fastening on my dress, weren't you?" I grabbed his hand, dragged him into the bedroom before he could react, and shut the door firmly behind us.

Alfie

June 1908

HE DIDN'T LIKE the Haymarket, but Victoria did and so that's where they went. She was paying, after all, even though Tar's money felt warm in Alfie's pocket. He'd paid for a haircut and a shoeshine, but the rest he kept hold of, just in case. He had another appointment in two days' time, but two private concerts didn't make a fella rich. Even though he felt like a millionaire walking in on Victoria's arm.

The Haymarket was a vast building that looked like any other theater from the outside. The clientele appeared respectable, white and well-dressed, and certainly there was no shortage of money flowing into the pockets of Mr. Corey, the owner. On his first visit, as a paid musician covering for the regular pianist, Alfie had been impressed, had thought it a fancy place. Until he'd looked a little closer. Downstairs, the pretense was mostly upheld. A band kept up a never-ending string of dance songs, the stage lined with cancan girls. The dancers' full skirts allowed for the showing off of more leg than was proper, but from the studied focus of many of the gents, anyone could see that was the point.

As many women as men sat at the tables, in couples or foursomes, the drinking growing heavier as the hour grew later. While some of the women were clearly with their husbands, many were not. Pairs of them would arrive together and then split up or take a whirl on the dance floor, only to part when approached by a male partner.

A man would arrive alone, striding confidently through the doors, stopping only to pay his entrance fee (the women didn't pay a cent). He'd set his hat on a table and sit down while a waiter came and took his order. Watching the dance floor carefully, this lonely fellow would drink a beer for Dutch courage before making a beeline for his prey. Or at least, the woman he thought was prey. For Alfie had noticed that many of the women on the dance floor were also keen-eyed, unashamedly putting themselves and their décolletage in the eyeline of these fresh young—or old—men.

There was nothing risqué to be seen, not on the dance floor. A gentleman would usually enjoy a few dances with his new friend, always maintaining the correct distance from her. The pair would retire to the table he had earlier procured, the waiter reappearing with champagne, which the woman would guzzle down quickly, as if her life depended on reaching the bottom of the bottle in as short a time as possible. Sometimes the gent would drink, sometimes not. And sometimes, after only a glass or two of wine, he would offer her his arm and they would leave the table, taking the stairs to the balcony above, where they could get on with the rest of their transaction in private. As Alfie and Victoria took their seats, he wondered if she knew all this. And if she did, was that the reason she'd brought him there?

Victoria was still an enigma to him, but he was drawn to her nevertheless. Or perhaps that was why. At first he'd assumed that he was just a casual amusement for her, but the night she'd sought him out at the saloon, she'd looked shy when she'd asked him to meet her on the corner by the Haymarket and given him a description of the carriage she'd be in. Tonight she had dressed up in her finery and she was chattering away ten to the dozen, as if this were normal. As if rich young white women sat in places of dubious reputation with Negro men every night. Alfie supposed that it was more common in New York than it had been back home. Which was why he'd had to leave.

"Have you been here before?" Victoria asked once they'd ordered drinks from a grinning waiter who'd winked at Alfie in a way that made him feel complicit in something he hadn't agreed to.

"I played piano here once," he admitted. "You?"

"No!" She shook her head vehemently. "You must know that . . . well, people like me aren't supposed to come to places like this."

"And yet here you are."

"Yes." She giggled, and it made her look younger. Her confidence had made him think that she was at least twenty, but maybe she was closer to Alfie's own age. He wanted to ask but didn't know how to without ruining what had become an enjoyable atmosphere.

"So, what brings you here now?" He didn't mean that, not exactly. He wanted to know what it was that she wanted from him. He needed to make sure that when they left the Haymarket in the small hours of the morning there wouldn't be trouble waiting. Inside the revolving door, anything went; that was acknowledged. Back out on the street was something else entirely.

"I wanted to get to know you," she said frankly. "And there aren't many places a couple like us can go to without drawing a lot of attention."

She wasn't totally naive, then. "I don't want any trouble. I had that before. That's how I ended up here."

"In New York?"

He nodded. "A girl I knew. Her family and mine, we sort of knew one another. My mama was their cook once upon a time, and I guess the mother of the family sent all their laundry and sewing jobs our way."

"You grew up together."

"In a way." Though it wasn't really what he'd call it. The Canning family was white and well-off. Not Victoria wealthy but certainly they had more money than the Aldridges. "I knew Lucy to nod to in the street. She was on speaking terms with my sister more than with me."

Lucy Canning had said barely a dozen words to him in his life. Even when she'd blown his life apart, she'd not spoken to him. It was lucky for him that the Cannings' maid was friendly with Jessie, had come running down to tell her that her brother had about half an hour, the time it would take Lucy's father to raise a posse on a Sunday morning, to get out of town. Half an hour filled with a rage that would make Mr. Canning forget that his daughter had spent the summer before in Savannah with her cousins. That the swollen belly that his wife had caught sight of, hidden for so many months beneath the clever layers of Lucy's dresses, sewn by Alfie's mother and sister, could not have been the fault of any man in Florida, whatever Lucy claimed. He wondered why she had named him, if it had just been pure panic and his was the first name that sprang to mind.

"Let's just say that she got into a tricky situation and needed someone to blame." He kept it simple. He didn't want Victoria to think that he was the sort of fella who'd hold a grudge against people like her. And he didn't think she was another Lucy Canning, although maybe there was a man down in Savannah who had thought that Lucy was just like Victoria.

"You don't need to worry," she told him. "This isn't the South. This is the twentieth century and it's New York City. I might not be able to vote—yet—but I'll damned well make my own decisions about who I get to spend time with."

She was passionate; he'd give her that. But her cheeks flushed red when she cursed and he guessed that part of her presence in the Tenderloin was due to the illicitness of the area, the company she kept, the liquor she drank. It was rebellion in the way that only the privileged knew it, but Alfie was too tired for principles. If she was paying, let him drink for free. If she wanted him to take her up that infamous staircase and show her what really went on up there, he'd do it happily.

In the end, she didn't. They drank and they took a little turn on the dance floor, but everything was chaste, and he felt, when she said she needed to leave, that her carriage was returning at midnight, that it was just as well.

With Victoria safely delivered, Alfie ignoring the sneer and the gob of spittle that her driver aimed in his direction, he oriented himself toward his boardinghouse. He couldn't call it home, not when he didn't even have a bed all to himself. He was passing the back of the Haymarket when he heard his name.

"Alfie?"

He turned, the voice so familiar but so extraordinary to hear in this city. Far from where he had last heard it. But there she was, looking small and shy. His sister. In the last place he had expected to see her.

"Jessie?" He walked up to her, unable to believe his eyes. She must have felt the same, for she put out her hand, touching his jacket, feeling the silk lining that she herself had stitched from leftovers from a wedding dress she'd made for someone with money. "What are you doing here?"

"Looking for you." Her eyes filled with tears. "You left me all alone, you know. I needed to find you."

He didn't know what to say. When he'd left, it had been in a rush, terror pumping through his veins. She knew that. Had she been blaming him that whole time? "You know I didn't leave you, Jess. Wasn't like I had a choice."

He hadn't had a choice then, but he knew he could have done more. Could have written home more, could have got a regular paying job like everyone else in his position, could have sent money home to his poor mother and sister. Instead, it had been easier to pretend that he was all alone in the world. And now here Jessie was. Proof that he wasn't. He should have been happy, but instead he felt overwhelmed with shame.

"You could've taken me with you." She grabbed his hands, clutching them tight as if he would otherwise try to run away from her again.

Alfie shrugged, looking away. "No, I couldn't. I couldn't protect myself, and besides, what about Mama?" He knew as soon as he mentioned her that she was gone. Saw that the tears in Jessie's eyes weren't just for him, but for them. For all that she'd lost. He tried to speak, but his voice broke. He coughed and tried again. "What happened?"

"Pneumonia. We had no money for a doctor."

Was it his fault? Did she blame him? He'd been supposed to be the man of the house, after all. He'd been selfish.

"I meant to write, only the longer I left it . . . ," he said, his words infused with sorrowful defiance. "I just wanted to get on my feet first. I wanted her to be proud."

"She'd have been happy to know that you were safe." And there it was, the accusation in her eyes. His fierce sister, not about to let him off the hook that easily.

He was saved by an unexpected interruption.

"There you are, Jessie!" A girl had emerged from a door in the wall behind Jessie. She sidled between the siblings, looking Alfie up and down. "You two know each other?"

"This is Alfie." Jessie didn't take her gaze off her feckless brother.

"Alfie? Your brother, Alfie?"

"The one and only." He forced a grin as he stuck out his hand to shake.

"Mary Grace," she said, her eyes narrowing as she looked back toward Jessie. "Now, why do you both look so vexed at one another? You know, Alfie, she's spent the last couple months looking for you.

And, Jessie, aren't you pleased? You finally found him! And all you needed to do was come to work."

Alfie took a step back and surveyed the building behind them. That door definitely belonged to the Haymarket. "You been working here?"

"No," Jessie said, just as Mary Grace said, "Yes."

"I was helping out for tonight," Jessie said quickly, "but I work at a hotel, the Gilsey House. As a maid."

"Uh-huh." He stared at his sister. He knew what could happen to young girls like Jessie when they first arrived in the big city. He'd never have expected Jessie to be so stupid, but then, he'd never expected to see her in New York at all.

"Is that all you can say?" Jessie demanded. "What do you think I am?"

"Hey!" Mary Grace butted in. "Look, this is . . . It's stupid to stand here arguing in the middle of the street at this time of night." She nodded in the direction of a tussle that had started just a few feet down the sidewalk. "You two should talk when you've had some rest. Alfie, you'll take Jessie for dinner tomorrow night. You'll pay and the pair of you will talk. Agreed?"

Alfie was too tired and deflated to protest. He'd hoped to return to Jacksonville one day, triumphant. To show Jessie that he'd made a success of his life. Instead, she'd found him out. Seen that he was hardly surviving, and not only that, he'd missed the chance to say good-bye to his mother. What a sorry excuse he made.

"I'll meet you outside the Gilsey House tomorrow," Alfie told Jessie. "What time d'you get off work?"

She hesitated until Mary Grace nudged her. "I'll meet you outside at six o'clock." She turned on her heel and marched off, Mary Grace trotting after her.

At least she had a friend, he reasoned, even if she was a Haymarket girl. Maybe it was as well their mother was dead. She'd be horrified to see them both now, in a dirty part of a filthy city, mixing with the riffraff.

He could fix it, though, he decided as he resumed his journey back to his uncomfortable bed. Jessie was angry, and he couldn't blame her. But he could set up a new home for the pair of them with Tar's money. Jessie would have some money from the hotel, and maybe he could talk to Victoria about setting Jessie up with some dressmaking work. Though on second thought, best to keep the pair of them apart for now, just until Jessie came around. And she would. He knew it for certain.

13

Saturday, 12 September 1936

"IT'S JUST A photograph," I said, unhooking my dress from the curtain rail where it had been airing by the open window and throwing it lightly onto the bed.

"I know that." Will sounded bemused, sitting on the bed watching me. "Do you?"

"Well, how dare she?!" I whirled round and he leaned away from me, an expression of mock terror on his face. I could hear music coming from the living room; at least I wouldn't have to worry too much about being overheard. "I mean, why now? Those photographs are ten years old. She could have given them to Claud at any time."

Will shrugged. "It's a nice gesture? Or maybe Joey just found them. She's at that age, you know? Wanting to see photos of the past, of her family, such as it is."

"But isn't that the point? *You're* her family and you aren't in any of those photos." I pulled my sweater off and let my skirt fall to the ground. "You don't think Bel did it on purpose?"

"Maybe, but it only sticks if I care. And I don't." He got up and held my waist, stroking down the silk of my slip with his palms, trying to distract me. "I'm used to Bel's games, and she only plays them when she's rattled."

I put my hands on his shoulders, leaning back so that I could meet his gaze. "Rattled by what?"

"Or who." He smiled lazily. "You know she's jealous of you."

"No." I stood back and reached for the dress. "Why would she be?"

"Why would she be jealous of a woman who has everything she wants? You're younger than she is, you don't have a kid to look after, and you're not a widow whose husband died in less than commendable circumstances. You can sing. You've traveled. Not a lot of people have that luxury."

"I thought she liked me." I frowned, though I was a little flattered.

"She does. Probably," he added. "What? You've never been jealous of a friend?"

"She was trying to talk me into staying in New York yesterday." I slipped the dress over my head and turned my back so that Will could fasten it, his fingers lingering against my back as he folded the last button through its loop. "Why would she do that if she was jealous?"

"Imagine," he said slowly, "that I stuck around. She'll be wondering how that'll affect her. She don't earn enough to pay rent and keep up with the latest fashions as well. And if I had to foot my own rent someplace else, I could still help out, but I couldn't cover her bills the way I do now. Maybe she's thinking that if she makes friends with you, you'll make sure she's looked after."

"You're thinking of staying put?" I latched on to the information most important to me.

He shrugged and shook his head. "This is the longest I've planned to stick around in years, that's all. She must think something's up."

"Bel should get a better job or learn to budget like the rest of us." I shot him a side-eyed glance when he laughed. "What?"

"Nothing." He shook his head and carried on laughing. "I just . . . Nothing."

"She must know that you can't pay her rent forever," I said, "but I'm not trying to stick my nose in. It's your business."

He kissed me then, and my stomach dropped, that exhilarating combination of queasiness and euphoria that I got from New York elevators. I was falling fast, and I knew that coming to Harlem had either been the best thing I'd ever done or the worst mistake I'd ever made.

Will retreated to the living room and I sat down on the bed, by the window, to do my makeup. There was a lot to think about— Eliza Abernathy, for one. I could have made an excuse not to go and see her on Tuesday, but something was telling me that it would be worth my while to keep on good terms with her.

"Knock, knock!" Bel's rap on the door was a vague courtesy; she was inside the bedroom before I could even look up from the mirror. "Oh, Lena, you look gorgeous. Of course." She plonked herself down on the bed beside me, and I bit the inside of my mouth, re-minding myself that if Will wasn't bothered, neither should I be. Maybe nothing was meant by it.

"Thank you." I reached for my mascara brush and dipped it into the mug of already-blackened water left over from the day before. "And you look nice. Of course." I rubbed the brush across the scuffed surface of the cake before tilting my head back, looking down into the mirror. "Lovely photos that Joey found."

"They are, aren't they? I just wish there was one with Will in." Her sigh was theatrical. That, or I was growing more cynical by the second. "It's just that, obviously, he missed my wedding, the christening . . . And he's never home these days."

I grunted, hoping it sounded as though I were agreeing, and carefully rubbed a rogue flake of black from my cheek. "It's a shame for Joey, but I suppose it can't be helped."

"Yes, it is a shame for Joey," she agreed. "She loves her uncle and he's hardly around."

"Do you want him to stay?"

"Joey would like that. She'd love to have him around more. But me and him—we'd be at each other's throats after . . . well, it's only been three days? Four? And already I can see he'd rather be in any other room than the one I'm in. Do you think he's upset about the photographs?"

Perhaps Will hadn't been as relaxed as he'd made out. Or there was something that Bel, knowing him for so many years, could spot that I just couldn't.

"He didn't say anything to me," I told her, trying to read her expression, but she was a closed book.

She paused. "I'd like a drink. Do you want a drink? Gin? Beer?" She got up from the bed.

"Bel, hang on a mo." I put down the brush and turned to face her. "*Did* you mean anything by the photographs? I won't go running to Will, reporting back, I promise. But I could talk to him if you like. I would like to help."

She stared at me aghast, as if I'd asked her to sell her soul to the devil. "No, you wouldn't. No one wants to help me."

"I do." I saw that she didn't believe me. "Look, I know it's none of my business, but I see you and Will together and it seems so daft to me, this rift between you. You're family."

"By marriage," she reminded me. "Not blood."

"So what? You've got someone who cares about you, even if the two of you don't always get along. Trust me, you don't appreciate what you've got until it's gone."

She sat back down. "He won't ever forgive me, Lena, so what's the point in trying?"

"It's not up to you to decide that. Or me," I added. "I can't say whether he'll get over what's happened, but he's never turned his back on you, has he? He stays in your life for a reason. I think you could stand to give him some credit for that. Try and mend bridges instead of knocking them down." It was a rubbish metaphor, but she nodded, understanding.

"Sometimes I think that everyone would be better off if I just wasn't here," she said quietly.

"That's not true," I told her. "Joey needs you."

"No, she doesn't. Me and her, we're nothing alike. I guess she got Henry's smarts. So clever. Too clever. I don't know what she's talking about half the time and she's only ten years old. She has to get Claud to get help on her schoolwork. And I don't even put the roof over her head; Will does that." She sighed heavily. "I guess it'd just be nice to be needed for once. I feel like I'm an obligation. Will pays my rent 'cause his mama made him promise to before she died. It's a duty, nothing more. Claud and Louis are better parents to Joey than I am. Did you know that Joey sleeps over here all the time? In this very bed. I can't even give her a bedroom of her own at home."

"But you do your best." I leaned over and hugged her, her stiffness dissolving as she let herself go. "My father did the best he could for me, and we never had any more than what you and Joey have. Love isn't about the roof over your head or how much money you have in the bank. It's about being together. When Joey gets home from school every day, you're there." She nodded, dabbing away a tear that broke free. "Any fool can see how proud you are of her. *She* knows how proud you are of her."

"Maybe." She pulled a face. "It's just . . . have you ever stopped for a second and wondered how your life turned out so different from how you thought? I mean, I never had high expectations, but I thought there would be marriage. A nice home. Nothing crazy, but maybe something like this." She swept her arm around to indicate the neat, light-filled bedroom, so different from the cramped and damp flat that she and Joey lived in. "Will does what he can, but he needs to look after himself. Despite his best efforts, one day he'll have a family of his own to provide for. I can only do so much on what Leon pays me."

I thought about our shopping trip and knew that it wasn't for me to point out that Bel's wardrobe was a damned sight too fashionable for a woman in her position. Would I, in her shoes, be any different? Not a fortnight before, I'd been living in a tiny room in Soho, all my wages going on nights out, makeup, anything that made me feel better about myself. It was a lie, but who wants the world to know the truth?

"You know what?" I said to her. "You just never know what's around the corner. This doesn't have to be it for you. Like I said, you have Will and Joey. You have friends. Life has a funny way of surprising you." I thought about my own circumstances. "Sometimes you get the chance to take a different path and you have to take a risk. It might not turn out to be any better in the long run, but at least you know you tried."

She smiled. "You're so wise, Lena. Tell you what—I'm going to give it a go." She got up. "Starting with teaching Claud how to make a mean martini. Want one?"

"Absolutely." I checked my reflection in the mirror. Pretty decent. "Let me come with you."

In the living room Claud was folding napkins into fancy arrangements on the table. Joey was sitting beside Will at the piano, picking out the upper octave of a simple duet as Will worked the pedals and kept the rhythm going. Louis was sitting on the sofa, polishing the shiny brass buttons on what looked to be his best suit jacket, and tapping his foot along in time with the music.

Bel made a cocktail shaker out of a glass pickle jar as I chipped ice from a block resting in the sink. The cupboard revealed a hodgepodge of glasses, and I picked out three champagne coupes that I thought would do justice to the strong martinis that Bel was shaking together.

"I'm not a big drinker," Claud warned, looking wary of the glass Bel handed to her.

"It's just a little something to warm you up for later," Bel promised.

"Cheers." We clinked glasses and I took a sip. God, it was strong! I saw Claud wince, but she gamely went in for another swig before setting her glass firmly down on the counter.

"Come on, ladies, let's get this dinner served before I start seeing double."

Quite honestly, I'd never seen so much food produced from one tiny kitchen. It seemed to take forever to cart it out onto the dining table, the piano stool and an old wooden box that Louis had found in the building's basement making up the chairs as we all huddled around the feast. It was a noisy affair that reminded me of meals at the Harpers', of sitting next to my best friend, Maggie, as her mother dished up Sunday roasts and Christmas feasts that she rustled up on her small wage and her quick-tongued ability to bargain with the local butcher.

I watched Claud smile as Will laughed at something Bel had said. There was a healing quality to meals like this. The sharing of food brought people together, put them on equal footing, and removed the obstacles that existed away from the table. That was how it seemed to me then, as we ate Claud's tender chicken and shoveled away vast quantities of potatoes and gravy, followed by the grand birthday cake itself.

When Claud bent her head to blow out her candles, I took a moment to close my eyes and make my own wish. What I wished for, I can't tell you. There's still a chance it will come true.

STOMPIN' AT
THE SAVOY

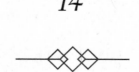

14

Saturday, 12 September 1936

I HADN'T BEEN to a party in so long that I'd forgotten how much I hated them, especially when I didn't really know anyone. The rent party card stated that the hosts were Gloria and Rosa, but I didn't even meet this pair until much later on. The apartment was crowded and hot, the Victrola struggling to be heard over the guests, everyone shouting to be heard. We dropped our entrance fee into the bowl on the side, and Louis and Bel took charge of the drinks, carting our beer and gin to the kitchen.

Will introduced me to people as we passed, but their names ran quickly in one ear and out the other, like water through fingers. He seemed to know everyone, and everyone was eager to catch up with the intrepid traveler, less interested in who I was. They talked and I looked around the room, feeling like an impostor among these men and women who were so at home. I wasn't used to being the stranger.

Almost everyone here was Black, save for a blond-haired, blue-eyed man with glasses who was talking to an equally serious-looking light-skinned chap in a corner of the room. Did he feel out of place? A break in the crowd gave me a glimpse of their hands, touching as they leaned toward each other, still talking but with no interest in what was happening in the rest of the room. Fingers brushed, interlocked briefly, fell away as a new man approached bearing gifts in the form of gin, but fell away gently and without fear. It was a comfort to see love worn so lightly. Surprising.

"This is Lena," Will said, dragging me away from the couple. "She came all the way from London to be here." A variation on the introduction I'd already heard several times.

"London, England?" Raised eyebrows on a succession of Will's friends, their brows wrinkled as if they couldn't contemplate it being a real city, not just a mythical place they'd read about, like Oz or Lilliput.

"That's the one," I said each time, giving them the full Cockney-sparrow accent until Will gave me a look. I tried not to drink too quickly, especially with the potent levels at which Bel was mixing the cocktails, but alcohol is an easy crutch to rely on in such situations.

It was all right for Will, the prodigal son returned. He was greeted with grins and expressions of joy, and I had to make do with sideways glances from the women wondering who I was and what I was to Will, the appraising looks from the men as they wondered why they hadn't seen me around before. In a lot of ways, the party felt familiar, like the bottle parties we had back in Soho. Everyone came and brought their own drink and some food to share, and paid their entrance fee. In this case, the proceeds went into the pockets of Gloria and Rosa and helped keep the tobacco-stained ceiling over their heads. If Maggie hadn't married so young, we might have done the same, sharing a flat and having friends round for drinks and the like.

"Will!" Claud maneuvered her way toward us through the crowded living room, dragging a tall, skinny man behind her. "Look who I found."

"Teddy, good to see you, man." The men greeted each other, and Claud stood by, a small, sly smile on her face.

"Teddy works at the Apollo," she told me, her voice low. This was who Will would have to speak to if he wanted a spot on the program for Amateur Night, then.

"It's been a while," Teddy was saying to Will. "You still a sailor?"

"Still sailing. Still not a sailor." Will laughed. "Good to see you, though." He pushed me forward a little, his palm gentle against the small of my back. "And this is Lena. She's staying with Claud and Lou for a couple weeks."

"Lena came all the way from London, England. Will met her at sea," Claud added.

"And brought her back home?" Teddy grinned, sticking out a hand for me to shake. "Pleased to meet you, Lena. Teddy Hughes."

"Lena's a singer," Will explained. "She had a job lined up on Broadway, but it fell through last minute."

Too late, I was realizing that this was a moment I should have been prepared for. Teddy Hughes was a man in the business. I felt that familiar jangle in the pit of my stomach. Opportunity opening up, a feeling like waiting in the wings for an audition to start. Stupid, really. I had no intention of staying in New York. If I was going to sing for this man, it would be for Will's benefit; that was all. If I kept telling myself that, maybe it would stick.

"Broadway, huh?" Teddy looked interested. "What happened?"

"A long story," I said, knowing he wouldn't believe me even if we had time to go into it. "Let's just say that I got a free trip out of it but not much more."

He seemed satisfied with that response. "So, you guys want to do Amateur Night this Wednesday?"

Claud had clearly laid the groundwork for us already. Now she was standing by, a huge grin on her face.

"Look, man, I know how many you get signing up. I don't expect no favors," Will said, though I could hear in his voice that he wouldn't turn one down if it was offered to him.

"You do know that this woman's had your name down in the reserves for the past year?" Teddy hoicked a thumb in Claud's direction. I wasn't surprised. "'Sides, you know I owe you big for helping out Bobby. His ma says he's a different kid these days, away from here."

Bobby was a sweet kid who'd been in Will's band on the ship. Young and with a lot to learn, but talented.

"Pleasure, man, really. He's a great musician. Give him a couple years and he'll make something of himself." Will was bashful. "So you can get us on? This Wednesday?"

"You'll have to come down that morning, show your face, but I can get you on."

"And Lena?"

I could see from Teddy's face that I was a different kettle of fish. No ties to the theater, no favors to be repaid. "Out-of-towners are a tricky sell. You know what the audience get like. If they think we turned away one of our own . . ."

"That's okay," I said, squeezing Will's hand. "I hadn't counted on doing anything other than sightseeing while I'm here. Honestly."

"Well, yeah, but I was planning on a duet," Will told Teddy. "That'd be all right, wouldn't it? Sharing the stage with a local?"

Teddy shrugged. "Sure. Whatever you want to do with your spot, it's up to you."

"Thanks, man. It's good of you." Will swallowed hard. "Guess this is happening, then."

Teddy grinned. "Just like the old days." He slapped Will on the back and went off to refresh his drink.

"See!" Claud crowed, dancing around Will with glee. "I told you! Didn't I tell you? This is just the beginning, Will. Louis!" She waved her husband over, eager to share the good news.

"It's just one gig, is all," Will said, trying to play it down even as

I saw the corners of his mouth twitch into a smile. "Crowd might boo us offstage."

"I bloody hope not," I said. "Does that often happen?"

"No, Lena, it does not," Louis assured me. "Will here is just doing his usual thing of imagining the worst possible thing that could happen."

"I am not!" Will protested. "I'm just a realist."

Claud went on and on about the local heroes who'd started out at the Apollo and had hit the big time, and Will didn't say a word, sipping his drink and looking like a man who'd made a terrible mistake. Another reminder that the Will Goodman I had met on the ship was not the Will Goodman of Harlem. If anything, though, it made me feel closer to him. His self-assurance had been a comfort at sea when I'd had no one to trust but him. On dry land, it was nice to know that none of us were perfect. It made me feel like less of a failure. We all had our flaws.

I took hold of Will's hand. "We just need to sit down tomorrow and decide what our song should be. Louis, Claud, what usually goes down well?"

Louis cleared his throat, and we settled in for his detailed analysis of the Apollo audience. It was as though he'd been preparing for this moment for months, waiting for the time when Will realized that he was meant to settle back in Harlem. And he was, I realized. He should stay here, with his friends and family, who loved him. I would have to give him up; it was that simple. Either that or work out a way for me to stay in Harlem too.

THERE WASN'T REALLY enough room in the apartment for dancing, but that didn't stop anyone from giving it a good go. Just past midnight there was an unspoken decision made, though, and the crowd began to thin, the party guests heading out to continue the night elsewhere.

"Word is, the Savoy Ballroom's where it's at," Louis called out as he passed. "Opening night!"

"Ballroom? Sounds fancy," I said.

"We're all dressed for it." Louis did a smooth turn, his brass jacket buttons glinting in the light. He was right: We did all look good.

Will shrugged. "The line'll be round the block this time of night. You okay with that?"

"If you say it's worth it, I'm in," I told him.

Though I was feeling a little tipsy for straightforward standing. When we'd been dancing, I hadn't noticed the effects of the last martini, along with sips of Will's beers along the way. Now I needed to sit. The sofa was vacated by a couple who were heading out with five or six others, and I slumped onto it, Will landing beside me.

"What happened to Bel?" I hadn't seen her in a couple of hours.

"Oh, she left ages ago. Found a fella who offered to buy her drinks if she'd go dancing with him. Too good to miss."

I couldn't tell if he was being matter-of-fact or derisory. "You know, if you stay home and give up on your wandering lifestyle, you're going to be spending a lot more time with your sister."

"I know." He fell silent for a moment. "I guess I should finally get over it, huh?"

"I don't think you need to forget about what happened. Just decide if it's worth holding on to all that when, as far as I can see, no one who was here tonight gives a damn about it. And Bel . . . I know I was angry with her earlier, but I can see that she wishes things had happened differently." I could understand why Bel had married Henry. With Will already in jail, she must have felt Henry was her only option. Maybe she could have done more to help repair Will's reputation since, but then he had insisted on running away. With him so absent, it was probably easier to ignore the past.

"I do want to put it all behind me," he said. "I just don't know. Maybe Wednesday night'll give me more of a clue about what to do. God bless Teddy for getting us on that bill."

"And thank Claud," I reminded him. "You're lucky to have her and Louis. I hope you know that."

"I do." He took hold of my hand. "I don't know what I'd have done without them. Spending this time with them—with you— makes me wonder why I stayed away so long."

"Aren't we all putting off something or other?" I looked to where Claud and Louis were slow dancing alone in the middle of the living room, everyone else around us finishing drinks, grabbing coats and jackets, and preparing to head out. "Except those two. They know what they want."

"Guess that's why I keep coming here. Hoping to learn how it's done." He reached into his pocket and pulled out his cigarettes. "The Savoy, then?"

Before we'd left home, Joey had been given strict instructions to finish reading one chapter of her book before going to bed. Bel had said that by the time we got back, it'd be morning anyway and she'd take Joey home then. If there'd been a chance at an empty apartment, I'd have suggested we take advantage, but since there wasn't, dancing seemed the next best option.

"Come on, let's go." I stole the lit cig from his mouth and inhaled deeply. "Take me out dancing before it's too late. I'll be back in London before either of us knows it."

He smiled and leaped to his feet, pulling me up to stand, calling over his shoulder to Claud and Louis, "You two lovebirds coming?"

And so the four of us left the dregs of the party behind us, glad that the mess wasn't ours to clean up the following day. Winding down the stairs and out into the mild September air, we felt as though the night was just beginning, the party just an aperitif to what would come next. Claud and Louis went ahead, Will and I at their heels, stealing kisses along the way. I felt light, full of joy. As if I had finally put the last few weeks behind me.

Alfie

June 1908

SHE WAS AN added complication and yet he was happy for the first time in months. Jessie, in New York! He could hardly believe it, kept his face impassive as she sat there with him in the saloon the evening after he'd first stumbled across her. She told him about their mother's last days and they both shed tears onto the battered and grooved surface of the wooden table they sat at. Jessie had been in the city for a few months already. She'd been swooped down upon as soon as the boat docked, but luckily it was one of the Good Samaritans from a mission up in Harlem who had gotten to her first, and not one of the less kindly folk who lurked around the docks, ready to prey upon the new, naive arrivals from the South. He knew that if he'd written home, had left an address, she'd have come straight to him. It would have been his fault entirely if anything had happened to her.

He'd found out where she was staying and was glad when her sour face gave away that she was hardly attached to the grim boardinghouse where she and Mary Grace were living. He'd told her his grand plan for renting rooms in a nicer part of town, and she'd actually smiled. She hadn't quite forgiven him for not writing home, but he thought that her resolve was weakening.

"Between the three of us we can rent somewhere decent," Jessie said, doing the math on her fingers.

"Three of us?" Her comment drew him out of the mire of his regrets.

"Me, you, and Mary Grace." Jessie looked at him as if he were stupid. "I wouldn't have found you without her help."

"You know what Mama would have to say about a girl like Mary Grace," he warned. Nothing good: loose; godless; a harlot. Mary Grace might not actually spread her legs for money—not yet, at least—but his mother would turn in her grave if she knew that Alfie was letting his sister consort with a girl with such a lack of morals. Thank goodness he and Jessie had found each other before she could do any damage.

"She goes to church," Jessie told him.

"Oh yeah?" She didn't look like a church girl.

"Sure. Abyssinian Baptist over on Fortieth. We've been the last few Sundays, ever since we moved downtown."

He knew the church. Had often passed it and felt duty tug at his soul, before he turned away. Pastor Isaiah back home would have been horrified, but Alfie didn't owe him anything. A man of God was worthless if he was also colored. He couldn't protect Alfie from the mob; he hadn't even tried, because he knew they'd run him down too. And what was the point of God if he let these things happen to good people? To his own people, who stood before all and preached his word?

"You want to keep an eye on me?" Jessie asked, and he nodded. "Then isn't it better for us all to be together? Besides, you left me all alone down in Jacksonville, so you don't really get a say in what happens to me now."

She spoke lightly, but he felt the burn of her words. He'd been a bad brother. He'd been a coward.

"Fine," he said, giving in. "But I don't want you to be going out until all hours just 'cause Mary Grace is."

"Cross my heart." She grinned and he found himself reciprocating. It felt good to be back with kin, with his sister. Leaving her behind had been the hardest thing he'd ever done, but what else could he have done? How was he to know that Mama would be gone inside a year? She'd always been a strong woman, never ill. If he'd known . . . But now he felt stronger, more able. And not only because they'd just eaten a feast, courtesy of his regular attendance at Tar's house, playing ragtime to the sickly madam of the house.

"Mr. Aldridge." Speak of the devil and he shall appear.

"Sir." Alfie shoved his chair back, catching it awkwardly as it threatened to topple. "Good evening."

They shook hands. "I'm sorry," Tar said. "I've interrupted your dinner."

"Oh no, sir, we've finished eating," Jessie told him.

"My sister," Alfie explained quickly. "Jessie Aldridge, this is Tar. My current employer," he stressed as he saw Jessie's confusion at how friendly he was with this white man.

"Oh, well, I'm very pleased to meet you, Mr. Tar," she said quickly.

"Just Tar. No 'Mr.' And the pleasure is mine." Tar took hold of her hand, bending to kiss the back of it, and Alfie saw that his sister was about ready to fall off her chair.

"Won't you join us?" Alfie asked, hoping to impress Jessie. She might have been in New York for a few months, but she'd never been in a black and tan before. Back home, there was no mingling of the sort that Alfie had become used to. The hierarchy was still there, but a man like Tar could sit at their table without any fuss or bother if he so pleased.

"Sure," Tar said, pulling up a chair. "Tell me, Miss Aldridge, are you a musician like your brother?"

"Oh no," she said quickly. "I sang in the church choir, but that's about all. I was a dressmaker back home. And up here I've been working in hotels. I'm employed at the Gilsey House."

"And how is that?" he asked.

"Oh. It's work, I suppose." Jessie looked embarrassed and Alfie knew she didn't want Tar to ask her about the specifics. A man like him wouldn't understand the drudgery of cleaning.

"But not interesting. Or personal." Tar pulled out his cigars, waving to the waiter to bring his usual. "I hate hotels myself. Never stay in 'em unless I have to."

"Tar has a house in London, England," Alfie informed his sister, sharing the new information he'd picked up on his recent visit uptown.

"You make it sound grander than it is," Tar said, holding a match to his cigar. "Honestly, it's just a small house, smaller than our New York home, but it does feel like home now that we've been spending summers there for the past fifteen years or so."

"You go to England every summer?" Jessie looked flabbergasted.

Tar shrugged and looked bashful. "My wife spent a great deal of her childhood there, so it's somewhere she loves."

"Ragtime has made it all the way across the ocean," Alfie told Jessie. "Tar thinks I should think about heading that way. There aren't many colored folk over there, but because of that they treat us like anyone else." He saw the look on her face. "But I ain't made no plans. I was thinking that maybe one day we could go together. Save our pennies and buy a passage to England."

"Oh, I don't think the Gilsey House will ever pay me enough for me to afford that," Jessie said, and Alfie knew that she was saying no. Not because of money but because, why would she want to go all that way? Jessie wouldn't have left the South if she'd had a choice.

But Tar didn't know Jessie like Alfie did. He took her at her word. "Jessie, you know, I have a solution for you. My daughter just lost her maid, and I'm sick and tired of her complaining about it. You said you're a dressmaker, but I assume you can carry out basic tasks? Cleaning and looking after a lady's toilette?"

"She can," Alfie said, getting in before Jessie could wreck her chances. He knew what Jessie was earning and he knew what Tar was worth. With both of them earning good money, they could get somewhere real nice to live. Maybe even save some money so that the trip to England wouldn't be such a wild dream.

The waiter delivered Tar's drink and the older man lifted his glass in a salute to the siblings. "Then the job's yours, so long as my daughter has no objections. Alfie's coming round tomorrow afternoon. He'll bring you over to meet her and you can start right away if the two of you get along." He pushed back his chair. "Now, please excuse me. I'm meeting someone and I shouldn't be late."

"What the hell d'you go and do that for?" Jessie hissed across the table once Tar had moved out of earshot, paying his bill before heading out of the main room. Through that back door were stairs that led to the private rooms above. All sorts went on up there, Alfie knew. Gambling, sex, private meetings with people who didn't want to be overheard or seen.

"What?" Alfie tried to look innocent even as he wondered what Tar's "business" was that night. "He pays well. Better than that shitty job you're doing. Isn't it easier to pick up after one person instead of however many you have to deal with at the hotel?"

"And his daughter? What's she like?"

He couldn't tell her the truth; she'd never go with him. "She's fine, I guess. I haven't ever met her properly, only seen her from a distance. She's pretty."

"I'll bet," Jessie muttered darkly under her breath.

"And she's fashionable. I reckon she gets her dresses made special." Alfie knew how to tempt her. "Even if working as her maid isn't so great, she might let you make a dress for her. Her mother's a wonderful woman. She's sick, though. Doesn't look like she's got long left."

It was a real shame when he came to think about it. Some days

Tar's wife was fine, almost like any other person if you ignored that she couldn't really walk or stand for very long. But she loved to chat about what was happening outside the four walls of her house. Music brought color to her cheeks, and Alfie found himself seeking out new music to share with her. He'd play a piece, or sing her a song he'd just learned, and they'd talk about it afterward. He could hardly believe he got paid to spend time with a friend, for that's what it felt like even though he knew their relationship was not as casual as that.

"Fine." Jessie finished her drink. "Tomorrow's my day off anyhow, so I'll come along and see what's what. But if I don't like it, then I'm not staying. And don't you look at me like that. You got me into this mess. I'll get myself out of it if I feel the need."

"I'm not saying a word." Alfie prepared to pay the bill, only to find that Tar had already settled it.

"I'm not sure I like that," Jessie said, giving Alfie a hard look. "A man like him, he prob'ly thinks he owns us now."

"It's just a couple plates of food, Jess," Alfie said, irritated.

Why couldn't she ever be grateful for good fortune? She was like their mother, always suspicious when anything went right for a change. Alfie was done with it. He'd been in New York longer and he was older than Jessie, even if only by a few minutes. If Jessie wanted them to set up home and live comfortably, then she had a duty to bring in as much money as she could.

"I can't wait to tell Mary Grace 'bout our plans," she said, brightening up as they made their way out into the warm summer evening. "She's working tonight but I'll tell her in the morning. I bet you she knows where to start looking."

"*I* know where to start looking," he retorted. "Look, Jess, I said she can live with us—if she wants to—but I'll find us somewhere. I know the lay of the land better than you do. And Mary Grace—she has different standards from us."

"Can you hear yourself?" Jessie marveled. "Looking down your nose at Mary Grace just 'cause she dances onstage. She don't just do it for the money. She loves to dance, that's why. She wants to work in one of the big theaters one day. The Haymarket's just to get used to it, that's all. When she gets some experience, she'll move on."

"Sure. Whatever you say. I barely know her." He wasn't in the mood to argue. Jessie had agreed to go to Tar's house with him tomorrow. Once she saw how Tar lived, she'd change her tune. She was imagining that he was rich like the families she sewed for back home. She didn't know yet that there was rich and there was *rich*.

The only worry he had was Mary Grace. Jessie had lost her mind to get so attached to a girl like that. She'd never have been friends with a harlot like her back home. Alfie had seen her at the Haymarket that night with Jessie, Mary Grace's skirt indecently short, ankles showing. Jessie reckoned that she wasn't as bad as he imagined. Perhaps he could stand to give the girl the benefit of the doubt. He wouldn't need to be the bad guy and Jessie would be safe from temptation. It didn't seem too much to hope for.

15

Saturday, 12 September 1936

"YOU REALLY DON'T come home very often," I observed when we finally joined Claud, Louis, and the other party stragglers at the back of the queue.

We'd been stopped at least five times on our way down, Will shaking hands with old buddies from school, musicians he'd played with along the way, friends who seemed surprised but pleased to see him. I wondered if Paul Robeson's wife felt like this when she went out on the town with him, the woman who got the looks, the brief moment of wonder, before the attention passed back to the man on whose arm she hung. The proud wife by her famous husband's side. I was proud, but that didn't mean I had to like being second best.

"Yeah," he admitted sheepishly. "Guess I sort of keep my head down whenever I'm back."

"Well, you're certainly Mr. Popular tonight," I said, tilting my head so he could kiss me.

"I've been telling him for years that people ask after him," Claud chimed in. "And don't you think I'm right?"

"Just say yes. It's easier," Louis muttered, earning himself a punch on the arm from his wife.

"Maybe you are right," Will said. He looked a little like a man just waking up from a strange dream. "Maybe I've been worrying about the past for too long."

"Haven't I been saying so for the past five years?" Claud asked him, shaking her head. "Time you listened to me instead of Bel. I know, I know." She held up her hands. "She's your family and you love her or whatever. And God knows I love Joey. I love that kid more than anything, which is why I've held my damned tongue as long as I have."

"Until a few highballs loosened it," Louis observed. "Is now the moment, baby? We're here for a good time, not to drag over the past."

"And why has our friend Will not been having a good time for all these years?" she retorted. "Because a certain someone's been filling his head with rubbish about what people think of him."

"Bel? What's she been saying?" As much as I'd enjoyed spending time with Bel, the idea of her talking nonsense about Will behind his back made my hackles rise. It wasn't his fault she'd been left alone with a child to raise. Henry was the wife beater, the adulterer, not Will. If he hadn't been cheating on his wife, he'd probably still be alive and Bel would be living a much easier life.

The three of them looked at one another, then answered at the same instant.

"Nothing much." Will.

"A lot of nonsense." Claud.

"A pile of bullshit." Louis.

"Language!" Claud smacked Louis's arm for a second time. "Though my husband does speak the truth."

"I don't think she means badly." Will looked at me, wariness writ across his face. "She just . . . Bel knows how bad I was when I got out of jail. It felt like all eyes were on me, wherever I went. All it took was a person to let on that they knew about what I did to Henry, and I'd have to leave wherever it was. I used to just panic. Couldn't breathe, couldn't act normal at all. I try not to feel like that anymore, but it's hard. I don't know. Maybe she's toughening me up. If I can't cope with Bel, how can I deal with the outside world?"

"She knew how sorry he was, and she kept reminding him until he left New York," Claud told me. "I say 'kept'—she's still at it to this day, and we all have to pretend it's all right, 'cause the one time I pulled her up on it, she kept me from seeing Joey for almost three months."

"That's true." Louis looked sad. "Don't get me wrong. I understand that she's got it hard, but Will, you need to have it out with her now that you got a few days. Tell her there's a chance you'll be staying and that she needs to get used to it and quit stirring the pot."

"Hey, hey, hey, I never said nothin' 'bout staying." But Will laughed and I knew the thought was stuck in his mind. The ease with which he'd been replaced on the ship had shown him that escape was possible if he wanted it.

"And what about you, Lena?" Claud turned her gin-loosened tongue on me.

"What about me?"

"Well, if Will were staying put, would that make you think about sticking around?"

Of course, I'd have been lying if I said that the thought hadn't crossed my mind, but I didn't want to tell Will that. For one thing, there was Eliza to think of, and the fact that I'd rather walk across hot coals than see either of her children—my half siblings—ever again.

"What would I do here?" I said eventually.

"What everyone else does. Find a job, get married, have kids, grow old, and die." Claud had all the answers, it seemed.

Louis burst out laughing, breaking the tension. "Baby, no more gin for you. Leave poor Lena alone. She's a grown woman. She don't need your help deciding what to do with her life."

Claud looked as though she disagreed with his assessment, but she allowed him to steer her forward as the line began to move. I dared to look up at Will, to see what he made of it all.

"I'm not expecting you to stay," he said quietly, so that the Linfields wouldn't hear. "You don't have to take my feelings into account. I know you have people to get back to."

Maggie. As good as family to me, especially now that Alfie was gone. I didn't count the Abernathys in that category—blood wasn't thicker than water, as far as I was concerned. The hunt for the woman who might or might not have been Alfie's sister had run aground. There were still Claud's church ladies to talk to, but I wasn't holding out much hope. Besides which, if I let myself consider why Alfie would have deserted his only sister, none of the options were good. Did I want to taint the memories of my beloved father? They were all I had left of him. On the other hand, if I found Jessie, she could tell me so much. About Alfie when he was young. His childhood and those ambitions that had sent him across an ocean to London. I might have cousins. There could be an entire branch of the Aldridge family just waiting to be discovered.

"I like this," I said to Will. "Us being together, I mean. I just don't know what happens next."

He nodded. "I know what you mean."

"Would you stay?" I asked. "Claud thinks she's got it all worked out, but what do you want to do?"

We shuffled forward another few feet while he thought about it. "I guess I'll know after Wednesday. It's a chance, you know? Amateur Night's a big deal. The biggest deal I've had to think about in a good long while."

"It's that important?" I was getting the terrifying feeling that I'd agreed to do something that was a lot bigger than I'd anticipated. Was it too late to back out?

"I don't know." The way he said it told me that it was. "Look, it might not amount to anything at all." But he wanted it to, so badly. I felt his grip on me tighten as his arm tensed just from his thinking about what this opportunity could mean.

"But it could," I said. "We'll sit down tomorrow and practice. Get Louis and Claud to listen in and tell us what they think. Louis seems to have a lot of opinions about music choices."

Will laughed. "That he does. I shouldn't laugh. Louis's been to a heck of a lot more Amateur Nights than I have. In the audience, of course, but he knows what goes down well."

"We don't have to make any decisions now, either of us," I said, feeling suddenly buoyant. It seemed so easy now that we had a date to aim for. "See how Wednesday goes and then we'll know the lay of the land."

"All right, baby." He pulled me close as we inched nearer to the entrance of the Savoy Ballroom. "Wednesday I'll make a decision 'bout what to do."

So much for my recuperative fortnight of sightseeing in New York. I had hoped to have a little peace and quiet to get over the ordeal that I had suffered through on the ship. Being totally honest, I'd let a spark of hope ignite that Will felt more for me than just the casual arrangement we'd silently agreed to. Before I'd arrived in Harlem and met his friends and family, I'd seen him as rootless, a man in search of somewhere or someone to call home. Foolishly I'd considered the possibility that he might think about coming to London for a while. Now that I was here I saw that of the two of us, I was the one who lacked a place that was truly their own. Homeless and without work, only the money in my carpetbag to my name, I had no security, no solid ground beneath my feet. Was it time to consider that there was an alternative to London?

"Will? Will Goodman?"

Will dropped my hand to hug this woman who had converged upon us, another two women behind her, neither of them shy in giving me the old up-and-down, trying to work out who the hell I was.

"Been a while, Glo," he said.

"Too damn long. Were you at the party? There were so many people, I didn't get a chance to get round to seeing everyone, and you were the last man I was expecting to see. I was beginning to think Bel had done away with you in secret and was just telling everyone you were at sea to cover her tracks." Glo smiled up at him winningly, her hand resting proprietorially on his arm.

"I get back every now and then, but usually I only get a couple days' leave." I coughed unsubtly and Will suddenly remembered that I was there. "You should meet my . . . friend." Friend?! "Glo, meet Lena Aldridge. She's a singer I met on the ship. And these are Florrie and Ada behind." He included the two women, who just nodded in my direction, straight-lipped and waiting for their leader to direct them.

"It's lovely to meet you all," I said, putting on my posh accent.

"You're not from around here," Glo said, eyes narrowing.

"No. I'm from London. England." I smiled brightly. I'd dealt with a variety of Glos over the years and I'd usually won, at worst accepting a draw.

"Lena and Will are signing up at the Apollo Wednesday night." Claud came to the rescue, and I got the impression that she too had a penchant for taking down Glo. "You girls should come down. Bring Wallace if he's back in town then." She gave Glo a meaningful look and the other woman took her hand back off Will.

"You and Wally?" Will's eyebrows shot up. "Really?"

"He's away working till the end of the month, but I'll make sure to let everyone know to come and support our favorite musician." She gave Will a wink and I felt my temper start to rise.

"God bless you," Claud said, tugging me forward as we finally reached the ballroom door. "Well, we won't keep you. Better get to the end of the line before it gets any longer!"

The women departed and I itched to ask Will about Glo. There had been something between them once upon a time, I could tell. I wasn't sure that Wally, whoever he was, would be enough to keep Glo from trying to get her claws back into Will.

"You don't have anything to worry about," Claud soothed quietly, reading my mind. "That ship has sailed—trust me. No way in hell that Will would go back there."

I'd be almost as sad to leave Claud behind as I would to leave Will. I couldn't remember a time when anyone else had been so welcoming, so keen to draw me into her circle of friends. She was going to help make my decision over where my future lay very difficult.

16

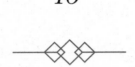

Saturday, 12 September 1936

INSIDE THE CLUB was madness. We lost Claud and Louis almost immediately, and I was glad that we seemed to have lost Glo and her troupe as well. I don't know what I'd been expecting, but the Savoy Ballroom defeated any ideas I'd had. The place was vast, a cathedral for swing, the band exercising their divine right to play music as if their lives depended on it. It was loud and glorious; people hadn't come to stand by and watch. They had come to dance. There was no time for chitchat, not even much drinking going on other than when the tired revelers dragged themselves out of the melee for water. Will and I hung back and watched couples swing and hop around the floor with ease, pulling off gymnastic moves that left me breathless just being in their presence.

The house band kept up a rapid fire of hit songs, and I saw Will watching them play with a gleam of green in his eye. I knew what he was feeling. The singer was just a slip of a girl, younger than me, and I wondered how she'd ended up singing to thousands of people on a Saturday night in New York City.

"She won first place at Amateur Night a couple years ago," Will told me, reading my mind.

"What do you actually win for first place?" I asked him, standing on tiptoes so that he could hear me.

"If they like you, then they offer you to play there for a week," he said. "But look, let's not worry 'bout that for now. Let's dance!"

I wasn't used to feeling like the worst dancer in a room, but here I was definitely the class dunce. I could just about hang on to the turns, and I let Will show off his moves until we were both out of breath, and if I was sweating, then poor Will in his jacket and tie was soaked through. It was the most fun I'd had in a long time.

It was after three in the morning by the time we'd made our way back outside and headed home.

"Ah, I haven't danced like that in years," Will said, his feet bouncing along the pavement. I'd never seen him so full of joy. "Whatever happens, promise me we can head back there next week."

"Promise. Besides, I need to get some dance practice in, I think."

"You held your own," he assured me. "Anyway, a lot of those dancers are professionals. They get paid to make the place jump, you know? Some fellas pay the women to dance with 'em, teach 'em some moves."

"I can see why."

We reached the Linfields' building and Will let us in, gesturing to me to take off my shoes so we could tread lightly up the stairs. As we crept up, the building was completely silent, and the living room lights were off when we reached the apartment. There was a slight glow emanating from my bedroom. I could hear rummaging. Had Joey woken up in the night?

"Damn it," Will swore, obviously hoping that Bel and Joey had already left to go home.

I pushed the door open gently, but it wasn't Joey I disturbed. The girl was fast asleep, curled up under the bedclothes. It was Bel who was rummaging, so absorbed in her activity that she didn't see me. She was counting money on the bed, sorting the bills into neat piles as she emptied them out from my carpetbag.

"What the hell's all that money?" Will startled me as much as he did Bel. He'd kept his voice low, aware of Joey's proximity, but there was a power in his delivery nonetheless.

"Will!" She stared up at us, wide-eyed. "I thought . . ."

I reached the bed in two long strides, sweeping the money up and pushing it back into my bag, snatching it away from Bel. "Why are you looking through my things?" I could feel the heat flare in my cheeks. No one was supposed to know about the money. I stared at her, and she was brazen enough to hold my gaze. She'd seen me with Eliza at the Sherry-Netherland, I remembered. Did she know who Eliza Abernathy was? She was a society figure, after all, known for being the daughter of one of the richest men in the city. Her photograph had been in all the newspapers over the years, let alone in the last week, since both her father and husband had been so brutally killed. The questions Bel had been pressing me with the night before . . . Had she put two and two together? I looked at her, torn between fear and anger. If she had even the slightest idea who I was, who Eliza Abernathy was, she could destroy everything.

"I wasn't stealing it," she said. "I didn't mean to. I just . . . I just . . ."

"That's your bag, Lena?" Will asked, and I nodded, not able to look him in the eye.

There was so much I hadn't told him. So much I hadn't been sure I'd ever *have* to tell him if we didn't have a real future. Only now Bel had gone snooping and turned up a wad of stolen money hidden away in my belongings.

Not stolen by me, I reminded myself. And really it depended on whose money you believed it was. Maggie had taken it from her husband's safe, and he was dead, so, by rights, it would have been inherited by her in due course. It was Maggie who'd made me take it and keep it. Said that I might need it in New York, little knowing just what a godsend it would turn out to be.

"It's all the money I have in the world," I told him, honestly. "It looks more impressive than it is, trust me. I wasn't planning on heading back to London so soon, and I didn't know when I'd get paid next."

"Bel, get out," he said, looking over my head to where his sister still sat.

"I didn't mean to," she protested. "It was just there and . . . it is quite a lot of money, Lena. I just wonder where it all came from, you know, and—"

"Get out!" He raised his voice, all of us glancing toward the slumbering figure in the bed, but she didn't wake. "Joey can stay. Let the girl sleep, but you got to leave now. Before I lose my temper."

"I won't leave my daughter with you in this sort of a mood." Bel collected her composure in an instant, looking as put out as if it was we who had been rooting through her private belongings, not the other way around. "Joey, darling, wake up. Time to go home."

"Just leave her, Bel," I said, though I could see that Joey was already beginning to stir, blinking her eyes against the light.

"I know when I'm not wanted," Bel told me. "And if you don't want me, you don't want my daughter neither."

"Mama?" Joey was confused as her mother took off her own coat and began to bundle her daughter into it, presumably judging it quicker than waiting for Joey to get changed out of her pajamas.

Will walked to the window, and pressed his hand against the frame as he pushed his forehead to the glass, eyes closed. I could see the tension in his back, even through his jacket. I shoved the bag back under the bed as Bel marched Joey out. We stood in silence until the door slammed hard, rattling the windowpane, and we heard Bel's heels on the stairs, making every last step heard throughout the house.

"She never did give a damn about anyone else," Will said, and I wasn't sure if he was talking about the neighbors or about us.

I went over to him and dared to put a hand on his arm. He didn't move an inch. "I can explain. About the money."

He turned his head. "You don't have to. It's your money, after all. Bel had no right to go through your belongings."

"Oh." I could feel the anger melting out of him. "I thought you might wonder if I'd robbed a bank or something." I tried to laugh. "I didn't. It does belong to me."

He pressed a finger to my lips. "I'm mad at Bel, not you. Anytime something good happens to me, she's there ready to sling a sledgehammer at it. That's what it feels like, anyhow."

I didn't know what to say. Whatever she'd done, she was his sister. I might not have grown up with siblings, but I'd lived in the same house as Maggie and her sisters and learned the hard way that it's perfectly all right to say nasty things about one's own sister, but it's a completely different matter for someone else to say the same.

"I should go," he said, but he didn't move.

"Do you have to?" I stepped into his arms and pressed my cheek against his chest. "Better to give Bel some time, don't you think?"

"Claud'll be mad at me."

"Not when I tell her what happened."

And so we fell into bed and I did my absolute best to take his mind off his sister and her shortcomings. Afterward, dozing as I heard the front door open and Claud and Louis stagger in, I realized that Bel was just playing a game. She wanted Will to feel unwelcome in his own home because she liked that he was never there. She wanted him away at sea, where he wasn't a daily reminder of how she had wronged him. I'd have felt the same, though I wasn't sure I'd have the guts to carry through with such a campaign. The photographs, the searching through my belongings, the *poor me* routine. It was all designed to show Will that he wasn't needed, that he wasn't wanted.

Why had she made such an effort with me, then? Even if she'd seen Eliza and realized something was up, that had happened on our shopping trip. She'd already been making overtures to become friends. Had she had some other sly plan up her sleeve? Was it my fault for trusting her after everything I'd heard? I'd ignored Will's reactions and thought him bitter. What a heel I was for not trusting him, for not believing that he had a perfectly valid reason for keeping his sister at arm's length.

I heard Claud giggling in the living room as Louis tried to steer her to bed, her drunken joy giving me hope. With her on my side we'd have no trouble thwarting Bel's attempts. I only had a little over a week to do it, but I was determined now. Will would stop running away. He'd stop right here in Harlem even if it took every waking minute for me to make sure of it. I'd been just as bad as him, happy to sing every night for pennies at the Canary Club rather than take the risk of auditioning anywhere with a bit of class. We were opposite sides of the same coin. Where I'd been paralyzed, stuck in the Canary Club out of fear that I wasn't good enough, Will had fled to the ocean. Maybe it was time for both of us to stop being scared. It was time for a change.

17

Sunday, 13 September 1936

IF I'D VAGUELY remembered that we were supposed to be going to church that morning, I'd also been convinced that Claud would be in no shape to enforce it. I was wrong.

Eight o'clock dawned, and less than five hours after I'd heard her trying to convince Louis to have one last whirl around the living room, Claud was banging plates of bacon and eggs onto the table, shouting through my bedroom door for us to get our behinds out of bed else we'd be late and if I wanted to talk to the church aunties, then I'd best be on time.

"Will you quit your hollerin', Claudette, for the love of God!" Will groaned and shoved his head under the pillow. So much for my halfhearted plan to sneak him out before the apartment woke up.

"Good night?" Claud could barely keep the grin from her face as we finally sat down to eat. She looked as fresh as a daisy, highly irritating to behold. My head pounded and I wasn't sure I'd be able to eat the food she'd bothered to prepare.

I grabbed for the coffeepot, just beating Will to it. "Yes, thank you. Though the ending was fairly eventful."

"Huh?" Louis looked up from shoveling scrambled eggs into his mouth.

"Bel." Will said it as though it was an inevitability.

Claud groaned. "What now?"

"We caught her going through Lena's bags when we got home," Will said, buttering a roll. "Then she had the audacity to act like we were in the wrong. Woke up poor Joey and dragged her home at that time of the morning, like the streets are perfectly safe."

Claud shook her head. "I'm so sorry, Lena. I don't know what gets into that woman sometimes. She goes months being on her best behavior and then she goes and pulls a trick like this. I hope nothing's missing, Lena. I mean, Bel's not a thief, but . . ."

"No," I assured her. "Honestly, I think she just let her curiosity get the better of her." Why was I defending her?

"She's acting up 'cause I'm around." Will sat back in his chair, his food uneaten. "And don't tell me I'm wrong. Like you said, she's fine most of the time, but anytime I'm back for more than a night or two, she starts up with something. Remember when me and Glo . . ." His eyes slid in my direction, then just as quickly away.

I knew it! I bloody knew it, the way she'd looked at him the night before. As if he were her rightful property.

"Gloria Wilson?" Claud snorted. "She's just as bad. In fact, I'd argue that's the only time I can vouch that Bel had your best interests at heart." She checked her watch. "Now, come on, eat up. Ten minutes, then we need to leave."

THE LAST TIME I'd set foot in church—not counting the rather monotonous Sunday service on board the *Queen Mary*—had been for my father's funeral. Alfie hadn't been particularly religious, but it had felt like the right thing to do. I hadn't really known what to do with myself after he'd gone, after so long watching his illness destroy him. Organizing the funeral, the wake afterward at Maggie's mother's house, meeting his old friends—it had all filled the deep hole that his absence left. It had always been the two of us. I didn't need anyone else until he was gone, and I realized that I had no one.

"Miss Marietta Coleman and Miss Ida Barker," Claud said, pointing to two middle-aged women, one in a slightly too-tight dress and the other wearing a very wide-brimmed hat. "Between the pair of them, they could name damn near everyone who's ever passed through Harlem, even if just for a night. They've been here since the beginning, since these streets were full of white folk."

"I'm not even sure if Alfie ever lived in Harlem." I tried not to flinch as one of the women caught sight of me and stared at me as if she was trying to work out who or what I was.

Claud grabbed me by the arm and began to drag me in their direction. "Don't you want to find your family?"

It was a question I kept asking myself. Was it really the wisest idea to dig up the past? Watching Will's relationship with his sister, being reminded that family was complicated, was off-putting. But then, what if Jessie was close by? What if she was just like Alfie, kind and funny and loving? I'd regret it for the rest of my life if I didn't try to find out.

Nobody was going into the church yet. Everyone seemed to have gathered outside, greeting one another like long-lost friends even though surely this was a weekly event. I was glad I'd made an effort to look demure. Marietta and Ida looked as though they'd not have much truck with slovenly girls.

"Ladies, good morning," Claud sang out. "I hope you're both well? I thought you'd like to meet our visitor all the way from England. Miss Lena Aldridge, this is Miss Marietta and Miss Ida."

"Pleased to meet you." I suppressed a wild urge to curtsy before them, for surely this pair were church royalty.

"From England?" The lady in the too-tight dress—Ida—beamed a wide smile. "I always wanted to go there someday."

"Ida's never even left New York State," Marietta told me. Her face remained quite stern, but there was a fondness in her voice. "What brought you all this way, Miss Aldridge?"

"A job opportunity," I said, hoping a simple explanation would suffice.

"Claudette is a pillar of the community. Her work with the children at the library is just exemplary," Ida told me, turning to Claud. "It's been wonderful to see how you've progressed."

"Miss Ida and Miss Marietta teach school," Claud told me. "They taught me and Louis. Will too."

"My gosh, is that William over there?" Marietta shaded her eyes and squinted in Will's direction. He was standing with Louis, and as I watched, I saw that bloody woman Glo stalking up behind him.

Claud must have seen the same as me, for she called out immediately. "Will! Will, come over here and say hello."

"Miss Marietta, Miss Ida." Will nodded respectfully, tipping his hat.

"Where on earth have you been hiding?" Ida scolded. "I haven't seen you at church in months. You better have a good excuse for it."

"I've been working on the ships, remember? But don't worry—they have a church service on board, and I make sure to go every week, even though of course it's not the same."

"How could it be?" Marietta sniffed. "I hope you're back home for good now?" I saw her glance at me suspiciously, clearly wondering how I fit into his future. I couldn't blame her when I was wondering the same.

"Nothing's settled just yet, but if you both are free on Wednesday evening I'll hopefully be performing at the Apollo. With Lena." He took my hand and I saw Marietta nod to herself.

"Oh, we'll be there, don't you worry. I always said, Lena, that our William had the voice of an angel," Ida told me. "If he hadn't been smart enough to get into college, I thought he'd do well on the stage."

"We don't have to start talking about the old days," he said, laughing. "Don't scare Lena off before Wednesday, Miss Ida. I need her."

I felt my breath catch in the back of my throat and didn't dare look up at him. Did he mean that? Or was it just something that had tripped out on his tongue?

People were starting to move toward the church doors and Claud realized that our window of opportunity was vanishing. "Ladies, we do have a favor to ask. Lena's father was originally from New York and she's trying to trace some family who might still be living here. You both would have been living in Harlem when her father left. I just remember you telling us all those stories when we were children. Perhaps if you sat down with Lena and had a chat . . ."

"We're having some of the church ladies over for tea after the service," Ida said as we began to walk toward the door. "Come on over. The more the merrier, though it is ladies only, I'm afraid, William. The young girls get distracted otherwise."

He looked relieved. "May I at least escort you inside?"

Ida and Marietta took an arm each and Claud and I followed, picking up Louis on our way in. Another insight into Will's life in Harlem. What would he find if our roles were reversed? Certainly, I'd never been a churchgoer. The people I called friends could be counted on the fingers of one hand, and really Maggie was the only friend I could say knew everything about me. (At least, she had until I'd left English soil. We'd have a hell of a time when I got home and tried to recount my recent adventures to her. It would take a few bottles of wine or more, I reckoned.) This life that Will had spent so long rejecting was ready to re-embrace him if only he'd stand still long enough to realize it. Did he know how lucky he was to have this?

If I'd discovered a church like this in London, I might have been a more regular worshipper. There was no dry Church of England vicar, this Harlem preacher as far removed from the judgmental Reverend Sullivan of Bethnal Green as you could imagine. There was a vibrancy to the preaching, an inclusion of the congregation. We weren't being spoken down to from the pulpit, the wise vicar instructing his slovenly and stupid East London locals.

I'd stopped going to Sunday school after the Reverend Sullivan's wife had made us draw pictures of Noah and his sons, telling us of the curse of Ham. *And all his descendants are so cursed, just like Lena's father.* Alfie had said that we needed never go back to that church, and it was the one time I knew of that he argued with Mrs. Harper, who was our landlady at the time. Still, she didn't throw us out and Alfie promised that he and I would have our own church service at home every week. While the Harpers headed out in their Sunday best, Alfie and I had walked down to the local picture house, where he played the piano and had a key to the back door. He'd taught me all the latest songs and we'd belted them out to the empty auditorium. It was our own style of worship, celebrating the gifts we had been given, and we always ended with a bowing of our heads and a reciting of the Lord's Prayer so that when we got home and Mrs. Harper asked, we could say truthfully that we had prayed and felt saved.

Song had been so much a part of our lives that I cried during the second hymn, suddenly missing Alfie as powerfully as when he had died nine months earlier. I knew I would never get over it, but it shocked me that it hit me so hard in that moment. Claud passed me a handkerchief without saying a word, somehow understanding, and Will squeezed my hand. Maybe it was only Brits who didn't think it usual to show emotions in public.

Miss Ida and Miss Marietta lived in a house five minutes' walk from the church. The brownstone was set out how I imagined Claud and Louis's had been before the floors had been sectioned off into apartments.

"They let out the top two floors to young girls who need a helping hand," Claud whispered, seeing me looking around. "They do good work."

As the churchwomen gathered in the spacious living room I thought I spotted some of those girls handing out cups of tea and setting out cakes and stacked plates on the coffee table. One side of the room was given over almost entirely to book shelving that reached to the high ceiling. Several Bibles and a lot of dry-looking texts lined the wall. The middle shelf, however, was for photographs. I wandered over and accepted a cup of tea from a girl who looked all of fourteen.

Posed photographs, Marietta and Ida in most of them, but not always together. Groups of children dominated the majority, but as the two women grew older, their subjects grew with them. The seven- and eight-year-olds of the early pictures became the girls who served us tea and cake.

"Oh Lord!" Claud came alongside me and picked up one of the frames. "Bet you can't pick out Will in this one."

"Will?" I peered over her shoulder. But of course, he was right in the front. A tiny boy with a cheeky grin, the crinkles around his eyes and the rounding of his cheeks just the same as they would be when he grew up. Behind him I thought I spotted boy Louis, and in the line of little girls, all of them with their hair neatly braided and their skirts falling past their knees to meet their socks, I recognized Claud.

"Simpler days." Claud sighed. "Do you ever wish you could go back and whisper in your ear when you were just a child? Warn yourself what not to do?"

I couldn't imagine that Claud had any dark secrets of her own. But I could well see her telling her younger self to keep an eye on Will, to stop him from bringing Henry Bennett to meet his sister. The past was a funny beast, though. If Will hadn't gone to jail, then I'd never have met him. Maybe he'd have ended up married to one of these women. Glo, perhaps, who was even now glaring at me from the corner of the room. People made mistakes, and I wasn't entirely sure that we weren't meant to. Our lives were formed from those errors of judgment. Even the bad times sometimes begot the good. Bel had married a philanderer, but he'd at least had the decency to give her Joey before he fell under a garbage truck. Will had been to jail, but would he have been any happier if he hadn't run away from Harlem? This homecoming felt fortuitous.

"Oh, my gorgeous boy." Ida sidled up behind us. "Do we have you to thank, Lena, for bringing him home?"

I started to shake my head just as Claud spoke a determined "Yes!"

Ida laughed. "Well, whatever it is, you do what you can to keep him here, understand? That boy thinks he lost his way, but he never did, not in my book. We protect our own. No shame in that."

"Amen," Claud said quietly, winking at me. "Sister Ida, you've been in Harlem for a long time now, haven't you?"

"You calling me old?" Ida laughed again. "Child, I arrived here before Harlem was Black. Etta and I, we were among the first, before everyone else got sick of living down in those disgusting rat-infested tenements downtown."

"Setting the fashion as always," Claud complimented.

"Always." Ida smoothed down her dress. She'd left her hat on indoors, presumably so the rest of us could continue to enjoy it. "Now, you're thinking I might have come across some long-lost relative, Lena?"

"Not so much long-lost. My father, Alfie. I don't know much about his life before he arrived in London, but he did live in New York. It's a long shot, I know, but I wondered if we had any relatives left over this side of the pond."

"Alfie what?"

I told her our surname, the year that I thought Alfie might have left New York, that he played piano and sang, just like Will.

177

"Aldridge," she said, and I could have sworn she looked worried. "And a musician? Well, there have always been more musicians than you could shake a stick at. Was he New York–born, or did he come up with all those other poor folks? They came up in droves from the South, you know, soon as they realized that slavery ending was just a technicality and not a new way of life. Hundreds of them."

"Maybe," I said, trying to remember where it was that Smiles had told me Alfie had originally come from. "Florida? And he had a sister."

"Etta, you remember that skinny girl from Florida all those years back?" Ida called over to her friend. "Wasn't her surname Aldridge?"

"Which skinny girl from Florida?" Etta came over, her stern disposition more to do with her ramrod-straight back and severe tailoring than with her personality. "There've been so many girls through here at one time or another."

"Years back. When we were just getting started. Remember, she was a seamstress. She didn't stay for long, ended up running with the wrong crowd. The Lord only knows what became of her. What was her name?" Ida tapped her head with her forefinger, gently teasing the information out of her memories. "Janie? No, Jessie! Didn't she have a brother?"

I held my breath. This was her. Jessie Aldridge. There was no way that Ida could have dreamed up the same name as Smiles had remembered.

Etta frowned. "I don't remember them the way you do. Only the girls who deserve to be remembered." She turned to me and Claud. "We treat all our girls well, but we expect them to be chaste, you know? We don't make any profit out of this arrangement. It's purely about making sure that these young girls have a safe place to live. Giving them a chance to walk on the right path. Those who don't, I don't care to waste too much time thinking about."

"Well, I don't know if that helps, but it's a name at least. And she definitely had a brother. She'd come to find him. I remember that, very clearly," Ida told me. "Such a shame we couldn't save her."

"Save her?"

"From temptation." My heart rate slowed as I realized that Ida was talking in metaphors. "She was a quiet girl and I thought she'd soon settle in, learn from us and maybe join us in our work one day. But as soon as that brother of hers showed up, she packed up and headed downtown, to the Tenderloin." She shook her head as if still unable to believe it all these years later. "She'd fallen in with a bad influence before that, if I'm honest. Now, apologies if that brother was your father, but he did her no favors. That place was a den of sin. Once those wayward girls leave us, we never see them again. It's a real shame. Still, people have to find their own way through life."

More people arrived and it was a relief when Ida and Etta moved away to greet the new guests. I hadn't appreciated her talking about Alfie that way. If he had cared for his sister even a fraction of the way he had for me, Jessie would have been perfectly safe, no matter where they lived. In truth, the Tenderloin didn't sound very different from my Soho. I was sure that Ida Barker would have a fit if she visited any of my old London haunts.

Claud started talking, but all I could think of was this new puzzle piece. Jessie was real. She'd started off in Harlem but moved down to the Tenderloin; that tallied with Smiles' account. But it seemed as though no one knew what had happened to the siblings once they'd been reunited. As far as anyone seemed to know, they'd both vanished off the face of the earth. Had Jessie and Alfie left New York together or had something caused them to split apart before then?

One thought crossed my mind: Might Eliza know? It looked as though our meeting on Tuesday was coming at just the right time.

Harlem After Midnight

Thursday, 17 September 1936, 4 a.m.

"YOU LET THE prime suspect go off in an ambulance with the victim?" McLennan looked at Garson like he was a prize fool.

"It happened too fast. I only just arrived on the scene. Before that it was just the rookie. Freeman. He's off at the hospital now, making sure nothing happens." Garson was fuming internally. As if McLennan would have been able to do things differently! The lazy bastard had only just bothered to show up, hours late. Even now, he'd only wandered into the bedroom and started poking around; even Garson had already had a good look.

"Alibis?" McLennan went to the window and looked out, as if he thought the culprit could be out there.

"There was a party. Everyone had been drinking. No one seems sure where anyone else was. Goodman is the main suspect because we know he was in the room with the victim earlier that evening, though he told Freeman that he was in the living room when she fell.

We got an eyewitness who can verify that he was, but he hadn't been there for long."

"So he could have pushed her and hurried back to alibi himself before the body was discovered." McLennan took a swig from a hip flask and Garson tried not to look appalled.

"Well, she's not exactly a body yet; she's still breathing, far as I know, but yes. That's what I was thinking."

"All right, well, let's go and speak to the residents."

As they walked out into the living room, Mrs. Linfield was speaking: "I don't think it's a good idea."

"Think what's a good idea, Mrs. Linfield?" McLennan boomed out, making the woman jump.

She shot a panicked look in her husband's direction. Garson wondered if there was more going on in this apartment than met the eye.

18

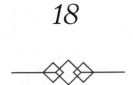

Tuesday, 15 September 1936

A TWO-DAY HANGOVER carried me through a Monday spent doing little more than exploring the local streets and having a picnic
with Will in St. Nicholas Park, lying back on the grass and watching
the turning leaves on the trees above our heads. I was glad to wake
up feeling somewhat close to normal on Tuesday. At least I felt normal until I remembered what day it was. I was due at the Abernathys'
at one o'clock.

I had thought about calling from the pay phone at the end of the
street, giving a polite excuse as to why I'd regretfully be unable to
attend. Eliza would surely have staff to answer her telephone for her,
after all. I could easily lie to a stranger, especially when I didn't have
to look them in the eye.

All in all, going to see Eliza seemed the easiest solution. An hour,
that was all, and then I'd have done my daughterly duty. She'd no
doubt try to palm some money off on me to assuage her guilt, and I

wouldn't think twice about taking it this time. It was amazing how just a week of peace and quiet away from the ship had changed my perspective on the matter.

"Will you be home for dinner?" Claud asked over breakfast.

I'd told a white lie, that I was going down to the main branch of the New York Public Library to do some research. I might pop in if I had time, I reasoned, so it wasn't really a lie at all. I intended to use Eliza to try to answer some questions about Alfie and Jessie. What was better, a woman who'd lived with my father, albeit briefly, or some dry old papers at the library? Trawling through births and deaths in the *New York Times* was not my idea of a good time.

I headed into Midtown on the subway and ducked into a post office to send my inadequate telegram to Maggie in London:

LEAVING NEW YORK WEEK ON WEDNESDAY. QUEEN MARY.
IF NO WORD FROM YOU WILL COME TO HAMPSTEAD.

I hoped that it was clear enough. I was counting on Maggie to have somewhere for me to stay when I got back. Eliza's money was my last resort.

I couldn't decide if I liked the straightforward layout of the New York streets or if they were depressingly unimaginative. I loved London's laneways and alleys, the history surrounding me as I walked my city's uneven and crooked streets. A city I could still get lost in after living there my entire life. Here, a man had been busy with his set square and ruler, meticulously planning streets and avenues that followed strict rules. Order had its advantages: I found Eliza's house easily enough on my own. Sometimes, though, I found myself craving chaos.

I stood before the town house and stared up at its ornate windows. It wasn't what I'd had in mind. The house had been my grandfather's before he moved into a more modern apartment. I'd visited there briefly the previous week, before going to stay with the Linfields, and it had been far closer to Francis Parker's sensibilities than was the home he'd given over to his daughter and her family.

Four stories tall, built from warm brick, ivy crawling up its façade, it looked like my dream of a home. A residence for the wealthy, of course, but without that cold, impersonal touch that was Parker's usual style. My nerves ebbed away slightly as I took the three steps up to the front door, flanked by rosebushes in beautiful terra-cotta pots, and I rang the bell.

"Lena!" I was shocked that Eliza herself answered the door, a beaming smile on her face, and stepped back to let me in. "I'm so happy you could make it."

I mumbled something about wanting to pay my respects and she looked at me strangely for a moment until she realized what I meant.

"Oh, darling, I'm so sorry. The doctor's got me on these fabulous new pills. It's impossible to feel even a twinge of grief on them, I'm afraid. Poor Jack. I'm sure if he were here, he'd be disgusted at me, but what's to be done?"

To give Eliza some credit, she was dressed very somberly still, befitting a widow of less than a fortnight. And I'd never held any illusions that she and Jack had been in love, either at the end of his life or at the beginning of their marriage. Not from what I'd heard from several close sources. That she'd not mentioned her father didn't surprise me either.

I followed her mutely along the corridor, beyond the staircase and into a comfortable sitting room. The day was cool but sunny and the large French windows let in the light. It was a room that looked lived-in. Cozy. A bookcase along one wall contained books with cracked spines. A corner was home to a tucked-away card table, and before the fireplace were arranged a large coffee table, a sofa, and two deep armchairs.

"I don't have much of an appetite these days, but I thought perhaps some sandwiches and cake?" Eliza perched on one end of the sofa and gestured for me to take the other. I nodded and sat down. "You look well," she said. "The color's back in your cheeks."

"Thank you. I do feel a little better. Especially now that I'm not fearing for my life any longer." I managed to force a smile onto my lips to reduce the sting. Though, of course, Eliza had nothing to do with the murders. Not directly.

"I agree with you entirely. I may never leave New York again after our ordeal. I'm glad to be home, sweet home. The children are the complete opposite, of course. The memories of their father are a little much for them. They traveled out to the Hamptons this morning. Unfashionable at this time of year, so they won't have those usual prying eyes keeping watch."

Carrie and Frankie were gone? I felt some of the tension ease through my shoulders and along my spine. My half brother and half sister, though Frankie, as far as I was aware, still didn't know that we were related. In truth, Eliza didn't scare me. Our connection still felt unreal, hypothetical. A fact that I had accepted because it made sense, like learning the alphabet in school, or accepting that the law of gravity exists even though I'm not interested in understanding it. She was my mother. The theory of it was sound, but the relationship, the irresistible emotional weight that family came with, was not. Having seen Eliza with her two perfectly golden-haired legitimate children, I wasn't sure th he knew how to be a real mother. Not the mother I had cra   hild, though Alfie was as brilliant a father as any could

"How have y   asked, trying to be polite.

"Oh, you kno   is." Her shrug was noncommittal.

A maid silently   eared bearing a silver tray of sandwiches, pretty éclairs, and iced biscuits, and placed them on the low table. She returned with the coffeepot, cups of fine china, and a bowl of perfect sugar cubes alongside the cream. I let Eliza pour for me and filled my plate with sandwiches: cheese and tomato, ham salad, and egg. Very English.

"Isn't this nice?" Eliza nibbled on an éclair.

"Why did you want to meet?" I hoped I sounded curious rather than combative.

"Because I didn't want to leave it the way things were. I know I'm not worthy of being your mother," she said, turning to look me straight in the eye, the most lucid she'd been since the day I'd first met her. "I abandoned you and I will forever be ashamed of that. And I know I could have done more this time around. Maybe you're wondering why I won't tell Frankie and Carrie about you. The only answer I have is that I want to do right by them, at least. We can tell them, one day, but not now. Not when they've lost so much, and Frankie, well . . ."

Frankie was a chip off the old block, as they say. An adult, yes, but a young man of privilege who was used to doing what he wanted, when he wanted, with very few repercussions. A child in a man's expensive tailoring. I didn't particularly want him to know that we were related. And if he found out who my father had been, well, I couldn't imagine his reaction would be pretty.

"Frankie's at a difficult age," I said, an attempt at diplomacy.

"He's at a crossroads," Eliza agreed, "and the silver lining of all that's happened is that I can try and shunt him onto the right path. He worshipped his father, but Jack wasn't always the best example to follow. I think Frankie's got it in him to be a better man now."

I wished her luck with her hopes. "The last couple of weeks have been difficult, for you far more than for me. I don't know what else to say."

"You don't need to say anything," she assured me. "This isn't about me trying to win you over or to suddenly prove myself. It'd be a waste of both our time. I have a lot to deal with. My husband was not a nice man, but I'd come to rely on him for a lot of things. The same with my father. I hope that one day we can have some sort of a relationship, but it doesn't have to be now. In fact, better that it isn't now."

"Oh." What was she saying? Was this a polite rebuff? An antici-patory meeting to ward me off in the future?

"Please don't look at me like that," she begged. "I'm trying to do the right thing—really, I am. But, Lena, I don't know what I'm do-ing. Father's lawyers are arranging everything and I'm just waiting to be told what I do next. I've never been in charge of my own money, and now I have a seat on the board of a multimillion-dollar company! Can you imagine?" I shook my head. "And Frankie is go-ing to want in on it once he finds out. That's partly why I sent them both away. I need to figure out who I am. What I want. I'm afraid that if I try and start a relationship with you now it'll all go wrong."

"I understand." In a funny way, I did. I felt at the junction of a crossroads, and Eliza was in a similar position. Even after sending the telegram to Maggie, I didn't feel entirely certain about where my future lay—here in New York or back in London. If I went home alone, would my friendship with Maggie be on shaky ground? If I stayed, would Will be ready to make a fresh start, and with me by his side? Eliza had to consider whether she wanted to be the new head of the Parker/Abernathy fortune or whether she should acqui-esce to her overprivileged young son. It would be a battle to keep him at bay, though I knew that her daughter, Carrie, would be on her side.

Eliza rested her hand on mine, and squeezed it. "Thank you, Lena. Perhaps it's rather uncouth, but shall we talk money now?"

"Money?" I'd half forgotten that she'd offered me fifty thousand dollars when we were at sea. Blood money to assuage her guilt. A lot had happened between then and now, and I'd tried to put the idea out of my mind in case she didn't come through.

Eliza put down her plate and stood, brushing crumbs from her lap onto the floor. "I've made the arrangements." She disappeared through the door, and came back a moment or two later with an envelope. "Here. You'll need to visit the Parker Godwin office in London. I figured it'd be a lot easier to do it through them since you don't have an American bank account. You just need to go in and see this gentleman, Winston Radlett. He was always my father's right-hand man in London. He knows who you are, let's put it that way. I've already spoken to him on the telephone, and he'll be expecting to meet with you when you get back. Take identification; your passport will do. He'll arrange for a monthly check to be drawn up. The details are all in the letter, further proof that we've met, and that you are who you say you are."

I took the envelope. It was unsealed and I was itching to pull out the letter and see what she'd written. "I didn't come here expecting this." Though I wasn't going to turn it down. Money wasn't everything, but it'd make my immediate future a damn sight easier.

"I don't care either way," she said, "but I wanted to show you that my word counts for something. This is a small step toward making things up to you."

She remained standing, and I realized that this was it. The finale to whatever this had been. Eliza Abernathy had written a to-do list and now I had been crossed off. It didn't really matter what I wanted. There was no option. Her final offer was in the envelope, and if I turned it down, she wouldn't be open to negotiation.

I got up and tucked the envelope into my handbag, biting my tongue to stop myself from thanking her. It was the least she could do, and there was more than a hint of payoff about it. But I'd come for another reason. Now that I knew for certain that the Abernathys were nothing more than a regular income, Jessie forced her way to the front of my mind.

"I wanted to ask you something else," I said. "About Alfie."

"Alfie?" She looked puzzled.

"He . . . I met someone who knew him, years back. Before he met you. They told me that he had a sister. I wondered if he ever mentioned her. If you knew what became of her. If she's still alive I'd love to . . ." Love to what? Meet her? Add yet another stranger to my tangled family? Perhaps it was a simple as having someone normal in my life. Someone who would be happy to learn that she had a long-lost niece. "Does the name Jessie ring a bell?"

Eliza pursed her lips. "Alfie told me nothing about his family. I always assumed he had none. He seemed lonely when I met him. A sad young boy. I grew up surrounded by people who were defined by who their families were. I liked him because he wasn't. He was just Alfie. Alone. I never heard him mention a sister."

I could see she was telling the truth. She didn't care enough to lie. "You must have a lot to arrange, Eliza," I said. "I'll get out of your hair."

Her shoulders fell visibly as she let go of the fear that I was going to make a fuss. "Take care, Lena."

I showed myself out, wondering why I suddenly felt so bereft. I'd been alone for almost a year, ever since Alfie had died. So why was it now that the loneliness was hitting me? Even Francis Parker and Jack Abernathy, men who could best be described as ruthless and self-serving, had family to care that they'd gone. If I'd died on that ship, who would wear mourning? Who would pay for my funeral and show their face in church to sing "Abide with Me"? Maggie? Probably. But the longer we spent apart, the less confident I felt in our twenty-year friendship.

And now the enigma of Jessie was making my skin itch. Who was she and where had she disappeared to? Alfie and Eliza had spent little more than a year together, but if Jessie had been in London, Eliza would have heard of her. I knew that Alfie hadn't been in London long when the pair of them met. So Jessie had stayed behind in New York. Was she still here? And if she was alive, then why had Alfie never spoken of her?

DREAM A LITTLE DREAM OF ME

Jessie

July 1908

"WELL, DON'T SAY I didn't warn you." Ida's arms were folded across her vast chest.

"I won't." Jessie looked down into her glass of lemonade, trickles of condensation running down the sides, the ice melted already in the summer heat.

She wondered why she'd thought it a good idea to journey back up to Harlem. It was as if she'd had a need to be scolded. Was that what she was missing now that Mama was dead? Someone to keep her on the good path, to remind her that she was supposed to be a good girl? Ida Barker had become that person. She'd come to Jessie's rescue when Jessie had first stumbled off the boat three months earlier. Thank goodness for Ida.

It hadn't taken Jessie more than two minutes after disembarking to realize she'd underestimated New York. She'd made the journey because what else did she have? No mother, no father. No brother if she stayed in Florida, but the hope of finding him if she took that chance. Ida had spotted her a mile off. *Gotta catch you young'uns soon as you arrive*, she'd said. *You're like baby turtles, hatching out. We leave you to your own devices and you might get swept up by a gull.*

The gulls were the men who hung around, waiting for fresh faces to offer opportunities to. Ida hadn't gone into specifics, but Jessie had worked out what she meant. Ida was a good woman, but she had very strict ideas on what young women were allowed to do. It was partly through Ida that Jessie had met her friend Mary Grace, but when Mary Grace had suggested that the pair of them move downtown, Ida had said that if Jessie moved to the Tenderloin with her new friend, she'd end up going the way of all bad girls. Still, what choice had Jessie had? She'd heard the music on the breeze, seen the young men who lived and worked down there, and known that finding Alfie meant taking that chance. And hadn't she been proved right?

"Alfie's doing well," she said, defending her brother. "He's got a well-paying job with a very good family. I'm going to work for them too. I start tomorrow."

"So well that you're still stuck in the Tenderloin? Jessie, you know I only want you to be safe. Safe from the likes of those people who would have you turn to sin. Mary Grace being just one example."

"Mary Grace isn't so bad."

She hoped that Ida didn't ask her what Mary Grace was doing for work. The Haymarket was the very symbol of everything that was wrong with the Tenderloin, as far as Ida was concerned—the home territory of the gulls. And Ida didn't even know the half of what actually went on there. Alcohol and dancing were the devil's instruments, in her opinion. It wasn't that Jessie disagreed, but in the short time she'd been in New York, she'd become accustomed to things being different than back home. Mary Grace might have a job that Jessie wouldn't take for love or money (not that she was much of a dancer anyway), but she was also fun to be around. She was kind and had taken Jessie under her wing in a way that Ida, with her constant scripture quoting and inflexible ideas on how to live, hadn't quite managed. Mary Grace had ambition. She wasn't content; she wanted more from life. The move to the Tenderloin had been based on necessity. Mary Grace planned to get out one day, but not to live like a nun in a tiny apartment in Harlem like Ida and Etta, her partner in her martyrdom. When Jessie had told her about the job offer from Tar, that she had reservations, Mary Grace had told her to stop being so dumb. To take the money, a vast improvement on what she'd been earning at the Gilsey House, and to use her new wages to buy herself some new clothes.

"Because I don't mean to be nasty, but you look like a poor Southern church mouse," Mary Grace had said, and Jessie had known she was right.

"Child, what do you want out of life?" Ida asked, and Jessie snapped her mind back into the present.

"I don't know," she said. "I guess I'm still figuring that out."

SHE DECLINED ANOTHER drink, suddenly tired of Ida's lecturing, and took the elevated train downtown, hopping off at Thirty-Fourth Street before realizing that she'd gone too far, that the new rooms Alfie had moved them to a few days before were back up eight blocks. Sighing, she set out to walk. It was just past midday and the city was sweltering, her dress sticking to her underarms, but it was nice to be outside. It was funny how quickly the smells and sounds of the city had become familiar. It was never quiet, even at night. The sidewalks were always thronged with people, and the streets full of traffic. Watching where you walked was vital, huge clods of horse shit everywhere, kicked up by the wheels of passing carriages and thrown about by unruly children. *What do you want out of life?* She honestly didn't know, but she had a feeling she might find it here, in New York.

She was turning the corner, barely a few yards from home, when she saw them. Brazen as anything. A woman, coming out of the door to the building. Alfie just a step behind. She turned and planted a kiss on his lips, and said something that Jessie couldn't hear, before skipping down to the sidewalk to her waiting carriage. Jessie could hardly believe her eyes. Her mouth open, she stared after the carriage as it set off, not taking her gaze away until it was out of sight. Alfie, by this time, had gone back inside.

Was he crazy? Jessie knew that what had happened back home had nothing to do with him. Just bad luck that his name had been plucked out of thin air by a desperate and unthinking girl who cared more about saving her own reputation than about the life of a poor Black man. Only now Alfie had lost his mind and decided that— what?—he might as well follow through on what he'd been accused of?

She marched up the steps, into the building, and up to the second floor, where the three of them shared two rooms. The bedroom was for Jessie and Mary Grace. Alfie slept on a makeshift cot in the other room, which did as their kitchen and living room as well. He was sitting at the table now, drinking a glass of milk and playing a game of solitaire.

"You're back early," he said, barely glancing up.

"Too early." Jessie stood, her palms resting on the table opposite her brother.

"Huh?" He looked puzzled. "Did something happen? Don't tell me that God-fearing old harridan upset you."

"Ida? No. No, I'm beginning to think that she's the only person in this city who isn't afraid to admit the truth. Well, her and Etta." Jessie couldn't see a pinch of remorse on his face. What had happened to Alfie?

"All right. Are you going to tell me what's wrong, then?"

"I saw you." She pulled up a chair and sat down, suddenly exhausted. "With that woman."

"Ah." And now he did have the decency to look a little ashamed. "Victoria."

"Who the hell is she? Are you crazy?"

He leaned back and stared up at the ceiling. "Maybe. I don't know. But if I am, so is she."

"Is that sort of thing . . . Is that even acceptable here?" Jessie shook her head. "I mean, in broad daylight for anyone to see. Has she no shame?"

"That's what I'm trying to figure out myself." He let a chuckle slip out and Jessie wanted to get up and slap him around the head. "Jessie, I know it's madness, but I figure that it's up to her. I never forced her to come here. She actually brought us a present. Well, really, it's for you."

He gestured behind him. That she hadn't noticed it she could put down only to her initial rage. There was barely room for the sewing machine. Almost new, from the looks of it. A Singer.

"I told her all about you. That you were a dressmaker and that you hoped to pick up business here once things got settled. I didn't ask her for nothing; she just brought it over. She was left it by an aunt who died, but Victoria's not a sewer."

No, Jessie couldn't imagine that woman sitting down behind that beautiful machine. Jessie could make good use of it, but she didn't want to be in debt to a woman who could ruin her brother's life. "It's too much. You'll have to send it back."

"Don't be dumb! It's yours. You can work at Tar's with me during the day and start up your dressmaking business in the evenings. Victoria said she'll pay you to make her a dress for when she goes to the races. She's got lots of important friends. If they like what you do, you'll be set. Forget Jacksonville; this is New York money. We'll be out of these rooms and into something better in no time."

"All you seem to care about these days is money. Spending all your time sucking up to rich people. What about what's really important?"

"Which is what exactly?" he shot back. "Do you want to live like this forever? Working your fingers to the bone just to keep a roof over your head? If that's what you really want, then go ahead. I won't stop you. You can keep going to see Ida and listen to her sermons and feel better about yourself even as your belly's rumbling 'cause you ain't got enough to eat. But did you ever think that if God works in mysterious ways, then he might just have sent these people to us? To help us. To help you start a new life as a dressmaker to rich New York women. To put me on the ladder to being a famous piano player."

She laughed then. "Famous? You play tunes for some sick old woman who just happens to have too much money. Victoria is just sucking up to you because she wants something. If she hasn't already had it."

As his face reddened she felt the swell of triumph, quickly washed away with guilt. She hadn't come to New York to fight with her brother. He'd changed over the months he'd been gone, but she could understand that. She felt different already herself. And he did make a good point. Jessie wouldn't be doing anything wrong by using the sewing machine. There was nothing wrong with taking a job in a wealthy family. She'd be a maid just like hundreds, thousands, of young Black girls in this city. "Alfie, you're a grown man now. You already ran from one lynch mob, so I guess you can do it again if it comes to it. Just promise me you won't ever bring her back here. I don't want any trouble in my own home."

"Agreed." He bit his lip. "But would you meet her? Not here, somewhere safe. I just think you'd like her."

"What do you see happening here, Alfie?" She sighed. He'd always had his head in the clouds and she'd always been the sensible one, holding on to his shoelaces so he didn't float up to the sun. "Where do you see yourself five years from now?"

He shrugged and smiled. "Damned if I know. But we're both young. We got plenty time to figure that out."

19

Wednesday, 16 September 1936

THE STAGE WAS huge, a gigantic floating platform that seemed to sway under my feet. It reminded me of being back at sea, my stomach bobbing with nausea. A spotlit microphone marked my place and my legs moved toward it, ignoring my brain's feeble pleas to run away and seek shelter. With the bright light in my eyes, I couldn't see my audience, could only hear them. The murmur that seemed to grow as I stood there, their impatience swelling like a thundercloud, ready to unleash a storm if I wasn't careful. I was vaguely aware of the house band behind me. Was Will there? My neck was stiff, fixed in place so that I couldn't turn to look. The music started, a tune I wasn't sure I recognized, although the lyrics suddenly swam into my mind. Gibberish that surely made no sense, and yet I knew that the words were the right ones.

Hearing my cue, I opened my mouth and . . . nothing. A croak. I tried again. No words came out, no soft melody, just a harsh, dry rasp, my lungs straining as I tried to force out the words. The music ground to a halt and the audience chatter grew angry. Tears flooded down my cheeks, blurring the lights into a kaleidoscope, and I tried to retreat but my feet were glued to the floor.

A hand was placed on my arm: "Honey, this isn't for you. Let me show you the door." Glo, with a red-painted smirk on her lips.

I wanted to shout, *No!* I wanted to slap that stupid grin off her stupid face. But I had no words. I focused everything I had on wrenching my arm from her grip, exploding free to find myself awake. Sitting up in bed. Daylight spilled through a crack in the curtains, and I felt my heart rate start to slow. I was safe.

I'd forgotten what it was to be nervous, to feel that bone-melting energy that could ebb and flow for hours until the danger had passed. I woke up early that morning with a sense of dark anticipation. That night heralded my return to a proper stage. In a theater where, from what I'd overheard, the locals could be brutal. I wondered if it was too late to back out.

Beside me Will slept on, like the proverbial baby, his face soft and peaceful. He had more to lose than I did, I knew that much. Claud had returned from work the night before with a list of all the people she'd told, all of whom seemed keen to come along and see Will. He'd smiled and thanked her, but I could see that he was just beginning to contemplate what this one performance could mean. If it all went well, then Will Goodman had returned. With word of mouth, he'd be able to get work locally without having to go back on the *Queen Mary*, though he'd assured me that, no matter what, he'd be taking that next crossing with me. If, however, the crowd didn't fall in love with him, if he held his own but didn't stand out, it would be business as usual. Out of sight was out of mind, and Will had been gone for the best part of a decade.

Even Claud wasn't up yet, so I took it upon myself to brew the coffee on the stove. An olive branch to make peace once she realized that Will hadn't actually left the apartment the night before. He'd convinced me that it would be all right. I'd been glad of the companionship more than anything else. I was trying not to think about the fact that I had only one more week before I left to go back to England. Unless I didn't go . . .

The visit to Eliza had unlocked the door to possibility. Money. When she'd first broached the subject, halfway across the Atlantic in the no-man's-land of an ocean liner, where nothing had seemed quite real, I hadn't believed in it. Eliza had been in a tricky position, discovering her bastard daughter, being trapped at sea not only with her oblivious legitimate family but with a murderer as well. In her position, who wouldn't say whatever they needed to in order to keep the peace? But now that I was safe on terra firma, the offer was still there. With a monthly stipend, I could make plans for the future. I could think about a home for me and Will. Would Will want that? Did I want that? And it was no good if Will was going back to work on the *Queen Mary*.

"Morning." Claud appeared in the doorway, her hair set in rollers. "What are you doing up so early?"

"I don't know," I said. "I didn't sleep well. Coffee?" I poured her a cup.

"Makes a nice change for someone else to make it for me." She retreated to the living room, and I followed her out, each of us curling up on one end of the sofa. "How you feeling?"

"Me?" Were my nerves that obvious? "I'm terrified about tonight."

She chuckled. "Lena, you'll be fine. If Will thinks you're good enough to be on that stage with him, then you are. I don't doubt it for a second."

"Logically, I know you're right," I said. "But what if something goes wrong? What if my voice cracks? Or the audience don't take to me. It happens, you know. Sometimes there just isn't that connection. This could be Will's only chance."

"And you don't want to muck it up," she said, finishing my thought. "Lena, only Will can ruin his own chances. He's been signed up to that damned Amateur Night more times than you could count on the fingers of both hands. He's always backed out. If you can get him to that theater this morning, he'll be a step closer to that stage than he's ever been."

I hadn't known that about him. That he'd walked away from opportunity so many times. Something else we had in common. "I'm not responsible for getting him there; it's all him."

"Well . . ." Claud smiled secretively. "He really likes you—you know that?"

My cheeks grew warm. "I really like him too."

"Sure, but I mean, I've not seen him like this for years. Trust me." Her eyes searched my face for signs of a response. "What are you thinking?"

I answered honestly. "I don't know. This is all . . . It's unexpected. I didn't come to New York looking for love. I came for work. I came because a man made me a promise that turned out to be a lie. And I like Will. But we both have pasts." An understatement if ever there was one. "There's a lot going on there."

"He served his time." Claud's forehead wrinkled; I'd disappointed her.

"I know. That's not what I'm bothered about." And yet there was something niggling me.

"And that stuff about him and Bel was just a lot of nonsense," Claud went on, her sales pitch regaining its footing. "A malicious bit of gossip spread about by Henry Bennett, long may he rest." She didn't wish him peace, I noticed.

"And Glo?" I said it quickly, getting the three letters off my chest.

"Glo?" Claud started to laugh. "Seriously? You got nothin' to worry about from that woman. Believe me. She ditched Will like a hot potato when all that trouble went down. He wouldn't take her back, and besides, she's been shacked up with Percy Wallace for years, on and off. Prob'ly off right now, which is why she had to throw that rent party the other night. Wally works the railroad, you see. Travels up and down the country, which leaves Glo enough time to get bored."

Glo's boredom was what worried me. "You can't forgive a betrayal like that," I said, trying to convince myself.

"Exactly!" Claud was triumphant. "So stop fretting." She drained her cup and went to stand. "You want some oatmeal?"

I didn't, but I knew she'd suggest making me something more elaborate if I turned it down. She'd just pottered back into the kitchen when Will appeared. He must have sneaked into the bathroom while Claud and I were talking, as he was fully dressed and shaved.

"Claud's making breakfast," I murmured, pointing toward the kitchen. After our conversation, I wasn't sure if Will and I were supposed to be sneaking around still or if it was accepted that he'd be staying with me from now on.

He kissed me as he sat down, his fresh-toothpaste mouth contrasting with the sour taste of coffee on my tongue. "You want to come with me to the Apollo? Head down about midday?"

"Yes, please." It sounded like a good idea. At least I could strip the fear of the unknown away from my threatening stage fright. A distraction was just the ticket.

THE WEATHER WAS mild, but the sky clouded over with the promise of rain. Will took my hand and we strolled south down Seventh Avenue. Late summer was perfect for city living. The temperatures were just right for walking, no jacket necessary. Again, it felt miraculous that nobody stared as we went. We were normal, the pair of us, just like anyone else in Harlem. In London, we'd have attracted attention. Those with manners would look away as soon as I caught them staring; those who didn't would gawp, openmouthed if they'd never seen a man with skin as dark as Will's before. I remembered it well from when Alfie was alive.

Where I'd grown up things were different. People had had time to decide if they liked us or not. Those who didn't would sniff as I walked by, or would spit on the ground if they wanted to make sure I knew what they thought of me. They were in the minority, but I still remembered their names: Doris Forster, Mr. Jenkins, the Wilkinsons who ran the fish-and-chip shop on the corner of our street. Alfie refused to eat anything from them, would walk two streets over to a chap who was a lot friendlier. His fish was fresher as well; at least it tasted that way to me. Maggie's mother upheld our boycott of Wilkinson's, but the boyfriend of one of Maggie's sisters had brought us a supper from there one evening, unaware of the standoff. Greasy, we decided. And the chips were hard in the middle, not properly cooked.

"You're awful quiet this morning." Will squeezed my hand. "You're not nervous, are you?"

"A little bit," I admitted. "Just stage fright, though. I'll be right as rain soon enough." I hoped.

We entered the theater through a back entrance, the door propped open with a wooden chair. I could hear music and the rhythmic tap of dance shoes against the rehearsal room floor. Heading down a set of steps, I took a deep breath: sweat, women's perfume, that particular odor that clung to stage costumes no matter how often they were laundered. It smelled like coming home.

Will pushed open a door and we were in a vast practice room, a few nervous people hovering close to a rectangular table, Teddy set up behind it with a very officious-looking list, a pair of spectacles giving him a more serious look than I'd seen from him on Saturday night.

"Are these others here for the same thing?" I asked Will quietly.

"Yep." He sounded as though he'd caught my nerves. "Guess we'd better go and show him that we're here."

We moved closer to Teddy, who was making a point of studying the piece of paper in front of him, ignoring those of us who were waiting. It was an act, to make sure that we were serious. I was giving him the benefit of the doubt. If I hadn't met him already and known he was a decent chap, I'd have said he was showing off his position of power.

He looked up finally, removing the glasses. "Well, now. Ev'rybody here to try and get a spot tonight, huh?" He got to his feet, slow and smooth, list in hand. "I assume your name's down here on my piece of paper already, else I'm afraid you've had a wasted trip. I got almost a full bill already—this here is the reserve list."

Will nudged me as Teddy began to read off names, people calling out "here" like we were back in primary school. A few names passed by without comment, Teddy crossing them off with a firm stroke, each one a missed opportunity. Had Will's name been crossed off that list before? How many lines would he have through his name if they were all added up?

"Will Goodman with Lena Aldridge?"

"Here!" Will answered for both of us, squeezing my hand.

"All right, now, I'm sorry—there ain't any more room. Alma May? Hattie Smith?" Two young girls put up their hands. "Come back Monday if you want to try again."

I felt sorry for them as they slunk past us. Surely if anyone was at the bottom of the list, it should have been me. "Does that happen often?" I asked Will.

"Every week," he confirmed. "We're lucky that Teddy got us on. This is a tough gig. Everyone wants to be onstage at the Apollo. Amateur Night can make or break a person at the start of their career. How d'you think Ella Fitzgerald got started?"

I remembered that effortless voice from Saturday night, hitting every note, every rhythm. I could still hear "I'll Chase the Blues Away," the sound of her preserved in my memory. "Big shoes to fill."

"Sure. But you're up to it. *We're* up to it." He was trying to convince himself as well as me. "Come on, let's go grab something to eat. We need to make a decision on what we're performing."

Some of the other contestants were talking to a fella at the piano, but I supposed that Will was my pianist. Just the two of us, onstage. The last time we'd performed together onstage—the *only* time we'd performed together onstage—I'd fallen back in love with singing. Not just as an everyday job but something more. Now that I'd seen who we were up against, seen their nerves and knew how they were feeling, my own premature stage fright eased a little. This wasn't my first theater, my first time on a stage. It had just been a while.

We stopped in at a basement restaurant halfway up on Seventh, Will proclaiming that they did the best club sandwich within five blocks. A sandwich seemed manageable, and maybe some French fries. My mouth started to water. Maybe I was hungry, after all.

At least I was until I saw them together, thick as thieves. At a table against the far wall as we arrived at the foot of the stairs leading into the restaurant. Bel and Glo. Laughing over plates of chow mein and glasses of cheap beer. Will saw them a split second after I did; I felt his grip tighten around my hand.

"Guess it's a free country," he murmured, and led me to a table as far from them as possible.

I tried not to look, but it was impossible. As hard as I tried not to, my eyes were pulled to Bel like a magnet to steel. She caught my eye and looked away. It was like that, then. No chance of us talking about what had happened the other night like civil adults. She had gone straight to the other side. Glo turned to look and smirked in my direction. I smiled sweetly, my eyes narrowed. I might be new to Harlem, but this was an old game. Whether it was Will's hand in mine, or a wad of ready money, I had something they wanted, and they were putting their heads together to work something out. They had another think coming if they thought I didn't have a few tricks up my own sleeve. I sat down feeling confident, not knowing that we were all just a few hours away from finding out just how deadly a game we were playing.

20

Wednesday, 16 September 1936

WHAT THE HELL was I going to wear? Claud and I decamped to my bedroom to go through my limited options. I tried on a red dress only to discover that there was a gravy stain right above the bosom. I wanted people to be captivated by my voice, not be staring at my breasts and wondering what it was that I'd spilled. I threw it off in a huff and stood in my slip, hands on hips as I considered my choices.

I'd left a trio of beautiful designer dresses in my trunk at the Sherry-Netherland, but I dismissed the idea of retrieving them. They had helped me to fit in on the ship, but no one would be turning up at the Apollo in a Schiaparelli evening gown. I didn't want people to start asking questions and I didn't want to attract Bel's attention again, not after she'd found my stash of money. God only knew what she was thinking. And now she was sharing her wild theories with Glo.

"Why not this?" Claud picked up the new ultramarine silk frock that I'd bought for the party.

"Everyone saw it on Saturday," I reminded her.

"Hmm." She looked from me to the dress and back again. "But do you think anyone remembers? And there'll be a hell of a lot of people there tonight who weren't at the party."

A hell of a lot of people. My stomach somersaulted, and I shook out my arms, trying to throw off the nerves physically. "Don't bloody remind me!"

"Although, actually," she said, thinking out loud, "they don't like a show-off on Amateur Night. You need to look like someone at the bottom, trying to get a foot on the ladder. Something plain, something humble. That's what goes down well."

She disappeared from the room, and I picked up one of the plain skirts I'd bought for everyday wear. I had a nice blouse to go with it, but it was clearly a daytime look. I'd never have worn it onstage in London. Not a chance.

"Here." Claud hurried back in holding a dress. "Louis talked me into buying this for a gala at the hospital, but I've never had another chance to wear it."

The dress was perfect. Plain black cotton but tailored with a cinched waistband in silk. The neckline was brave without being scandalous and, when I held it against me, the hem hit just below my knees. The ideal frock for a woman who wanted to look like she'd made an effort without being too flashy.

"Are you sure?" I asked, already half into the dress.

"Of course," she assured me, helping me with the zipper. It was a perfect fit. "Lena, I'd rather someone got some wear out of the dress. I'm not sure it even fits me anymore. And even if it did, it wouldn't for much longer." She paused, pressing her lips together before deciding to confide in me. "I've only told Louis so far, but . . ."

"You're pregnant?" I grinned at her in the mirror. "Congratulations!"

She blushed. "It's early days, but my obstetrician is very positive.

We've been trying for a while, you see. Things haven't worked out so far, but I feel like this one might just stick around."

I did hope so. I'd seen how Maggie had suffered, losing one baby after another before giving up. Claud and Louis deserved happiness. "Will doesn't know?"

She shook her head. "We thought that it was safer to wait before telling anyone. Our parents don't even know! And once we start telling one person, it gets impossible to stop the news from spreading."

I could well imagine. "My lips are sealed," I promised.

"I hate asking you to keep a secret from Will, but I am planning to tell him soon."

I just smiled. She had no idea how many secrets I was keeping from Will. My mother, the truth about who had actually been behind the murders at sea, the real source of the money in my carpetbag. Adding Claud's secret to those was nothing. Telling him everything wouldn't change what had already happened. And it wouldn't have stopped what was going to happen later that night.

MY EVENING MEAL consisted of cigarettes and a small brandy to settle my stomach, my skin buzzing with nerves, palms sweaty as I tried to get ready. My face was shiny, so I pressed too much powder on, my skin masklike until I washed it all off and began again. I checked the time: eight o'clock. Plenty of time. The show didn't begin until eleven, ready to be broadcast countrywide. An entire nation. So many strangers, listening to me, judging me. They wouldn't even see my sweating forehead or admire my borrowed dress. We'd played through the song a few times, and Louis and Claud had applauded enthusiastically, but I felt under-rehearsed. Claud claimed that was perfect, that those who'd practiced themselves to death lost the soul from their voice; I wasn't so sure that was the case.

"One song," Will reminded me, looking casual as he lounged on the bed, dressed in his suit with just his shoes to go on when it was time to leave. "Three minutes or so. That's all."

True enough, and yet it didn't make me feel any better. What if they hated us? What if they hated *me*? An outsider. It was all I could think about as we walked along to the Apollo, Claud and Louis having already left to grab seats; we'd not see them again until after the show, but they'd been dressed to the nines, Louis with his fancy brass-buttoned jacket and Claud in a dress that rivaled the one she'd lent me. Their excitement was both lovely to see and unhelpful in that it reminded me what was at stake.

To "die" onstage was not unheard-of. It had never happened to me, but everyone in the game had heard of it happening to someone else. So often I'd competed against other singers, other actresses, in auditions, but I'd never been in an actual competition before, with a prize. With an audience who knew that their reaction could make or break a performer.

Backstage was quiet mayhem. I wasn't the only one in the grip of stage fright. A young girl pressed her back hard into the brick wall of the corridor as we waited, as if she wanted to disappear. Will chatted away with some fellas he knew, sharing cigarettes and making jokes. I ran through my warm-up and checked the list. We were up second to last in the running order, which meant almost an hour to wait, listening to everyone else. It could be a good position if we stood out from the crowd, or bad if the audience got bored before we took to the stage. I had to trust that Teddy, who'd done well for us so far, had placed us there for a reason.

"You guys are together? You and the tall guy?" A woman a little younger than me came and joined me. She looked relaxed, but I had heard her warming up. "Rosa." I introduced myself and we shook hands. "I'm on fourth."

I looked at the clock. Ten to eleven. We could hear the cheers of the audience as the featured band finished another big number. They were getting ready to wrap up. "Good luck," I said. "Have you been on before?"

"It's my third time," she confessed. "First time, I was so nervous, I forgot my lyrics halfway through and had to scat the whole last verse. Not my finest moment—the crowd didn't exactly punish me, but they knew I messed up." Good to know. The golden rule: Just keep going. "Second time, I placed third."

"Blimey," I said, "well, you must be good."

"I sing all right," she said, modest despite the pride in her eyes. "I take it you're not from round here. *Blimey.*" She tried to imitate me, giggling but not in a mean way.

"I'm from London. It's my first time here," I confessed. "In New York and here at the Apollo."

"Welcome." She grinned and offered me a Lucky Strike. "I recognize your man, though."

"Will? He's from here, from Harlem," I confirmed, taking the cigarette.

She clicked her fingers together. "Will Goodman! He was in my class at school. I knew I knew him from somewhere. Been a while since I set eyes on that man. Well, a few of us Harlem old-timers are heading out after the show, if you want to come along. I'm sure Will'll want to catch up."

"I'm sure he will." Was there anyone in Harlem who didn't know Will?

The MC took to the stage, about to announce the start of Amateur Night.

"Damn! Never gets any easier."

Rosa sighed the words as she disappeared in the direction of the restroom, and I knew what she meant. My heart began to speed up and I put a hand against the wall to steady myself. The young lad who was on first looked as though he was about to be sick, and it was Will who steadied him, pointing him toward a strange-looking object, what looked like a tree stump. The boy put his hand to its polished surface and almost forgot to take his banjo as he ran onstage.

Will came to join me. "Here we go. Not long to wait."

"What is that?" I pointed to the tree stump.

"Tree of Hope," he told me. "It's for luck. You gotta rub it before you go onstage."

Superstition. I was used to that in theaters. It was something I had missed about working at the Canary so long. Every night there was much like the one before. There were no nerves or excitement, no rituals to create good or bad luck; if you were at the Canary, then it was taken as given that you were on your downers. I should be grateful for this opportunity. And if it went badly, then so what? No one knew me here, and in a week's time I'd be on a ship heading for Europe. I had nothing to lose. *Nothing to lose. Nothing to lose. Nothing to lose.* Repeating it to myself, I felt my heart rate slow, my breathing return to normal. That scared young lad was doing well with a jaunty rendition of "I Got Plenty o' Nuttin'," his voice deeper and carrying far more gravitas than I'd have given him credit for. He'd make an excellent Porgy once he learned how to grow hair on his chin.

"He's good." Will looked relaxed but it was an act. I could see the way he was looking around at our competition. Weighing them up. I might have nothing to lose, but for Will it was a different matter.

The acts ticked by like seconds on a clock face, each song seeming to last mere moments before the next singer was pushed on. Rosa did a serviceable rendition of "Body and Soul," though I thought it lacked expression. The audience reaction was decent but not as enthusiastic as it had been for the young Porgy.

"Do you know her?" I asked Will. "She knew your name."

"Rosa?" He frowned. "Sure. Haven't spoken to her for a long while, though."

She was beaming when she clattered her way back offstage. "You were amazing," I told her.

"You really think? The audience seemed to like it, anyway. That's the main thing." Her attempt at bashfulness wasn't quite coming off.

"You're a shit liar," Will whispered.

"Just being nice, that's all," I hissed back, glad that at least Rosa didn't seem to have noticed. God knew I should start making some friends to make up for the enemies I seemed to be collecting. Between Bel's defection and Glo's blatant designs on Will, I couldn't rely just on Claud and Louis to be on my side.

Before I knew it, we were up. I put my hand to the stump, hoping to draw strength from the sturdy elm wood. As I stood on the edge of the stage, my heart felt like a rock rising to block my gullet. My underarms itched with cold sweat, and I felt the same moisture break out on my top lip. Why was I doing this to myself, this strange torture?

"Take a deep breath and walk." Will gave me the instructions I needed, my legs and lungs obeying.

I knew enough not to look out into the abyss until I was safe behind the microphone. I knew that if I needed it, the solidity of the piano to my right would prop me up. Even so, I kept my eyes fixed to the floor, hoping that the audience would think me caught up in the moment and not sense my absolute terror. There came the scrape of the piano stool as Will took his seat, the piano standing between us. It was then that I took another deep breath and looked up.

They were almost on top of me, the people in this packed house. The closest boxes hung almost over the stage, their occupants watching me, their faces full of curiosity. They would have been able to hear the pounding in my chest, I was sure. Where were Claud and Louis? Up in the balcony, Will had said; that was their usual spot. Too far back, seated in darkness. I found the outline of a woman in the front row above my head and made her Claud. I heard murmuring and foot shuffling, and then Will began to play the opening bars. "Dream a Little Dream of Me."

We'd chosen the song after hours of hair pulling, Will determined to find the perfect song for a duet. Easy enough to play that he wouldn't need to think too much about what his hands were doing on the keyboard. A song that lent itself to harmonies that suited both of us. A song we'd both sung a thousand times before. This time it felt different. I sang the first line, and I felt the supportive silence of the audience, as compelling as gravity, pulling the lyrics out of me. They wanted to hear the song, and I wanted to show them that I could do it justice. After the first verse I dared to glance at Will, our eyes meeting as we both smiled. We knew we'd done ourselves proud. Our voices glided over each other effortlessly, just how we'd practiced, only this time there was something else. I'm not a regular churchgoer by any means, but I knew what it was to feel moved, to feel a higher power that couldn't be explained.

And then, just like that, it was over. The MC shooed us offstage with the audience cheers echoing in our ears. I was as giddy as a child who's eaten a whole bag of penny sweets. I didn't even hear the last act, barely able to contain my excitement.

"You done good." Rosa didn't look as friendly as she had before. "Audiences do like a good romance. I always say that the winners have as good a story as a voice. Sometimes better."

Was that a dig? If so, I was too overcome to fall into the trap. It wasn't as though Rosa's opinion counted for anything in the contest.

"Everyone onstage!" The command went up and we dutifully filed on in the order we'd performed, Will taking my hand. I made sure that we stood close together, adding fuel to our story—if Rosa was going to be a cow about us doing well, then I might as well prove her right.

The process of choosing a winner was quite democratic, though terrifying for those of us in line. The MC went along the row, holding his hand above each contestant's head. In turn, the audience would let their appreciation be known. Little Porgy got a roar that shocked me, the stage vibrating with the tremors from the stamping feet. The next act got a far more lukewarm response, and I saw a tear slip down the cheek of a young light-skinned woman whose nerves had forced her voice to wobble off-key through the first few lines of "What'll I Do."

Rosa did all right, but it wasn't going to be third time lucky for her. Will squeezed my hand as the MC drew closer, the audience brutal in their judgment. "Maybe Rosa was right," I said, looking up to him as our turn came, and he took the hint, bending to kiss me lightly on the lips, nothing too salacious but enough to tell the audience that our tale was a true one. Whether it made a difference or not, they were generous in their applause and their cheers.

"In third place, for the second time in a row . . ." The MC brought forward Rosa, whose grin looked fake.

I was sure we'd done better than Rosa. We had to have placed, but could we have actually won? I held my breath and waited.

Jessie

September 1908

THE JOB ITSELF was easy. She had only one spoiled brat of a girl to look after, and she was out of the house a lot of the time. The money was good. Very good. The housekeeper, Mrs. Callaghan, was a firm but fair Irishwoman who would send Jessie to the mirror if she had a hair out of place but would also make sure that Jessie's dinner was kept warm if Miss Elizabeth kept her late sewing the hems of one of her fancy party dresses, only to change her mind and demand that a different gown be pressed.

Alfie was round every week to play his concerts for an audience of one, and although Jessie rarely caught more than a glimpse of her brother—they rarely crossed paths at home, she out all day, he out all night—she could hear his music wherever she was in the house. She didn't see much more of the lady of the house. She was ill; Jessie knew that much. The poor woman never left the house and left her rooms only when Alfie was present. It was quite an undertaking, moving her downstairs when he arrived to give his concert. Tar would carry her down the stairs as easily as if she weighed less than a bag of sugar. Jessie was usually roped in to help Mrs. Callaghan carry the far heavier wheelchair down so that their mistress might be mobile if she needed to be. Alfie said that sometimes she liked to sit by the window in that great chair, watching the people on the street. Jessie understood that. It must be awful to feel closed off from life. To be trapped indoors permanently, for Mrs. Callaghan only shook her head and made the sign of the cross when Jessie asked if there was any chance of recovery.

All in all, there was only one problem, and that was Tar himself. Jessie couldn't put her finger on it, but he just always seemed to be present, turning up when she least expected it. For a busy man (according to Mrs. Callaghan, who thought that the sun shone from his backside), he was at home an awful lot. Gentlemen in expensive suits would arrive at the house most weekdays and be shown into Tar's study. Hours would go by, food and drink served to them as they discussed business, and even Miss Elizabeth wouldn't cause a ruckus when her father's men were in the house. So yes, he was busy. And yet he would appear out of nowhere. In the laundry room as Jessie starched her mistress's shirtwaists, in his daughter's bedroom moments after Miss Elizabeth had slammed the front door shut as she headed out with friends. Alfie didn't have a bad word to say about him, and he'd not stood closer than three feet from Jessie, and yet the hairs on the back of her arms stood up when it was just the two of them in a room together.

"I'm in your way," he said one Saturday afternoon as she was taking a scrubbing brush to the hearth in her mistress's bedroom. He didn't leave, though.

"No, sir," she said. Against her better judgment, she rocked back on her heels. She tried to keep their exchanges down to as few words as possible, the bare minimum required not to cause offense. Alfie would kill her if she lost this job or made trouble for him with Tar. "Can I help you with something?"

"No." He turned as if to leave. "Yes. Actually . . . I remembered that you used to be a seamstress. I have that correct?"

"I used to do piecework back home," Jessie confirmed. "And I used to make dresses. I fix up all Miss Elizabeth's clothes for her."

Tar grimaced. "That girl will be the death of me, I swear. If it weren't for her mother, I'd . . . well, anyway. I wondered if you'd ever hemmed a pair of men's trousers."

"Of course." She breathed a sigh of relief. Just work. Work that she was used to. She had Ida's voice in the back of her head the whole time, reminding her that men were after only one thing. But Tar didn't seem like that. And Alfie wouldn't bring his sister into the home of a man he didn't trust.

"Let me show you my problem." Tar walked out of the bedroom and Jessie scrambled to her feet, hurrying after him.

To her great relief he led her downstairs toward his study. She'd never set foot in the room before, but the general maid, Annie, and of course Mrs. Callaghan were in and out all day. It was a very "gentlemanly" room, she thought. The downstairs of the house smelled mostly of furniture polish and whichever flowers Mrs. Callaghan had placed in a giant bouquet on the hallway table, ready to greet visitors. Tar's room held the aroma of tobacco smoke from expensive cigars and a deep, savory cologne that Jessie had smelled whenever he'd passed her by in the hallway. Leather from the bound books that lined the bookshelves behind Tar's great mahogany desk. The room was dark; even with the drapes pulled back, their heavy navy blue velvet keeping out prying eyes, for the study faced onto the street.

Tar went behind his desk and pulled out a drawer. "I have some pins here. My tailor often comes to the house, but he's taken the day off to go to Coney Island with his family and I need these trousers ready for tomorrow."

Labor Day, Jessie realized vaguely. He handed her the pins and walked past her, closing the study door before going to stand in front of the window.

"Is there enough light here for you?" He was a silhouette, the light surrounding his torso, his face obscured so that she couldn't see his expression. "There's a lamp on the desk, if you need it."

"No, sir." She gathered herself together. Hadn't she pinned men's pants before? Not just Alfie's, but her father's a long while back, and Pastor Isaiah's. "If you just move here." She gestured toward the spot she meant, but he didn't move until she dared to move close, shepherding him without touching him. She knelt before him and examined the trouser legs, treating them as if they were being worn by a statue and not this imposing flesh-and-blood man whose eyes she felt burning into the top of her head.

"Are you liking it here?" he asked her as she placed the first pin, tackling his right leg first. "I love my daughter very much, but she can pose quite the challenge."

"We get along," Jessie said. And she didn't mind Miss Elizabeth that much. Her temper was mercurial, but Jessie could see it was for the attention and not because she was a cruel mistress. The three of them—Tar, his wife, and his daughter—rarely spent time with one another. Mrs. Callaghan had taken her to one side in Jessie's first few days and explained that Miss Elizabeth was suffering. Already grieving for her mother before she'd taken her final breaths.

Jessie paused when she felt the hand rest on the top of her head.

"Do you ever get lonely?"

"Sir?" Jessie tilted her head slowly, not daring to cast his hand away but desperate to get it off her. "I don't know what you mean. The house is full of people. I'm hardly ever alone for more than a few minutes."

He didn't speak, but he did move his hand, and so she hurried on with her pinning, torn between needing to do a good job and wanting to be off her knees as soon as possible. She moved on to the left leg.

"I can't remember a time when I wasn't lonely. It doesn't matter how many people there are in this house; it's not the same as it used to be." When Jessie dared to glance up, Tar was staring down at her. "Before my wife got ill, this was a happy household. My daughter did as she was told. Was happy to. It was my wife, Eleanor, who sat at the piano every day, not your brother. Talented though he is, it's not the same." He chuckled. "He's *too* good. Eleanor always played with a heavy hand. Made mistakes. Young Alfie plays like a professional."

"He does get paid for it," Jessie said, the words slipping out before she could stop them. "Doesn't that make him a professional?"

"I suppose it does." Tar smiled. "You really are a breath of fresh air, Jessie. That's what I was trying to say in my clumsy way. I'm glad you're here. This is a more pleasant house to live in because of you."

"Glad to be of service, sir." Jessie lurched to her feet, the last pin placed. "I have to go. Miss Elizabeth wanted me to pick up some books for her, for her studies, and I must go now, before they close. I can sew these pants when I get back, if that's all right with you."

"Her studies, huh?" Tar shook his head. "A waste of her time, but these are the things I do to keep a civil daughter. Well, I'll leave these in my dressing room. You can collect them from there and have them back to me by tomorrow." He turned toward the window, Jessie dismissed.

IT HADN'T BEEN much, that hand resting on her head, but it was the first contact. Jessie had survived that, and so next time, when he took her by the wrist, she didn't flinch. When he asked if she could measure him for a waistcoat, offered her a month's wages to stitch it together from the glorious piece of silk that he had already purchased, she said yes without a second thought. And if he accidentally brushed her breast as he lowered his arms, well, that was just an accident. She didn't think he'd even noticed.

Alfie came the next week and told her excitedly about the new opportunities that were suddenly coming his way. Friends of Tar's who had heard of his skill and were keen to have their very own pet Negro to play tunes for them. *It's just something we have to put up with,* he said. *But if the benefits outweigh the costs, what harm is it?*

He made a strong point, Jessie thought. So when Tar asked her to read to him one evening, she agreed readily. She wasn't a strong reader, but she knew how. Tar didn't mind that she spoke slowly, resting the book against the solid wood of the desk and moving her finger beneath each word so that she wouldn't lose her place. He brought them both cocoa and slugged brandy into both cups. She didn't complain, just took tiny sips and was careful not to finish it too quickly in case he suggested having another. It was innocent enough, though. Only an hour, a dollar bill in her hand for staying after her duties were done. Easy work.

It became a ritual. Through the end of summer, leaving September behind for the cool fall days of October. Jessie tucked away the dollars in an old purse that fit into a tear in her mattress. She didn't even tell Mary Grace about the extra money. When the purse's bulge got too great, she would swap out the single notes for the crisp five-dollar notes that she was handed every Friday in her wage packet. Money for a rainy day. This luck couldn't last.

In late October, Jessie got caught in a hailstorm on the way back from fetching a pair of shoes from Lord and Taylor for Miss Elizabeth. Her mistress never gave her any money for the journey—it was only a twenty-minute walk under regular circumstances—so Jessie was soaked by the time she returned. Her sneezes alerted the master of the house, who called her down. It wasn't their usual rendezvous time. Barely an hour before dinner, after all, and she longed to go home and get changed out of her wet clothes, but she could hardly say no.

Tar lit the fire in his study, and instead of sitting at his desk, he moved the armchair before the hearth. "Come. Sit down and get warm," he ordered. "Coffee?" The pot was already sitting on his desk, so Jessie didn't see the harm in saying yes.

She knew they weren't friends. A girl like her, a man like him, they could never be equals. And he was married. A lot older than she was, old enough to be her father, for she was the same age as his own daughter. But they had spent so much time together by then that she had simply forgotten to be afraid. She took the cup and tasted the burn of the brandy beneath the cream and sugar, but she was so cold that she loved the warmth of it. The fire was burning her face but slowing her shivers.

"Wait there," Tar said, and she did because she didn't want to move from that glorious heat. He came back with a robe of dark red silk embroidered richly with thick black thread. Jessie was so caught up in its luxury that she didn't realize at first that it was meant for her. "Come on, then," he chivvied. "I can promise you, girl, you've nothing I haven't seen before."

She knew it was true. Alfie had told her already that a lot of the white men who went to the black and tans went there to ogle colored women. Mary Grace had cackled and said that wasn't the half of it and made Jessie glad that neither of them knew about her odd arrangement with Tar. Tar's wife, ill as she was, could not have been performing her wifely duties.

The old version of Jessie would have made her excuses and left. But this new Jessie had grown to like her master. Through their innocent nightly ritual, he had never been less than a gentleman. He'd never suggested that there was anything more to their arrangement, so when he helped her to undress, she let him, her wet maid's uniform falling in a heap on the floor. Her chemise had stuck to her skin and she turned her back to him as she pulled it over her head. When she felt his lips brush the nape of her neck, she jolted away, but when his hands steadied her, weighing down her shoulders, she didn't pull free. Was there any harm in making each other feel less lonely? He slipped the robe around her shoulders and helped her to tie it at the waist. And then he left her alone, and she was surprised to feel disappointed. Just like all those other evenings, they sat and talked before that roaring fire as they sipped lukewarm coffee laced with brandy. Tar listened to what she had to say, and when she shifted in her seat, the silk of her robe caressed her skin, and, for a time, Jessie felt like more than a shy little girl from the South.

21

Thursday, 17 September 1936

"CONGRATULATIONS!" CLAUD HUGGED me tightly before doing the same to Will. "Second place! My goodness, I'm so proud."

We'd lost out to Little Porgy, but I couldn't begrudge him his success. The poor lad had just arrived in New York from somewhere in Kentucky and needed the twenty-five dollars far more than I did. From the queue of people waiting to congratulate Will as we stood outside the front of the theater, I thought he'd won the prize he needed anyway.

"Everyone's heading over to our place to celebrate," Louis told us. "Bel couldn't get the night off, but she said she'll come by soon as she can."

Maybe it was because of the glow of goodwill following our success, but I supposed I should take the chance to speak to Bel when I could. Leaving words unspoken was never a good idea. I'd found that out the hard way before. So, she'd been nosy. She'd gone through my belongings. But could I really blame her? I was a stranger, after all, a stranger who had moved in with two of her closest friends and was sharing a bed with her brother. Wouldn't I have done the same?

"You gonna talk to her?" Will asked as we started to walk. Either he was a mind reader or he knew me so well already that it scared me a little. Our time was running out.

"I think I should," I replied. "I overreacted. What she did wasn't so bad."

"Nothing she ever does is *so* bad," he said. "Her biggest talent is making poor decisions."

I smothered a smile, not wanting to encourage him. Bel and I had gotten along before the snooping incident. We could get along again. At least that was my intention before we arrived back at the Linfields'.

"So, Lena," Claud said as we headed up to the apartment, "what are you thinking now?"

"Thinking?" I knew what she meant, but I wasn't sure how to explain my feelings even to myself.

"Girl, you just placed second! At the Apollo! If those fools hadn't fallen for that kid's cute face, you'd have won. Lord knows you got a better voice than him."

"Oh, I don't know about that." Little Porgy had been good. Really good. I'd probably have been rooting for him if I'd been in the audience and not onstage. "Anyway, the poor boy has no money. Imagine being all alone in the big city with hardly a dime to your name."

It was a lame excuse. Being out there on that stage had felt incredible. Like I should have been doing it my whole life. It had made me realize that I really had let my life slide into a routine of mediocrity, avoiding the challenge of auditions and applying for jobs in fancier clubs and hotels. I'd told myself that I was doing it for Alfie. Doctors weren't free and neither was the sanatorium where he spent his last days. A good daughter would take the regular work and the guaranteed wages. At first that had been true, but I knew that Alfie would have told me off later. If he'd been watching over me these past nine months, he'd have been disappointed. But not tonight. Tonight, he would have been proud. I just didn't know how to explain any of that to Claud.

There was booze left over from the rent party, and a whole group of musicians arrived from the Apollo with more. I was enjoying being the center of attention, alongside Will, when Bel arrived. But she wasn't alone. She came with her posse: Glo, the last woman I wanted to see, and my new friend Rosa, who smirked as she caught me staring. I saw Glo's lips moving, though I couldn't hear what she said, and both Bel and Rosa laughed. Had Rosa known who I was all along? Bel didn't say a word to us but led her troops straight toward the kitchen, probably to get drinks, although I didn't put it past her to be doing a little plotting on the side.

"Here comes trouble." Louis sighed.

Claud's eyes narrowed. "What the hell is wrong with her?"

I knew why I didn't like Glo, but it seemed as though Claud disliked her even more than I. "What's going on?"

"I'll explain later," Claud whispered as Bel came toward us. "Why, hello there! Nice company you're keeping."

Bel stood defiant before us, one hand on her hip. "Who, Glo? She's been a real pal to me, you know. I don't know why you think so badly of her. You were happy enough to go to her party the other night."

"Half of Harlem went to that party, and you do know why I don't like her. You're no fool. Why d'you think she's suddenly giving you the time of day? Something to do with your brother would be my guess."

I looked at Will but he was suddenly fascinated by the last half inch of gin in his cup. Any idiot could work out what Claud was insinuating. That Glo was cozying up to Bel in order to get closer to Will.

"You can tell her she's wasting her time," he said, the words rattling out machine-gun fast. "I ain't interested in her. Can't she see I'm with Lena?"

"I'm pretty sure that's the point," Claud muttered, shooting Glo an acid glare over her shoulder. "The cat's not interested in the mouse once it's dead."

"Am I . . . the mouse?" Will looked offended, but I had to stifle a laugh.

"It's not a game!" Bel was talking to Claud but looking at her stepbrother. "Can't I have friends of my own? Does it always have to be about Will all the time? I've said I'm sorry a thousand times but it's never good enough for any of you." She paused and took a deep breath. "Will, can we talk? Just the two of us."

He stared at her for a moment, then nodded. "You want to go to your place?"

I stopped myself from protesting. If Will left, there would be no guarantee he'd return anytime soon, but I didn't want her to have won.

"Can we go to your room?" Bel asked me. "Sorry, but Joey's fast asleep back home. I don't want to wake her up if . . ."

"Of course," I said quickly. It had to be a better solution than them both leaving.

I could see Glo out of the corner of my eye, her expression one of frustration as she saw Bel and Will leave without so much as a word to her. Satisfaction is such a warming feeling.

"Are you going to tell me about Glo and Will?" I asked Claud. "All of it."

"Why not? You already know most of it." Claud took a gulp of her drink as fortification. "Once upon a time, they were a couple. He thought it was serious between them. Once he graduated, he planned to propose, only when Will was arrested, she disappeared. Into thin air. Didn't go and see him in jail. Didn't check up on him or ask any of us what was going on. Nothing. She'd got with Wally before the trial was even over."

I hated her even more. What sort of a person did that to someone they were supposed to love? The magnitude of what we'd achieved that night suddenly felt overwhelming. When I'd met Will he'd seemed so steadfast, so sure of who he was. It was why, amid the turbulence of those days at sea, I'd been drawn to him. Now I could see that, yes, that was the person he was, but he was more like me than I'd realized. He'd fought to get himself an education, only to have it ripped away thanks to one stupid decision. The girl he'd thought would become his wife had betrayed him, and his sister had refused to stand up for him. All things considered, it was no surprise that he'd chosen to leave Harlem behind and put the pieces back together as far away as possible.

"Will always said it was for the best, but I know he was cut up about what happened." Louis glared in Glo's direction. The living room was almost full, the gathering turning into a real party, which was just as well, as otherwise I was sure Glo would have noticed the three of us shooting daggers in her direction.

"We don't like her," Claud said, as if that hadn't been made abundantly clear. "But she knows she made a mistake letting Will go."

"What about this chap Wally, though?" Poor man.

"If she had any sense, she'd just marry him and make do. But our Gloria has always had her sights on someone with status. Someone with the cash to keep her from having to work. She's a shop assistant, see. Likes the store discount, hates the customers. Her big dream in life is to have a husband who can support her so she can still shop but hasn't got to worry about doing an honest day's work."

When Will was a jailbird, she hadn't given two figs about him. What had changed? Was she just bored of treading water with Wally or did she see potential in Will now? Placing second at the Apollo didn't mean much alone, but it would maybe open a few doors for Will if he decided to stick it out in New York and start over. Anyone who'd heard him play knew he was good.

"Will doesn't have any money," I said, thinking aloud. What was it that Glo was hoping for?

"'Course not." Louis laughed. "But he has the potential to earn a decent living and he's popular. Trust me, if Will stays home this time, he'll be recognized in every restaurant and drinking spot in Harlem before long. Wally can't show her a good time when he's away more often than not."

The thought of another woman with Will was unsettling, but it wasn't as if I was a virgin before we met. I was confident that Glo was in the past as far as he was concerned. I was less happy about the glances that Glo and Rosa were taking turns to fire in our direction.

"Well, I'm glad that Will and Bel are finally having things out," I said, changing the subject. Out of the frying pan and into the fire.

Louis winced. "Yeah, you think we should go check in on them? They've had time to either kiss and make up or else have one hell of a fight."

"Give 'em time, honey." Claud patted her husband's hand. "They're grown-ups, after all. It's about time they sorted out their differences."

Claud made a good point. If Will Goodman was going to put down roots in Harlem once more, then he'd see Bel all the time. He'd probably have to move in with her, I realized, once finances came into the equation. I doubted he could afford rent on two apartments.

"Lena. You got a sec?" It was Rosa who'd sidled up to us.

"What's the matter?" I asked, keeping my expression straight. I didn't want her to know how bothered I was that she'd—well, she hadn't *lied*, exactly, but she hadn't been entirely honest with me either.

"Maybe we could step outside and talk?"

I glanced at Claud and Louis and got an eye roll and a shrug as answer. "Fine."

"Claudette never did like me or Glo," Rosa commented, taking the cigarette I offered her as we stood on the landing outside the apartment door. "Too good for the likes of us."

Was she including me in that statement? "You were all at school together?"

"Sure were. Course, some had parents who had a little more money. They could afford to go and study to become doctors and the like. Rest of us had to go out and work for a living soon as we were old enough."

"I get it," I told her. "I left school as soon as it was allowed."

"Then, just watch out. I know you and Glo got off on the wrong foot, but I ain't got no reason to see you get chewed up and spit out."

"Spit out?" I shook my head, not understanding.

"D'you think I'll ever be able to afford to live in a fancy apartment like this one? Well"—she reconsidered—"maybe if I ever get those magical four first places at the Apollo. But most of the time I'm just another lowly shop assistant with big dreams that I should've outgrown."

"I still don't see what that's got to do with me."

"I'm just saying that they don't like outsiders. They tolerate Bel 'cause she's family. But Glo—they got rid of her soon as they could. Poisoned Will against her."

"I heard she ditched Will when he got into trouble," I said.

Rosa's laugh was dry. "Sure. That's what he thinks, but it ain't true. Glo spent days trying to find out where Will even was. They took him away and no one would tell her where to. Will's mom told her to stay away 'cause of what Claud had been saying. Bel didn't dare stick up for her, too busy staying out of sight for her part in it. Glo would have supported Will if his so-called friends"—here she stuck an arm out, pointing with menace toward the apartment door and, I presumed, Claud and Louis—"hadn't stopped her. They filled Will's head with lies, and by the time she found out where he was, he didn't want to see her."

"But why would they do that?" It seemed like a lot of effort if Glo really hadn't done anything wrong. "Look, Rosa, you're a good friend. Glo's lucky to have you and—"

"It's not about Glo," she insisted. "Or not just about Glo. It's not even about Will necessarily. God knows he's been through enough tough times of his own."

"So it's just Claud you don't like." I knew about rivalries, how the effects of small actions could fester and turn nasty. I didn't think that Rosa was a bad person, but neither could I imagine Claud ruining two people's lives over a mild dislike of a former school friend.

"Okay." She tapped cigarette ash over the banister and smiled. "I'm wasting my time. Still, it was good to meet you, Lena. See you around." She disappeared back into the apartment, leaving me to stare after her.

See you around. Did she think I was going to be a permanent fixture in Harlem? It would explain why she and Glo had gone to such desperate measures. I laughed to myself, casting her accusations from my shoulders. The events she'd talked about were from a decade ago. Plenty of time for Glo to talk to Will about them if she'd wanted to. If they had even happened.

I went back inside. I needed a drink. I couldn't see any sign of either Will or Bel, which meant that they must still be talking, and that put my bedroom out of bounds. A couple of musicians had struck up a jazz tune, a wild cacophony that I didn't recognize. I went to the kitchen, which was thankfully empty. A half-full bottle of rum stood beside the sink and I decided that since it had been left there, it was anyone's. Finders keepers. I poured an inch into my glass, then added another for good measure. It might be a long night.

I'd only taken a small sip when the music suddenly stopped and I heard a thumping on the apartment door. A neighbor complaining about the noise? I lit a cigarette before turning to see that half the room had already emptied out.

"What's happened?" I asked anyone who was listening.

"Police are downstairs." The trumpet player who'd been so lost in his music just a minute or two earlier was now pulling on his jacket, grabbing his instrument case.

I followed him out and down the stairs, to where a crowd had gathered in the hallway.

"They're not letting anybody leave," someone said.

I bumped into Teddy, and was glad to see a familiar face. "Have you seen Will?" I asked.

"He ran outside," he said. "Here, I'll help you get through."

He shepherded me through the chaos, at least twenty people between us and the front door to the building. I didn't know what I'd expected to see out there, but it was certainly not what I got. On the front steps of the building lay a dark shape that I slowly came to realize was a person. A woman, her body sprawled awkwardly down the steps, although her modesty was protected by the position of her bent legs, the black skirt slightly raised to an inch above her knees. Her head was resting on a police officer's jacket. Will was there, bent into a crouch by the body, and I pushed forward between the spectators as he put out one shaking hand toward the woman, her face turned away from me.

"Will!" I called his name and his head snapped up, the tragic expression on his face changing to one of relief. "Oh God, what happened?"

"Lena?" He struggled to his feet, his legs unsteady. I slid down the last two steps and he yanked me into his arms. "They said that . . . they said that it was . . ." He was gripping me so tightly that I could hardly breathe. "Your passport. But it's not you. It's . . ."

"I'm fine, darling. I'm fine." I pushed him back gently. "My passport? What do you mean?"

"I answered the door when they knocked," he told me. "They said your name. But it's not you. Oh Jesus, it's Bel."

"What?" I took another look. The blond hair was familiar

enough. The red-painted nails and the shoes that had been re-heeled any number of times. Bel, lying there like a broken doll.

I still couldn't see her face, didn't want to. I saw her hand twitch and I had to stifle a sob. She was still alive.

"Will, how? How did this happen?"

He ignored me, falling back to his knees beside his sister, taking her hand.

"Ma'am?" The police officer was by my side, looking concerned. "Are you Eleanor Aldridge?"

"Yes." I watched Will, tears running down his cheeks as he tried to talk to Bel. To comfort her.

"The ambulance is on its way. She had your passport in her hand." The police officer showed me quickly but made no move to return it. Evidence, I supposed. "We thought . . . well, you know." He shrugged, embarrassed. "She fell. From up there."

I looked up. The window two floors above us was open, the curtain fluttering out on the breeze. It was my bedroom window.

22

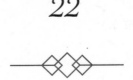

Thursday, 17 September 1936

I TOOK A sip of the brandy-laden coffee, but it had gone cold. To my left I could hear the whispered conversation taking place between Louis and Claud. Will had been allowed to go to the hospital with his sister. Bel was in a bad way, but she had survived her fall. Just. I'd asked him what had happened, but he hadn't been there, he told me. They'd had words and he'd stormed out just a few minutes before. He'd been talking to Teddy when the knock came.

"What about Joey?" I asked, suddenly remembering the little girl. How did you tell a ten-year-old that her mother was gravely injured?

Claud checked her wristwatch. "I'll go and fetch her in an hour or so. May as well let her sleep for now. She won't know the difference."

It was five o'clock in the morning, still dark out. "I suppose Will'll send news as soon as there is any."

"Bill downstairs has a telephone," Louis told me. "Will knows he can call there. Besides, I need to get to work soon. My shift starts at seven, but I'll go and see how Bel's doing beforehand."

"Send Will home, soon as you get there," Claud said. "No point both of you staying."

"I have work to do, honey. I can't stay with Bel when my patients need me," Louis reminded her gently.

"But if anything happens—anything changes—they'll come find you." She was very certain. "Will has to come home. Joey'll need him."

"I'll let Will decide what he wants to do," Louis insisted, keeping his tone moderate. He looked shell-shocked, his usual relaxed demeanor having disappeared. A stocky man, he looked diminished in a way that seemed impossible. In a matter of minutes, he had changed from an outgoing, confident man who always had a smile to this smaller and sadder figure. I hadn't asked him what he thought about Bel's chances of survival; I saw it in his manner and the haunted look in his eyes.

"The police," I said. "What do they think happened?"

Claud shrugged. "You know as much as I do."

Which wasn't exactly true. So many people had been in the apartment when Bel fell from my bedroom window, but I wasn't one of them. I'd been out in the hallway with Rosa when it must have happened. If we'd been a minute longer out there, we'd probably have heard the knock at the door of the policemen instead of that of the nice doctor downstairs. Something to thank Rosa for, I supposed. I was lucky not to be caught at the scene of yet another tragedy after my week at sea, and the murder that had gone before it. God bless jealousy. I thought about Rosa's warning, that Claud and Louis would close ranks against me. She was wrong; there was no hint of my being shut out. This was all just one big, horrible accident.

"What was Bel doing in my room alone?" I wondered out loud. Stupid, really, because I knew exactly what she'd been doing, even if Claud and Louis didn't. She'd had my passport in her hand. Whether she'd meant to leave the apartment with it, I didn't know, but I was pretty sure she'd been looking for my stash. Good thing I'd moved the banknotes, tucked them into an old hatbox hidden at the top of the wardrobe. Could she have been searching for the money when she fell? I didn't see how, but then, I couldn't really understand how she'd fallen at all.

The police officer who'd been there since the start—Freeman, he'd said his name was—walked out of the bedroom as I was staring at the door, wondering when I'd be allowed in. I wanted to have a wash, get changed. I'd been in this situation before, though. I knew that it was better to be patient and to do what I was told.

"Hey," Louis called to Freeman. "You gonna tell us what's happening?"

Freeman glanced over his shoulder toward the bedroom. I'd seen two men go in there with him, plainclothes detectives, I supposed. "Out of my hands, sir. Detective McLennan's in charge. Garson's his rookie." He walked a little closer and lowered his voice. "Just answer the questions. Don't argue with 'em. They don't care much, so long as the case gets resolved quickly."

Louis and Claud exchanged a glance. It didn't take a genius to work out what Freeman was implying. There were only two scenarios: Bel had fallen, or she'd been pushed. If she'd fallen, then it was just a horrible accident. If she'd been pushed . . .

But was it even possible? Who could do such a thing? Yes, Louis and Claud looked on edge, but this was their home. Their quiet life shattered. What had happened to Bel was upsetting, even if she had been up to no good (which I knew was the case). On the mantel I saw once more the photograph of Bel, Henry, Louis and Claud, the baby Joey in Bel's arms. At least Joey had somewhere safe to be. The poor girl would have a nasty shock when she woke up.

Freeman left and we sat there in silence, listening to the low voices of the detectives in the next room.

"Maybe I should go and fetch Joey now," Claud worried aloud. "You think they'll need to talk to her? The police, I mean?"

"Don't see why. She wasn't here," Louis pointed out.

"I know. But d'you think they'll want to be the ones to tell her? I don't think it's a good idea."

"Think what's a good idea, Mrs. Linfield?" The older detective—McLennan, had Freeman called him?—emerged from the bedroom with his younger colleague in tow.

"Oh!" She looked completely guilty, even though I knew her comment had been innocent. "Joey. Josephine," she corrected. "Bel's daughter. She's all alone. I don't want her to find out about her mother from someone else."

"And she's how old?" McLennan leaned against the wall, looking casual, but his gaze was sharp. He was an old bear of a man, his still-thick hair and beard grizzled gray with faded red. He was in his fifties if he was a day. He didn't look particularly antagonistic, but neither did he appear friendly.

"Ten," Claud said.

"Ten years old and she's been left on her own all night?" McLennan nudged his partner, who whipped out a notebook and pencil. "Is that usual?"

Claud looked to Louis, who I could see was trying to appear calm. "Bel works evenings at a club. Leon's, if you know it. Joey's a sensible girl. Straight-A student."

"Leon's." McLennan looked thoughtful. "What does Miss Bennett do there exactly?"

"Missus," Claud corrected him. "Mrs. Bennett. She's a widow, not . . . Anyway, she works behind the bar. Just a straightforward job. She wants to be home for Joey when she gets home from school. Have a meal on the table, you know? She works while Joey sleeps. It's a very safe building."

"Uh-huh." McLennan looked unconvinced by this arrangement. I could see the frustration writ across Claud's face, but she knew as well as I did that there was little point in pressing the issue. This man would believe what he wanted to believe. "So she worked last night and then she came here? Did she often do that?"

Louis explained about Amateur Night, about our moderate success, and I saw the younger cop give me a curious look. A look of interest, as if he knew the magnitude of what we'd achieved the night before. Garson, his name was, I remembered. He was about my age. Young enough to have an open mind when it came to Bel?

"Let me get this straight." McLennan lined up the facts. "Mrs. Bennett missed her brother's performance. Because of work," he added quickly, sensing that Claud was about to jump in. "But she was here by half past midnight. Leon's doesn't close until two."

"I guess she got off early. A favor maybe? You'd need to ask the folk at Leon's." Louis sounded calm, but I could see the sweat breaking out on his forehead. He wiped it away quickly with a handkerchief. "She wanted to speak to Will."

"And where is Will?"

"He's with her at the hospital right now," Louis said. "That first fella, Freeman—he said it was fine for him to go."

The detectives exchanged a glance, and I wondered if Freeman would be in for it later when they caught up with him. Will would be a pretty obvious suspect if there was any evidence that Bel had been pushed.

"Talk me through what happened after you left the Apollo," Garson said, moving things along.

"We all got here just after midnight. The invitation was open, so there were quite a few people here by the time Bel arrived. Twenty or so. She wanted to talk to Will, alone, so they went to the bedroom to talk. That was the last I saw of her." Louis swallowed hard. "I saw Will after that, though. He was talking to Teddy over by the piano when we heard what had happened."

McLennan took control. "You were all in this room, all twenty or so of you, except for Mrs. Bennett? And none of you heard or saw a fully grown woman fall from a third-story window?" He looked incredulous. "Do any of you think that she would have thrown herself out?"

"No." I said it without thinking, my cheeks flaring as Claud and Louis both shot looks in my direction. "I mean, this must have just been an awful accident. Couldn't she have just leaned out too far?" I asked, trying to picture the windowsill. Waist height, maybe just below for Bel, who was an inch or so taller than I was. If she'd left the light off in the bedroom to avoid detection, had wanted to read something, the small print on my passport, for example, could she have leaned forward to see in the glow of the streetlamp?

"You tell me." Garson made a note in his book. "Where were you when it happened, Miss . . . ?"

"Aldridge." I pointed toward his pocket. "That's my passport you have there. And I was in the kitchen when I heard the commotion, but I'd only just come in from the hallway. I was talking to someone out there."

"Who?" He looked up, his pencil poised.

"Rosa." I looked at Claud, helplessly.

"Rosa Marin," she told Garson.

"Ah." He flicked back a few pages, presumably checking that he had her name written down. I assumed the police would be speaking to everyone who'd been at the party. "So I guess that gives you both an alibi. So long as she says the same as you."

"I suppose so." I wasn't sure I liked the way he was looking at me, as if my presence in the hallway was just a little too convenient.

"Let me just get this all straight. Miss Aldridge was out in the hallway until just before the alarm was raised, and then she was in the kitchen. Mr. Goodman, the brother, had been in the bedroom with his sister before coming back in here. And you two were both in this room too?"

"Yes, sir." Claud spoke quickly, and I saw Louis blink a few times. I tried to think back. I'd had to push through the bodies to get to the kitchen when I'd returned. I hadn't even seen Rosa, and she had been only a few steps ahead of me. I couldn't remember seeing any one of them, not Will or Louis or Claud.

Garson flipped his notebook closed. "All right. I guess that'll do for now. With a bit of luck Mrs. Bennett will be able to tell us what happened when she wakes."

God, I hoped so. I'd seen enough death over the past few weeks to last several lifetimes. Whatever I thought about Bel, she didn't deserve this, even if she'd fallen while trying to rob me. Which re-minded me . . .

"Can I go into the bedroom?" I asked. "My belongings—they're all in there. I'd like to get changed." I wanted to check that my money was safe. And I needed to sleep, but I doubted I could bear to lie down in that room after what had happened.

The detectives exchanged a glance. "There's a photographer coming," McLennan told me. "Garson will wait here until he ar-rives. After that, you can go in."

"Are we free to leave?" Louis asked. "I have to work at the hos-pital. I can tell you exactly where I'll be. And my wife has to go and fetch Bel's daughter. Bring her back here so she's with family."

"Sure." McLennan nodded. He didn't look too concerned about the Linfields both leaving, and I hoped it wasn't because he'd already decided what had happened. "Perhaps you can come to the hospital with me, help me find your friend."

Louis nodded reluctantly and went to change his clothes. Claud didn't bother, simply pulled on a pair of low-heeled shoes and a jacket before hurrying out the door to retrieve Joey. McLennan set-tled himself into the armchair opposite me and lit a cigarette while he waited. He looked as comfortable as if he were in his own home, with the confidence of a man who knew exactly what was going on and who needed to pay for it.

23

Thursday, 17 September 1936

I CLEANED THE kitchen and made a pot of coffee rather than sit under McLennan's sharp gaze. The place was spotless by the time the photographer arrived, and he was done by the time Claud returned with Joey. The girl was somber, her belongings packed into a blue suitcase that Claud carried while Joey slung her school bag down by the wall. Her face was clean, but her eyes were swollen, and she followed Claud like a shadow. McLennan had gone, thank goodness. Garson had replaced him in the armchair, and he was less imposing. Less terrifying for Joey, I hoped.

Claud handed me a brown paper bag. "Cookies and fresh milk," she whispered. "Ida from the church is going to come round later as well. She teaches Joey at Sunday school. The more familiar faces, the better, I figure."

I nodded and fanned out the cookies on a plate, then almost dropped them as I went to take them out and walked straight into Garson.

"A cookie, Detective?" I asked, hoping to distract him from my fluster.

"No. Thank you." He took a step back. "I was coming to let you know that you can go into the bedroom now. We've been through everything, and you can take what you need."

"Thanks," I said. "I'm not sure I feel like sleeping in that room any longer, though. I can't bear the thought of what's happened."

Garson looked a little uncomfortable. "Don't feel as though you have to stay here, miss. Long as you let us know where you are, you can leave. My sister works reception at the Hotel Olga up on 145th Street. If you tell her that Sam sent you, she'll give you a good rate."

"You're Sam?"

He nodded. "I'll be on my way, but you can expect to hear from us soon." He left, but the atmosphere in the apartment remained somber.

"What do you think of him?" I asked Claud as she settled Joey on the couch, tucking a blanket around the little girl, who had yet to utter a word.

"Who? The cop?" Claud sat down and looked up at me. "I think, 'Thank God.' Though I wish to heaven he'd been the one to go to the hospital to talk to Will."

Thank God? "You know him?" I asked.

"No." She reached for a cookie. "But he's one of us, isn't he? Least he'll listen to what actually happened. If we got stuck with just that Irish cop, I'd be worried." She bit the cookie in half and chewed, making it look like a trial rather than a joy.

Garson was colored. Able to pass like Bel. Like me. It made sense, then. His sister at the Hotel Olga. A hotel where Black people were welcome—I knew that even in Harlem that often wasn't the case. "I was thinking that I might move to the Olga," I said.

Claud swallowed a mouthful of milk, wiping her lips with the back of her hand. "I hate to say it, Lena, but that's probably a good idea. You can afford it?"

"I'd always banked on staying in a hotel anyway. It was only because you were so kind that I ended up here."

"So much for your vacation." Claud sighed and stroked Joey's forehead; the girl's eyes were open, but she didn't say a word, just looked up at Claud. "Baby, your uncle Louis'll send word soon. Promise. And later on, we can go and see your mama."

The lack of knowledge was killing us all. Was it good or bad that we hadn't heard anything? It had been hours now. When I went to my bedroom and looked out the window, the street was going about its morning as if nothing had happened. I looked down on the hats of people striding past, and not one tilted back for its wearer to look up. No mark left to show where Bel had fallen. Had landed. Staring down onto the steps below, I started to feel dizzy and moved away, my hand propped against the wall to my left, steadying me.

This was just a terrible accident, I reminded myself. Nothing to do with what had happened on the *Queen Mary*. I knew who had been responsible for those deaths. I leaned against the wall and tried to take deep breaths, my lungs constricting as I fought the panic. A lot of people had been in this apartment when Bel fell. Only one had been on board the ship, and he had had nothing to with the murders. I knew that for certain. I trusted Will, even though he had secrets of his own to hide. Or was I being a total fool? I cursed Rosa. If not for her, spreading her poison on the very night of Bel's fall, I'd not give two seconds to considering Will's part in all this.

But she had cast doubt on the trustworthiness of not only Will, but the Linfields too. Was she spending her morning telling anyone who would listen how she'd never trusted Claud or Louis? Was she running around reminding everyone she knew that Will was capable of violence? Hadn't he served time for it? Had a criminal record for a split second of madness, letting the red mist control him?

Even if I didn't believe it, the police might. McLennan would. A man who could lose his temper long enough to put another in the hospital could reasonably be assumed able to get angry enough to push a woman much smaller than he. That an open window added the fatal ingredient was just dreadful luck. If Bel had been a foot away, she might have fallen to the floor. He might have had time to catch himself, staring down at her, realizing how unbalanced the power between them was.

"Lena, are you all right?" Claud stood in the doorway. "You don't need to leave right now. You should wait until we hear news. Come and sit down." I could see that she was worried about me.

I followed her to the living room and sat down. She should be concerned about Joey; that was enough for her to worry about. Claud dropped a measure of brandy each into two mugs and took them to the kitchen, then topped them with cold milk.

"You're going to need a new bottle of brandy at this rate," I said, the poor attempt at a joke falling flat.

"Louis will call with news soon," Claud said, taking up her position back by Joey's side. "You need some sleep, Lena. Drink that and go lie down. Will can take you up to the Olga later on."

It had only been a half idea to leave, but Claud had happily taken it as concrete, and when I set foot back in the bedroom, I knew I couldn't stay. My carpetbag had been emptied out on the floor and my belongings looked a pitiful heap: a couple of paperback novels, a scarf, the fake contract I'd signed for the Broadway production that never was. I stood barefoot on the edge of the bed to reach the high shelf in the wardrobe. My money was safe.

I looked around, and other than my upturned bag, there was no obvious sign of disturbance. The bedspread was dented only from my feet. Otherwise, the bed had been left made, from my efforts the day before. The window had been left open as it had been discovered, the wind outside picking up so that the curtain billowed. I allowed myself a morbid moment, pressing my hips to the sill and leaning forward to see what was possible.

You'd have to lean out quite a way to fall. Which didn't mean that Bel hadn't fallen. If someone had startled her, if she'd not wanted to get caught with something she shouldn't have had, then perhaps she had leaned out that far. If she'd wanted to throw something down to be retrieved later on, for example, like a passport.

I ran through the sequence of events in my head, according to what was known. Everyone had been having such a good time. No one seemed to remember Bel rejoining the party. She'd gone through my belongings and taken my passport. Why? And where had Will been when all this was happening? Bel must have stayed in the bedroom after he'd gone.

"Don't think badly of her." Claud walked into the room. "She's not a bad woman, whatever this was." She gestured around us.

"She didn't trust me." The thought exploded, clarity bursting a bubble in my brain. "She was snooping to find out if I was who I said I was."

Claud shrugged. "It sounds more like the Bel I know. She was so desperate for Will to forgive her. To let the past be behind them. She liked you. I know that much, but she'd have wanted to make sure you were going to be good for Will. For all three of them."

"Three?" I was slow to realize. "Her and Joey. Their family."

"They rely so heavily on Will." Claud perched on the end of the bed. "And Joey is everything to Bel. She opened a college fund for Joey the week after she was born. People look at Bel and think she's a loose woman. She wears nice clothes because she learned how to sew. She tailors her skirts and looks after them. Alters them as the fashions change. Any spare pennies she has, they go into that college fund so that Joey can have the best education, but it only worked as long as Will was happy to provide the roof over their head."

"Does Will know this?" A daft question. Of course he did. "How's Joey doing?" I asked, changing the subject slightly. Just talking about Bel made me feel guilty. Thinking that if I'd just taken the time to talk to her face-to-face after the snooping incident, this might not have happened. She could have told me her concerns. I could have showed her my passport, proof that I was who I said I was.

"She's coping, I suppose." Claud looked down at her hands, clasped in her lap. "Soon as I get the word, I'll take her to see her mother. It'll be better once Bel wakes up. She can tell us what happened, what the hell she was doing in here." Her sigh was heavy, and I could see how exhausted she was, not just physically but in her soul. "Stupid girl."

"I'll wait until Will comes back, but then I'll get out of your hair," I told her. "I feel . . . in the way. You've been so kind. So generous, Claud, but this is . . . Joey needs to stay here until Bel gets well enough to leave the hospital. You need the room."

Claud didn't argue. We looked at each other and I thought I saw her mouth twitch, as if there was something else she wanted to say but didn't feel able to. That she was sorry. Or that she wished things could be different. I felt the same way.

Through the silence I heard the unmistakable ring of a telephone from beneath our feet, and our eyes met. Claud jumped to stand up, shaking off her lethargy, and I followed her to the front door. As she opened it, a woman in her fifties appeared at the top of the stairs. Betsy, the wife of the doctor downstairs. Claud yanked my arm, dragging me out onto the landing, pulling the door closed behind us. From the look on Betsy's face I could tell before she opened her mouth what news she brought. Claud had known the same. It was why she had brought us outside, so that Joey wouldn't hear.

Bel Bennett had died.

24

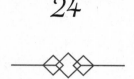

Thursday, 17 September 1936

IT WAS HARD not to think of myself as some Angel of Death. Everywhere I'd been for the past few weeks, corpses had fallen behind me. From Soho to the Atlantic Ocean and now as far as Harlem, the bodies were piling up.

I packed my belongings quietly as the family gathered in the living room. Will looked like a shell of himself when he returned, just after eight, Louis holding him up as he staggered in to tell his niece that she was now an orphan. I couldn't bear to listen, to hear that little girl's life ripping apart. I was a coward, but at least I wasn't in the way. It wasn't my pain to share.

"Do you want me to go up to the hotel with you?" Will asked, walking in as I tried to decide whether it was better to slip away or wait until I could say good-bye.

"I'm so sorry." Useless words, but I didn't know what else to say. Our embrace felt awkward, as if we were two strangers, not two people who had spent the past few nights sharing a bed. "Don't feel as though you have to come. Poor Joey . . . I just can't imagine how that little girl is feeling."

"It's hard." Will's voice cracked and he swallowed before going on. "I'll come with you. I need to get some air and . . . This isn't . . ." He stopped and tried to gather himself together. "Lena, I care about you a lot. More than almost anybody, but—"

"You have to look after your family," I said, forcing a smile through the pain. "You have to put Joey first. And it's not as though you don't know where I'll be. I'll come over whenever you need me to. I'd like to help."

"Let's go get you settled in at the Olga." Will picked up my carpetbag.

The walk was only around twenty minutes, heading across to Lenox and then up to 145th Street, but it felt twice as long. Will didn't speak and I didn't know what to say. No one watching us on the street would have thought us lovers, for we walked with clear air between us, no more hand holding or shared smiles. I understood why, but it was difficult not to feel rejected, difficult to fend off the guilt about feeling that way when Will had just watched his sister die.

"I won't come in with you," he said, slowing down as we drew close to our destination, the three-story hotel building squatting on the corner. "It'll be easier if you go in alone. Less questions that way. Just in case someone recognizes us, or . . . You know how people talk."

He meant to protect my reputation, I knew, but it stung nonetheless. "Should I come over tomorrow morning? Claud must need help, with Joey." What did people do after a bereavement? Bring food? Help out with the cooking and cleaning? All those mundane tasks that felt both monumental and pointless when there was a person missing. Gone, forever.

"I'm sure Claud would appreciate it." Will stopped just shy of the doorway, still holding my carpetbag.

"All right." I reached for the bag, but he didn't let go straight-away. I took a risk: "Do *you* want me to come over?"

He nodded, and I could see that his eyes were damp. "I don't know what to do," he said, so quietly that it was barely a whisper.

"No one does," I told him, wanting to reach up and wipe the tears from his cheeks but knowing that he wouldn't want me to. Not out in public, where people were watching. Ready to judge him for everything he did in these hours after his sister's death. "Nobody could."

He let go of my bag and took a step back. "Come over tomorrow. Please. For Claud. And for me. You're as welcome now as you ever were."

"Promise?" I managed a small smile.

"Cross my heart." He placed a hand on his chest to mark the vow. "Get some rest and we'll talk then."

I didn't want to watch him walk away. Instead, I turned and pushed through the door into the hotel. The Olga was the best hotel a colored person could stay in here in New York, so Will had said. It was no Ritz, but it was pleasant enough. The furnishings were what you'd expect from a top-class hotel: mahogany furniture, brass polished to a high shine, the staff in starched and well-kept uniforms. As I approached, the girl behind the desk smiled, bidding me a good morning.

"How can I help?" she asked.

"I'm hoping you have a room free," I said, trying to sound perk-ier than I felt.

"Just for this evening?"

"No." I paused and then realized that there was no chance that I'd be returning to the Linfields'. Not to stay, at least. "I'll need a room until next Wednesday." She was taking her time checking the book, and I remembered Garson's words. "Sam Garson sent me. You don't happen to be his sister, do you?"

The girl looked up. "Ivy's out the back. Did you want to speak to her?"

Damn. "Oh, no, I don't know her. It was just his recommendation, that's all."

She smiled. "Sam's a doll. He wouldn't have sent you here for no reason." She straightened up and quoted me a price that was cheaper than I'd expected. The "special rate," no doubt. "The room isn't the biggest, but it has something of a view, at least."

I paid the deposit, glad that I'd transferred some of my cash to my purse before leaving the Linfields'. The key was a heavy brass affair that I was to leave at the front desk whenever I left the hotel. As much as I was grateful to Garson, I couldn't help feeling that he'd been keen to keep an eye on me. While I was at the Olga, he'd be able to check in and know if I was in residence or not at any time of the day.

I declined assistance and carried my own bag to the room on the first floor. I was glad to be no higher, all things considered. As hotel rooms went, it was certainly compact, but it had everything I needed. A bed with clean sheets, a wardrobe to store my meager belongings, and the bathroom just two doors down, at the end of the corridor. Locking the door behind me, slipping on the chain to be sure, I kicked off my shoes, then lay down on the bed.

It was the last thing I remembered until a pounding fist against the door jolted me awake. The hotel room was shrouded in darkness, the only light emanating from the streetlamps outside the window and from the fraction-of-an-inch gap beneath the door. I sat up, my head thudding and a stale taste in my mouth. What time was it?

"Lena?" It was a woman's voice. "Lena, you in there?" She knocked again. Rosa.

I stumbled off the bed and turned the key, struggling to release the chain. "What are you doing here?"

"That's a nice welcome." Rosa stood there, arms folded. "I thought you might need a friend."

"I have friends, thank you." I wanted to close the door on her, but some sixth sense stopped me. "How did you know I was here?"

"You aren't at the Linfields. There're only so many other places a woman can go in Harlem, and I didn't think you had the guts to try and get in at the Theresa." She named the most luxurious hotel in Harlem, one that I knew had a whites-only policy.

"You've heard about Bel, then."

"Girl, everyone's heard about Bel. And they're all talking about it. About *you*." She jabbed a finger in my direction.

"I wasn't even in the apartment," I argued.

"Thanks to me," she reminded me.

"Have you come to collect some sort of reward?" I wasn't in the mood for Rosa's games. Whatever it was that she wanted, I knew I wasn't going to like it.

"No. Look, there's a restaurant I like a couple doors down. Have you eaten? My treat."

Annoyingly, I was quite hungry. Rosa was turning out to be relentless—the least she could do was pay for my meal.

I followed her out and down to the street to a cozy local restaurant. It wasn't busy, just half of the tables occupied, but it was late for dinner in these parts. Almost eight o'clock and I could see from the waiter's face as he led us to our table that he hoped we'd be quick.

"A chicken sandwich and fries," Rosa said, batting away the menu. "And a coffee."

"I'll have the same," I said, and the waiter's demeanor thawed before he marched away to deliver our order. "Now, what's all this about?"

"I want to know who killed Bel." Rosa's face was serious suddenly. "It was somebody in that apartment and you either know who or you're in the best place to find out."

"The police are looking into what happened," I said, not committing to her opinion that Bel had been pushed. "Why don't you speak to them? Detective Garson's the man to talk to."

"The police don't care." She fidgeted with her napkin, shaking it out onto her lap before picking at the corner stitching. "How do you prove that someone was pushed when there's no eyewitness?"

She made a good point, though it was one that made me feel less anxious. If that was the case, then it would make it harder for the police to pin it on Will. "I wasn't there. As you know."

"If the guilty person confesses, then they don't need any witness," she pointed out. "The Linfields, Will—they're thick as thieves. None of them would betray the others. Same thing happened when Will went to jail. Claud and Louis both said they hadn't seen anything when everyone knew they were right there. And the defense claimed that Henry's blow to the head made him unreliable. It was Bel's testimony that did for Will. She stood up in court and told the judge that Will had confessed to her. That he'd begged for her forgiveness, but she knew that she had to do the right thing and tell the truth."

My mind reeled. "She turned on her own brother?" Even after everything I'd been told, I hadn't realized she'd been the prosecution's star witness. I could hardly believe it.

"Stepbrother," Rosa reminded me.

"Why? She wasn't there. She didn't need to say a word." It didn't chime with what I knew. Why Will gave her money, why she was still so close to the Linfields. Rosa's claim that they'd tried to cut her out didn't match what I had seen over the past week. The photograph of them as godparents to Joey. And then it clicked. "Bel was already pregnant. She must have married Henry straight after the trial. And it's so much easier to be a married mother than one bringing up a child all alone, out of wedlock."

Rosa shifted in her chair, looking less confident. "Maybe. But my point still stands. Those three, they don't let anyone else in and they'll protect one another, no matter what. You've already been cast out, haven't you?"

"It was my idea, actually," I spat back. "I wanted what was best for Joey."

"And isn't it best for Joey that the truth comes out?" Rosa asked. "You just need to keep your ears open. Listen to see if one of them says something that doesn't sound right. Unless they've already cut you out."

"I'm going round there tomorrow," I said, indignance overtaking my better judgment about keeping quiet about my plans. "Look, Rosa, I'll keep an ear out. That's all I can say."

We fell silent as the waiter came with cream, sugar, and a pot of coffee. He departed briefly to bring our food, but I was no longer hungry. After he served us I shook salt on the fries as Rosa chewed a mouthful of bread and chicken.

"Where's Glo this evening?" I asked. "Did she send you to do her dirty work?"

"Glo's got nothing to do with this," Rosa told me, unconvincingly.

"Really? And would she be happy or sad if Will got blamed for what's happened to Bel?"

She poured herself a cup of coffee and took her time adding too much sugar and a slug of cream. "Obviously you know they were together back then. Glo thought that they'd get married once he graduated from law school. She had it all planned out, you know? Nice house, nice clothes, cute kids. The dream."

So far, she hadn't given me anything that Claud hadn't shared. "But she lost interest once he couldn't give her those fancy things."

"Glo didn't know what to do. I told you that Claud and Louis wouldn't tell her anything. Later on, she wanted to talk to Will, to tell him what they'd done, but he wouldn't see her. Wouldn't answer her letters. Cut her off completely. Bel was the only person who'd give her the time of day."

"But Bel was the one who'd sent Will to prison." I knew I was being unfair. These people shared a history that I hadn't been part of. Will wasn't a man to hold a grudge. Unlike Claud, he had been civil enough to Glo when we'd run into her.

"Bel was in love with Henry. She had to choose between her fiancé and her stepbrother. And her child," Rosa said. "I think that Will understood that. He knew what Henry was like. A charmer of a gentleman until he didn't care what you thought of him any longer. As soon as you needed him more than he needed you, he became a different person."

"But none of this explains why you think that Bel was murdered," I said. "Is this really just about Bel, or is this you and Glo trying to settle an old score?"

"Can't it be about the truth?" She smiled sweetly before she took a sip from her cup.

I wanted to believe her, but every word she'd said to me during our short acquaintance felt directed. She was Glo's puppet—I was sure of it—and she didn't look devastated by Bel's death. The pair of them were up to something, and I was certain it had more to do with past events than with the tragedy of the night before. What really worried me was that the way Rosa told it, there was one obvious suspect if Bel's death hadn't been an accident: Will. I'd been with him before it happened; I'd seen his face when he'd returned from the hospital. I refused to believe he could have killed Bel in cold blood. My dilemma now was whether to warn him, adding more problems to his overburdened state of mind, or to take on Rosa and Glo myself.

25

Friday, 18 September 1936

I SLEPT FITFULLY that night, waking at three a.m. to finish eating the chicken sandwich that I'd carried up to my room after getting rid of Rosa. To her credit, she had at least paid the bill. I hadn't slept properly in weeks, and when I finally gave up at quarter to seven, the morning light dribbling in through the crack in the curtains, my head was pounding as though I'd been at the gin. I wished that I had been. At least that way I might have just passed out.

The advantage to being up early was that the bathroom at the end of the hall was free. I had a quick wash and got dressed, then sent down my dirty clothes to be laundered, a positive note to being in a hotel. Here on a corner of busy Lenox Avenue, the street sounds were magnified. The beeping of horns, the shouts of people greeting one another on the way to work, the newspaper vendors calling out headlines. It was, I supposed, Harlem proper compared to the Linfields' quiet and genteel street. I watched people go by for a while until I judged it a civilized hour to visit the bereaved.

Claud had told me to keep my key until I left New York. I supposed it was easier that way, and when I arrived back at the apartment, I saw why. I was far from the first visitor that day. At the front door I crossed paths with a couple I recognized vaguely from church the Sunday before. Sober in their expressions, they looked as though they'd popped round before work, he in a suit, she wearing a nurse's uniform under her coat. We exchanged mild pleasantries as I headed up the stairs to the apartment.

Inside, Claud was directing events. She had pulled the dining table out, and its surface was covered with dishes. Had everyone the Linfields ever known brought food? Macaroni cheese, three different sorts of pie, a potato salad, two fruitcakes. Other dishes were covered with tea towels, and she had a coffeepot beside it all, along with empty cups and saucers waiting for visitors to come and claim them.

"You're here!" Claud threw her arms around me, startling me a little. "Thank God! Have you ever seen so much food in your life?"

I shook my head, mute. There was something unnatural in her behavior, a touch of the manic that told me that Claud was not all right. "Can I help with something? Where are the others?" Where was Will? I wanted to ask, but I didn't know if it would be seemly under the circumstances.

"Louis's at work and Will's gone over to Joey's school to talk to the principal. I mean, I'm sure they've heard what happened, but it's just easier if he arranges it all properly. Joey can't go back yet."

"No, of course not." I glanced over at the bedroom that had been mine, the door closed firmly. "Is she asleep? How's she doing?"

"Hardly said a word." Claud poured out two cups of coffee and handed me one. "She's asleep. I hope. Will slept out here last night." She patted the sofa as we sat down on it.

I pulled out my cigarettes and held the pack out to Claud. "He was in a bad way yesterday."

"Mm." Claud lit her cigarette and looked away as she blew out her first lungful of smoke. "It all seems so unfair!" She turned to face me, her eyes tearful. "I thought that we were finally putting the past behind us. You came here, and Will was happy for the first time in so long. And he and Bel were getting along better than they had in so long, believe it or not. I honestly thought that this was going to be a new start for all of us." She pressed her palm to her belly, and I knew she was thinking of the baby. Of how she had been ready to relinquish her care of Will and give it over to the new life inside her.

"I'm so sorry," I said, for what felt like the hundredth useless time. "What's happened is awful, but there's always a way forward. Once the police have finished investigating what happened."

"The police are the last thing we need," she said, raising her voice. "Can you imagine what'll happen if they decide it wasn't an accident? They'll come after Will. He has a record, Lena. They won't care about what really happened."

Maybe it was just an odd choice of words, but it sounded to me as though Claud herself was of two minds about it being an accident. Either that or she knew for certain that it wasn't.

"How do you think it happened?" I asked, hoping that I sounded puzzled rather than interrogatory.

"I don't know. Bel . . . well, she was a risk taker. I loved her like a sister, but I always worried about her. I knew how tired she was of living like she was. My fear was always that some smart-looking fella over at Leon's would turn her head. Pretty girl, good figure still. There're plenty of men who'd push their morals to one side and slip a few lies into a girl's ear to get into her bed. Another Henry, or worse. I never thought it would be this." She stared off into the distance.

It sounded as though Bel's friends and family had all underestimated her. Like Claud said, Bel must have had plenty of chances to fall in with the wrong man, but she hadn't. Rosa had made one good point, at least. "She was a good mother."

"Yes. She was." Claud leaned back against the sofa cushions. I doubted she'd slept more than an hour or so, and her skin looked as gray as the line of ash that was growing longer at the end of her cigarette.

"What'll happen to Joey now?" I kept my voice low, knowing that a girl as smart as Joey would be very capable of eavesdropping in order to find out what the grown-ups didn't want her to know.

Claud shrugged, her shoulders heavy. "I guess it's up to Will. He's her next of kin. Henry's mother might have something to say, but she moved out of Harlem five years ago and I haven't seen her since. Bel takes Joey to see her pretty often, but they're not close. According to Bel, she thought Henry could do better for himself, which just goes to show how blinkered some mothers can be."

There was a knock at the door. "Shall I go?" I asked, hoping to ease some of Claud's burden.

"No." She stubbed out her cigarette and brushed ash from her skirt. "Thank you, but trust me—let me handle it. I got a spiel going now. So many people! I know they care, but they're also nosy as all get out."

I was glad she'd kept a little of her sense of humor despite the somber occasion. She was quick to welcome the visitor in, and I recognized another friendly face from the church. Miss Ida.

"Good to see you again, dearie," Ida said, handing over a huge casserole dish to Claud. "Careful not to spill! I see you got a lot of food already, but you can't go wrong with a little chicken soup. Soothes the soul." She lowered her voice. "Feed the girl up even if she says she ain't hungry."

"Thank you." Claud took the dish with both hands, sagging a little under its weight, and I jumped up to clear space on the table. "Can I get you anything, Ida? Please? I got three pound cakes that need eating up and the coffee's still warm in the pot."

"That sounds lovely, Claudette." Ida lowered herself into one of the armchairs with a sigh. "Gosh, it's been an age since I last paid you a visit. A crying shame it's taken this sad occasion for it to happen."

"Uh-huh." Claud busied herself fetching plates and slicing thick slabs from one of the cakes on the table. So much food. We could have fed everyone who lived on the street and had leftovers. "You know, I might just take in some soup to Joey. She didn't eat a thing last night." She handed us our cake and then disappeared into the kitchen with the soup dish.

"My husband passed ten years ago, and I remember how awful it was in those days right after it happened." Ida put her plate down in her lap, the cake untouched. "Everyone in the neighborhood just descended. In one way it's nice, makes you feel wanted. Like the person who's gone was loved. But it's also such a pain in the behind! Entertaining is the last thing you want to do. And yet here I am, doing the exact same thing. Can't stay away. You can't, can you? You got to show your face at a time like this."

I laughed, shocked at her candor. "My father died recently, but it wasn't like this. It was a long illness, and a lot of his old friends had moved away or lost touch with us before he went. It was a nice funeral, though. Close friends, the sort that are as good as family."

"Your father." She broke off a corner of cake. "You mentioned him the other day. What did you say his name was again?"

"Alfie. Alfie Aldridge. Alfred, I suppose, though no one ever called him that."

She chewed thoughtfully. "And did you manage to find out about the girl I mentioned the other day? Jessie?"

"Nothing more." Events had overtaken me. Finding Jessie had been moved to the back of my mind when there had been Amateur Night to think of; now that Bel was dead it seemed disrespectful to even contemplate resuming my search.

"Your father didn't tell you anything about her?"

"It was only ever the two of us in London. I knew he sailed from New York to get to Europe, but he never liked to talk about what had gone on before that. Just that his parents had died and there was nothing left for him in this country. No mention of a sister or any living relative at all."

"A man who doesn't like to talk about his past is usually hiding something," Ida mused. "Not that I mean to say anything against your father."

"No, no." I waved away the idea that she'd caused any offense. "In truth, I've wondered the same." One of the secrets he'd kept from me, my mother's identity, I knew he'd kept with the best of intentions. But then, that was a secret that had almost killed me. "Is there anything else at all you can tell me about Jessie?"

"Oh, it was so long ago." Ida glanced at me. "I just know that she came to New York looking for her brother, your father. Now, I never met him, unfortunately, so I'm not sure what else I can add that helps you. If I'm honest, it was a strange time. A time of change. Folk like us didn't live in Harlem the way we do now. Around that time, thirty years or so ago, there suddenly began this movement. Colored folk moving up north to the big cities 'cause they'd had enough of being treated like dirt down in the South. I met Jessie at the docks, straight off the steamer and with not a clue how things worked in a city like New York." She shook her head, but I could see it was a fond memory. "A scrawny, scrappy little thing, she was. Before I took over the Sunday school, I saw it as a calling, if you like. To go down to the docks when I could, when I knew a steamer was due in. Those girls, so many of them were chasing after family members, or just a new life. No idea how big the city was. Some of them were from towns with less people than could fit into the foyer at the Apollo Theater."

I tried to imagine Alfie living in a small town and failed. He'd always loved London. The bright lights and the opportunity. But what if he'd learned to love the city? What if he'd loved it precisely because it was so far away from what he'd grown up with?

"I'd love to find out more about Jessie," I said. "Anything you can tell me at all."

"All right, then. Let me speak to Etta and see what she remembers 'bout her." Ida set her attention on the pound cake, and I did the same, suddenly ravenous.

SOLITUDE

26

Friday, 18 September 1936

WILL ARRIVED HOME just as Ida left, not outstaying her welcome. He looked as tired as Claud, and I longed to hold him but no longer knew if it would be welcome. Everything had changed and there was no place for romance now.

"How's the hotel?" he asked cordially.

"Comfortable," I assured him, and hesitated before adding, "Rosa came to see me last night."

"Rosa?" He looked concerned. "What did she want?"

"She's upset." I waited for him to join me on the sofa. "She thinks that someone pushed Bel."

"And she thinks that someone is me?" Will rubbed his eyes with his hands. "Based on what? The fact that she hates my guts?"

"Does she? Hate your guts?"

He shrugged, annoyed. "I don't know. She did. There's all this old history between all of us. I don't expect you to understand."

"And yet I do," I shot back. "I know how family history has a habit of catching up with you. I'm on your side, you know. I just need to know if I should be steering clear of Rosa and Glo. If there's anyone else I should be wary of."

"I'm sorry." He placed a placatory hand on my knee. "God, Lena, my head is . . . I don't know what's happening. I was just at the school, and the principal, he had all these dumb questions. When will Joey be back? Do I want them to send work here or to Bel's apartment? Did I want any of Joey's schoolmates at the funeral?" He looked lost. "How am I supposed to know all these things? I get that they're simple questions. I should know the answers, but I don't."

I squeezed his hand. "You'll work it out. You love Joey, and whatever happens, she's in the best place, with people who love her."

He pulled me to him then, and I felt his heart rate slow against my cheek as I rested against his chest. In that moment I wasn't thinking of Bel, or of Joey. I felt only my own personal, selfish devastation that this had ruined whatever chance there had been for us. The more time I had spent with Will, the more I had considered that there might be a place for me here. A new start. Away from the memories of Soho, of my last few days with Maggie. I had no job in London, no place to live that was my own. No family. And here, in New York, I had thought that maybe there was a chance to have those things again. New and untainted by memories.

Claud came out of Joey's room looking somber. "She's eating. That's something. How'd it go at the school?"

Will gave her a brief version of the conversation he'd had with Joey's principal. "I guess we just see what happens. She's a bright girl. I'm not worried about her missing a couple weeks of school."

"She's way ahead," Claud agreed. "She could have skipped a grade, only she didn't want to. She wanted to stay with her friends."

"She's got sense," Will said. "Her teacher spoke highly of her but they're asking the impossible, wanting to know details so soon. I don't even know where we'll be living next week, let alone anything else."

"You'll take Joey in, then?" Claud asked gently. Her hand rested on her belly and I knew she was thinking that she was in no position to take on a ten-year-old full-time.

"She's my niece," Will said simply. "And I want to. I ran into Teddy and he reckons he can get me some work with the house band at the Apollo. It'll take some time, but I'm hoping I can earn enough to carry on paying rent on Bel's place. I got some savings to get us through the first few months, at least."

I thought of Bel's grim little apartment, the tiny bedroom and the lumpy sofa that Joey slept on. It wasn't much, but at least Joey was used to it. And it was a bigger space than the cramped quarters Will had shared on board the ship.

The rest of the afternoon passed in much the same vein, Will and Claud discussing the grim realities of funeral arrangements, who was left to be informed, what paperwork needed to be done to inform the authorities that Mabel Bennett was no longer to be counted among the living. Neighbors and friends popped in periodically and Claud was up and down like a yo-yo, refilling the coffeepot while I washed up cups and plates, an inconceivable amount of pound cake vanishing from the plates on the table, only to be replaced with new dishes, of casserole and fried chicken and pie.

"By the time we eat half of this, it'll be the funeral and it'll all get replaced." Claud sighed. "When we're sad, we cook."

When I was sad I usually smoked and drank gin, but it didn't seem suitable here, so I replaced the booze with stodgy food. Chicken, and potatoes in a cheesy sauce. Will picked at his and Claud waved me away when I offered to dish some up for her. She sat and worried away at the dry skin around her fingernails whenever she wasn't pouring out hot drinks for guests or heating up food in the oven.

"What time will Louis be home?" I asked, desperate for a change from this sad, repeating chain of events. There was nothing I could do to help, other than the washing up. I felt in the way, but when I'd offered to leave, Claud had assured me that I wasn't a hindrance.

Besides, where would I go? The soulless hotel room didn't call to me, and I was worried that I'd have another visit from Rosa there or, worse, one from Glo. They'd never dare come round to the Linfields' for any other reason than to pay their respects. Whether they would do that much or not remained to be seen. It was a relief when Claud cursed for the second time that day.

"Out of damned milk," she growled, emptying the last of the bottle into a jug.

"Let me go down to the store and get some," I offered. A breath of fresh air would do me a world of good.

I refused Claud's offer of money and hurried down the street. The closest store was only a five-minute walk away, so I went on to the next, the cool late-summer breeze refreshing me. I needed time to think. In a week I'd be on a ship, heading back to England alone. Unless I wasn't.

When Alfie had been ill, I'd told myself that the sacrifices I was making, the exciting roles I didn't audition for in lieu of taking more regular employment, were just temporary. His illness would not go on forever; I didn't want it to, much as I knew that my heart would be broken when he died. The pain he was in, the racking coughs and the struggle for breath, was too much. But then, when he was gone, I had found comfort in the familiar. Singing at the Canary Club was easy work. A couple of hours a night for a steady wage that paid the rent if nothing much else besides. The same with my relationships. An affair with a married man offered no challenge. No fear of commitment. He would never leave his wife and I would never have to make changes to my lifestyle.

It was only when that lover had left me, my best friend's husband had been murdered, and the opportunity of a lifetime had been handed to me that I shook myself out of that rut. With Will, I saw a similar situation, except that he had been jolted from one rut straight into a new one. He had his niece to think of, and her own needs were surely more important than his own. Would he want me to stay if I suggested it, or would I just be making his life more difficult?

I bought the milk and grabbed a copy of *Cosmopolitan* so that I had something to read back at the hotel. On the way back I wondered if Maggie had sent word. I should make time to check with the Sherry-Netherland to see if any messages had been left. I felt aimless and despondent as I reached the foot of the steps leading up to the Linfields' building. It was so damned unfair. Less than two days ago it had seemed as though Will and I had the world at our feet. Now everything was ruined and there wasn't even anyone to blame. Just a terrible, awful accident.

I stared at the steps. There was no sign that anything out of the ordinary had happened. Had there been blood or had I imagined it? Someone must have cleaned the steps, swept them. There wasn't even a stray leaf to be seen.

"Miss Aldridge?"

I jumped, clutching the railing to steady myself, and heard a chinking sound as my foot struck something. "Detective Garson!" I looked down at the object. A piece of china.

"You settle in all right at the Olga?"

"Yes, thank you. I didn't see your sister, but her colleague was very helpful." I gave him my most charming smile. "You wouldn't mind carrying this up for me, would you? We ran out of milk."

As he took the paper bag from me, I quickly bent and grabbed the curved fragment from beside my foot. "I can be ever so clumsy." I clutched the piece of china, barely the size of my palm, and hoped he didn't ask what it was that I'd retrieved, though it was probably nothing anyway.

He stood by to let me open the door with my key, and a nagging pull in my gut told me to be careful with him. "How long are you staying in New York?"

"I sail back to England next week," I said, leading the way up-stairs to the apartment. "In a way, I wish I was staying longer, after what's happened. In another, I worry that I'm in the way. I'm just a guest, after all. I didn't know Bel very well."

"She was well-known around here," he said, and I glanced back at him over my shoulder, unsure if he was casting aspersions or just stating a fact.

"Everyone seems to know everyone around here," I said. "In such a big city, Harlem is its own little village, it seems."

"True, that." He laughed. With everyone else so somber, his lightheartedness felt misplaced. I hoped he wasn't about to upset things.

I turned the key in the lock and called out as I stepped into the apartment: "I'm back! And Detective Garson is here." I didn't think he could accuse me of sending up a warning flare, but something told me I should.

Will got up from the sofa. "Sam. Long time no see."

I held back a groan. Was there nobody with whom Will didn't have a history in this corner of the city?

"I wish it were under happier circumstances," Garson said. "But I'm afraid to say, Will, I need to take you down to the station."

"What?" Claud flew out of the kitchen. "What the hell is going on? You can't just march in here and take him away like this."

Garson held his hands up. "I'm not arresting nobody. Not yet, anyhow. Will, you just need to come and give a statement. Tell us what exactly took place between you and your sister that night. Because as far as anyone else has told us, you were the last fella to see her alive."

Will nodded, resigned. "All right, then. Let's get this over with." He grabbed his jacket from the arm of the sofa and pulled it on.

"Will, hold up a minute." Claud put out a hand to stop him. "I'm sorry, Detective, but how do we know to trust you? What's to say you haven't been sent down here to avoid a scene?"

Garson gave a half smile. "Guess you don't, Mrs. Linfield. But if you'd prefer a scene, I can make the arrangements."

Will gently removed Claud's hand from his arm. "It's all right, Claud. Just . . . let Louis know when he gets home. He'll know what to do."

They left and I didn't need to look at Claud's anguished face to know it was bad. The last one to see Bel alive had been Will, a man who had been crossed by his sister in the past and who had a criminal record to prove that he had a history of violence.

I opened my hand and looked at the piece of china that I'd rescued. There was a smear of black bisecting it. I sniffed at it. I couldn't be entirely sure, but it looked very much like mascara. I had been using one of Claud's old mugs to dip my brush into ever since I'd arrived; I never cleaned it properly, just changed the water each day. Slovenly, but there we go. If this was it—and what else could it be?— then it must have fallen along with Bel. Had she grabbed at it as she fell? I squeezed the shard, feeling its edges bite into my skin. The mug hadn't been on the windowsill; it had been on the bedside table. If Bel had fallen naturally, she wouldn't have been able to take it with her. A struggle, though, a second body wrestling with her, might have knocked the mug with enough force to send it hopping out into thin air.

Harlem After Midnight

GARSON ALMOST FELT sorry for him, that sad man sitting in the chair opposite. Will Goodman didn't look like a thug, but then, not every brute wore his inner self on the outside. The meekest-seeming of men could be the most vicious. And this man had a history that suggested he was capable of violence.

"So, why did your sister remain in the room after you left?" he asked, not for the first time. "You gotta understand how this looks. I can see that you would go there together, for a private conversation, but it wasn't her room. It was your friend who was staying there. Miss Aldridge."

"Lena."

"And you two—you and Lena—you were what, a couple?"

"I guess." Goodman shrugged and Garson sighed.

"C'mon, now. Don't you want me to help you? You got to answer the questions, else my partner out there'll come in, and you really don't want that." Garson didn't want it either. McLennan rarely did more than shout and slam things about, unless he got really riled up, but he'd never let Garson forget that he'd not been able

270

to get a civil answer out of his fellow Negro. That, more than anything else, angered him about Goodman's refusal to give a straight answer.

"I left her there because I'm a fool," he said eventually. "She talked about leaving town, about making a new life for herself. I said, fine. Go ahead. She started crying and I told her I'd had it with her tears. I walked out because—" He paused and looked Garson straight in the eye. "I walked out because I was angry."

"Angry enough that if she'd come at you, you'd have defended yourself?" He was getting close; he could feel it.

"That never happened." Will shook his head, vehement in his denial.

"So humor me. If she had attacked you first, would you have pushed her?"

For a moment Will said nothing. And then he nodded.

Alfie

December 1908

LIFE WAS GOOD. The rent was paid, and Alfie had plenty of money in his pocket for the first time ever. Even his gambling luck had changed. Word had gotten around, and Alfie found himself working several afternoons and evenings a week, giving concerts in the opulent drawing rooms of the great and good of Manhattan.

Not only that, but he hadn't realized what a relief it would be to have Jessie close by. That unsettled feeling he'd had since arriving in New York had finally subsided. He always hung around in the kitchen after he'd finished his performance for the lady of the house, the cook happy to waste a half hour or so chatting and feeding him the corn bread and leftovers that she served up to the other household servants. Jessie would steal away for a while (her fickle young mistress allowing) and the twins would talk, more than they had in years. They made plans for Jessie's half day, every Wednesday, when Alfie would usually take her to see a show at the theater. He put up with Mary Grace joining them, because it made his sister happy. In fact, he'd never openly admit it, but the girl was growing on him.

She was rough-spoken, and he still doubted that her dancing gig at the Haymarket was as straight as it seemed, but she was just hustling, same as everyone else. She dressed appropriately when she sat with Alfie and Jessie in their usual restaurant, and he'd never seen her drink alcohol. On Sundays she was in church alongside them. In latter days, he'd made a point of meeting Jessie later, making the excuse that he had business to conduct, so that she had time to talk to Mary Grace alone. He was glad that Jessie had such a good friend. He knew how lonely he'd been in those first few weeks in New York. The big city was no place to be alone.

On the afternoon of the Monday before Christmas, he went shopping for a present for Jessie. He'd noticed that the dress she wore to church was getting a little ragged, even as skilled as she was at patching it up. Of course, Alfie had not the first idea of where to buy material, or what might be in fashion for young ladies these days. Victoria was his proxy, a woman who was only a little older than Jessie and who would be welcomed into the shops that sold what Alfie needed. He didn't need to make any attempt to know that he certainly wouldn't be. She came to meet him at the Marshall Hotel, a thick, paper-wrapped parcel under her arm.

"I think she'll be very pleased," she said, and pressed her lips chastely to Alfie's cheek. It was still early, and although anyone frequenting the Marshall was used to seeing white women in the company of Black men, it didn't do to be too brazen. "And look—I even got them to tie a ribbon around."

It did look a pretty present, Alfie admitted. He'd ordered coffee for three, hoping that Jessie wouldn't be late. As a rule, she wasn't, but Mary Grace had the habit of holding her friend up.

Victoria fidgeted with her napkin. "You have warned her, haven't you?"

"She knows I want to introduce her to someone special." Alfie smiled. It was funny to see the usually confident Victoria so nervous. He hadn't known if she'd be interested in Jessie at all; he still wasn't

273

convinced that this wasn't all just a game to her, something to alleviate the stagnancy of a privileged lifestyle. "Jessie can be a little shy. If she's quiet, it don't mean that she don't like you."

"It seems to me that you're covering all eventualities," Victoria complained. "If she visibly likes me you'll say *I told you so*. And if she seems reluctant, you'll say she's just timid."

Alfie looked up and saw his sister loitering at the dining room entrance, looking around the room anxiously. He half stood and waved until she spied him, relief washing over her face. He knew that Jessie hated this sort of place. The Marshall was busy, full of people who might be Black but would still look down on a simple maid. It was a place for the ambitious. That was why Alfie had made it his preferred choice. You had to live in the manner of the life you wanted to have.

He and Victoria both stood as Jessie reached them. Alfie moved to pull out a chair for his twin and she looked at him strangely. Had he never done that before for his own sister? He supposed not. Back home, there hadn't been anywhere that warranted such a genteel action.

"Jessie, please meet Victoria Russell. She's a dear friend of mine." He placed emphasis on the word "friend," though he knew that Jessie was no fool. He remembered her reaction to seeing Victoria before and prayed this meeting would go well. "Victoria, this is my sister."

"I'm delighted to meet you." Victoria's words were welcoming, but Alfie detected a strange tone to her voice. He shot her a glance, but she was staring at Jessie.

"It's lovely to meet a friend of Alfie's."

Jessie behaved as he'd expected. Her words were polite and measured. She didn't exactly approve, but she knew that her brother wouldn't listen if she protested, so she'd just make do. Later he would wonder if he'd been too secure in his belief that Jessie needed him.

Conversation over coffee was pleasant and, as agreed beforehand,

Victoria made her excuses to leave after half an hour or so. He'd hoped that when it was just the two of them, Jessie would open up and tell him what she really thought. He was braced for her consternation, for her to ridicule him for his stupidity. For what Black man ran from a lynch mob only to go on to commit the very crime he had been falsely accused of? Alfie Aldridge might be a fool, he knew, but he also liked Victoria. This was New York, and the North was a different country from the South.

"You liked her?" he probed eventually.

"She seems very nice," came the measured response. "Wealthy."

"Her father's a lawyer and her mother's family are well-off," he admitted. "She's educated, but then, so are we in our own way."

Jessie allowed herself a short laugh. "In our own way? Yes, I suppose you could say that. I can read and write, which is something. But if you like her, then so will I. Just as long as you know what you're doing."

"Is that it?" He looked at her, bemused. This wasn't the Jessie he'd known for nineteen years. His sister had always told him what she really thought.

"Forgive me," she said, pushing back her chair. "I should go home and rest. Tar's girl has me working my fingers to the bone at the moment. She's at a party every night, it seems. She takes no care of her dresses and expects me to fix any tears or frays the moment she throws them in my face."

She did look tired, so he let her go once they'd exchanged gifts. It was a light, rectangular parcel that she gave him. A book, he guessed. He hadn't read for pleasure in so long that he couldn't fathom a guess at what it might be. A novel, though. It had been their nightly ritual when they were children, taking turns to read to each other from the latest popular book. Jessie would be spending her Christmas serving Tar's household, but he'd see her in the evening. He'd have to suffer the day with Mary Grace, but at least she'd offered to cook, and with luck Jessie wouldn't be kept out too late.

He didn't miss much about his old life, but those precious moments with his sister made him wonder how he could have left her behind so easily before.

"I TOLD YOU she'd like you," he crowed to Victoria just a few days later. She'd spent the holiday with her family, of course, but she had paid for them to spend a Friday night in one of the Marshall's well-appointed rooms.

Was it because she was a few years older or because she had seemingly limitless access to funds that she so easily walked up the stairs of the hotel on his arm? Everyone knew where they were going. What they were planning to do. Victoria held her head up high and asked for champagne to be brought up. They were lying back in bed now, drinking that champagne out of fancy glasses and listening to the rain hit the window beyond the drawn curtains, the fire keeping out the winter chill.

Victoria shifted her weight a little, moving so that she could face Alfie. "She seemed a little distracted, don't you think? I mean, I hardly know her, but still, her mind was elsewhere. You had to ask her several questions twice."

Had Jessie been distracted? He supposed so when he thought about it. She was probably just tired, though. He'd seen the dark circles under her eyes, and she'd not been eating well, the way she usually did. She'd been like that for a few weeks, Tar's daughter creating more and more work for her to do. "You think she took against you and doesn't want to show it."

"No, not exactly." Victoria drained her glass. There was clearly something on her mind. Something she didn't want to say.

"Just tell me what you're thinking. I don't mind if you two didn't hit it off first go-around. There's always time!"

Victoria turned toward him, her brow furrowed. "I might be wrong, that's all. I don't want to cause trouble where there is none."

"What on earth are you talking about?"

"I never wanted to say anything before. It's just gossip. I don't know if any of it's true." She bit her lip. "This man who you work for—Tar, as you call him—how well do you really know him?"

"He's just a fella who pays me to play piano. That's it. We're not friends." Alfie laughed. "Can you imagine? A man like that wanting to be friends with someone like me?"

"But you got Jessie that job with him?"

"Yes." Alfie thought about it for a second. "He ran into us downtown. He offered the job to Jessie when he found out that she was working her fingers to the bone at the Gilsey House. Why? Do you think he's treating her bad and she don't want to say?"

"Maybe." Victoria shook her head and looked as though she wished she'd not spoken. "It's probably nothing."

"Then you may as well just tell me." Alfie tried to laugh it off, but he had a sinking feeling that Victoria was about to douse his good mood.

"It's just something my mother said the other day. She knows that family, and ever since the wife got ill, they seem to go through maids like water through a sieve," she said eventually. "Honestly, don't take it too seriously. They're not the only household to do so."

"What would his wife getting sick have to do with . . . Oh!" Alfie guessed what Victoria was insinuating. "No, Jessie ain't like that. She'd tell me if Tar had overstepped the line."

"I'm not saying she is." Victoria put her hand up, softly caressing his jaw. "It's probably nothing. Like I said, just idle gossip. Ignore me." She let her hand slide smooth as satin down his neck, his chest, and she leaned forward to kiss him. "Jessie would tell you if something was wrong." She moved her body over his. "Let's not talk about this now."

"All right" was all he managed, the blood in his head fleeing from the terrible thought that Victoria had placed there, toward the destination of her hand.

YOU BETTER
GO NOW

27

Friday, 18 September 1936

THE WAIT FOR Louis to return home felt unbearable. Claud could hardly speak and took to pacing up and down the length of the living room. I couldn't help but imagine the worst. Garson had looked too on edge, as if he was suppressing something, as he took Will away. I'd glanced out the window as the pair of them walked toward Garson's car, two women across the street clearly gossiping, their eyes firmly on Will. People would know by now. They'd be sitting down to dinner and talking about Will and Bel.

"Do you think he did it?" Claud asked me. Her tone was a little accusatory, as if she was expecting me to wash my hands of Will now that things had become complicated.

"No, of course not," I said. "Will doesn't have it in him to harm . . ." I'd almost said *anyone*, but I knew that wasn't true. "He and Bel had their struggles, but why would he push her?" I thought back to Saturday night. When we'd caught Bel snooping, he'd looked not angry, just disappointed in her. Worried that I might judge her harshly. "Besides, he isn't the type to lie about it even if he had done it."

"That's true," Claud said, finally sitting down. "After the fight with Henry, Will admitted everything. Why he'd done it, what his intentions had been, the lot. Even when the lawyer asked him . . ." She paused to catch her breath. "Will said that if Louis hadn't grabbed hold of him, he'd have kept hitting Henry. That he might not have stopped until he was dead." She looked at me. "He told them everything. If he's saying nothing now, then he's innocent."

It made good sense, and I trusted it, but I knew what the police would argue. That Will had learned what happened when you were too honest. That his stint in jail had toughened him up and prepared him for the real world, where before he'd been just a young, idealistic student.

Louis's key sounded in the lock and Claud leaped across to open the door before he could turn the door handle.

"What's happened?" he asked, putting down his bag and pulling Claud into a tight hug.

"Will's at the police station," I told him. "Detective Garson came to take him away."

"Garson? All right." Louis let go of his wife. "Then I'll need to go and make a telephone call. Wait here. I know someone. An old college friend of Will's who takes criminal cases."

"Criminal cases?" Claud's panic rose.

"Honey, that's what this is. You understand?" Louis kissed her on the forehead. "If they charge Will, then the best-case scenario is manslaughter. That's if they believe that it was an accident."

He didn't need to tell us the alternative charge—murder. My heart beat faster. Surely they couldn't think that. Even if they used Will's temper against him, they'd see that it could only have been an awful accident. A struggle gone wrong or something of that sort.

"Uncle Will didn't do it."

We all whipped around to see Joey, a battered old teddy bear under her arm as if to emphasize her youth and innocence. She was dressed in pajamas that were a little too big for her, an old cardigan that must have been Claud's wrapped around her torso, falling almost to her knees.

"Darling girl, you shouldn't be out of bed." Claud started to fuss, but Joey dodged out of her way.

"I'm not tired, Aunt Claud. I want to help Uncle Will."

"Sure you do, honey, but this is where the grown-ups have to take charge." Louis strode over and patted her on the head. "It'll all be fine. Trust me. Whatever else happens, your uncle Will isn't going to jail."

"Cross your heart?" she asked.

"Cross my heart. Swear on my life."

He used his finger to place the X across his chest, and I heard Claud take a quick breath. I knew what she was thinking; I was thinking it too. That it was too cavalier of Louis to make such a promise when none of us knew what would happen. How would he explain it to Joey if he was wrong?

"I know Uncle Will didn't do it. He told me the other day that he was going to stay in New York. That the three of us were going to get a nicer apartment and live all together. Why would he say that if it wasn't true?"

Will had made plans to stay? He hadn't said a word to me, or to Claud and Louis, judging from their faces.

Louis left and Claud pushed Joey back toward the bedroom. I knew that I should probably go and leave them to it, but the thought of that sad hotel room made me wince, and I wanted to be there in case Will came home. It was worth clinging to the scrap of hope that Garson really did care about getting to the truth and not just taking the easy route to closing the case.

"I'll make some cocoa," I shouted through to Claud.

She didn't reply, so I went ahead and put the milk on to warm in a pan on the stove. The tin of Hershey's Breakfast Cocoa was only a quarter full, and I added it to a mental shopping list for the next day. If nothing else, I could repay the Linfields' kindness by taking care of a few groceries while they had bigger worries. I added spoonfuls of sugar to three mugs and poured the milk in slowly, making a paste first, the way my father had taught me. That way you didn't get the lumps of the amateur cocoa maker. There was a half bottle of whiskey tucked up high on a shelf, and I added generous glugs to two of the mugs. I took one laced, one unadulterated cocoa through to the bedroom, where, in a reversal of the usual bedtime scenario, Joey was reading to Claud.

"Here." I handed Claud her mug, being sure she got the boozy one, Joey reaching eagerly for the other. "Warm milk always helps me to sleep."

"Did you want to stay and listen?" Joey asked. Her eyes were puffy from crying, but she seemed as well as a ten-year-old child could be following the death of her mother. "It's *Emil and the Detectives*. It's about a boy the same age as me. He lives alone with his mother because his father's died. When his mother sends him to stay with relatives, he gets robbed and has to find the thief."

"Not my choice," Claud muttered, as if Joey hadn't shown herself to be quite capable of making her own decisions. "Don't you think we should read something happier?"

"This is happy, Aunt Claud," Joey informed her. "Emil gets the reward money in the end. Which maybe I shouldn't have told you, but I figured you'd work that much out."

Claud rolled her eyes and drank from her mug, raising her eyebrows at me as she tasted the whiskey. "Someone else has been making interesting choices."

We heard the click and creak of the front door; Louis had returned. Claud looked from me to Joey.

"Aunt Claud, I'm perfectly all right," Joey said. "I'll just sit here and read my book. Go and find out what's happening."

When Claud and I went out Louis was alone in the living room, midpour with a glass in one hand and a fresh bottle of rum in the other. "You're going to want to sit down for this," he said, his face grim.

We did so, waiting patiently for him to join us. I lit a cigarette and tried to stop my hand from shaking. I knew what Louis was going to say and I wanted more than anything for it not to be true.

"Will's been arrested for Bel's murder," he said, sinking down heavily into the armchair.

I had braced myself for his words and yet they shook me even still. It was nonsense. There was no way that Will had done this. But someone had. My hands began to tremble and I clasped them tight, pushing my palms together as hard as I could to stop myself from bursting into tears.

"According to what evidence?" Claud cried out. "The police barely looked around the apartment. They just took a few fingerprints and then left."

"It wasn't helpful in this case," Louis said gently. "There was never any suspicion of a stranger being in the room with Bel. We've all been living here for the past week, Will included. Our fingerprints were all over everything anyway."

It was so unfair. Will didn't deserve this. I'd brought him bad luck. If I hadn't come to Harlem, Bel would still be alive and Will would be safe back on the *Queen Mary*. This was all my fault. Bel had been tempted by my money, by my life perhaps. Was that why she'd taken my passport? I knew what it was to live a life that had ground to a halt, the temptation that any new opportunity posed. Bel and I—we had far more in common than I liked to admit.

"Why would Will want to harm Bel?" I asked. "Have the police said what motive they're trying to pin on him?"

"Jealousy." Louis looked doubtful as Claud snorted. "Revenge? Everyone knows what happened ten years ago, and Will has the criminal record to go with it. Bel didn't go to watch him perform at the Apollo the other night and Garson thinks it's because the pair of them were estranged. That they'd fallen out, and that something happened that night. The straw that broke the camel's back, as it were."

"But Bel had to work! It's as simple as that, not this fairy tale they've drummed up to pin it all on Will." They couldn't just make up a story like that, could they? "Can't Leon tell them that?" He'd looked like a man who was familiar to the police, but he was also a businessman, and there would have been a whole host of drinkers in the bar who could vouch for Bel's attendance that night.

"Apparently she wasn't at work at all," Louis said, and my heart sank. "She lied about that. Maybe for the very reason that Garson says. He thinks that she was happy with her current living arrangements and didn't want anything to change. Think about it," he invited us, as if he'd already bought into Garson's version of events. "Will stays on his ship, well away from Harlem, and hands over her rent money every fortnight. If Will decided to stay here, then that'd mean less money for his sister."

"Then get Joey to speak to Garson," I said. "Didn't she tell us already that the plan was for the three of them to get a better apartment, together?" I tried to ignore the needle-sharp pang that hit me when I remembered that Will had started setting out his future and hadn't told me. "Why wouldn't Bel want to live somewhere nicer?"

"And if Bel was worried about losing out on money, wouldn't that lead to her being mad at Will, not the other way around?" Claud made a good point.

"Yes, except that Garson thinks that she did do something. God knows what, 'cause it's all conjecture right now, but he thinks that Bel threatened Will. She sent him to jail, after all, and she let the rumors about him persist. Bel skipped out on work, made a big song and dance about talking to Will alone, and then she winds up dead and Will has no alibi. What was it she wanted to talk to him about? Will won't say, which isn't helping."

I could see how, to a police detective, Will looked incredibly guilty. "Neither of you heard anything that night?" I asked, desperate. "What were they doing in the bedroom?"

Claud and Louis exchanged a glance. "I heard them arguing." Claud sighed. "Though it was more of a squabble. The door was open a crack and I peered in to make sure everything was all right, but they were barely talking louder than we are now. No shouting or pushing. Nothing that would suggest violence."

Louis nodded. "Question is, how do we explain that if we get asked? Soon as we confirm that there was some sort of falling-out between them, that's just more ammunition against Will."

Everything was happening so fast, I felt breathless. Will had been right here, in front of me, just a few hours ago. If I'd known it could be the last time I saw him free . . . "Will we be able to see Will?" Would he trust me enough to tell me what they'd been arguing about, if he wouldn't tell the police?

"I don't know." Louis scratched his chin, his fingernails rasping against stubble. "He's got a lawyer, at least, the fella I called. MacAllister, his name is, and he knows the history between Will and Bel. He thinks that with a lack of evidence we have a small chance of at least getting bail."

"I have money," I said. Wasn't that what it came down to very often? Those with access to funds avoided the worst of it. Much as with the rest of life. "I can help if you need it. For bail."

"Thank you, Lena, but that won't be necessary," Louis told me. "We look after our own here. We got money put aside for a rainy day. And today it seems to be pouring cats and dogs."

I glanced at Claud, who had her hand pressed once more against her belly. Could they really afford to pay for Will's bail? For this lawyer who was surely charging a pretty penny, friend or not? "Honestly, I'd like to help Will," I said. "Please let me do something."

"Guilty conscience?" Louis asked, and for the first time I felt something shift between us. The aura of frustration that had surrounded him since he'd returned to the apartment spread out toward me. "We don't need anything else from you, Lena. You've done enough."

"Louis!" Claud was as shocked as I. "What's got into you?"

"I'm sorry," he told me, but he didn't look it. Not really. "I just can't help but think that none of this would have happened if you hadn't come here. Haven't you been thinking the same thing?"

My presence in Will's life had been the lit match dropped into the dry tinder of his relationship with his sister. "But how could I have known? How could any of us have?"

He lowered his head into his hands. "I don't know, Lena. Really, I don't. But I think you should leave now. Just for tonight. Come back tomorrow when we've all had some sleep."

It seemed like a good idea, so I didn't bother to argue. I'd return the next day, rested, and we'd make a plan. I didn't realize that they'd already made one without me.

28

Saturday, 19 September 1936

YOU'D HAVE THOUGHT that I'd have trouble sleeping, after everything that had happened, but in fact I slept like a baby that night. The best sleep I'd had in weeks. A few doors down from the Olga was a small restaurant that did hot coffee, and in the morning I treated myself to a plate of waffles. Indulgent food, but I needed it, even if the waistband of my skirt said otherwise. It was almost ten o'clock by the time I'd finished, but I knew that Claud would be at home, the dutiful wife sitting in to wait for news and take care of her goddaughter. I hoped that Louis would be at work. His tone of the previous evening still rankled, even if I half agreed with him.

I still had my key, but in light of recent events, I let myself in only through the main entrance, and knocked on the Linfields' apartment door. Claud answered, not looking surprised that I hadn't just let myself in.

"George is here," she said, and then, when I looked confused: "Will's friend from college. The lawyer."

His best hope, then. I followed her eagerly into the living room, where I was to be sorely disappointed. George MacAllister was, well, not what I'd expected. A skinny white man who looked like he still should have been in school, though he must have been older than I if he'd studied with Will. His suit was wrinkled, and his spectacles sat wonkily on his nose. He was a mouse, not the lion I had hoped would fight for Will's freedom.

"Miss Aldridge?" He stood up from the armchair, Louis's usual seat, juggling a cup of coffee and a plate of pound cake that Claud had no doubt foisted upon him. He held out a hand and I leaned forward to shake it, his grip surprisingly firm. "I'm glad to meet you. I know that Will was keen that I speak with you."

"Really?" Perhaps I should have been less surprised, but after the way Louis had spoken the day before, I was beginning to wonder if I had any right to still be lingering. I went to sit beside Claud on the sofa. She squeezed my hand, and I knew that George MacAllister had not come with good news.

"I was just saying to Claud that this is going to be tricky," he said, "but that I think we have a chance."

"A slim chance," Claud muttered.

"It's too soon to give up hope." His tone was that of a stern father. "Now, I don't think that bail is an option. We go before the judge this afternoon, and I want you to set your expectations accordingly. Problem being Will's place of work. A ship that leaves from New York on Wednesday. The prosecution will argue that even with the shipping line notified, Will has too many friends who could sneak him on board, and he'd be on his way to England before anyone knew he'd vanished."

"That's ridiculous!" I said. "So he just has to rot in jail until the trial?"

"The other option is for me to try and get the case thrown out. There were a hell of a lot of people at the party. The police don't have any evidence that Will pushed Bel, or that he was even in the room when she fell. No evidence really that she didn't just fall of her own accord, only the fact that it doesn't make sense. Why would she have been leaning out that far? We don't know." He stopped to take a sip of coffee. "My argument is that there's no real motive there either. Will paid Bel's rent, had done for years. There was no suggestion that the arrangement was going to cease. Will has a prior criminal record, but he behaved well in prison. The only instance of violence they can pin on him is the fight with Henry Bennett. Will was never abusive toward his sister; in fact, the incident with Henry is proof that he was more than willing to defend her."

"That's good, then," I insisted. "They're just putting two and two together and coming up with five. Will's an honest man. Truly, I believe that."

"Ah." MacAllister's face fell slightly. "See, that's another slight problem. Will lied about his past to get his first job on the ships. A little white lie, as far as most of us are concerned, but a lie nonetheless."

"How can they know that?" Claud clung to hope.

"They just put two and two together and checked with the shipping line," George told her. "Where did Will get his references from? How did he explain the gaps in employment? The jury will decide if they think he lied or not. Even if he didn't lie explicitly, the prosecution will say that an honest man would have told the truth even if it meant losing out on work."

"That's stupid." I could feel the rage bubbling up in my stomach. This was an impossible situation. How was Will supposed to defend himself against such petty arguments? "I mean, are they trying to say that anyone who tells a tiny white lie must be capable of murder? Without that tiny lie, Will wouldn't have got a decent job. He wouldn't have been able to pay Bel's rent all these years. He'd be stuck doing menial work, earning pennies and barely able to support himself."

"That's not the point, though." George stood up and began to pace back and forth before us, as if practicing for court. As if we were his jury. "Think logically. It's a game, Lena. They will throw anything and everything they have against Will. If he cheated on a term paper at college, that shows a man who will take shortcuts to get what he wants." He held up a hand to Claud, who was half standing, indignation heating the air around her. "I know, Claud, I know. Will never cheated. It's just an example of what they'll be doing if we end up going to trial."

No way to prove that Will wasn't in the bedroom when Bel fell. No need for the prosecution to prove that he pushed his sister to her death.

"I wish I'd told her to leave." Claud looked miserable. "God, how I wish. I knew whatever she wanted to talk to Will about, it was nothing good. I should have checked up on them. I've stuck my nose in enough times when things have been rough between them. Why'd I choose this one time to keep my silence?"

I knew her regret. If I hadn't been distracted by Rosa . . . "But we know that Will was with Teddy when the alarm went up," I said. "Teddy's said as much."

"Sure." George nodded. "But the patrolman says it took him a while to rouse the residents downstairs. I guess the music up here stopped any of you from hearing him knocking. Even Will admits that he'd only had time to exchange a few words with Teddy. That's his only alibi, that and he stopped by the kitchen to get a drink. But no one can confirm that. He reckons it was at least five minutes between him leaving the bedroom and reaching Teddy, but as far as the cops are concerned, he had time to push Bel and make a beeline for Teddy to cover his back."

I tried to pay attention as George ran over the events of that fatal night. The police claimed that the murder had been a spur-of-the-moment thing, a violent push driven by passion and rage. I remembered the mascara-stained mug. I didn't think that the police were wrong about what happened. I just knew that they had the wrong man. Someone else had a reason to be angry at Bel, and there was one person who would be more than happy to talk.

ROSA AND GLO'S apartment seemed paradoxically smaller without the crush of people within it. During the rent party I'd not really paid attention to the décor, but as I sat waiting for Rosa to mix me a gin and juice, I took the time to have a proper gander. Artwork hung on the walls, Harlem tableaux of brownstones and brown folk, children playing and cars driving past. I recognized the Apollo in the background of one, and the subway station at 125th and Lenox. Hardly enough to call myself a New Yorker yet, but I felt stupidly pleased to have pinpointed the landmarks.

"Glo paints," Rosa said, returning with the drinks.

"She did these?" I was surprised, but I didn't know Glo at all. I just knew that I'd been glad when Rosa had told me she was at work. "They're really good."

"They do add some color to the place," Rosa agreed. "So, what's new?"

"They arrested Will," I told her, and took a sip of gin. "We got him a lawyer, but without anyone to corroborate that he wasn't in the room when Bel fell . . ."

"And you don't think he did it?"

"Of course not. And I don't think you do either."

"I don't know anything. Like I said, I just want to find out the truth." She pulled out her cigarettes and I guarded my silence, knowing that she had more to say. "What if he did do it?"

"I don't believe that." I shook my head and took a cigarette from her case, joining her in a nicotine haze. "But I do think that Bel was up to something. And I think you know what it was. You talked to her that night."

She didn't answer for a moment, but I could see that she was thinking. Whatever was going on, I already knew that it wasn't just her secret. "She wasn't herself," she said finally. "She came to see Glo that afternoon. I wasn't here—I was rehearsing for the Apollo—but Glo mentioned it when I got home. Said that Bel had come to pay back five dollars that she borrowed months ago, and that she'd been all excited about something. She told Glo . . ." She gave me an apologetic look. "She said that you weren't who you said you were. That she was worried about Will and that she had a plan. She said you'd regret trying to take her brother for a ride."

I thought about the money that Bel had found. Did she think that I'd stolen it? That I was some sort of master criminal? Was that what she'd been arguing with Will about?

Rosa went on: "Then, when we were at the party, she asked me to go speak to you. Distract you. She said that she wanted to speak to Will alone and she was worried that you'd walk in on them. She wanted me to give her more time."

"So, she wanted to tell Will that I was a bad influence? He's a grown man. There's nothing Bel knew about me that Will didn't." Ignoring the fact that there was a hell of a lot that Will didn't know about me.

"I don't know." Rosa looked genuinely mystified. "She just said something about Will deserving better, that she was going to give it to him straight. Glo thought it was weird. Like she was settling up. Wally did that to her before he left town for good last month. Paid off his bills, settled old debts, then left for Philadelphia."

The passport. Bel had died clutching my identity in her hand. Could she have been planning to take it, along with the money? We didn't look that much alike, skin tone aside, but I'd heard it was easy enough to doctor a passport if you knew what you were doing. Had she been about to skip town?

"Did Bel know anyone—" How to phrase it . . . ? "Not to be rude, but anyone crooked?"

Rosa laughed. "You ever go to Leon's? You can hardly take a step without bumping into some fella with a scheme."

I remembered the bar, and Leon himself. "I suppose that answers that." So if Bel had had my passport and a wad of cash, she could have gotten herself some shiny new identification. In my name but with her likeness. Ready to start over somewhere new.

"Look," Rosa said, "I like you. Against my better judgment. Bel and Will, they had a strange relationship going on. I never believed that story about Will being in love with her. It was too neat, that whole spiel. Coming out when it did, right after he'd gone to the Tombs and she was trying to make it up to Henry. I know Bel wasn't always straight with people."

I chose my words carefully. "Did Bel ever say why she didn't trust me?"

Rosa shrugged. "Honestly, I thought it was just Bel being Bel. I figured she didn't like that Will might be moving back here permanently, and she didn't like the competition. Nothing more than that."

I walked back to the Hotel Olga shortly afterward, not wanting to be in the apartment when Glo got home from work. My conversation with Rosa had been more confusing than enlightening. Bel had wanted to tell Will that I was no good for him, but then what had happened? I'd hoped to find out something to use in Will's favor, but telling the police what I knew would skew the balance against him.

Because what it boiled down to was that Bel had told Will something he hadn't wanted to hear, and shortly afterward she'd been pushed to her death.

29

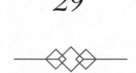

Sunday, 20 September 1936

"A DREADFUL BUSINESS." Ida shook her head and sighed heavily. "Of course he didn't do it. William doesn't have a bad bone in his body. I never bought the tall tales that Bennett boy spouted neither. I can smell a liar from fifty paces, and Henry Bennett could hardly open that mouth of his without spilling untruths from it."

"I'm glad you believe him," I said, and sipped weak, too-sweet coffee from the china cup she'd given me. I'd gone to church that morning, but the Linfields had been absent. From the sideways glances I caught directed at me, I was glad they had, Bel's death on everyone's mind. I'd sought Ida out after the service and hovered until she invited me to her apartment for coffee and cake. "It all seems so hopeless, though. Will can't prove he didn't push Bel, which seems ridiculous when the police can't prove that he did."

"He's in my prayers" was her answer. "Mark my words—the good Lord will see to it that justice is done."

I wasn't so sure. God hadn't exactly stepped in when Henry Bennett was beating his wife and sleeping around behind her back. In fact, he'd let her one protector get punished for protecting her. Although, come to think of it, he had sent that garbage truck to send Bennett to hell, so there was a slim chance that Ida was right.

"Now, don't look so glum. Remember I said I'd ask around about your aunt Jessie?"

I perked right up. "Oh yes! Did you find out anything from your friend? Etta, was it?"

"Etta, yes, but no." Ida reached down the side of her armchair. "There was another girl. Not Jessie but a friend of hers named Mary Grace. A jezebel if ever there was one, and I warned Jessie not to go with her, but young girls have no common sense. Mary Grace's great ambition in life was to dance on the stage, if you can believe that!"

I winced. Had Ida forgotten what I did for a living?

"They moved out of Harlem and down to the Tenderloin, against my advice." She sniffed as though her nose was still out of joint following this slight. "There were a lot more colored folk down there in those days, and a whole heap of dens of iniquity for a girl with loose morals. I hardly saw Jessie after that, maybe once or twice more. I assumed that she got too busy to remember me. Found herself a husband or took up the dancing herself; either way, I forgot about her entirely."

Ida seemed less innocently benevolent now, reminding me more than a little of my former landlady in London. She had loved to lecture me on my loose morals. Of course, I'd been having an affair with a married man at the time, but it wasn't as if she'd known that. I'd hated the old bag, the feeling mutual, but I'd also been convinced that the woman hadn't always been so virtuous herself. I was now getting a strong whiff of the same sour sort of hypocrisy off Ida Barker.

"You mentioned this friend. Mary?" I tried to move her back to the point.

"Mary Grace, yes. Well, like I said, I forgot about Jessie. Mary

Grace too, until Etta reminded me." I nodded and hoped that this wasn't just a chance for Ida to get some morality tale off her chest. "I was talking to her yesterday, after I'd been to see you and Claudette, and she pointed out that Mary Grace has been in our congregation for the past ten years! Can you believe that? I never knew. Didn't recognize her."

No longer the jezebel, then. "She's changed since she was a girl?"

"I'll say." Ida shook her head in giddy disbelief. "Mrs. Grace Butterworth. That's her name these days; that's why I never put two and two together. Her husband's a bank manager and they have two wonderful children who went to our Sunday school when they were little. Samuel and Antonia. Samuel's following in his father's footsteps, and lovely Antonia got married this past spring to a very impressive young man from Chicago."

"And Mrs. Butterworth might remember Jessie. She might know where she is now." I sat up in my chair. "Where can I find her? Was she at church this morning?"

Why the bloody hell didn't you introduce us? was what I wanted to ask, but you catch more flies with honey than with vinegar. Ida seemed pleased to mete out her knowledge in tiny drips, but I was running out of time, and my last few days in New York had to be focused on freeing Will. Finding Jessie had started to feel like an impossible task, but if Grace Butterworth could give me an address or a clue, I'd be daft not to go and see her. If nothing else, it was my duty. If Alfie really had cut off all contact with his past, then Jessie wouldn't even know that he was dead. Someone should tell her.

"Now, actually, she wasn't at church today and neither was her husband. It might be that they're away. They do visit Antonia in Chicago every couple of months, now that there's a baby on the way."

Any slight hope I'd had of getting a definitive answer about Jessie Aldridge faded quickly. "Oh well. Thank you for letting me know, Ida. I do appreciate it."

"Well, dear, you can't just give up like that. Why don't you call around to the apartment tomorrow? They just moved to the Dunbar. Eighth Avenue between 149th and 150th. At the very least, the doorman might know when they'll be back."

It seemed worth a shot. I left Ida's shortly afterward and wandered aimlessly for a while. I'd always struggled a little with Sundays. A day of rest when I felt the lack of purpose in my life more keenly. The clubs were closed, the theaters dark. No family to cook a lavish Sunday dinner for, to settle down before the wireless with. I'd been to church more often in the past eight days than in the past eight years. Not enough to get on God's good list. Was there any point in praying that Will would survive this ordeal?

Three days until the *Queen Mary* was due to take me back to England. My ticket was secure, still tucked away in my safety-deposit box at the Sherry-Netherland. Just a few days earlier I'd been considering whether to give it up. Whether New York could become the home I'd envisaged when I'd left from Southampton less than a month earlier. Of course, then I'd thought I had a job here. That I had connections that would make starting my new life easy. Even once those plans had evaporated, there had been Will.

Was it too soon to call it love? It was more than I'd felt for any man before. I barely knew him and yet I believed totally that he was innocent. Not that I didn't think he might have it in him to get angry. To lose his temper and give a little push. To be horrified as his stepsister toppled from the window. I knew he was capable of that, as was I. In the heat of the moment these things can happen. What I didn't believe was that Will would have let Bel suffer. He wouldn't have left her on those steps, all alone, waiting to die. He would have owned up to his mistake; I was sure of it. Will Goodman wasn't a coward.

There had been so many people in the apartment, and yet no one had seen anything. No one admitted to seeing her fall, and yet someone must have. Bel hadn't thrown herself out of the window. She'd been rifling through my personal belongings; that much was known.

She had my passport in her hand. I had hidden the money, but wouldn't she have continued searching until she found it? She wasn't a quitter when it came to self-preservation, according to anyone who'd known her. The problem was that any way I looked at it, Will had the strongest motive. She'd engineered the meeting with him, had taken him away from the party to . . . what? Confront him? Sit him down and tell him her concerns about me? It was too easy to imagine an argument flaring, hot tempers clashing. One push. An accident, but one that would see Will jailed for the second time. His new life crushed before it had even begun. And why hadn't Will told me about his plans to stay in Harlem with Bel and Joey? Because I hadn't told him the truth, that I was thinking about staying too?

I had wandered too far up St. Nicholas Avenue. Having cut through Colonial Park, I found myself on 149th. Wasn't that close to where Ida had told me that Jessie's friend lived? I retrieved the scrunched-up paper from my bag, Ida's childlike handwriting marking the address. The Dunbar Apartments. I carried on along until I found the building. I had nothing to lose, after all. If the woman was in Chicago, then there was nothing I could do about it. At least I'd know I tried.

Much as I tried to convince myself that there would be no one at home, by the time I arrived at the apartment door, my heart was thudding. I took a few deep breaths before ringing the bell, silently hoping that there would be no answer. I didn't want to find out that Alfie had kept his family a secret. With everything else going on, I couldn't have the memory of my father shaken. But then I heard footsteps and had to brace myself.

The woman who answered the door—Mrs. Grace Butterworth—was handsome and well-dressed. She was clearly well-to-do, as her address implied, and her smart dress didn't look like just Sunday best.

"Yes?"

"Oh, hello." I hadn't thought how to start the conversation. "I'm terribly sorry to bother you but—you are Mrs. Butterworth?"

"I am." She tilted her head, looking interested rather than annoyed at my interrupting her on the Lord's day.

"My name is Lena Aldridge. You'll think me foolish, but I was given your name by Ida Barker and . . ."

"That old bag?" Grace's demeanor slipped. "Are you a friend of hers?"

"No," I said hurriedly. "No, I was only led to her because I was looking for . . . Well, I was hoping you can help me to track somebody down. Ida thought you used to know her. I'm not from here, you see."

"I can tell." She gave me the once-over, her sharp gaze raking from my shoes to my hat.

"And so," I went on quickly, before she could dismiss me, "Ida thought that you might have known this woman. Jessie Aldridge? She said that you had been friends at one time."

"Jessie?" Grace Butterworth looked shaken. "You'd better come in."

I followed her into the apartment, down a carpeted hallway, and into the living room. The Butterworths were not poor. Bold, bright paintings adorned the walls, and a large vase, big enough to fit a small child, dominated one corner of the room. The furniture was modern. Apart from the latest issue of *The Crisis*, resting open on one sofa cushion, where Grace had no doubt abandoned it when I'd rung the bell, there was no clutter.

"Lemonade?" Grace offered. "I can't abide hot drinks."

"Yes, please." I sat down on the opposite side of the sofa while she bustled off to the kitchen. I heard the clink of glasses and the fizzy pop of the bottle top. Where was Mr. Butterworth?

"My husband has gone to Chicago," she said as she came back, handing me a cool glass as she answered my unasked question.

"Ida said that your daughter lives there," I said, trying to make small talk.

"Yes. Antonia." She smiled. "I have a meeting tomorrow and

then I head out. Our grandchild's due any day now. And Terrence, he dotes on Toni. Has done since the day she was born." She paused, her face turning serious. "But you didn't come here to talk about me."

"No," I agreed, "and I might be wasting your time. I'm sorry if that's the case, but you might be able to at least clear something up for me."

"About Jessie?"

"Yes. You'll have noticed that we share a surname. My father lived in New York before he moved to England, almost thirty years ago now. He died recently and when I found myself here, I wondered if perhaps . . . He never spoke of family, you see, never mentioned a sister. I don't know why." My throat was dry, and I took a sip of the lemonade, its sweetness making me wince. "Did she happen to mention a brother?"

Grace nodded slowly. "Alfie. I knew him, briefly. That was my first year in New York. Before I met my husband."

"I don't suppose—"

"I knew him well," she said. "I can tell you exactly why he left New York."

Jessie

January 1909

THE SNOWSTORM HAD left the city looking like a faraway fairy-tale land. Jessie looked out of her mistress's bedroom window to the park across the street, its trees sparkling in the sunlight, their branches like glass, long stalactites hanging from the iron railings. The road between the house and the park gates was a smooth blanket of pristine white. It was after eight o'clock, but the usual morning deliveries had been rendered impossible. The roads were impassable, and the city had come to a standstill. It looked beautiful but Jessie knew how treacherous the ground was. She'd struggled to get to work the Friday before, finally arriving an hour late, and had been ordered to remain resident in the servants' quarters over the weekend. A woman in her condition should not be traversing the length of the city in such weather. Though of course, no one knew about her condition. Only Mary Grace.

"You got to tell him," her friend had insisted the week before.

"At the very least you can get some money for it. Then get out of that house!"

"I need that job! And what am I supposed to tell Alfie?"

"You just take the money and then you get rid of it," Mary Grace had said, her arm around a sobbing Jessie. "Worry about Alfie afterward."

"Get rid of it?" She hadn't understood.

"There are ways and means." Mary Grace had pressed her hand firmly against Jessie's stomach. "You're too late for the easy option, for pills and potions and whatnot, but I know a woman who knows all the tricks. She ain't cheap, though. That's why you need the money."

The price the woman charged was more than Jessie usually earned in a month. Why this old hag lived in a dirty tenement like anyone else was beyond Jessie. The woman lived on a street lined with whorehouses; she must have more business than she could cope with. But then, perhaps not everyone took that road. The path to hell, Jessie thought as she'd sat in church the Sunday before, Alfie at her side, ignorant of his sister's torment. Her mother would have whipped her and then told her to accept her fate. A baby was a blessing, until it grew older, and then everyone would see it for the curse it was. A bastard. Another mouth to feed. That was without even thinking about the looks. The child wouldn't look like Jessie. Everyone would know what she'd done.

There was only one other person she trusted to tell. She told Alfie that she would have to stay late at work one night, but instead she traveled up to Harlem.

"You've put on weight" was the first thing that Ida said to her when she opened the door. "You must be doing well for yourself."

Jessie avoided answering. She'd come for advice, not to give a confession. Her pride wouldn't let her admit to this woman that she'd been right, though not in the way she'd thought. It wasn't the Tenderloin that had ruined Jessie.

"I know you do good works," she said as Ida placed a hot cup of cocoa before her. "The mission, the girls you rescue. I wondered . . . I have a friend who's found herself in a certain position." She took a breath, feeling Ida's keen eyes on her. "There's going to be a baby, and she wishes that there weren't. Is there any hope for someone like her? Getting rid of the baby would be a sin, but she also can't afford to keep it. Are there still places for babies like that?"

Ida grunted, but Jessie saw her shuffle herself into a more comfortable position on her chair, ready to begin her proclamation. "My first piece of advice is to cut off all ties with that girl," she said. "Is it someone I know?"

Jessie knew Ida was thinking of Mary Grace and shook her head vehemently. "Just someone I used to work with at the hotel, is all."

"Oh." Ida looked a little disappointed. "Well, girls like that, they are damned either way. She can take the baby to an orphanage, but all she'll be doing is condemning that poor child to a life just like her mother's. Better she honor her responsibility and pay the price for her actions rather than expect the city to take care of them."

Jessie left feeling worse than before. It wasn't as if she'd anticipated a magical solution, but she had hoped that Ida would give her a second option. Really, it was ridiculous. Mary Grace would have laughed if she'd known who Jessie had turned to for help. A judgmental self-proclaimed martyr. How could she be expected to offer advice that wasn't tinged by her own beliefs? Ida had been right about Mary Grace in one regard. She had lain with more than one man without worrying about whether a ring would be forthcoming. But Mary Grace understood the risk and knew what to do if the worst happened. Without her, Jessie wouldn't have known what to do.

"**WHERE IS MY** new dress?" Miss Elizabeth slammed into the room. "I wish to pay a visit to Loretta Kingsland, and I know she will be green with envy once she sees it."

"But the snow—"

"Has stopped falling." Miss Elizabeth paced to the window and raised the sash, needles of icy air shooting into the room. "See? I can see people in the park, walking. You can go home, Jessie, once you've done your work. Don't say I'm not generous."

Jessie ran to fetch the dress from the press, knowing that her mistress's patience was on a short fuse. Imagine if she knew that her maid concealed her half sibling beneath her apron! But she could never find out. The only other person who needed to know was Tar. And only because he was the source of the fee that Jessie needed to put this sorry incident behind her.

She'd been foolish. Of course one thing had led to another. She'd felt sorry for him, and he'd been gentle at first. The small gifts, just trinkets really, had turned her head and made her feel as though she were something to this man, no matter how removed their stations from each other. She saw Tar's wife each day and she saw the woman shrinking, weakening. When Tar sobbed onto Jessie's shoulder, she had known him to be genuinely heartbroken. He was just in need of solace, she'd reasoned as he'd kissed her. His wife could no longer provide for his needs, she'd reminded herself as he suggested that they lie down and hold each other. For comfort. But then comfort had turned into desire, and she had not wanted to turn him away. She was ashamed to say that she had been as eager as he by that point. He was a handsome man still, despite the many years he had on her. And when the small whispers of doubt crept into her head, she dismissed them. She knew perfectly well what her brother and Victoria got up to at the Marshall Hotel. If a woman from a well-to-do family like Victoria's didn't see the harm in it, why should Jessie?

She'd been too cowardly to confront Tar while she was trapped indefinitely in his house. How would he react? Angrily, she feared. Back home, there had been a young woman from church who was found dead one morning in a ditch on the outskirts of town. Her married lover had fled the night before. He'd known that the child she was carrying would alert his wife to his misdeeds and in a panic had thrust a knife into her belly. Mary Grace had warned Jessie to stay close to the door when she told him, so that she could run if she needed to. She didn't think that Tar had it in him, but she would pay attention all the same. Ignoring sage advice was what had gotten her in trouble in the first place.

Miss Elizabeth went out after the midday meal, and her mother was resting in her bedroom. It had become an odd ritual, for Jessie to bring Tar his hot drink and to be invited to sit, knowing that she was expected to listen to his wise words, before letting him undress her. In the beginning it had been exciting. She had felt chosen; he'd told her as much. Now that it had become more of a habit, she wasn't so sure that Tar would not be just as happy to thrust himself into any girl who was willing. He liked her because she was clean. Innocent and free of disease. He'd known from the beginning that he was the only man she'd ever lain with.

"Is something the matter?" Tar sipped his coffee, looking perplexed. Usually, Jessie poured his drink and sat right down, waiting for his address to begin.

She fumbled with her apron strings and shifted her weight. The heavy desk was between her and her employer. The door was closed, but she knew she could turn on her heel in an instant and be out of the room before he was on his feet. "Sir, there's something I need to talk to you about." She took a breath. "I need money."

He sighed heavily. "Money? Come on, Jessie. Don't I treat you well? And I pay far better than your previous job. You've told me so yourself."

"Oh yes, sir. Ordinarily I wouldn't . . . I mean . . ." She had to do this. There was no other way. "I—there's a baby." She couldn't look at him, fixing her eyes on the brass paperweight that kept his papers anchored to his desk. "There's a woman who can help me, but she needs to be paid."

The silence grew so heavy that Jessie felt an affinity with those papers, pressed down onto the solid wood by the dense metal. When she dared to raise her eyes to see his expression, he was staring off into the distance, his fingers steepled as he sat back in his chair.

"It's illegal," he said finally. "You know that?"

"Yes, sir," she replied. "I don't want to do it, but I can't afford a child. And my brother—he doesn't know. I can't bear to tell him."

"And yet you have not asked if I would support you." He spoke slowly, and she detected a note of approval that made her feel a little nauseated. "It is an inconvenience, I suppose, but I'm impressed by your pragmatism, Jessie. I suppose it is an advantage of your race, not to be ruled by emotion."

Jessie dug her fingernails into her palms. How had she let this man anywhere near her? "You will help me?" She felt sick that she had to ask, but what else could she do? If she waited any longer, then her condition would be clear to anyone. Once she began to show, questions would be asked. Miss Elizabeth wouldn't tolerate her as a maid any longer and she'd be out of work, unlikely to get hired anywhere else.

Tar reached into his pocket and pulled out a key, then unlocked the drawer where Jessie knew he kept petty cash. He'd often delved into it to pay for his daughter's trinkets when Jessie had been ordered out to fetch ribbons and collect shoes from stores where her credit had run too high. "How much?"

"Forty dollars," she told him. So much for her, and so little for him.

"Here." He handed over a wad of notes with a sigh. "It gives me no great pleasure, Jessie, but I shall have to let you go. The carelessness is as much my fault as yours, I know, but I cannot risk gossip. This will tide you over until you can find employment elsewhere. I shall have the housekeeper write a reference and get it to Alfie later this week."

"But Alfie . . . What will I tell him?" She hadn't thought this would happen—stupid, really. Of course he wouldn't want her around. Reminding him of his mistakes. She took the money and stuffed it into her pocket without looking.

"You're a sensible girl. You'll think of something." He sounded pleased and, to her own shame, she felt better for having won his approval. "My daughter is known for her capricious temperament. You're her third maid since last summer. Alfred won't think anything of it."

WHEN SHE GOT back to the boardinghouse Alfie was out, probably with Victoria. How was it fair that he could conduct his affairs practically in front of the world, and yet she was condemned? Jessie pulled out the wad of banknotes and spread them out on the small square table they squeezed around to eat breakfast. She counted them three times to be sure: one hundred dollars. More money than she'd had in her life before. Enough to pay the woman to cleanse her of her mistake and then—what then? Sixty dollars left over. But what could she do with it, when Alfie would ask questions? Mary Grace would have a plan, but her plans were of the sort that had gotten Jessie into trouble in the first place.

Having peeled away four ten-dollar bills, Jessie fashioned a make-shift envelope from a sheet torn from a copy of *Cosmopolitan* magazine; Victoria gave her read copies to Alfie, thinking that Jessie would be grateful to read articles about the Vanderbilts or about going to the theater in Holland, as if Jessie would ever travel to Europe (though she did admit to occasionally enjoying some of the stories). She folded the rest of the money and tucked it into the metal tin where the three of them placed their rent money each week. She could move it later, but for now that would do.

She would go now, that instant, she decided. If the woman was at home, then it would be a sign that it was meant to be done. If not, then she would return and wait for Alfie to come back. She'd tell him it all, face his disappointment. Hadn't he faced hers not so long ago? They weren't so terribly different, after all.

As she made her way down the street, heading toward the house where the old woman lived, the sky was clear for the first time in days, the sun beaming blinding light off the mounds of snow that lined the road, the few people who braved the conditions taking tentative, sliding steps. Jessie strode forward, her decision made. Women had to make difficult choices every day. She knew this. She accepted this.

30

Monday, 21 September 1936

I HADN'T EXPECTED to end up in a cemetery during my trip to New York, and yet there I was. Grace Butterworth had picked me up from the Hotel Olga that morning in a snappy little blue car with no roof, her hair tied up in a headscarf and her face half-concealed with sunglasses, like someone out of a movie. We spoke barely two words on the journey up to the Bronx, a new area to me, and the Woodlawn Cemetery. The resting place of the aunt I never knew I'd had.

"Alfie used half the money she left to pay for the funeral. We thought she would have liked it here, out of the busy city. Not quite home, but as good as we could give her. I added the headstone later, after I met Mr. Butterworth." She allowed herself a small smile as she led the way along the path. "As soon as I could afford it."

She must have come quite often, I realized, for she didn't hesitate as she found her way through the labyrinth of headstones and monuments. Was that why Alfie had never mentioned his sister? He knew that there was someone left to look after her.

"And all for the love of a man," I said, knowing that I had skated on thin ice more than a few times myself in that regard.

"I wouldn't call it love." Grace came to a halt, removing her sunglasses and snapping the arms closed. "Here she is. Jessie Loretta Aldridge. Only nineteen when she died."

The grave was neat and well-kept. Grace had done a good job. The headstone was white marble. It looked like Jessie was someone important. She had been important, to Grace at least. To Alfie.

"It was my fault," Grace said quietly. "I introduced her to the woman. She was well-known in the neighborhood, but if I hadn't told Jessie about her . . . Some of the girls at the Haymarket had used her before. Occupational hazard, I suppose." She paused and I let the silence expand. There was no point in hectoring her over something that had happened three decades earlier. It was clear that my aunt's death had affected her greatly. "She used a knitting needle. I didn't know. I mean, I thought that was what desperate girls resorted to. I thought that a woman who made a profession out of helping girls in trouble would have come up with a safer method, but . . . It didn't stop her from charging one hell of a fee." She reached into her handbag and pulled out a pack of cigarettes. "I always thought that the price of something—if a thing was expensive, it gave you a guarantee. That it meant it was worth it. I was wrong."

"How did Jessie afford it?"

Grace lit a cigarette, inhaling deeply before blowing the smoke up to the sky. "He gave her the money. The man she worked for, in his big house. He paid her off, gave her the fee for the abortion plus an extra wad of cash, a bonus for being a good girl, and expected to hear nothing of it again. Oh, and he let her go, of course. Not that I wouldn't have tried to talk her out of going back anyway."

I wondered if that man had shed a tear for Jessie. If he'd even ever known what had happened to her. I knew the hypocrisy of men like that. They were happy to have their fun, immoral or not, and they would never have to pay for it. Women and girls like Jessie were the ones who had to suffer. To choose between breaking the law and being consigned to lifelong poverty, all their dreams washing down the gutter. Because no man wanted to marry an unmarried mother. The pious churchgoers loved nothing better than to turn their backs on those less fortunate than themselves. Not much had changed since Jessie's day, and I knew girls who'd been faced with the same impossible choice that she had.

I'd brought some flowers, white chrysanthemums, and I laid these on the grave, staring at the carved date of Jessie's death. "Alfie left New York just a few weeks afterward."

"Alfie didn't know what to do with the rest of the money," Grace said. "I met my husband that winter and I wanted to move away from the Tenderloin. Don't get me wrong—I wasn't ashamed of what I was. A dancer," she clarified before I could assume the worst. "But Terrence is from a far better family than my own. He was clever and he already knew some of the most upstanding men of the time. Alfie split the money between us. I used mine to rent a room up in Harlem, and Alfie bought a steerage ticket to take him to Europe. He had some money saved up from his concerts, and he said that things would be easier there. That he was sick and tired of trying to make a go of it here when people only saw a trained monkey at a piano."

I wasn't so sure that anyone in England had treated Alfie any better, but then, if he'd not gone to England, I'd not have been born. I looked at my aunt's grave and saw how lucky I'd been. My life had depended on the loss of hers. And her life had been lost at the whim of some wealthy man who hadn't given her a second thought. Just threw some money at her and expected that to be the end of it. I shouldn't have been surprised, but still . . .

"What was the man's name?" I asked Grace as we headed back to the car.

"The man?"

"Jessie's . . . The father of Jessie's baby."

"Oh." She tilted her head, trying to remember. "I should know this. He died quite recently, and I remember reading it in the *New York Times* and thinking, *Good riddance!* It just doesn't seem fair that he got to live a full life. He was so much older than Jessie. Easily old enough to be her father." We were almost at the car when the name clicked back into her head. "Parker! That was it. His name was Francis Parker."

My jaw dropped. I now knew exactly why Alfie had really gone to England. What the hell had he done?

GRACE WAS IN a rush to make her luncheon meeting and I had her drop me at the Linfields' apartment. Our good-byes were cordial, but I could tell she was eager to get me out of the car. Almost thirty years of pain had been brought back, and I could tell that she needed time to be alone with her thoughts. My own head was spinning with Grace's revelation, though she had no idea that was the case. I'd managed to hide most of my surprise behind the fact that Francis Parker had been a well-known figure. It stood to reason that most people would be shocked that such an upstanding figure in New York society had buried such a scandal.

Did Eliza know? Jessie had worked in her house, the very house that I'd taken tea in just a few days earlier. Alfie had been in that house. Had their affair begun here in New York? But no. Eliza had been very clear that they'd met in London. There was no reason for her to lie about that. Which meant that Alfie had—what?—traveled to London that summer with the intention of seeking out the Parkers. Was his affair with Eliza some sordid revenge for the death of his sister? Was I alive only because he'd wanted to show Francis Parker what it was like when a loved one was ruined by the callous behavior of a man?

Suddenly I missed Maggie terribly. If she was in New York, I'd have gone straight to her. She'd know what to do with this information. She'd pour us stiff drinks and we'd talk for hours, until we fell asleep, or I felt better. She was the only living person who knew Alfie even a fraction as well as I had—or thought I had. I knew that she'd calm me down, talk me out of some of the wild theories that were whirling around my mind, and remind me what a kind man Alfie was. That whatever he might have done in the midst of his grief, he'd made up for it since, at least where I was concerned.

But I had to put all that to one side momentarily. I was running out of time. My ship sailed in two days, and I still had no idea if I wanted to be on it. Less than forty-eight hours to clear Will's name. This time when I knocked on the apartment door, nobody answered. I used my key; the alternative was to go back to the impersonal hotel room at the Olga, and I reasoned that since Claud hadn't asked for the key back, I was still welcome.

The apartment was quiet. Ominously so. Where had they all gone? It was Monday morning. The lawyer had thought that today he might ask for bail for Will. Were they all at the courthouse? I didn't know where that was. It hurt a little to think that they might have gone without telling me. I didn't want to think that Glo and Rosa might be right. I was an outsider now.

Sitting down in the living room felt wrong in the absence of my hosts. The bedroom—formerly mine, now Joey's—had its door propped open slightly. An invitation if ever I saw one. I knocked gently, in case they had left Joey home and asleep, and when there was no answer, I pushed my way in.

The bed had been made and Joey's belongings, such as they were, had been put away. On the table on one side of the bed, farthest from the window, was the christening photograph, Joey in her mother's arms. I picked it up and sat down on the bed, staring at Bel's beaming face. She looked happier there than I'd ever seen her in real life. And yet when that photo had been taken, her husband had only just died. Her stepbrother had still had months to serve on his sentence. Claud too looked happy. The only smile that looked forced was Louis's. A man doing his duty, nothing more.

I put the photograph back and looked around, hoping for a clue to drop out of thin air into my lap. Will needed it. He needed something, or else I might never see him again. Was there any point in my staying without his blessing? I could feel Claud and Louis pulling away from me, gently preparing me for departure. The trio had closed ranks, just as Glo and Rosa had told me they would. I didn't understand it. Why didn't they trust me?

I remembered Claud, her hand pressed against her belly, shyly admitting that there was a child to think of. A child that meant everything to her and her husband. Was Claudette Linfield strong enough to overpower Bel? Would Will cover for her, knowing how prison would destroy her life and that of her unborn child? I could believe that he would, but I didn't believe it was what happened. Bel was taller than Claud, scrappier. If they'd wrestled it would have been Claud flying out the window, not Bel.

Walking around the bed to the window, I looked out once more. The street was quiet, a contrast to the road outside the Hotel Olga. Claud and Louis lived in a little oasis; I could appreciate it for that now. I could understand how terrifying it would be to contemplate leaving this safe apartment, this sanctuary. Beneath the window was the other bedside table, the one on which had sat the mug that I'd found smashed on the steps below. How was it only now that I saw how odd it was that it was this window that Bel had fallen from?

If Bel had been standing in the center of the room, or even if she had been resting my carpetbag on the bed, then this wasn't the closest window. She would have had to walk around the side of the bed. I followed her footsteps, her path suggesting that she had been inching away from someone. Moving away from them, backed into a corner. Perhaps using that mug as the only makeshift weapon available to her.

I stood in front of that window and looked out. I knew that both windows had been shut when I'd left for the Apollo. Bel had opened this one for some reason. She had taken my passport, small enough to hide in the crook of an arm or in her handbag as she left. If she'd heard someone coming, might she have thought of throwing it out, retrieving it later?

I was getting a headache from thinking so hard, so many hypotheses crammed into my brain, and no way to know which, if any, was the truth. I pulled out the drawer of the bedside table: nothing there. As I slammed it, the table rocked, and I heard a clink as something dislodged at the back. Pulling the furniture forward, I spied a glint of something small fallen onto the floor behind. I reached down and came back with a button. A bold brass button from a man's suit jacket.

The silence of the apartment was broken by the sound of a key turning in the lock. They were home. And I still didn't know exactly what had happened, but I did know who was responsible.

Alfie

May 1909

I'D GIVE ANYTHING *to ruin that man*, Mary Grace had said. They'd been drunk the night of the funeral and she'd said that if it weren't for Terrence Butterworth, she'd have thought about inquiring about the vacant maid's position at Tar's house. Tar didn't know Mary Grace. He didn't even know that Jessie was dead. Mary Grace would go there and teach that man a thing or two about messing with the wrong girl.

Too dangerous, Alfie had told her. It was all well and good planning revenge, but he knew that Tar wasn't stupid. He'd easily smell a rat and God only knew what a man like that would do to a girl who tried to trick him. He'd sat there and listened to Mary Grace's wild schemes, which would come to nothing, and thought about the money that was left over. Even if he split it with Mary Grace, there was enough to buy him a ticket on a ship heading to Europe. It felt like running away, but did that really matter? There was no one left alive to judge him. No Jessie to come after him and berate him for being a coward and a terrible brother. He wished now that she'd not found him. Back home she'd had friends, the church, a real community. If only she could have forgotten about her useless brother.

Alfie hadn't gone back to Tar's house. He didn't want Tar to know about what had happened to Jessie. It wasn't a grief that he wanted that man to have any share in. Every time he heard the man's name, forever on Mary Grace's lips as she ranted daily, his heart hardened a little more, until it was like a boulder in his chest, restricting his breathing as he tried to sleep at night, pushing down on his stomach when he tried to eat more than a mouthful of food. A week passed, then two, three. He avoided the usual places in case Tar was there, and he saw Victoria only once, at the Marshall Hotel. It was the last time. They had sat in the lounge, over coffee, and he had told her that he never wanted to see her again.

She'd known, he realized, and she hadn't said anything. Not explicitly. Her cryptic comments at Christmas only now made sense to him. Through tears, she claimed she'd been protecting Jessie. That she hadn't been entirely sure, and how could she make such a claim when she'd met his siser only that one time? Would it have made a difference? He'd have been angry, he knew. He might have made a scene at the house, dragged Jessie behind him, ashamed and embarrassed, and made Tar answer for his rancid behavior. But probably the outcome would have been no better. Either Jessie would have gone to the woman regardless, or her life would have been ruined. Once Tar had gotten his dirty hands on her, there had been no possible happy outcome.

He said none of this to Victoria, though, just sat quietly listening as she pleaded for forgiveness. *Look at the risk I take for you*, she'd said. *I could end up like Jessie. You think it would be easier for me, just because I have money? Do you know what it would do to my father if he saw me here, with you? If it didn't kill him, he'd kill me. His only daughter! He'd cut me off without a dime. He'd be a laughingstock around town and I would have done that to him. Me! Who loves him!*

So it was thanks to Victoria and to Mary Grace that Alfie set sail for England with revenge on his mind.

IN THE END, she had come to him. It was fate, he reasoned. All right, so he'd manipulated his way to being at the party. It was easy. Everything in London felt easy after New York. He'd learned from past mistakes. Knew the value of talking to people, of keeping an ear out for opportunity. One of his other wealthy New York patrons, a very good friend of Tar's, had been over the moon to find out that Alfie too had decided to travel to London. Mr. Olsen was set up for the summer in a huge house overlooking Regent's Park. Alfie had spent the past month entertaining his guests at various soirees, listening in to the gossip as he did so. It was so easy for these people that they didn't think to wonder how a skinny Black kid had made it across the ocean. Even if they did, they wouldn't guess at the truth.

As soon as he'd heard about the party—to celebrate the engagement between Olsen's eldest daughter and the son of some lord or other—he'd made it his mission to get hired for it. Olsen knew everybody, and he liked Alfie because Alfie made himself likable. He'd learned in New York what these people liked. A malleable Negro who kept them in the loop of what was fashionable, musically speaking. He could play the pet when he needed to. Before, when Jessie was alive, he hadn't realized that was how they thought of him. Now that knowledge helped him. He'd known how to suggest to Olsen that he put Alfie forward to work at the party. He'd bring a little American flamboyance to the proceedings. That was how he came to be sitting on a wall outside the kitchen of a house in Richmond, a House with a capital *H*. Big enough that with four hundred guests invited, he'd worried that he wouldn't even set eyes on his quarry.

But now here she was. Elizabeth Parker, though she'd reinvented herself since he'd last run into her. She was now Eliza, and she was weaving, too many glasses of champagne fizzing around in her veins.

The puppy fat was gone, and she looked like a young woman now. Like a woman who had lived a little. Her mother had died just two months earlier, for which he was sorry. Mrs. Parker had been a nice lady. She'd deserved better than her immoral husband and spoiled daughter.

"Don't you get bored?" Eliza's opening gambit was enough to make Alfie seethe. Bored? Of working two jobs to pay rent?

He let an easy smile form on his lips, knowing that he had one over on her; she hadn't recognized him. She'd barely glanced in his direction when he'd been working for her father. At the time he'd taken it as a slight. Now he was thankful. It made everything easier.

"Of what? Taking in the beautiful night air? Enjoying this pipe?" He inhaled, savoring the taste of fine tobacco, a gift from Olsen. He'd recently taken up pipe smoking. He thought it made him look older, along with the mustache. It helped him step away from that foolish boy who had let his sister die because he hadn't taken care of her properly.

"Of being a rich man's puppet." She flung herself down on the stone wall beside him. "Don't you get tired of it?"

For a second, he was tempted to tell her the truth. To shake her world and let her know just who her father was. But that was not the plan. What was his plan? To ruin Tar's daughter. To have her be seen in polite society with a Black man, and to let the insidious gossip ruin her reputation, just as Victoria had risked. Not just like this, sitting on a wall. Innocent enough. But to have her be seen in a compromising position.

"I'm my own man," he told Eliza now. "I do as I like."

"You play what they tell you," she said.

"Do you really think all these people had heard ragtime before I played it to them?" His grin was genuine now. Stupid girl. She didn't know what he knew.

"My father likes that sort of music," she said with a shrug. "I don't much care for it."

She was making it so easy for him. "What music do you care for? Beethoven? Bach?"

"Too bland," she replied.

"I could play you some Debussy if you like. Certainly the man's private life is anything but bland."

Eliza took his pipe from his hand, and coughed a little as she inhaled, though she tried to hide it. Alfie bit his lip to stop from laughing. Girls like Eliza Parker didn't like to be laughed at, perhaps because they didn't shy away from laughing at others. He had to play her game for now.

"I should get back to it," he said, getting to his feet and relieving her of his pipe.

"I wouldn't bother if I were you." She put a hand on his arm, the light pressure and warmth of her palm encouraging him to sit. "They're doing speeches. They'll take an age. Olsen loves the sound of his own voice."

Alfie couldn't disagree with that; it had made his task far easier than it ought to have been. "Aren't you a friend of the happy couple?"

Her nose wrinkled. "She's a dullard whose only ambition was to marry a man with some sort of title. I suppose at least she has fulfilled her purpose at the age of twenty. She can die happy now, which is more than you could say for most people. And I don't know him at all, but I can tell you that his breath stinks and rumor has it that he's only marrying Emily for her money. He has a mistress on the side already."

"It sounds like a match made in heaven," Alfie said, and Eliza's burst of laughter startled him into joining in. "But these are your people, are they not? People like you don't associate with people like me. Not unless you want something."

"Well, maybe I want something." She worried her lip and gave him a wide-eyed look that some other man had probably told her was becoming. Alfie found her rather obvious, but that was good.

"I don't think that I have what you want." *Don't make it easy*, he reminded himself. It was how he'd snared Victoria, although on that occasion it had been accidental. He'd been scared after what had happened in Jacksonville. He hadn't wanted to draw any more attention to himself.

She grabbed the pipe back from him, exchanging it for a silver flask. "I stole some of the host's whiskey."

He unscrewed the cap and took a swig. It was a fine, peaty spirit. Expensive. He took another mouthful. "Not bad."

She propped the pipe on one side of her mouth, trying to look nonchalant, though he could tell she was trying not to inhale. "You know how much that stuff costs?"

"Do you?" In his experience rich women didn't know what anything cost. They had maids to go to the store, and their fathers, and then husbands, paid the bills. "Thank you, though." He passed back the flask.

"So, how d'you learn to play piano like that?"

"My father taught me the basics. The rest I learned myself. I got a good ear."

"My mother used to love ragtime." Her eyes grew shiny with unshed tears. "She used to pay a boy to come play for her twice a week."

He had to tread carefully. "A boy?" Was that why she hadn't recognized him? The extra year had put a few pounds on him, he supposed, and he'd grown the mustache for the purposes of disguise.

"Some Negro kid who didn't have a lot going for him. She took pity on him, but she loved the music. And he played almost as good as you do. I used to hear him from my bedroom. Mama would be in the drawing room, watching him, and listening, for hours. Poor boy must have got cramp in his fingers!"

He chuckled alongside her, remembering those afternoons in New York. Mrs. Parker had been a lovely woman. Hopefully she was resting in peace now. Maybe Jessie and she were in a better place, together.

"Would you teach me?" Her question surprised him.

"What? To play piano?"

"What else?"

He shrugged. It hadn't been part of the plan, but the best plans were malleable, had give in them. Look at Mary Grace. Her plan had been to dance on the stage. And now she'd met some fella from a good family and had given all that up to get married. She was happier for it. He'd always assumed that she would be the one taking her chances with a backstreet abortionist, but he'd been proven wrong. It didn't do to judge people too quickly. He even kind of missed her, his only living link back to Jessie.

"So, what do you say?" Eliza was waiting for an answer.

"I say that you can't afford me," he said, baiting her.

"I can pay whatever you're worth. One pound for an afternoon," she offered. "We have a very nice pianoforte in our house and my father is at work from eight in the morning and never gets home before eight at night."

"But there'll be a chaperone?" He knew it was expected, though he also knew that the Elizabeth Parker of old wouldn't let that get in her way.

"Of course. Just come to our house a few hours, once or twice a week, and teach me to play Debussy." She grinned and handed back his pipe, then held that same hand out for him to shake.

It was a pretty good deal. Getting paid to seduce the daughter of his greatest enemy. Earning money for something he'd intended to do for free.

"All right, then." He shook on it and watched her walk away.

The funny thing was, he found that the new Eliza wasn't half as bad as he remembered. Would he feel remorse later on? He didn't think so. Francis Parker had destroyed his sister, had as good as killed her himself. He didn't expect consequences because, for men like him, they didn't exist. Not up until now.

31

Monday, 21 September 1936

I WALKED INTO the living room and was confronted by all three of them: Claud, Louis, and Will.

"You're home!" Despite everything, I couldn't stop the smile from springing to my lips. Will was free, at least for now.

"I got a good lawyer." He looked a little sheepish, but MacAllister had done well.

"Where's Joey?" I asked. I really didn't want to have this next, difficult conversation in front of her.

"I took her to her grandmother's. Henry's mother sent for her," Claud explained, seeing the puzzled look on my face. "I thought she could do with a change of scenery until things are a little more settled here."

"Oh. Good. I . . ." I squeezed the brass button in my fist. How the hell was I supposed to do this?

"We didn't expect to see you here when we got home." Louis

was trying to keep his tone light, but I saw the look he shot in Claud's direction. I'd been right. I was no longer welcome.

"No, well, I was out with Grace Butterworth, and I found out some things about my father. Why he left New York. I suppose I just didn't want to be alone."

"What did she tell you?" Will stepped forward and pulled me into his arms. "Baby, what's the matter?"

"Grace Butterworth?" Claud was confused. "I didn't realize you knew her."

I savored being in Will's embrace for a moment before gently extricating myself. "She knew my father. And Jessie, my aunt. She took me to the cemetery to see her grave."

"You found your family?" Will drew me down to sit on the sofa. "I'm sorry I couldn't be there."

"You did have bigger fish to fry," I tried to joke, but even I couldn't raise a smile. "She told me some things that . . . make sense. About my father, and how he met my mother. She was very generous with her time."

"Mrs. Butterworth is known for it," Claud told me, sitting down in the armchair. "She does a lot for the civil rights movement. Holds dances and charity dinners to raise money, that sort of thing. She's a handy lady to know."

"What's happening?" I asked Will. "They let you go. Does that mean—"

He shook his head quickly. "George got me out on bail, that's all. Claud and Louis lent me the money."

I looked across at the couple. Louis stood with one hand resting on the mantelpiece, watching his wife. Blood money? "I found out something else," I said.

"Found what?" Claud snapped the words out. She'd seen me walk out of the bedroom. I could see her fingernails pick at the stitching on the chair arm.

I opened my hand, the brass button resting benignly on my palm. "Isn't this yours, Louis?"

"Where . . . ?" He cleared his throat and tried again. "I don't know if it is mine."

"It is," I said firmly. "From your best suit jacket. You wore it to the Savoy, and you had it on the night of the Apollo. I found it behind the bedside table next to the window Bel fell from."

"Lena, please. Don't do this." Will was staring at the floor, his jaw clenched as if he was trying not to cry.

"You knew?" Realization washed over me like a bucket of ice-cold water. I should have known. How had I not guessed? The three of them had pulled together, slowly closing me out, just as Rosa had told me they would. Though it wasn't for the reasons she'd given. It was because they'd come to a decision. An agreement that was so twisted that I couldn't know. Nobody could know.

"You're going to let Will take the blame for something he didn't do?" I aimed the accusation at the Linfields, but only Louis flinched. "Don't you have any shame?"

"It was Will's decision," Claud told me, her face as hard as stone. "We're family." The implication: *You're not part of this.*

"George thinks that the evidence isn't strong enough," Louis told me earnestly. "They can't prove that Will was in the bedroom when Bel fell."

"Don't you mean when she was pushed? Because he wasn't in the room," I pointed out. "It was you, Louis. You were in the room with Bel. Why? What happened? Did you struggle with her? Is that how your button came off?"

"Damn you, Lena! Would you shut your mouth?" Claud sat on the edge of her chair, fury writ across her face. "This is none of your business."

"Will?" I looked at him, and his eyes slid away to meet Claud's. "Why would you do this?"

"They can give Joey a family," he said quietly. "And there's the baby to think of. Joey loves Claud and Louis. She can have a good life here. Besides, like Louis said, they don't have any real evidence against me. It'll probably all be fine."

"Do you always have to be so bloody honorable?" I felt my eyes fill with tears. "You were just about to get your life back and you're going to risk it all?" I stared at Louis, who at least had the decency to look ashamed. "This is madness!" I got to my feet, stumbling a little. "You're happy to let Will go to prison? Worse! If they decide it was murder, this is Will's life we're talking about."

"It was an accident," Louis told me. "Honestly, Lena. Please believe me. I never meant . . ." He leaned against the wall, his face drawn. I wondered if he'd slept much since it had happened. "I saw Will come out and I could see from his face that Bel'd had nothing good to tell him. I was sick of it, that's all. I'd had a few drinks. It seemed like a good idea to try and talk to her. Find out what she was up to and try to put a stop to it." He took a deep breath, closing his eyes, and I saw a tear slip down his cheek. "She was going through your things, searching through them like she was looking for something in particular."

"I guess we're not the only ones with a secret," Claud said, and my cheeks flamed with both shame at the truth and anger at the audacity of her.

"She was robbing you, Lena," Louis told me. "She jumped up when she saw me and grabbed the passport. She kept saying that it was for Joey. It was so Joey could have a better life, with Will and with us. She was leaving. She was going to take your passport, and she was skipping out on her family. On her daughter."

I could see the anger in his face then, the emotions fainter than they must have appeared the week before when he'd confronted Bel.

"Louis was just trying to stop her from leaving," Claud told me. "Wouldn't you have done the same? I know I would've if I'd known."

"Bel's dead," I said quietly, and she flinched. "How did she fall?"

"I begged her," Louis said. "I told her to think of Will. Everything he'd given up for her already. He was just getting his life back, but she didn't give a shit about that. She was going to saddle him with her daughter and vanish."

"She wasn't taking Joey with her?" I glanced at Will and he shook his head, staring down at his hands as they rested in his lap. "You're sure?"

"Lena, she told me so. She said that Joey would be better off with folk who hadn't screwed up their lives the way she had. In her head, we'd all become one happy family without her." Louis sighed. "I got angry. Tried to grab hold of her, to shake some sense into her. She dropped the money and ran around the side of the bed, and I . . . I followed her. She had the passport, see, and I knew she was crazy enough to take it and leave."

"You were both struggling for the passport." I understood then how it had happened. Those sash windows had their sills set at waist height. Easy enough to tip someone's balance with a little bit of force. "Force" being the vital word. I could believe that Louis hadn't entered that room with anything but the best of intentions. What I didn't believe was that the fall had been purely accidental. "She was going to throw it out the window and you wrestled for it. So why not just tell the police it was an accident?" I tried to keep my poker face.

"No one'll believe that," Claud said, proving that she was no idiot.

"I did." Will spoke up. "But then, I guess I know Bel too well. Knew." He swallowed hard. "And she knew that I wouldn't let her down. That I'd take care of Joey. I still have to do that, however risky it is."

"Bloody hell, Will." I took hold of his hand and squeezed it tight. "This is a dangerous gamble."

"There's no evidence." Claud was firm. "George said that they have a very weak case against Will. If we can hold strong, then there's no need for anyone to go to jail."

"You don't know that!" I spoke to Will directly. "If this goes to trial, if they show photographs of sweet, pretty Bel to the jury. If they talk about your violent past, or use the gossip that Bel spread about you, they will believe that you killed her. It doesn't matter if they can prove it or not. The story is there, ready for people to trust in." I wiped the tears from my cheeks; none of us had dry eyes.

"Will's a brother to me. I won't let him go to jail—or worse—on my behalf." Louis spoke in earnest, his eyes on Will. "Will, you know that, right? This is just . . . because there's no reason for anyone to get punished for this. It was an accident. I swear on my wife's life, the life of our unborn baby."

"It's what we agreed, Will." Claud leaned forward, her hands clasped tightly over her stomach, and I hated them both in that moment. Emotional blackmail. Happy to trade Will's life for the cozy family that Claud and Louis had dreamed of.

"I'm sorry, Lena." His eyes finally met mine, and I saw that he'd made his choice.

"So, what happens now?" I asked Will.

He shrugged. "We wait for MacAllister to get in touch about a court date. What else can I do?" There was such misery in his eyes that I couldn't bear it. "You won't say a word, will you? Promise?"

"Don't make me do that," I begged.

He looked up at his so-called friends. "Leave us, would you?" Without a word, Claud and Louis vanished into their bedroom and left us alone.

"You have to," he said, his voice firm, his gaze unwavering. "I don't expect you to understand how or why, but I owe Claud and Louis so much. I wouldn't be here now if it weren't for them. And I'm not doing this to be noble. It's partly my fault. For leaving Bel in that room, knowing she'd already been through your things. For running away for so long instead of dealing with what happened ten years ago." He reached into his pocket, pulled out a clean white cotton handkerchief, and handed it to me so I could blow my nose.

"You don't owe them your life," I said, pleading. Did he really trust in the same system that had already tried to throw him away once? "If they find you guilty . . . Do you trust Louis to do as he said and tell the truth?"

"Lena, I have to do this. And you have to leave," he continued. "Take the ship to England on Wednesday. For my sake. I'll write and let you know what happens. But I can't do this with you here." He managed a small smile. "I honestly believe this is all gonna work out, but it's too hard with you here."

"This is mad." My voice was a whisper. "I can't just leave you now. England is too far away. What if you're wrong? About what the police have, about Louis and Claud? I won't be able to get here in time."

"To do what?" He cupped my cheek in his hand. "I didn't want to lie to you. I wanted to spare you this. Because there's nothing you can do. I can't force you to go, but if you say a word about this to anyone, then I can't see you again. Claud will make sure no one believes you. And you don't have any evidence. That button in your hand could have come from anywhere." He leaned forward and kissed me. "I don't want things to turn nasty. You don't deserve that."

He was serious, and I knew that he was right. Claud would easily be able to discredit me. My motive was obvious—I'd do anything to clear Will's name, even blame Louis. The button, missed by the police, was no proof at all.

"You're sure about this? There's no other way?" I watched him nod and felt a crack in my chest.

Through tears I wrote Maggie's address on a scrap of paper and gave it to Will. I felt so useless. We'd probably never see each other again. Was this really how it was going to end? It felt like some gruesome trick of the universe. Not even two weeks ago I'd been set up to take the blame for a series of murders. I'd been lucky to escape my fate, only to pass it on to the one person I knew who didn't deserve it. That Will had been let down by the people he trusted most made it even worse.

"You'd better write as soon as there's news," I said, sniffing back tears. "Or—no—a telegram. I can't wait for the mail. Promise me!"

"Baby, I promise." He kissed me then, pulling me close, and even though I knew it was good-bye, there was something there. Love? Or at least its possibility, crushed under the heel of Claud's sensible shoes.

If only I'd hidden that damned carpetbag better as soon as I'd arrived at the Linfields'. If only Bel hadn't been such a devious snoop. If only, if only, if only . . .

"You'd better go." He kissed my hands and then let them fall, taking a step back. Cutting himself off from me. "Have a good trip back to England, and if you see the band, please don't tell 'em anything. Just that my sister died. No need to go into details."

I used a clean corner of his handkerchief to wipe away the mascara that had run and formed shadows under my eyes. "You take care of yourself, all right? And if, for any reason, you do change your mind before Wednesday . . ."

"I won't. Lena, I don't want you to go," he said, walking me toward the door and holding it open. "It's just that, right now, I need you to. I'm tired of running away from Harlem. I need to do this. But I do wish we could have had more time."

I turned once more to look at him, his eyes as damp as mine. Of all the outcomes I'd envisaged, even knowing that a good-bye was the most likely, I had never imagined this pain. The guilt and shame of knowing that my presence had led to this, that I might have indirectly harmed the one person who had inspired me to make a fresh start.

"Me too." I turned and fled, unable to bear it any longer.

JUST ONE OF THOSE THINGS

32

Friday, 25 September 1936

DÉJÀ VU. STARING from the deck of the most luxurious ocean liner in the world, the ocean far below me, I tried to judge the distance. Farther than Bel had fallen. If I jumped, would I die? Or would the waves catch me, soften the blow so that I was merely stunned? Even if they did, I'd likely drown before anyone realized I was gone. Morbid, but I'd seen so much death in the past few weeks that it was hard not to wonder if it would soon be my turn.

I glanced around me, and no one on the Promenade Deck was paying me any notice. I'd done my absolute best not to talk to anyone since I'd boarded two days earlier. My old pal Danny was my steward again for this crossing; I'd requested him specifically. New people weren't to be trusted. Danny was from my neck of the woods. We knew each other even though we'd met only as I'd traveled from Southampton to New York, full of hope. He didn't ask me why I was going back so soon, just smiled and told me it was nice to see me again. He brought my meals to my cabin without a question, never once suggesting that I should consider a visit to the dining room. I supposed he felt sorry for me. He couldn't know the truth of what had gone on during my previous crossing, but he'd know that the man I was traveling with had been discovered dead, his body lying beside a note that confessed to several murders. He'd know that things were complicated.

I checked my watch: I'd made it to the half hour of fresh air that I forced myself to take each day. I didn't want to draw attention to myself, and as much as it was a struggle, I knew that the relief I'd feel when I got back to my cabin and locked the door behind me would make it all worthwhile. My bed would have been made in my absence, Danny always knowing exactly when I'd stepped out. Ten minutes after I arrived back, he'd knock on the door with a pot of coffee and the lemon shortbread that he knew I loved. It was those small things that were keeping me going. A little bit of kindness went a long way.

"Afternoon, miss." Danny winked as we approached each other in the corridor as I slunk my way back.

"Danny." I nodded and smiled.

"Glad to have bumped into you," he told me. "I have a small favor to ask."

"Oh?" I paused, wary.

"See, the bandleader for tonight, he's lost his voice. And I did hear a rumor that you sang a little on your last crossing with us."

I stared at him. "It was only a song." Will had made me get up and sing as he played. It had been a test. Him trying to work out who I was when I didn't even know myself.

"But you are a singer, aren't you? I mean, miss, do tell me if I've overstepped the mark, but it's your job." He looked a little nervous now, confounded by my lukewarm reaction. "Say no, of course. It's just that they're a bit stuck for tonight, and when I mentioned your name, the chaps in the band said they knew you."

Oh God. A lump swelled in my throat. Will's old bandmates.

And if they knew that I was on board, they'd want to know why. I'd hoped to avoid them. They'd have questions that I didn't want to answer. I could feel the sweat start to gather on my upper lip.

Although . . . did I have to lie? Only by omission. Will's sister had died, unexpectedly, and he'd stayed in New York to take care of his niece. All true.

"It's the Starlight Lounge?" I asked. It was a small, exclusive venue at the top of the ship. Something to add to my curriculum vitae next time I went for an audition. And that would be soon. I had no job to go back to. Someone out there would be impressed by a gig on the *Queen Mary*.

Danny nodded. "You'll do it?"

Perhaps it was a way of closing a circle. The beginning and ending of my relationship with Will. At least it would be a way of killing a couple of hours. There was only so much reading a girl could do of a night.

"I'll do it."

Back in my cabin, pouring cream into the coffee that Danny had delivered as per our usual routine, I wondered what Alfie would have made of everything. Had he known, all those years ago, what events he was setting in motion? I hadn't mentioned anything to Grace Butterworth because I wasn't sure if he would have confided in her. She'd appeared genuine when she'd struggled to recall Francis Parker's name. Would she have mentioned anything if she'd suspected that Alfie hadn't let his sister's death go unavenged? Was I reading too much between the lines?

If you'd asked me a few weeks earlier if my father was capable of plotting a cold-blooded revenge against the Parker family, I'd just have laughed. He wasn't that sort of person. He never held a grudge, unlike so many other people I'd met along the way. He'd always encouraged me to rise above. To let things go. Was that attitude adopted after his own plan had gone somewhat awry? I doubted that he'd intended to end up holding a literal baby, that the rest of his life would be diverted to the outcome of his decision to pursue Eliza Parker, later to become Abernathy. Was my own life so chaotic because I'd been conceived with the intention of destroying someone's life?

I smoked a cigarette and considered ordering a martini, only to decide not to. I had a show to do that night. A rehearsal to go to in less than an hour. Getting half cut wouldn't help anyone. I couldn't change what Alfie had done. I'd never know if he had actually set out to target Eliza, or if their meeting in London had been by chance. Perhaps that was a good thing. I couldn't imagine confronting Alfie with such a question. Hearing an answer that I didn't want to contemplate. What was done was done. Hopefully, after everything that had happened, it was at an end. I had the business card for Eliza's lawyer and I'd be well compensated for my troubles. Alfie had learned not to hold grudges. I should learn from his mistakes.

I'D WORRIED THAT the Starlight would bring back bad memories. I'd watched a man die there just a few weeks ago. Somehow, without the Abernathys' presence, the ship felt different, though. The scandal and intrigue of my outbound trip had been mopped away as easily as a spilled drink from a tiled floor. Everything was back to normal. New passengers. The tables arranged in a different configuration. A complete exorcism. Thank goodness.

"Good to see you again, Lena." Deon, the bass player, had greeted me earlier as I met up with the band in the tiny music room, the only free space for us to have a quick rehearsal before the evening performance.

I shook hands with him, then with Bobby and Leo, whom I'd met on the way over to New York. Winston was the standby for Will. The permanent replacement, I supposed, though I wasn't sure if he knew that yet. I'd stuck to my earlier plan, sharing scant details about

Bel's tragic death and Will's decision to care for Joey. They didn't press, which I was grateful for.

"We'll stick to our standard set list. No requests," Deon promised. Since Winston's voice was a hoarse whisper at best, Deon had stepped up to make the decisions for the evening, though I would be the voice of the band onstage.

It was all far too easy. I knew every song on the list. The rehearsal had gone smoothly and now we were in the center of the Starlight Lounge. I'd love to say that everyone's eyes were on me, but we were background noise at best. No one present loved Porter or Gershwin, or possibly even music at all. We were there to add a little class to the proceedings. To ensure that conversations had a backdrop, that a certain ambience was maintained. Nothing more.

I remembered that at some stage I'd envied Will having command of his own band, singing for the great and good, but now that I was standing where he had for so long, I wondered how he'd borne it. The Canary Club had hardly been salubrious, but its clientele had loved the music. There was very little else to recommend the venue. I'd thought that standing up there behind the microphone would make me feel proud, but instead I felt sad. Sad that Will had run away for so long. Sad that when he'd finally dared to make a change, someone else had destroyed his new beginning.

"You ready?" Deon asked me in a low voice, and I half turned, nodded.

This was something new, but also familiar. The one constant I'd had in my life was my voice. Getting up and showing it off in front of other people, whether they cared or not. Singing had been my bread and butter; it had been my greatest joy. Whatever happened when I got back to London, I had a voice and it would help me find my way to wherever I was supposed to end up.

33

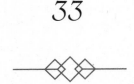

Friday, 2 October 1936

I WAS BACK where it all started, sitting at a table in a Soho restaurant and staring with incredulity at my best friend.

"Are you bloody crazy?" I asked. It was too much. I gulped back my glass of champagne, and a disquieting sensation of déjà vu washed over me.

"It makes good business sense," Maggie told me, her face serene. "I knew you'd overreact."

"Overreact!" My voice was hoarse with the effort of not screaming. It was a busy lunchtime service, and the waiters here already despised us.

I'd been back in London barely a week, after an absence of less than a month, but it was as though time had sped up while I was away. The city I'd returned to felt at least a year older. I'd left Maggie with her life in tatters, but she'd fixed herself right back up, stronger than before. With her husband, Tommy, dead, she'd inherited the lot. Including the seedy nightclub where he'd met his death, his demise prompted by enemies who didn't like Tommy's dodgy dealings or the extra money he was scooping up via the brothel he operated in the flat above. Maggie had to be insane to contemplate getting into business with the very men who'd strong-armed her into offing her own husband.

"I started thinking while you were away," Maggie said.

"Could have fooled me," I muttered.

"Just listen, would you? Brian came to see me, and we talked. About how things might work out now that Tommy's gone. He had some good ideas for the club, and it means that the lads can keep their jobs. And then, when you telegraphed to say you were coming back, I thought that you could help me. You know all about the music side of things, after all. I'll need help with that."

"Brian? DI Hargreaves?" My heart sank. It was worse even than I'd thought. Hargreaves was not only the very man who'd started this whole ball rolling in the first place; he'd also been involved in the murders on the *Queen Mary*. If he ever found out the truth of what had gone on there, I'd be in deep trouble, added to which, I had a growing suspicion that Maggie had ulterior motives when it came to the detective inspector. Talk about jumping from the frying pan into the fire. "Isn't he married?"

"He and his wife are going through a difficult period." Her cheeks flushed, confirming my fear. "And you can't talk. You're hardly whiter than white yourself when it comes to married men."

Touché. "At least James Harrington never killed anyone." I lit a cigarette and sat back in my chair, watching her. I never should have left London. Everything had been a mess ever since.

I'd had such high hopes when the taxi had pulled up outside Maggie's Hampstead home. She'd opened the front door with a friendly face, and I'd jumped out of the cab and almost raced up the path to hug her. Our first night together had lived up to expectations. We'd gotten drunk on rum and chain-smoked until I felt sick, and I'd cried on her shoulder as I told her about Will, and she'd cried on mine as she described Tommy's funeral and the wake, the guilt she'd felt as his family sobbed at the graveside and she had to stand there knowing that she'd killed him. Over the days, though, she'd become more reserved. I'd felt a barrier grow up between us, and I was now finding out the reason why.

"I knew you'd do this," she said, gesturing with her hands at the sour expression on my face. "Look at yourself! Judging me, as if your life's so bloody perfect. If I'd told you at home, you'd have stormed out or started shouting. I needed time to think about what to say, and I wanted to be sure that all the details were sorted."

"I know my life isn't perfect. I'm just worried about you," I said. "Hargreaves is dangerous."

"Tommy was a fool. He got what was coming to him." I couldn't disagree. "We talked, me and Brian, and he'd rather that I take over the club than start over with someone new. He went over the books with me, showed me how it works and how much money I could be making. Imagine! Little old me in charge of a business empire!"

I'd have been proud of her if I didn't know that Hargreaves was using her. Of course he preferred to have Maggie instead of someone with more experience running a nightclub. He could tell her whatever he wanted, and she'd believe it. Plus, he got to spend nights in her bed. He was getting a fantastic deal while she was getting short-changed.

"If you don't like it, you can leave," she said. "I gave you a load of money before you went and deserted me. It'll more than pay for a few months' rent somewhere decent."

"Deserted you?" My eyebrows shot up. "Are you having a laugh? You told me to go. I only got mixed up in all of this because of you and bleeding Hargreaves."

"I know, I know. I just . . ." She had the decency to look sheepish. "Look, Lee, I'm sorry. I should have kept you out of my mess. But now it's up to you if you want to stay out of it." Little did she know that it wasn't entirely her own mess. I could hardly tell her the full story now, though, when she was mixed up with Hargreaves. "You're my best friend. Can you just trust me on this? And if it's a mistake, I'll own it, but I feel powerful for once in my life. The Canary Club is mine. No one else's. Not Tommy's anymore. I can make it a better place. For the girls who work there, for Vic and the lads. I've got some really good ideas, Lee. Imagine if the Canary was the club everyone was talking about. Where you could get a proper cocktail and dance to the hottest music in Soho. Not just a front for a knocking shop."

"I suppose miracles can happen," I said. I hoped she could pull it off. It wasn't that I didn't think Maggie capable. I'd just seen it before, with Tommy. How her best-laid plans had been cast aside to keep him happy. If Brian Hargreaves hadn't been involved, I'd have been over the moon for her. "Let's talk about this later, shall we? You can tell me about all these exciting plans tonight." I pulled out my purse and counted out what I thought I owed.

"Where you off to?" She sounded put out.

"I've got to see a man about a dog." I said it to annoy her; it was one of Tommy's favorite sayings. "I'll be home for dinner. The dog's in Mayfair. I'll bring us some treats from Fortnum's and we can celebrate the new Canary tonight."

Mollified, she smiled and nodded. "Mrs. Wood's making her famous beef Wellington, so don't be late."

I stepped out into the busy street, the narrowness of it comforting after New York's wide avenues. It was good to be home, even though there was no Will Goodman in London. At least I knew he was safe.

He'd kept his promise. A telegram the very day I'd arrived back in London had confirmed that the charges against him had been dropped. The autopsy had been inconclusive, with no evidence to indicate foul play. Louis's button had been the only clue, and the police had missed it. The day before, I'd received a letter, presumably sent at the same time as the telegram. It was brief, to the point. The most male of missives, void of emotion until the last line. Will wrote that he had started working at the Apollo. He included an address that I recognized as Bel's; he'd moved into the old apartment to keep things as normal as possible for Joey. He was her new guardian, and she was coping as well as could be expected. There was no mention of Louis and Claud, and I wondered if he was struggling with the new aspect that the old friendship had taken on. I knew only too well what that was like.

I would write back over the weekend. I wasn't ready to give up on him, and I still hadn't decided what form my new life would take. If Maggie managed to make a success of the Canary, then I would be happy for her, but I would never sing there again. I didn't need to any longer. I had an appointment with Winston Radlett at Parker Godwin. He was expecting me at three o'clock sharp, which gave me just about enough time if I jumped in a cab.

I'd telephoned his office from Maggie's house the day before, and it sounded ever so simple. I just walked in and showed him my passport, and he would authorize a check to be drawn up. Eliza had kept her word. My bank manager was about to become my best friend instead of my mortal enemy. No more debts. I could find a place of my own to live, close enough to Maggie that I could visit easily but without running the risk of bumping into DI Brian Hargreaves in his smalls first thing in the morning. Depending on how much money Eliza's guilt was blessing me with, I could even think about buying property. Or I could travel. Paris had fabulous jazz clubs, I'd heard. And Maggie and I had never made it to the South of France like we'd talked about.

My father had made mistakes, but he'd always been an optimist and he'd always told me to make him proud. It was about time I did just that.

Acknowledgments

Writing never gets easier, and so first I have to thank those who read early chapters and told me to keep going. Lou Kramskoy, Ruth Ivo, and the much-missed Karen Clarke, who, I don't think anyone will mind my saying, was the absolute best of us.

I'm lucky enough to have an agent who is not only supportive and a great cheerleader but who understands what I'm trying to write, often before even I do. I can honestly say that I wouldn't be where I am without Nelle Andrew.

I'm so grateful to the wonderful Berkley team for their constant support and belief, especially my incredible editor Amanda Bergeron. Thanks also to Sareer Khader, Jessica Plummer, Tara O'Connor, Lauren Burnstein, and everyone else involved.

Thanks to my incredible UK editor, Manpreet Grewal, and to the wider team at HQ/Harper Collins: Claire Brett, Becci Mansell, Angie Dobbs, Halema Begum, Georgina Green, Fliss Porter, Angela Thomson, Sara Eusebi, Petra Moll, Rebecca Fortuin, and Mel Hayes.

To all my friends and family: I love you. Thank you for being there for me.